To Tommy Cocke and Family

May you enjoy this tale about my Grandpa Shaw's family after the Civil War.

Waldon Merrill McLellan

12/98

One Step - Two Step

A Civil War Sequel

Waldron Murrill McLellon

BUTTERNUT PRESS, PUBLISHERS
FERN PARK, FLORIDA

ONE STEP—TWO STEP,
A CIVIL WAR SEQUEL

Published by: Butternut Press, Publishers
1913 Winnebago Trail
Fern Park, Florida 32730-3015
Tel\Fax: 407-339-9244
e-mail: wally79497@msn.com

Manufactured in the United States of America
Library of Congress Catalog Card Number: 98-93140
ISBN: 1-884489-02-8

Publisher's Cataloging-in-Publication
(Provided by Quality Books, Inc.)

McLellon, Waldron M.
One step-- two step : a Civil War sequel / Waldron Murrill McLellon. -- 1st ed.
p. cm.
Preassigned LCCN: 98-93140
ISBN: 1-884489-02-8

1. Afro-Americans--History--1863-1877--Fiction. 2. Afro-Americans--West Virginia--Fiction. 3. West Virginia --History--Fiction. I. Title.

PS3562.A3184064 1998 813'.54
QBI98-1134

DEDICATION

To
the African Americans
of the United States
after the Civil War
and their unrelenting struggles
to improve
their individual and collective lots

PROLOGUE

In the era of Reconstruction, many former Negro slaves remained in the South and made their lots there. Over the years, as the Civil War defeat receded in time and Southern bitterness overcame resignation, oppression restarted, and intensified once the reconstruction occupation was terminated. Formerly vociferous northern abolitionists did little to help on a long term basis, essentially abandoning the Negroes' protection and improvement after freeing them from slavery. Southern Negroes were increasingly restricted by whites and their votes discouraged by threat and eventually a poll tax, the latter not eliminated until the middle 1900s. They were cast back not into slavery-by-ownership but into economic bondage, for the white man controlled the politics, the wealth, the jobs, and how much to pay for labor. No redistribution of land occurred, the famous, "forty acres and a mule" being a myth. Those Negroes that escaped to the North found less of a hazard but still suffered the trauma of personal adjustment from a plantation life to that of freedom.

Hannibal and Hester were two of the fortunate escapees, associated with a well-known, influential man in West Virginia. They had saved his life in his daring 1864 escape from a Confederate POW camp at Columbia, S.C. (LEATHER AND SOUL, A Civil War Odyssey). Starting from a position of advantage, with a friend and a farm, free and with a nest egg, they could count on advancing as far as their ambitions and abilities could take them. But always, undercurrents boiled in Virginia converted to West Virginia and on the Ohio side of the bordering river. A state with a varied heritage and people, some former Confederates in West Virginia opposed Negroes' rights and privileges. This tale follows Claude Shaw, Hannibal and Hester as they and others adjust to a new reality in the troubled peace after the end of the Civil War.

Both books are based on information on the life of the author's GGPa James Claudius Shaw, Captain, 7th Ohio Cavalry.

SPRING 1865

1

COLUMBIA, SOUTH CAROLINA

A thread of smoke curled up from the log cabin in the trees, its haze and acrid smell spreading lazily into the cool damp of midmorning. A few sunrays slanted through holes in the leafy cover, their glinting passage adding to the beauty of the setting. The sunlight increased the oppressive dampness as it vaporized sparkling water drops, jeweled necklaces adorning the leaves. Little splats among the chirps and scratchings of the small birds testified to the wet canopy, and augmented the yeasty scent of decaying forest mulch.

"Dat's de place," Hester shrieked. "We dere."

Brakes screeched when Hannibal hauled on the reins of the team and brought the carriage to a stop before the cabin door. He was still gentling the horses when Hester leaped out of the rear seat and ran into the old hut.

"She mighty anxious, Claude," the Negro said. He chuckled. "Old Granny Mandy be right s'prised."

Claude Shaw stepped down from the carriage, dressed still in his Captain's uniform, though the shooting war was finished. He stretched and worked out the creaks. "I expect they're about over it from the squeals."

A cacophony of sound filled the air, two happy women in the cabin chattering away. Before Claude could enter, the doorway was occupied by the ancient figure of Granny, her cane preceding her. She braced herself against the jamb and waved her stick at the planter, late of the Union cavalry. "Come bek, did yuh? Dat ring still in de wall jest like I say. Come on in an' git it." Her grinning face took in the two men. "Yer lookin' mighty fat. Musta fed up right good since de last time I seed yuh."

Claude stepped to her side and picked up her small frame, squeezing tight and planting a big kiss on each cheek. He whirled her around in a little dance.

"We're back, Granny, and safe. Come to get you."

She squirmed and protested, but with a laugh. He set down her wriggling body and headed for the carriage while Granny straightened her clothes.

"Body don' need no pawin'," she feebly protested. But her eyes were bright and tears glistened on her cheeks. Hester hastened to help her inside.

"Tie 'em off, Hannibal," Claude said, "and come on in. We need to tell Granny of our trip and the plans."

The big Negro led the horses to a grassy spot and fastened them on a long lead. He and the planter fished their saddlebags from the boot and carried them into the cabin. Granny surveyed the two from her chair, turned from the fireplace now that the weather was warmer. She patted the arm of her seat.

"Git overchere, Claude an' tell me 'bout de 'scape. Hester been runnin' on all jumbled. Can't git it straight." A thought struck her. "Git yer ring fust. It right at de axe mark dere behint de table."

Claude and Hannibal went over to the wall and the Negro unsheathed his knife. Granny's aim was off but they discovered the jewelry after excavating only a foot of clay chinking between the logs. Claude rubbed away the dirt and put the gold circlet back on his finger, hidden since their escape in November. Clenching his fist, he exposed the bright yellow decoration to the light from the fire. "Pretty, ain't it," he said. He felt whole again, his journey complete.

Granny held out his silver belt buckle when he neared her

chair. "Hid it good when you left. Warn't gwine sell it off." He hadn't expected return of the buckle and was of a mind to refuse, but a glance at the regal old Negro dissuaded him.

"Hurt you bad when I gave you the buckle last November," he said, humbling himself. "I won't offend you again." He bowed and accepted the piece. "I thank you for the gift."

They all fell silent when Granny tapped her stick, then fluffed up her skirts and settled into her seat. She sat very erect, a queen surveying her subjects. Granny tapped again and said in an imperious way, "Tell me of de journey."

"After we escaped last November first, Granny," Claude began, "your walnut dye and paper got us safe to Greenwood." He fell silent and shuddered at the recollection of a Union cavalry officer, dyed brown and dressed as a mulatto, while he wandered the woods with Hannibal. With forged papers to boot, imitating the handwriting of an important Charleston friend. He could have been shot as a spy. But it had worked, by God! Granny had saved him and the others.

"Big doin's at Camp Sorghum atter you folks 'scape," Granny said. "De Major fit ter be tied. Den de Minns come by an' head upcountry. Dat old bounty hunter real mad at de river trick." She chortled and rocked back and forth. "It fool him real good." But she was silent on the savaging Athey Minns had subjected her to, simply adding, "I put out de warnin' an' tol' Jenny an' de rest ter he'p."

Shaken out of his absorption with her tale, Claude said, "We know that, Granny. We got captured by Captain Hartsill and Captain Starr." He laughed grimly. "That Hartsill was hung by Rufus and Judah and all his troopers killed."

"Heard 'bout dat," Granny said. She laughed. "Liked dat 'about Judah cuttin' ol' Gill. He nuthin' but white trash, allus mistreatin' de gels when he lived over here close."

"Beulah helped us," Claude continued, "then Paul, young Owdoms and Sam, David's grandson. Sam took us on to Granny Owdoms at DueWest. It was near there that I killed young Jeremy Minns, but Sam got hurt a little."

Granny struck the arm of her chair and uttered a short, grim laugh. "You kilt all de Minns?"

Hannibal quietly interrupted. "Claude shot Jeremy up past Greenwood, Granny, den we kilt old man Minns an' Jared over ter Dalton. Hester run a pine spear thoo Minns."

The old woman cackled. "Allus tol' dat no-good Athey he'd git his comeuppance. De Debbil got him burnin' in Hell." Her face turned solemn and she put her forefinger up to her lips. The Negroes froze into rigid alarm but Claude raised the flap on his pistol holster, tensed to draw. A rustling sound carried through the door, followed by the entry of two young blacks. The youths stopped short, their mouths open, at the sight of Claude and the Negroes.

Granny raised her stick and sharply asked, "What you doin' here, Jed?"

"Hear'd de team an' wagon stop, Granny, fum up in de quarters," the bigger one replied. His eyesight shifted warily around the cabin and settled on the fireplace. "Me an' Bub's hungry. Reckened maybe we git a sop o' cake an' gravy." He and Bub remained at a respectful distance, out of range of Granny's hickory cane.

An imperious wave summoned them both closer. "You 'member de Lieutenant an' Hannibal?" she said. "Dey free now."

When the two nodded to Claude, she told Hester, "Git 'em one o' dem corn cakes, and gravy fum de pot."

Hannibal moved over toward the door. "Dey hep you while Hester gone?" he asked. "If dey don', I beat 'em good fo' dey leave."

Jed protested vehemently but Granny's blow with her stick silenced him. Bub was gulping his cake and spooning gravy from a bowl. He moved behind Hester and settled down out of view.

"Dey right good, Hannibal," Granny said. "Jed purty nice 'bout comin' 'round an' Bub mostly do what I say. Dey don' need no beatin'." Her face softened. "Dey my blood kin, twice removed, so I he'ps 'em like dey he'p me. Jed better; Bub jest rambunctious."

The two young Negroes smiled at her compliment and moved off to the table, eagerly attacking two more corn cakes and a bit of blackened meat that Hester offered them. With the visitors busy at the food, Granny returned to Athey Minns. She listened avidly as Hannibal and Hester told her of the last big fight when Gabe, their giant Negro friend, and Minns' son, Jared, killed each other and Hester finished Minns. That November action had left the fugitives free of pursuing enemies, only to hazard the Union lines by surrendering at Dalton. Granny wept at Gabe's passing, but rejoiced at the gruesome death of the bounty hunter.

"Ol' Athey beat me an' Jed an' Bub more'n onc't," she said. "Dat spear tear him up inside so he don' die quick. I happy 'bout dat." She hugged Hester tightly to her. "You done me proud, gel."

The girl smiled and preened, staying close to Granny's chair. Jed and Bub sidled over, their food exhausted. They hesitated until Granny told them to speak up.

"Ol' Minns' brudder Wiley been nosin' 'round," Jed said. "Dat preacher jest as mean as Athey. An' he fit his name. He a sneaky ol' weasel." Jed's lips curled down, disgust evident. He spit into the fire and wiped his mouth on his sleeve. "He an' Joshua askin' ever'body what happen ter ol' Athey. Ain't nobody know 'til now."

"Who's Joshua?" Claude asked.

Granny exploded. "Worse'n Athey," she said heatedly. "His oldest boy. Come bek fum de war an' right off beatin' on me an' Aunty Florinda 'bout Minns. Ketched Bub too."

Bub nodded and slipped off his shirt. Half-healed scars crisscrossed his back. The sight sickened Claude.

"Can't tell 'im nuthin'," Bub said. "Don' know nuthin'."

"Where are they now," Claude asked.

"Swingin' 'roun' north an' east," Jed replied. "Due bek 'bout three days, what I hears. Den dey s'posed ter git on west."

Claude's face wrinkled, his doubt showing. How did these Negroes know so much? "You keep tabs on the Minns?"

"Dey got two, three other boys heppin' 'em," Granny said.

"Dey our folks an' pass on 'bout dose Minns so's we be ready."

Hester had been circling around their cabin assembling Granny's things while the planter talked to the old woman and the Negro men. Her bundle was pitifully small when the girl announced to Claude that they were ready.

Granny shifted in the chair and her tears welled up. Her tremulous, "We got ter go? I been living in disyere cabin nigh onter thirty year. Don' know no other." She grasped the arms of her chair, then stroked the tops, polished from use. Her head dropped and she wept.

Claude knelt at the chair and put his arm around the trembling shoulders. "We're takin' you with us to West Virginia, Granny. Hannibal an' Hester'll be married soon and have a farm. You can live with them."

"Dat right," Hannibal boomed out heartily. "Claude plannnin' big weddin'. Can't hev it th'out you givin' Hester ter me."

Hester hugged and coaxed the old woman from the other side. "Claude promised me a white dress an' you a new red one, Granny. You got ter come."

At the mention of the new clothes, the old woman perked up and threw off their grasp. Her eyes gleamed and she braced the planter. "You buy me red taff'ta, Claude, one dat rustle? An' a silk bandanna?'

"Bright as yuh want," Claude said, falling into colloquialisms imprinted during his escape. "Git yer some fancy wimin's underthings, iff'n dey strike yuh. You jest say de kin'."

"You don' need ter talk like us, Claude," Granny said."Not fer me. I b'lieve yuh. But I ain' goin' 'less I sees Miz Ashley fust. An' Massa Rance, if he ain't off on bizness."

She struggled up. "You tek me up to de big house?"

Claude forced her back down into the chair and gently stroked her head. "That woman'll be coming down here, Granny," he said firmly. "You waited on Miz Ashley for all those years. She'll visit you this time, if I have to bring her at pistol point."

The Negroes recoiled from him and uttered cries of fear.

"Massa Pickens don' let you do dat," Hester burst out. "He right rousty you touch Miz Ashley."

"I'm not going to touch her," Claude said. His cold voice continued. "I'll ask her nice, but she's coming and him too if he's there."

The Union officer quick marched to the big house and clumped up the steps, his heavy leather boot heels resounding on the wooden porch. He fidgeted at the delay after his banging of the ornate clapper, an animal head bronze on a set of massive, painted doors. Surprisingly, a white man opened one side, a stocky, balding gentleman in the remnants of a Confederate uniform.

The southerner bowed without his face revealing even a flicker of surprise. "Rance Pickens, Captain," he said. When he invited Claude into the foyer, he made his excuses. "Most of our house help has abdicated, temporarily, I hope, so we're forced to our own contrivances."

Claude introduced himself before stepping forward. "Captain Claude Shaw, 7th Ohio Cavalry, sir. Visiting Granny Mandy in the quarters. May we talk?"

"Yes, Captain," Pickens said pleasantly.

Once the heavy door was swung shut, the limping southerner led Claude through the hall into a comfortable room, albeit with faded furniture and drapes. A woman rose as they entered, a thin, rigid statue in a well-worn dress.

"Captain Claude Shaw has come to visit, Ashley," Pickens said. "He's interested in Granny Mandy."

Claude bowed but the woman did not return his greeting.

"I expected as much," she said sharply. Her angular face and compressed, thin lips emphasized her bitterness while she inspected him. In contrast to her husband's hospitality, she did not invite Claude to sit. "Heard from Aunty Susan that Hester was with him. That girl was my best maid and she ran like the rest."

"Hester was free, Miz Pickens," Claude gently reminded her. "I too owned slaves up in Virginia" -- he choked a little and his voice rose and strengthened -- "but it was wrong, wrong to do so."

"You free your slaves?" Rance asked.

"Yes," Claude vehemently replied. "Once President Lincoln decided, I sent word to my wife to free those at the home place. I was campaigning in Tennessee." He sighed regretfully. "It was long after I should have."

"But why do you want ours?" Ashley burst out.

"I wouldn't be alive today," Claude said, "without Hannibal and Hester down there with old Granny Mandy. They saved my life more than once. Killed old Minns doin' it."

Rance Pickens' eyes widened. "Athey Minns is dead?"

Claude nodded. "And Jared and Jeremy. I killed Jeremy near Greenwood when they were chasing us and left him there. Expect he's buried nearby. Jared died fighting a Negro. Gabe was our friend and Jared shot and stabbed him. He broke Jared's neck. We buried them together in the forest outside Dalton."

"But what about Athey?" Pickens asked.

"He's in the woods east of Dalton. He shot me and was about to kill me when Hester ran him through with a pine splinter. Then she stabbed him." Claude laughed grimly, more in exultation than pleasure. "Athey Minns won't be bothering anybody any more."

A sharp intake of breath drew their attention to Ashley. "You must be the Lieutenant that escaped last November." Her face grew even more forbidding when she addressed her husband. "He's the one from Sorghum, Rance, the one that they couldn't catch."

Claude rubbed salt into the bitter woman's wounds. "That's right, Miz Pickens. And Granny and Hester helped me."

"I congratulate you, Captain," Rance said, and bowed. "Not many prisoners made it, particularly with that old Indian Athey Minns after them. And him with Old Blue. That bluetick was the most famous tracking dog in these parts. Athey and Blue caught dozens of runaways."

"I've got Blue at Greenbottom," Claude said. "That's my

place up in West Virginia," he explained. "Four thousand acres of bottomland along the Ohio River for him to run in, and the mountains behind."

Ashley cut short any other talk with a curt, "What do you want of us, Captain?"

Claude was all business. "I'm taking Granny Mandy up to West Virginia to live with Hannibal and Hester, her kin. She don't have many more years and we can make her easy. I ask you to come to the cabin and see her off."

A forbidding cloud stole over Ashley's face and her jaw set.

"Granny Mandy worked for you folks her whole life," Claude reminded them. "Will you not wish her well?"

"Let her come up here," Ashley spat out. "She's nothin' but a nigger slave and we're white folks."

"She can't walk all this way, Ma'am," Claude replied. His brittle request turned into a command. "I want you to come to the cabin and see her."

Rance stepped into the breech. Taking his wife's arm he forced her toward the hall. "Get your shawl, Ashley, while I put on a coat. Captain Shaw is right. We'll say goodbye at the cabin."

"It ain't right," his wife burst out.

The iron in Pickens' tone subdued her. "Granny was my Mammy when I was a baby and saw to my upbringing. We'll visit her before she goes."

When the three figures entered the cabin, Granny welcomed them from her chair. Rance swept off his cavalry hat with its flowing feather and bowed to her. "We've come to see you off, Granny."

She patted her lap. "Come here, boy," she said lovingly. Rance bent his stiff knee at the chair, groaning, with his arms around her and his head in Granny's lap. She gently stroked his bald top and recalled the past. "You had de most purty curly hair, boy, when youse a chile. I use'ter comb it up nice. Now gone jist like de Ol' Massa." Her ramblings went on with her little white son entwined in her being while her eyes dripped tears.

Silence enfolded the cabin until Pickens stirred and rose.

"You've got to go, Granny," he said. "Captain Shaw promises to take good care of you." He turned a sharp glance on Claude and a veiled threat came out. "I'll hold him to that promise."

Claude stared him down. "She'll be well treated. Granny saved my life."

Rance rummaged at his belt and produced a clinking leather sack. He withdrew a small gold piece and handed it to her. "Don't have much, Granny, but you'll go off with this. It's little enough for all our good days before the war."

Granny accepted the gift graciously with a nod and a smile. She turned the gold eagerly in her palms, where the yellow glittered against her seamed skin. Emotion overcame her and the old woman dropped her head and wiped her eyes on her apron, sniffling. "Mighty good o' yuh, Massa Rance. I let Hannibal keep it fer me 'til I'se needs some pretty."

A sob from his wife drew Rance to the woman's side. "Don't, Ashley," he said. He gently held her and stroked her back while the others, except for Granny, looked on uncomfortably. A triumphant gleam sparkled in the old servant's eyes.

A moment later, Ashley forced herself into composure. "You were a good maid, Hester," she said, biting off her words. "I wish you and Hannibal well. Write me about you and Granny once you're settled." She felt for the clasp of the strand of red brilliants garnishing her thin neck, but Hester demurred.

"Don't want your pretties, Miz Ashley. You done give me plenty. Teachin' me to read and write was mighty fine. I kin make sure our chil'ren git some learnin', more'n Hannibal an' me. Dat's enough."

A swift loading of the carriage followed the peaceful goodbyes, first the baggage in the boot, then the Negro women. Claude braced the southerner before entering the vehicle. Loitering at the step, he held out his hand. "The war's over, Captain. Will you settle for a truce? Or even friendship?"

Ashley frowned and her jaw muscles ridged hard. But Rance

limped over, finally, and grasped the proffered hand. "You're right, Claude. We've all got to go on and leave the past behind. Friendship is fine with me." The two gripped tightly, the locked gaze of the wounded veterans adding to the burying of the hatchet.

"I'm a merchant too, Rance," Claude said. "I do business as well as farm. Had a lot of factoring with Pinckney Middleton of Charleston before the war. Maybe we can arrange something to get us all started again."

Pickens' face lightened and he smiled at last. He straightened his shoulders and faced Claude confidently. "My wife is a Middleton and I know Pinck. I'll write him and will look to hear from you." He stepped back. "Old Pinck took a leg wound and can't dance any more but his mind's still sharp as ever."

"Good," Claude said. "Give him my regards."

When the carriage pulled away, Rance waved and shouted but his wife retreated into the dour silence of her first meeting. Nearby, Bub and Jed fidgeted before melting away into the trees.

"You'll regret this, Rance," his wife told him when the carriage disappeared from view. "His kind of folks killed all our kin." Venom replaced her kindness with Hester. "Stay clear of Shaw. He ain't nothing but trouble."

Her husband sighed, her bitterness and angry blows piled onto the South's humiliating defeat. Silence accompanied a few steps before his shoulders squared and he tensed his body. Seizing her arm and restraining her angry pulls to escape, he forced her to side him on the path to the big house. "The war is over, Ashley; we'll do business with the devil himself if we need to. I don't aim to lose this plantation."

2

Ruts in the road beyond the Broad River rocked the carriage violently, their upsets throwing Granny and Hester back and forth. The long, trying journey tired both and added to the women's woes of bruises and sore muscles. A gusty wind drove infrequent squalls of light, misty rain, penetrating the small shelter of the carriage top. By the time the light dimmed in the overcast of the late afternoon, presaging an early dusk, the women were shivering and wet and the men's gum coats dripping.

Granny drummed on the resonant floor with her stick and called out, "Need cabin, Claude, I'se hongry an' col'."

"We's gittin' wet," Hester shouted. "Ain't no reason ter go on tonight. Yo' git us some shelter, Hannibal."

The two men on the seat ahead waved in understanding and continued in conversation, swaying with the rocking motion. But Claude mercifully broke the two day trip to Greenwood with a stop at Saluda. The travelers perked up at the sight of a fence a mile past the river, a repaired boundary with some light colored, unseasoned rails. A ragged white man worked at the side of an opening, setting a post for a gate. His homestead cabin rested in a grove of oaks behind the fence, in the midst of bare spots and grown up weeds. Farming tools rusted at the side of a dilapidated barn. But the house seemed sound, with a well-formed stone step and a curl from the chimney rising into the drifting overcast. Hannibal pulled up at the lane, where Claude swung his stocky body down to greet the man. He was surprised to see the lanky farmer pick up a rifle from a hidden cover.

Claude stopped and raised his hands. “Hold on,” he said. “We’re just passing through and need shelter for the night.”

A suspicious gaze searched them all in silence. Finally the man spit a brown stream and lowered the rifle. Claude relaxed and let his arms drop. But his eyes never shifted from the southerner while he rested his right hand handy to his pocket pistol, a small caliber substitute of less weight than his holstered cavalry weapon. When a few drops fell from his campaign hat and distracted him, he cleared the rest of the water with a violent toss of his head. Claude’s tension eased when the farmer cradled his long gun.

“Can’t be too keerful, these times,” the man said. “You still a Yankee soldier?”

“Captain Claude Shaw, Seventh Ohio,” Claude replied, “but no more. War’s over.”

“Jess Abert, Reb,” was the challenging return. “You needin’ shelter fer the night? Goin’ on upcountry termorrer?”

Claude nodded. “Can we stay with you folks? Be happy to pay.”

At the mention of money, the wary expression of the man relaxed and his creases smoothed out into a roughhewn but gaunt face. He pointed on down the road to a cabin in a grove of trees. “Got too many kids fer you here an’ don’ let niggers in noway. You kin use the cabin down the trace, yonder.”

“Nobody there?” Claude asked.

“Nope,” the farmer told them. He shifted to outside the gate in the rail fence, dragging a lame foot. “The widow and her chil’ren left after her man was kilt in the war. I grew up with him, so she gimme the place free an’ clear.” He hesitated a moment and said mournfully, “Forest allus was wild but he made a good soldier. Saved me oncet when I got this bum foot.”

“Lot o’ good people hurt in the war,” Claude said, “both sides. Hope it will be well.” He shifted to the necessaries. “We need some meat. Got any deer or turkey?”

The man shuffled his way to a shed off to the side. A whole

unskinned deer hindquarter rested on his shoulder when her returned. Claude offered him a silver dollar once the meat was stowed in the carriage.

Ebert bridled and reset his rebel cap. "Ain't needin' no pay from a Yankee," he said. His tone sharpened. "And ain't no guestes o' mine pay fer no gift."

Claude pushed the money on him, irritated at the reb's refusal. "The war's over, man, and your woman and kids probably could use something. Take it for them."

Grudgingly, the farmer inched forward and accepted the silver. He turned it over in his palm and his brow wrinkled at the sparkle of the new metal.

"It's a new United States dollar," Claude explained. "No more of those Spanish Dollars around."

The rustic put the piece to his mouth and bit it, then growled with pain and spit. Holding his jaw, he looked at the befouled piece, its surface now discolored with tobacco. "Recken it be good," he said. "I thank ye fer the gift."

* * *

A slight wind rustled in the overhanging trees and the fire had burned to coals when Hannibal woke Claude.

"Got some fellers out dere," he whispered.

The planter reached for his weapons after pulling on his boots. Hannibal already had partially covered the coals. The darkened cabin left their bundled blanket rolls in shadow, sleepers to the intruders. They woke the women with hands over their mouths, cautioning them to be quiet. A knife to each armed them, but Granny seized her trusty stick and held out both hands, ready to punish anyone who came near. At Claude's insistence, she crouched by the trembling Hester in a corner away from the fire.

"Dey's comin' in, Claude," Hannibal muttered.

The two men hid on the hinge side of the plank door and watched the latch string raise the bar.

"Don' like this," an intruder murmured.

"He had a whole sack o' thet silver, Jobe," the other said. "We kill 'em, we kin git it all. An' the kerriage an' team too."

The door swung very slowly, its leather hinges making only the slightest squeak. When the door was well-opened, the intruders slow-footed into the cabin, eyes fixed on the blanket rolls. Knife blades glinted in the weak light from the fireplace.

When they were completely inside, Claude slammed the door and shouted, "Hands up."

The two invaders jumped off the floor as they whirled around, only to be stuck in the belly with gun barrels.

"Drop the knives," Claude hissed, jabbing his pistol barrel in deeper. Two blades hit the dirt floor with little thuds and the prisoner's arms shot toward the roof.

"Toss on some lightwood," Hannibal called out.

The resinous roots snapped and crackled when they blazed up, the fire growing brighter when Hester added shredded pieces. Two lighted candles added to the spectacle in the cabin, where Granny threatened the men from the side. Claude stepped back, his pistol leveled at Abert's belly. Increasing yellow light revealed a slim, teenaged youth beside the man, a young and frightened boy. Sweat beaded his brow and he trembled as he sought the protection of the older thief. Ignoring the pistol's threat, the farmer clutched the boy to his side and comforted him.

"Scairt, Pa," the boy gasped out.

His father stroked his hair and patted his back. "They ain't gonna hurt you, none, Jobe."

Claude's pistol rose and fell, his rage giving way to pity. "Thought to kill and rob us did you?" He flayed Abert. "We would have paid more if you had asked but you just had to have it all, an' to kill us to boot!"

"Ain't got no money, ner nuthin' now." Abert's shoulders slumped and his quavering voice oscillated between strangling and crying as he ran on. "Family 'most starvin' since the surrender. No seed ner a hoss ter plow with." His shrillness turned passionate. "How's a man ter git started agin when he ain't been left with nuthin'?"

The challenge struck Claude hard. It was a complaint that paralleled his own, but his credit in West Virginia was good and he was operating on borrowed money until he got his businesses and plantation in order. Now a defeated reb's agony and a boy's fear melted his indignation into softness, into a desire to help. He recalled his statement to Wood Stephens when the reb helped them escape to Union forces at Dalton. "I'll kill no more boys in this war," he had promised. Nor a father either, he knew now. The two rebs were safe from his gun, and he would help them if he could.

He braced Abert. "You give your word you'll be peaceful if we put away our pistols?"

The farmer reddened and looked him in the eye. "Yes," he promised. He bristled when a doubtful cast shadowed Hannibal's face. "You ask 'roun' an' you'll find Jess Abert's word allus good."

Claude relaxed and offered his hospitality. "Sit," he told them, "while Hester gets us some coffee. Then we talk."

The farmer perked up at that. The two intruders sheathed their knives and squatted on the dirt at one side of the fireplace, with Claude and Hannibal watching warily from the other side. As the heat took hold, a stink of sweat and mustiness arose from the rebs' drying clothes. It was enough for Hester to wrinkle her nose but she stirred out some coals and set the coffepot on them. Soon the aromatic brew scented up the cabin. When the coffee was poured into tin cups from Claude's kit, the first was handed to Granny, warming herself in a chair close to the fire.

The farmer accepted his steaming cup reverently, muttering thanks as he cradled it. He sniffed the brew and sighed before taking a sip. "Real coffee, boy," he said. "Ain't had none o' thet since sixty one." A quick slurp was rolled around in his mouth, then swallowed. He held the cup close as he slowly sipped the rest, savoring its taste.

Claude got down to business. "I could have killed you folks when you came in," he said reproachfully.

Abert nodded. "You could and had thet right," he admitted.

He looked at his boy and shook his head. "Could've kilt Jobe too. Robbin' you don' seem sech a good idee now."

"You own this land?" Claude asked.

Abert nodded. "'bout two hunderd acre. Maybe eighty real good fer crops, rest timber an' swamp." At sight of Claude's questioning face, he added, "Sold ter me by the Cullen's fer thirty dollars gold fer savin' their boy's life at Petersburg. Took 'bout ever'thin' I had to git the coin."

He stuffed a small tobacco leaf in his mouth and wadded up another quid. "The Cullen big house 'bout a mile over yonder. I farmed this little piece fer 'em on shares 'fore the war. Good loam in the bottom, an' wuth lots more."

Charging money as a reward for saving a life? It was unbelievable to Claude that the Cullens had been so rough on Abert. Why had they not presented the land to him? "They didn't give you the land for savin' their son? Can't believe they charged you hard money."

Abert shrugged resignedly. "Ol' Miz Cullen wanted but the Kunnel said he gonna lose the hull place 'less he pay on a debt to his banker in Columbia. Ever'body owin' these days."

Claude chuckled as the barb struck home. How true, he thought. Me too. And this reb, down to his boot straps, needed help to get started. He was destitute but trying. A gospel came unbidden into Claude's mind; the tale of the good Samaritan intruded into his normally cautious business approach. He braced Abert directly. "How much money would it take to get a mule and harness and some seed to start with, say corn, beans, potatoes. Notice you already got a plow and other tools."

Before the farmer could answer, Hannibal objected. "He need more'n feed, Claude. Got ter have cotton ter put by a little money next fall."

Claude shook his head firmly. "Food's enough for the first year. He can sell the surplus for profit, beyond what he keeps for his seed and stores. Get ahead faster growing crops for a full belly."

Abert confirmed Claude's estimate. "Food powerful skeerce.

Corn crop and taters bring good money." He pondered a moment. "They's hogs in the woods ter eat offen. Ketch a few and git my pigpen started."

Claude persisted. "Well, how much of a loan you need?"

Abert mulled over the question, turning his quid and spitting while he pondered. His son fidgeted, bursting to talk, while Claude grew more impatient.

"You got something to say, boy?" Claude asked.

Jobe's help spilled out rapidly. "Kin git that ol' mule of Prentiss', Pa, fer a few dollars. Miz Prentiss can't handle him and he's too old fer workin' cotton. She jist lets him run in the pasture. We kin ease him a little when he gits tired."

His father's face brightened. "Ain't no others 'round, that's sure, so he'll have ter do. Miz Prentiss sell?"

"Yes, Pa," Jobe replied eagerly. "She be glad to have some hard money. Tol' me so just yestiday."

Abert summed up his needs with slow, deliberate caution. "Five dollars fer the mule, Captain, maybe fifteen fer seed corn an' taters an' beans." He spit into the fire and wiped his mouth on his sleeve. "Say ten fer eat'n corn meal ter tide us over, ten fer harness an' tools. Kin git some tomato and punkin' seed free." Hope gentled his face, the corners of his mouth curling up. "Forty dollars? Give ye an IOU an' pay after the crops are sold."

Claude couldn't believe the total. "You can do with that little?"

"Yep," Abert replied, and his boy nodded. "Ain't no hard money 'roun' here. Union coin will buy it all mighty cheap."

Claude went to his luggage while Hester poured the last of the coffee to divert the farmer. Abert bent over the fragrant cup and smelled it, then passed the vessel to his son. "Finish it boy," he said. "Ain't gitten rid o' this chaw."

Claude fished two five dollar gold pieces and thirty silver dollars from the small handbag that carried his "bank." He exposed his belt pouch on return, palming the coins as if he had just recovered them. Handing the loan to Abert, he said, "I'll shake with you and have your word. Ain't no paper necessary if a man's word is good."

The farmer started at that and straightened up to attention, his glowing face and erect, confident posture replacing the gloom and defeated slump of a few minutes before. He took Claude's hand forcefully, inarticulately expressing his thanks. "Ye'll git it all back, Captain, an' then some. Jest give me directions to yer homeplace an' I'll fetch it with the boy."

Claude clapped Jess Ebert's hard, muscular arm with his free hand. Strong men made good friends and he sensed he had acquired a lifelong ally, if ever he needed help. "You're both welcome at Greenbottom," he said. "It's on the Ohio River below Gallipolis. I'll look for you and Jobe. Letty will welcome you both as well as your wife."

"Matty's a fine woman," Ebert said. "Jobe an' I couldn't never do 'thout her."

A thought struck Claude. The poor woman must be in rags after Ebert being gone so long. Reaching into his purse he fished out five more silver dollars and handed them to the farmer.

"Take these to her as a present from my Letty."

He raised his hand against Ebert's opening mouth, shutting off any protest by the fiercely independent reb. Jobe whooped and danced a jig.

"Now Momma can have some pretties," he shouted.

"I recken so, boy," Abert added. With a proud, erect bearing he said, "I thank you for the gift to Matty, an' the loan."

* * *

Their inquiry for David and Sam at Doctor Verdery's produced only a saddened widow dressed in black. Mrs.Verdery ushered Claude into the spacious living room and sat him down with a cup of chicory while she cried for her dear departed.

"The bloody flux ran through Greenwood in February when the weather turned warm and everything dripped. David went first." She sniffled and touched her nose with a lace handkerchief. "The Reverend prayed over the old man but it didn't do him or my husband any good. Buryin' David in the rain got the Reverend all wet. He and Sam passed on the next week." Claude's condolences did not help, the widow continuing her lamentations.

With the visit done, the party made it to DueWest by full dark and burst in on Granny Owdoms. Her grandson, John, raced to her side and was clutched tight until she recognized them. "Back, air ye?" the old Negro said, "got all de way ter Dalton?"

"Yes," Claude said. "We came back by Verdery's but Sam was dead. Can't help him." He undid his tight gunbelt and hung it over the back of a chair. Loosening his coat and scratching his middle as he stretched, he said, "You interested in goin' to West Virginia? We got room for you and John, easy."

"I tink on it," she said."

* * *

Rance Pickens warmed before the fireplace, the damp chilling his bones drawing him closer to the small fire. He was hunched down in his chair, almost asleep, a shawl over his shoulders, though it was warm outdoors when the sun was high. Ashley rocked nearby, her hands busy with her needles, crocheting a spread during the long silence of married companionship.

"It's only right, Rance," she said.

His reverie snapped, he sat up and asked, "What, Ashley? What is right?"

Ashley's grim face creased, its mean cast boding ill. "I've sent for Wiley Minns. I'm going to tell him about Athey's killing and that nigger-lover Shaw."

Rance bounded out of his chair and exploded, "You didn't?" He trembled uncontrollably as he walked the few steps, his agitation carrying him to a confrontation with his wife. "Why would you stir up that viper? He's nothing but a jackleg preacher, feeding on folks' fears with his hellfire and damnation."

A small smile crossed Ashley's face, her mouth settling into a thin crease. Hate and shadows accentuated the cruelness of her eyes. With her hair drawn back severely, its tightness and her single-minded purpose made her skull resemble a death's head, herself a harpie.

"Those Yankees ruined us," she said bitterly. "Now Shaw and Hannibal," she choked on the Negro's name, "those villains have taken Granny and Hester. Probably Jed and Bub will run off too. Leave us with nothing."

Rance swayed and groaned. "Don't do it Ashley," he pleaded. "Minns'll kill Claude." He could not be still but hobbled back and forth on his game leg, his stick tapping. "Claude and Pinckney are our chance at business again."

Ashley laughed at him. "You think that Yankee will help you?" She clawed at his feelings again. "No honor in him, or that Pinckney. They'll help themselves, not you."

His face bloated and darkened as his anger increased. Rance leaned over and slapped her hard. "Don't you say that about old Pinck. He's your own cousin and he and I been friends since we were boys. He don't cheat people."

She faced him boldly, her breast heaving, not cowed by the blow. Ashley rubbed her red cheek and poured salt on his hurt. "That's what you've come to, Rance, striking a woman. Not much left of your honor either."

He sagged down and the anger went out of him. His weak, "I'm mortified, Ashley," tried to make amends, but she resisted his attempt to kiss or hug her.

After her work was stuffed in a knit bag, she rose from her chair and banished him from her bed and love. "You'll use the back bedroom from now on, Mr. Pickens. Aunty will make it up." With an imperious, contemptuous smile, Ashley swept out of the room.

"Damn," Rance said. He went back to his chair and settled into its familiar curves. His wife's increasing tantrums at their poor circumstances occupied his mind, replacing the plans he had been making to approach Pinckney. What was he to do with her? They had almost no money, and neither the fine gowns nor the party gaiety of the earlier days. Most of the young gentlemen were dead and the rest impoverished. Their daughter would have to take her chances, even marrying a trader, if offered. Aye, that was what was worrying Ashley, in addition to her hate of Yankees. He needed to talk to Pinck, and soon, for Nancy was a good thirteen now and would need prospects at sixteen. And he had to restart his plantation. No slaves to do that, so it was business of some sort. Rance fell into a troubled sleep as he tried to solve the impossible. When Aunty checked him, he was mumbling a little and his body quivering, his dreams unknown.

"Yo' sleep tight, Marse Rance," she whispered and kissed his head. "Dat ol' witch upstairs ain' gwine hurt you. Not long as I'se here." She tucked in his shawl and left him to his visions.

* * *

Two days later a preacher called on Ashley, privately, while the master was away to Charleston. The Reverend's black trappings, string tie and felt hat covered a tall but bulky, plump frame. A wrinkled raggedness marred an otherwise clean appearance. When the hat came off, Wiley Minns' round face was made even larger with massively projecting black sideburns and a trimmed goatee. Topping the hairiness was a slick black thatch, combed down smooth. A pair of dark eyes peered out from deep sockets, rimmed above with bushy eyebrows.

Aunty answered the banging of the front door knocker, her disapproval apparent. "What yo' want?"

"Miz Ashley sent for me," Minns said.

Aunty's lip curled. "Yo' dat Minns?"

Minns' face flushed and he raised his beefy hand. "Don't you git uppity with me, nigger. You call me Reverend Minns or I'll hide you." When he reached for her she drew back and opened the door wide.

"Miz Ashley 'spectin' yuh. Yo' jest foller me."

She scurried up the wide, ornamented staircase with the preacher close behind. Turning down the hall, Aunty entered the front bedroom, a spacious chamber with a couch and chairs before a fireplace. Ashley sat on a flowery, upholstered lounge with one foot bandaged and resting on a stool before her.

"Reveren' Minns," Aunty announced, and made way for the preacher.

He bowed to the woman, "At your service, ma'am."

She nodded. "Take one of those chairs, Reverend," she said, then realized he was looking at her foot. "I beg your pardon for not getting up, but I fell on the stairs yesterday."

"My sympathies, Miz Ashley. They can be treacherous. I hope it's not broke or hurtin' much."

"Just a sprain," Ashley said. "Be up and about in a few days."

Aunty fussed about the couch, straightening Ashley's light shawl and adjusting the stool and dress to keep the ankle modestly covered.

Her mistress dismissed her with a preemptory, "Close the door when you go out, Aunty. I don't want us bothered while we talk." She called after the retreating servant, "I'll ring when I want coffee."

"Yes Ma'am," Aunty answered. "Get cook fix it right now." A slam of the heavy bedroom door voiced her displeasure. "Taint right," she muttered, "Miz Ashley alone in dat room wid a no-count, white-trash preacher." She sputtered on as she hustled to the kitchen, where she vented her anger on the cook.

Once the door was shut and Aunty's footsteps died out in the hall, Ashley went immediately to the heart of her intelligence. "Your brother's dead, Reverend. Athey and the boys, Jared and Jeremy, all gone."

His eyes closed and his breathing deepened. "May the Lord be with them," he intoned in a singsong. With the prayer done, he leaned forward, intent on the woman. "I heard 'bout Jeremy. He's buried up to Greenwood. Joshua and I visited his grave. But there wasn't no word on Athey."

"We found out just the other day," Ashley said, "from a Union Captain, Claude Shaw, the one that escaped from Sorghum last November. You remember?"

"What about him?"

"He was here with his servant, Hannibal, and my maid they stole. Told us that he killed Jeremy and that Athey and Jared were killed just east of Dalton."

Minns face grew bleak, a stony, "How?" his only word.

"A nigra, Gabe, killed Jared but was killed in return. My maid, Hester, killed Athey with a knife. They're buried east of Dalton in the woods."

The big frame seemed to expand as Wiley Minns tensed his imposing muscles. "Where is Shaw now?"

"Stole Granny Mandy and went off to the west. He's picking up some nigras that helped him along the way, then heading back to his plantation up on the Ohio River." She thought a moment. "Greenbottom, they told us."

"He an abolitionist?"

"Virginian," Ashley said disgustedly. "Turncoat that went with the Union. They're the worst kind."

Minns nodded and fell into thought. His face changed from a reflective calm into one with a set jaw when he next spoke. "Killin' 'em all ain't the way to get even, though that's what Josh will want. I'll have to keep that boy with me."

Ashley licked her lips and her face broke into a smile, but her eyes were bleak. "What will you do?" she said. "I want that nigger-stealer caught and thrashed or worse."

"Best way is to break him first," Minns said calmly. "Bankrupt him, humiliate him, make him sin. After he's humbled before the Lord, when he ain't got nothing, then vengeance can be taken."

The lack of a killing fever did not meet Ashley's experience with the southerner's sense of honor. First a cold-blooded intent to ruin, then kill? "How would you do that?" she said.

Minns smiled and put her off. "We got ways, Miz Ashley. Me and Josh will see it done right. Just don't you worry your head on it."

A pull on the bell rope was answered by Aunty with a tray and a severe frown. The old servant poured the cups of chicory and fussed around the room while the two conspirators finished with small talk. Minns bounded down the steps close after Aunty when Ashley dismissed him. He grabbed the Negro by the arm and struck her hard on the buttocks at the front door, repeating the blows as she struggled.

"Don't you cry, damn you," he said, "or I'll give you worse."

Aunty wrenched free, her blazing eyes and twisted face promising her threat to him. He laughed and strode to his buggy. It creaked when he hoisted his bulk into the seat and its axles protested as he drove off down the lane to the main road.

3

A they Minns' log house north of Columbia lay nestled in its hardwood clearing, a thin tendril of smoke drifting lazily away from the chunk rock chimney. It was the time of false dawn, with the family and dogs still bedded down, and only a light breeze rustling the leaves. When the sky lightened, nature's alarm clock sounded off. The red cock's crowing rousted out the hens and lesser roosters and stirred the house. Beds squeaked and water splashed as it was poured from a pitcher into a bowl.

A singular bloodhound on the wide porch yawned and stretched, first forward, then back down on his haunches to waken throughout. Great ears hung by his pendulous jowls. But he was not colored the red-brown or multibrown shades of the blood line. Instead he carried a bluish cast around the chest and was spotted over the body. A lighter frame suggested the half-breed, it and longer legs with light tan feet identifying the bluetick of a parent's line.

When a skinny, teenaged boy showed in the cabin doorway, yawning and scratching his ribs, the hound patted forward and wagged his tail. The boy automatically petted him and felt behind those massive ears. He inspected the dawn while he stroked the itch of the compliant hunter. A bluing sky with scattered clouds greeted him. "Gonna be a fine day, Red," he said. "Clear an' not too hot." He pushed the hound away. "Now git, 'til I'm back from the outhouse."

Red obediently flopped down on the porch while the boy walked down the hill to the tilted board and bat structure, askew on a rock foundation. Its tattered roof edge and darkened boards testified to long use. A few minutes passed before he showed, hitching up his pants. He went to the well and splashed water over his head and face before returning to the house. The dog rose to meet the boy when the latter bounded up the steps to the wide porch.

"Wantin' some cornbread?" the youth asked. Red grinned and wagged his tail even harder. The boy tossed his head and ran his fingers through his flying, long black hair. He shook off the water droplets and tied it back Indian fashion. Only then did he pat the slobbering dog. "Mama be up soon. An' Josh." A rattle inside was followed by sounds of the fire being stirred and chunks thrown on. He grinned. "Kate's bangin' 'roun' in thar. She'll fix us somethin'."

As if to confirm his message, a musical voice sounded from inside the house, "What you want, Jasper?"

"Be right in," he yelled back. Jasper laughed and petted Red. "You see, she allus makes us somethin'."

Red's body stretched out and he sniffed at the door, his snuffling nose investigating the odors. A sizzle of frying meat was followed by the pork's mouth-watering odor. Red pushed his head into the opening when the compelling scent grew stronger. Jasper slapped the dog in the face and crowded him back. "You ain't 'llowed in thar, Red," he said. "You know that."

The hound sank down but his tail still wagged and his mouth dripped saliva on the porch floor. He lay flat on his belly with head stretched out and his tail extended, a living doormat. But his brown eyes never left the boy. When Jasper disappeared inside, the hound inched forward into the door opening, savoring the coming treat. He did not have long to wait. A few minutes later, Jasper reappeared with a steaming tin plate full of food for himself. He carried another with a slab of cornbread soaked in grease from the meat trimmings stacked on it, a big feed for Red. The dog's neck bulged when he gulped it down and licked the plate. He was sitting up, begging from Jasper, before the latter was finished with the plate in his lap. His grin entreated for another piece of pone from the boy in the rocking chair.

Jasper laughed. “You ain’t nothin’ but an empty hole.”

The boy broke off another morsel of pone and fished out a piece of pork rind. They went down Red’s gullet to join the rest. When Jasper had cleaned his plate, he put it down for the hound to lick, a vigorous effort that slid the tin across the irregular planks of the porch in a clattering journey. Red sat up and belched when he could wring no more from the two plates. At Jasper’s “Here, Red,” the dog flopped down next to the rocker to receive a welcome petting. The two were dozing with full bellies when a buggy and team showed in the lane below the house, the vehicle’s creaking and swaying demanding their attention.

Jasper started up and shouted, “Ma, Ma, it’s Uncle Wiley come to visit.”

* * *

The morning sun was orange in a bluebell sky by the time Wiley was fed and had belched in appreciation. He and Joshua rocked in two of the chairs on the porch, while picking away at their teeth with splinters. Jasper propped his back against the cedar post at the steps, with Red stretched out alongside. A snore arose and the dog kicked and yipped, his vocals adding to his belly grumbles. The boy absentmindedly petted the hound as he followed the men’s discussion of the market for whiskey, now that the war was finished.

Ma Minns joined them once she had set Kate to the cleanup. She was wiping her red, wrinkled hands on her ragged, drab apron when she came out onto the porch, a spare, toil-worn woman with a premature stoop and a tired face. Settling into the last rocker with a sigh, one with a tattered quilt in the seat, she reached into the bag at the side and took out her knitting.

Wiley waited until her hands were busy. His somber voice and gloomy mien were funereal. “Know what happened to Athey and the boys."

Ma Minns brushed back a wisp of stringy, graying hair. Resignation lined her face with creases and she let her hands fall into her lap, but she did not cry. "Recken from yer tone, Wiley, that they's dead."

"Kilt, Ma. Heard it from Miz Ashley herself."

Joshua stopped rocking and leaned forward. He swore and pounded his fist on his knee, muttering angrily. Jasper's start woke Red, who sat up. The boy was a marble statue, frozen by the news.

Wiley worked his cud and spit over the porch rail. "Got all the particulars four days back. Been thinkin' on it ever since."

Joshua's low, ominous, "What happened, Unk?" presaged even more trouble than his clenched fists and flashing eyes. Strung tight, he quivered and inched his chair forward, straining to hear the rest.

"That Lieutenant Shaw that 'scaped from Sorghum last November, him with the nigger Hannibal, he kilt Jeremy up by Greenwood."

It was too much for Ma. She wept, her apron covering her face. "He was my smartest boy, allus thinkin' an' he could read." She moaned, her misery rising and shoulders sagging. "Spected him to get more schoolin' an' be more'n a whiskey stiller."

Wiley went on remorselessly, intoning the tragic details. "Reverend Verdery there read the service. Jeremy's in the church yard, buried proper and resting with the Lord. Josh and I seen the grave ourselves. Got a good headstone."

"And Athey and Jared?" she asked.

"Kilt east o' Dalton, Miz Ashley says. A nigger, Gabe, done Jared and her maid stabbed Athey to death with a knife." His voice broke a little and he blew his nose. "I got to find 'em and bury 'em proper."

"Goin' with you, Unk," Joshua said. His determined voice rang out clearly. "Atter we git em' in the ground, then we kin kill that Yankee an' the niggers."

"No, boy," Wiley replied. He raised his palm when Joshua

protested. "You be quiet now. I got me a plan. Been studyin' on it hard."

"Don't you git kilt too, Wiley," Ma cautioned. "Ain't no need lookin' fer more trouble."

A contemptuous, "Ain't no bother, Ma," burst out of Joshua. "Ain't nobody killin' no Minns 'thout we git back at 'em."

Wiley looked upward and clasped his hands together as if in prayer. "An eye for an eye," he intoned piously. "It's the law."

Kate shuffled out of the door and took a seat on the arm of her mother's rocker. The half-grown girl put an arm around the bent woman's shoulders. Ma wept, small sobs escaping her and tears running down her cheeks.

"I can't bear losing you too, Josh," she pleaded. "Don't go, boy, the signs ain't right."

"Got too, Ma," Joshua said firmly. "Ain't no Minns less'n I settle with that Shaw and his nigger."

Wiley swore and tried to calm the angry reb. "Damn it, boy," he said, punctuating his remarks with a threatening fist, "you listen to me. We ain't gonna kill 'im, not right off."

Rebellious, Joshua sneered. "You call yerself a Minns? Ain't no Minns gonna put up with that an' not git even."

Wiley sighed and patiently explained. "More ways than one to kill a man, Josh. First, you an' me gonna take Athey's gold and ruin that Yankee. I know where he hangs out. Once he's ruin't, when he ain't got nothin', then we kill him and all those niggers."

Mollified, Joshua pursued the plan for revenge. "He got any boys, Unk? I git them too fer Jared an' Jeremy."

"We find out once we're up on the Ohio. Fetch out Athey's gold."

Joshua lugged his father's heavy leather sacks out of the cabin, one at a time. Each of the three was stuffed with bright yellow coins, mixed Spanish and U.S. Wiley shucked his coat and spread it on the porch. He poured out two sacks, the gold coins forming an imposing pile of glittering metal on the black background of the coat lining.

"Where'd Athey git all this coin?" he asked. "I knowed he had some but not all this."

"Been sellin' whiskey last thirty years I know of," Ma replied. "He allus wanted gold. Wouldn't never take none of that paper money." She sighed and bitterly added, "kept it mighty close too. Couldn't hardly git 'im to give me none fer clothes an' sech fer me or the children."

"How much we got?" Wiley asked.

"I counted it, Unk," Joshua replied. "Bout eight thousand each bag."

Wiley's eyes gleamed. He fingered the coins and let them clink. "We take two sacks with us to do those business dealin's agin Shaw. We break him good."

"Kin I go too, Uncle Wiley?" Jasper said. "I'm gittin' big enough and shoot real good."

"No, boy. You care for your Ma and the girls an' run the whiskey business. We probably need more gold later."

Ma's face lightened and she beckoned Jasper to her chair. She grasped him tight and hugged him. "When you're growed, boy, you kin traipse off, but I need you right now."

"Yes, Ma," he said. He pulled away and made his stand, his lower lip protruding pugnaciously. "If they have trouble, I'm goin' up to help."

Within two days Wiley and Joshua had modified the buggy to create three hidden strongboxes for the gold, each well camouflaged and lined with soft skins to prevent noise. They rode out the following morning, Joshua on his horse Spots siding the preacher in the carriage. Red padded alongside, a loss Jasper had cried over when Josh announced his intention. They needed a good tracker, Josh had told him, and Red was the best, even better than his father, Old Blue.

The buggy squeaked when Wiley turned before leaving the clearing. "You're the man here, now," he shouted at Jasper. "You take good care of your Ma and Kate."

Kate and the boy shook their fists in the air. Their, "Kill

'em all," echoed down the slope.

The venom of the preacher had infected the young. But the travelers left over Ma's tearful entreaties, her warnings and dire predictions ignored in their blood feud desire for revenge.

* * *

Claude and Hannibal had little luck at DueWest in convincing Granny Owdoms or any of her brood to go with them. A day of hard persuasion left the Negroes unmoved. Old George had listened silently, shifted his cud and spit, and issued a polite no before limping off. And all the young children had clustered around Granny. Claude gave up and drove on, passing by the thicket off the Saluda River where Aunty Emma had doctored his bayonet wound during his escape in '64. Only a rock chimney and charcoal identified her cabin site, with blackened tree trunks from the fire and a few graves nearby. The Negroes and planter walked among the mounds, Claude wondering about their friend, a kindly Negro who had helped him so much.

"Don' even know where to put a stone," Hannibal said. "Can't tell which one."

"We can say a prayer," the planter responded. "It's about all we can do."

Hannibal insisted on the right, his loud, firm voice resonating in the glade with the first prayer of his ministry. "Oh Lawd. Here lie your chil'ren in de wilderness. Dey was good folks, Lawd. Take dem to your bosom in de free lan'."

Two days later their carriage rolled up to the Calhoun place about noon. The big house above the Seneca River was empty except for house servants when Claude called. A maid greeted them warmly at the door and sent them down the lane to Granny Esther's cabin in the quarters.

Sissie was playing with a rag doll when they approached. She ran screaming into the structure. "Granny, Granny, it's dem come back."

Granny Esther showed at the door of the cabin as Claude

and Hester alighted from the carriage. She was as scrawny as ever, hobbling with her cane, but just as feisty. "Made it, did yer?" She laughed, her eyes twinkling. "Figured Rufus' git ye thoo dem Rebs. Come on in an' set."

With Granny Mandy and Granny Esther ensconced in the two chairs in the rude cabin, the others sat on wood chunks. Two children rested in bunk beds along the walls, Esther's sick cabin remaining a haven for the Negroes still at the plantation. It had the same sour sweat and pone smells Claude remembered, a refuge for him in his time of need during his escape.

An hour of joyous talk took the Grannies through all the details of the escape and the fugitives' return. The two old women bonded immediately with their tales of outrage and success over the rebs, but Sissie soon tired of the visit and left Granny Esther's lap for her nest behind the sacks. Hester tucked her in, the slim, little girl drifting off to sleep when hidden.

Claude was curious about the vacancy at the big house. "Where's the overseer, Granny? Nobody there when we called."

"Hawkins took his missus over toward de Spartans atter he come bek fum de war." She giggled. "Mistress big as a barrel and he mighty mad."

"Not Hawkins' child?" Claude asked innocently.

"Rufus knocked her," Granny Esther said. She chuckled, then broke out in a cackle. "When dat nigger baby born dishere summer, 'spect old Hawkins kill 'er." She spit contemptuously. "She so mean we was gwine do it, but ol' Hawkins kill 'er fer us."

The planter nodded, deep in thought. So that was where Rufus had dallied that night at Calhoun's. A mistress with her husband gone and thinking he was a white man. Well, served her right for bedding Rufus. He conjured up a picture of the Negro. She couldn't have picked a finer person. Rufus might be a Negro but he was as strong and good a man as one could find. Claude wondered where the redhead and Judah had gotten too. Would they ever take up his offer to visit Greenbottom?

Hannibal reminded him of his protesting stomach when the Negro said, "I'se hungry, Hester. Fetch in some o' dat ham and de cornmeal."

"You got ham?" Granny Esther said delightedly. "Ain't had none since de winter."

The two old women offered much advice from their chairs while Hester, young and supple, stooped and stretched and carved and sweat to get the meal together from the travelers' stores. When it was ready, hot pone, left-over boiled beans with onion, and burned ham slices, she served Claude first. He took the tin plate and another and presented them to the grannies.

"You served me, Granny," he said. "Only right for you to get the first helpin's." He bowed his head as a thought struck him. "Say a blessin', Hannibal."

Silence ruled the group. Hannibal screwed up his eyes and said, "Lawd, we ain't much on good prayin' yet, but we thank you fer dishere food an' dat all o' us is free an' safe. Let us work in your ways. Amen."

Their amens finished, only rattles and crunches and swallows and gurgling sounds marred the cabin's silence while they filled their bellies. A long drink by Hannibal preceded a rumble as he expelled his gas in a great belch.

"Dat good," he said. "You gonna mek a fine cook, Hester."

Beads of sweat coated Hester's face and loose tendrils of hair swirled from under her colorful bandanna. She flipped her big fork at him and smiled. "Cook what you bring in. Up ter you whether it good or not."

Somnolence occupied their late afternoon, the men snoring on the floor and the grannies in their chairs. But Hester, curious, visited Iris at the big house to soak up all the gossip. The striking young woman was her usual ingenuous self, coy and scheming.

"Yo' got room fer me?" she said innocently.

On her guard, Hester fended off the question. "Yo' ask Claude. It's his carriage."

Iris' eyes gleamed. "Dat Hannibal mighty fine lookin' man an' he ain't yours yet. Like ter go 'long." She stared at Hester and shot out a barb. "Maybe he like me better'n you."

Instantly Hester seized Iris with her left hand and

jerked her up close. With her enraged face next to that of the other girl, she pulled a knife from her waist and stuck it against Iris' throat. "You mess wid Hannibal, I kill you," she hissed. Pushing on the knife, she pricked the girl's neck. A red trickle ran down Iris' smooth brown skin and wet her bosom. Hester shuddered and drew the blade back when the stream increased.

The vixen laughed at her. "You ain't got de sand ter kill me." She wrested loose and felt of the greasy blood on her neck. "I sees Claude. Maybe he tek me."

Hester broke and ran for Granny Esther's cabin. It took an hour of tears, wails and strangled sobs before Claude and Hannibal got her story straight.

Hannibal laughed and hugged her tight. "Don' want no Iris, Hester. Want you. We git married up to Claude's."

"That's right," Claude said. He reassured her. "I won't take Iris. She wasn't nothin' but a troublemaker when we were here."

Granny Esther nodded, "Iris allus in fights" her only comment.

When Iris appeared at the cabin, she had cleaned off the blood and washed out her dress. The girl shyly asked Claude for passage and raged at him when refused.

"You ain't seen de last o' me, you no-good trash." She turned away from the planter and railed at Hannibal who held Hester in an embrace. "I gits you in bed, you find I better'n dat skinny bitch you got holt of."

Iris' continuing tirade was ended by Granny Esther's flailing stick. The old woman drove her from the cabin, beating her about the head and shoulders until she ran out of the door. Iris continued her imprecations and threats as she retreated.

"I'se git even wid all o' you."

"You reckon she means any of that?" Claude asked.

"Iris sneakin' an' connivin', Granny Esther said, "but ain't likely she leave dishere place." She reconsidered. "Iffen she show up, don' you give her no openin'. She allus tek 'vantage an' plenty poison."

They ended the day on a note of jollity once Iris was expelled. After another big feed from Claude's stores, snores filled the cabin through the night. An overcast sky and dewy grass awaited them, a cool, but damp morning well-suited for their early start.

Claude's leave-taking of Granny Esther was poignant. She clutched him and whispered when he bent down to hear. "Second sight workin' last night, Claude. Yuh got big trouble fum dem Minns. Seed it right plain."

"The Minns? They were all killed."

She shook her head. "His family comin' atter yuh, Claude. You be keerful."

He rode off troubled, turmoil in his heart. He knew of the blood feuds of the mountaineer in western Virginia. They took in a whole family, brothers, cousins, in-laws. And Minns had been half-Indian as well. Well, so much for peace, he thought bitterly. Got to watch our backs until we can kill them too. That damned war never will end.

* * *

The Peavey family had farmed a piece of bottom land next to Claude's huge plantation for three generations, but Jubal Peavey's main acreage extended up a bordering, timbered hollow to the south. His meets and bounds rose from the river road opposite Greenbottom. They meandered to the higher land and extended along the ridge lines, encumbering perhaps 500 acres of mountains and private hollow. With the river road splitting his farm at the base of the hills, old man Jubal Peavey chose to locate his clapboard house on the rounded knob of his family's original log cabin. About one hundred feet back, its yard fronted the road to the north. A lack of trees allowed a fine view of his small acreage of bottom fields and the river beyond, with Ohio in the background. When he encased the cabin in 1850, the ancient timbers lay within the house walls and created a natural fortress in the front. Unpainted, with weathered poplar siding, the two story house sat solidly on a stone foundation. A porch at the front allowed comfortable sitting, both to see the road and to greet and visit with passing friends. Cedar shingles finished off the roof of the picturesque dwelling, but debris and bare ground around the yard in front depicted a casual attention to cleanliness. Peavey's barn, corncrib and outbuildings lay around the slope behind, along the small creek issuing from the hollow. The valley provided a contained pasture for Peavey's few cattle and gave access to the woods for his free-ranging pigs.

Cooling breezes blew from the north on this Sunday morning and carried away the chimney smoke. On the porch, Jubal puffed on his pipe, comfortable after a heavy breakfast. He had appropriated the only rocking chair and had his lame foot propped up on a wood chunk. A passing buggy drew a wave and a "Howdy," answered in turn by the passer-by.

A young, overalled man in a nearby chair sat up and shoved back his hat, craning his black moustached head after the buggy. "Didn't see 'im, Gramps," he said. The splints of his chair protested when he shifted his bulky yet tall frame around. Hickory legs screeched on the floorboards. He spit tobacco juice into the front yard, then tilted his chair back and propped one booted foot on the porch railing while slumping against the inclined splints.

The seat's precarious balance on two flimsy legs drew a caution from his grandpa. "Goin'a go over back'ards, Hank, you don' watch it."

The young man laughed and tilted the chair back even farther. "Like my comfort, Gramps," he said. "Who went by?"

The wind played with old Peavey's long, gray beard and curling white hair while he puffed slowly on his pipe. His angular, spare frame was encased in a linsey shirt and rusty black pants, frayed at the bottom. Jubal blew several smoke rings before deigning to identify the traveler. "It was that Shaw nigger, Isaiah," he said. "Don't recken Miz Letty goin' to church this mawnin' with that nigger out gallivantin' in the buggy. No kids with 'im neither."

"What you recken he's doin', Gramps?"

"Can't say, Hank, but it won't be he'pin' us." Bitterness tinged his reply. "Those damned uppity Shaws still got niggers ter he'p. We ain't got none left with them all runnin'."

Hank laughed. "Not all, Gramps. Member you hung two when we caught 'em trying to git 'cross the river last winter."

It set off the old man and he swore violently. "Rest o' 'em wouldn't dared try, hadn't been fer that young Shaw boy an' his nigger he'pin'. Ol' Claude wrote them Shaws to free all o' his. Miz Letty done it once she knowed they wouldn't run."

"Warn't 'til after he escaped, Gramps. Said Hannibal saved his life. She freed 'em all then, not when he fust tol' her."

"Don' matter," the old man protested. "Claude owes me fer them five niggers we lost. Worth five hundred each at least. Goin' git the money er take it outen his hide."

Hank shook his head and laughed derisively. "Nope," he said, "you know Claude's right stubborn. He ain't goin' pay you no money."

Jubal scowled as he grimly staked out his ground. "We Peavey's don't put up with nobody interferin' in family business. Claude's family done jest thet. We git satisfaction, or he'll go to hell."

4

Claude's carriage bounced down the badly rutted lane from Clarkesville, Georgia, and advanced slowly toward Jake's blacksmith shop. Its creaks sent a loud announcement of the travelers' arrival long before they came in view on the winding track. While his dog faced them with raised hackles and loud barking, Jake ducked hurriedly into the house and came out with a rifle. He cradled the weapon in his left arm and stood spread-legged across the lane at the turn around before the shop and barn. Two horses showed in the pasture beyond, their ears pricked at the sound and sight of visitors. But their peaceful interest was not shared by Jake. His ominous stance matched the overcast sky with its hint of rain.

The rangy man's threatening attitude put Claude on alert. "Ready your pistol, Hannibal," he said in a low voice. "He's mighty edgy."

When Hannibal pulled up close and stopped the team, Claude raised his right hand in greeting and called out, "Howdy, mind if we light?"

"Git down if ye want. You got shoe or harness trouble?"

"No," Claude replied. "Horses are fine. Just stopped by to see Jessie Mae."

A face appeared at a window in the nearby farmhouse, then the door slammed as Jessie Mae ran down the steps and into the bare yard. Rumpled and dumpy, with her graying hair flying, she looked no different to Claude than the previous November when she had helped them.

"What you want with me?" Jessie Mae asked.

Claude had stepped down from the carriage and the women were exiting the vehicle, accompanied by stretching and lamentations of miseries. The planter took a few steps toward the farm woman, his action instantly offset by Jake's move to her side.

"Remember me?" Claude said. He swept off his campaign hat at her puzzled stare. "I'm Claude Shaw. You helped Hannibal and me escape last winter."

Jessie Mae's face lighted up and a peal of laughter sprang from her lips. "You was the dyed one, the Union Lieutenant?"

"That's right, Jessie. And we left you a bear skin for some eggs and such."

Jessie put her hand on Jake's arm. "They's the runaways I tol' you 'bout, Jake. They ain't gonna hurt us."

The man relaxed, his aura much less edgy. With the introductions over, Claude and the farmers went into the cabin while the Negroes sought the backhouse. Granny hobbled into Jessie Mae's kitchen on Hester's arm a few minutes later and took a chair, while the girl stood behind her.

Hannibal leaned against the door frame, his strong body and passive, brown face quiescent while he concentrated on the news. Claude had told the farm couple of the Minns demise and the rudiments of their escape. Joy best described the climate in the family at the news of the man hunters.

Jake could hardly contain his satisfaction. "Those two horses, Claude, they was Minns'. We kept 'em while their hooves growed an' I doctored 'em. One had a bad split and t'other was damaged from hard ridin'. They's comin' back healthy now."

The avarice of the man permeated his talk. Divining his drift, Claude thought, well, why not? Jake had boarded the animals and treated their injuries. Probably reshod them, too. Why shouldn't the farmers have them. "They're yours," he said. "Only right after you kept 'em so long."

Jessie Mae expressed their hidden doubts. "Got to have a

bill o' sale, Claude. You sure we can have 'em?"

Claude reverted to his military roll as Captain of Union Cavalry. "I'm confiscating both horses in the name of the United States as rebel property of Minns."

Jake's face fell. "You gonna take 'em?"

"No, Jake," Claude said. "I'll sell 'em to you for a dollar each as unfit mounts, and give you a bill of sale. That'll make it right."

Jessie Mae clapped her hands and ran around the table to hug and kiss the planter. Her tears wet his cheek until he shied away. "Ain't no need, Jessie. You helped us and we'll help you now."

The somnolent Granny reared up in her chair and smiled. "Allus knowed Claude had good sense," she said. Hannibal nodded, his white teeth showing in a delighted grin.

Don't know how I'll square this with my conscience, Claude thought. But Colonel Garrard will back me. He always went with our decisions in the companies. No different here. Turn in the two dollars and a copy of the bill of sale to the quartermaster. Won't be no fuss.

A feast of venison and chicken with dumplings fed them all to repleteness, stuffed as they were with sides of cornbread and beans and some of Claude's real coffee. Jessie Mae sent the wanderers off with several sheets of corncake and a package of roast venison, just as she had victualled Claude before.

Jake shook Claude's hand forcefully before they left and pledged his troth. "You done us a good turn, Claude, and we're mighty beholdin'. You need he'p on somethin' up your way I'll come a'runnin'."

Whether the pledge was made in sincerity or not made no difference to Claude. "Jessie saved us," he said, "and I'm grateful."

A freshly watered and rested team trotted out of the farmyard while Jessie Mae and Jake waved goodbye. Claude's course set them toward Gainesville and farther south to his savior at Blackshear's Place.

By late afternoon they had endured a small shower and were on the road south. A deep mudhole had delayed them, a place in the rutted trace that looked sound but suffered a soft bottom. The right rear wheel had gone in to its axle, blocked from exit by a steep spot of hardpan. Hannibal and Claude were spotted with red dirt and tired, and their boots were wet, after an hours-long struggle to rescue the carriage.

Hannibal shifted in his driver's seat and swore. "Damned boots er pinchin'."

Claude held up his foot, its cover coated with mud streaks and the leather dulled. "Got to dry these out or they'll wear blisters. Look for a place to camp."

A grassy place enticed them. It lay in a meadow by a bend in the creek, a watering point from the looks of the beat-down brush and sloping creek bank. Many tracks showed in the soft green turf.

Hannibal recognized the ground first and waved his arm toward the slope to the east. Its magnificent hardwood timber bordered a wide but weed grown meadow invaded by bushes and small trees. "Dat's where old Hartsill was, Claude."

The planter started and craned his neck. Familiar points stood out from their November escape, the windfalls, the steep slope they had decided not to climb, the low, horizontal branches of some oaks. "We'll stop here while we rest the team," he said.

With the horses settled and Granny and Hester on a blanket by the water, Claude walked slowly over toward the timbered slope. Hannibal limped behind, favoring his right foot.

"Dere's one, Claude," Hannibal said. He thrashed through the bush and tramped down the growth, exposing a recent grave. "Most likely Rufus' man. Dey carry de sojers back to a church-yard."

They found two graves and a set of scattered bones on their trip to the trees, but no clothing.

"Spect all de clothes taken by de niggers who bury 'em," Hannibal said. "Ain't gonna th'ow away good things."

Claude nodded. "You're probably right."

Two rope ends hung from low oak branches where they entered the trees. On the ground under one lay a rawhide noose and some remnants, but nothing else to indicate that Hartsill or Gill had ever been there.

Hannibal shuddered and rolled his eyes. He sidled nearer to the planter. "Dis ain't no place ter spend de night," he said. "Dey's hants 'roun'. I kin feel 'em."

The planter shivered and riveted his gaze on the swinging ropes. He could hear the screams of Gill when Rufus' men hanged him, then Lieutenant Hartsill's defiance. At least the rebel officer had died a man. But Hannibal was right, it wasn't any place for a night camp. He broke from the site and ran down to the carriage, with Hannibal besting him in the race, sore foot or no. The Negro was on his seat and had the reins in hand before Claude could load Granny Mandy and Hester.

"Where we rest ternight?" Granny said from her blanket. Her cross tone continued. "I'se tired and Hester 'bout wore out fum all dat jouncin'."

The girl chimed in with her complaints. "Time we stop, Hannibal. Dis is a nice place. How come we can't camp here."

Claude took Granny by the arms and half-lifted her into the carriage. "There was a bunch o' men killed here, Granny. Hartsill 'bout hung us until Rufus came 'long. We ain't sleepin' in no graveyard."

At that fearsome news, Hester seized the blanket and hustled into the vehicle. She settled next to Granny and said, "Git on, Hannibal, don' want no hant 'round me."

Five miles farther on, a woods trail diverted to the left, long untraveled from the high weeds in the tracks. Hannibal took the overgrown path and drove around the wooded sidehill until they were completely hidden from the main road. He stopped the carriage on a raised bench, thickly carpeted with leaves. Willows sprouted at the toe of the slope and a small gurgle testified to the fresh water of the rivulet in the soft ground beyond.

"Be hid good here, Claude," Hannibal said. "Seen too many tracks out 'round de trail. Some bunched and don't seem ter be up ter no good."

"You think they're bandits?"

"Possible." Hannibal wet his fingers and felt the wind, then looked around at the site. "Wind blowin' away fum de road an' dey can't see our fire. We be safe here if we fort-up and keep de team close. Take turns guardin'."

A cool night for good sleeping was unbroken by any rain but dew settled, sparkling on the weeds in the morning sunlight. Claude rousted the women out just after sunup. The fire crackled and chunks of ham with venison sizzled on skewers leaning over the fire. A flat of cornbread rested on an inclined, flat stone next to the blaze, heating while the meat roasted.

Granny stretched and hobbled off with Hester, sliding around the side hill and into cover of the willows. Sleep had disappeared from their scrubbed faces when they returned to the fire. Meat dripped and sparks flew as Hannibal turned the sticks.

The old Negro squatted and braced herself with her cane. Her sharp eyes took in the food. "Smellin' mighty good, Hannibal. Dey 'bout ready?"

He pulled sticks for Granny and Hester and broke off pieces of the warmed cornbread. A sack of salt sat on another rock before them. Two other flat rocks served as seats on the damp ground. The women ate hungrily, without talk. One skewer and some pone sufficed for Granny, who wiped her mouth with the back of her hand and grunted when she was done. The old woman sat and digested her fare and stared into the fire. But Hester tore at the meat and reached for another skewer when it was finished. Her mouth glistened from the juices of the ham. Hannibal stuffed her until she waved him away and went to the creek for a drink and wash. Claude ate his meat and pone standing while Hannibal picked up his fare at the fire.

A stir from the grazing horses alerted them. Hannibal ran to the two animals and seized their bridles, crooning softly to them as he stroked their heads and necks. Thuds of hoofbeats carried faintly from the road along with some unintelligible talk. Though

Claude's horses' ears were pricked up they made no sound under Hannibal's gentling. The Negro stayed with them until the trail sounds faded to the South.

"Who you reckon they were?" Claude said.

Hannibal's gloom gave the planter no ease. "Ain't no reason fer a party like dat dese days, Claude. Don't feel right atall."

Granny woke from her trance-like stare into the fire. "Dey gwine try ter kill us on de trail," she said. "De fire ain't neber wrong."

Hester gasped and ran to Hannibal, inserting herself into the crook of his arm. "I'se scairt," she said.

Claude prepared the group just as he had his company of troopers. He reminded them of the two sawed off twelve gauge shotguns in the carriage. Union cavalry weapons his troop had used in the war, the guns were housed in holsters mounted right and left of the men.

"We'll reload both the shotguns with buck and check the pistols and rifles. If they come at us, Hannibal'll take the left and I the right. Weren't more than eight or ten from the sound. We can kill 'em all."

"Where we goin' next, Claude?" Hannibal said. "Still south?"

The planter was uncompromising. "Told all those that helped us that I'd be back." His voice grew steely and his jaw muscles bulged. "Ain't no trash keep me from Blackshear's Place. Granny Pearl mighty helpful to us."

When they turned into the south trail, Hester and Granny lay flat on the floor of the carriage with clothes piled over them. The alert men scanned not just the sides but the fresh tracks in the soft ground. Claude kept his right hand on the stock of his shotgun, ready to reclaim, cock and fire it.

A flash ahead at a little point of dense evergreens caught Hannibal's eye. "Dey's at the cedars," he whispered. Passing crows added to the warning, cawing wildly and shying away from the copse.

Before they reached the trees a rider entered the trail and held up his hand for them to stop. Hannibal halted the carriage about fifty yards back.

"Easy, Hannibal," Claude said. He cocked his shotgun as he spoke.

"Come on up," the man yelled.

Claude challenged him. "What you want?"

His question was answered by a rebel battle cry and a bunched group of mounted men that charged from behind the copse. Claude waited until they were within twenty five yards, then fired both barrels of his shotgun. He was dimly aware of booms from Hannibal's piece on his left. Two horses screamed and fell and the shots emptied six saddles. Cursing, the remaining men pulled up, firing pistols while they tried to control their rearing horses. Aimed fire from Claude's Navy Colt cleared one more saddle before the last two men broke and galloped away. But one clutched his side at a shot from Hannibal. Their hoofbeats rapidly receded on the trail.

Claude trembled while he repeatedly tried to reholster his weapon, finally making it on the third thrust. His shaking increased as he recovered from the horror of the action. Granny's tremulous call from the carriage and Hester's sobs steadied him.

"Hester an' me all right," Granny sobbed. "Dey gone?"

Hannibal answered in a loud voice, his pistol still raised and his eyes watchful. "Ain't no mo' trouble."

With his worst fright over, Claude reloaded his pistol, but his shaking hands spilled a few grains of powder. He was almost done when the carriage rocked. It startled him into raising his weapon but it was just Hannibal swinging down from the driver's seat. The Negro inspected the team and harness while Claude reloaded the shotguns.

"Dey ain't hurt," Hannibal told the planter. "Now I look at dose bandits."

A shot rang out a moment later and a second followed close on. Claude jumped down from the carriage and ran to the Negro when he turned over another fallen man. But that one needed no more balls from Hannibal's ready pistol. Claude shrank away from the man he had killed and the gaping hole where his nose had been.

"Ain't no more 'live, Claude," Hannibal said.

He holstered his weapon, then bent down and began to search the bodies while the planter silently watched. Within a few minutes Hannibal had recovered all their weapons and valuables. Claude couldn't bring himself to touch the dead. It seemed a desecration of the remnants of the Confederate uniforms on them. Tattered, dirty, and dead, more bodies for the worms in the ground. The war was over for them and their failed cause, but they still were soldiers and deserved respect. When Hannibal had finished with the seven corpses, he loaded the weapons in the boot of the carriage and sacked the wealth. Claude was surprised at the amount, a pile of coin and a stack of worthless Confederate bills that would serve only as relics of failure.

"We give that to all helped us 'long the way," Claude said. He shuddered. "Don't want none o' that money. See blood on it ever'time I count it out."

Hannibal shrugged. "Ain't no reason to fret. They tried ter kill us an' we did dem."

He dragged the men off the trail and placed them in a row in the surrounding woods. The line looked so typical of a battlefield that Claude wept. He stood over them and said his prayer as he had so many times before. Then the two men caught up the loose horses, unsaddled them and drove them off, leaving their recapture to any adventurers passing by. When their carriage squeaked away, they left the row of men unburied and the two dead horses in the trail where they fell.

* * *

The Reverend Wiley Minns and Joshua tarried in Union, West Virginia, after several days of passage north. Joshua, used to the saddle from his soldiering days, had protested when his uncle stopped at the ramshackle inn.

"We ain't gittin' up to Ohio by sittin' 'roun', Unk. Got to move on."

Wiley had shifted his ample buttocks and scooted sideways on the hard seat to ease himself, then called to the dog. Red wagged his tail and limped up, favoring his right front foot.

"Gonna stop couple days, boy," Wiley said. "You're young, but I'm 'bout wore out and Red needs some linament on that foot."

Joshua swore. "That damned Shaw be back 'fore we even git there, Unk."

Wiley's disdain showed in his face and a deprecating wave of a fat hand. "Ain't no matter. We go after his business when we're ready. Can't do it instanter. Ain't like one o' them cavalry charges you made."

The preacher stepped down from the buggy and went inside after tying off the team to the hitchrail. Joshua followed while Red picked a dusty spot next to the building and flopped down with a sigh.

With a room arranged, Wiley continued his commanding manner. "Bring in the guns and bags, Josh, then take them horses to the stable out back." He looked sharply at the youth. "Probably rain from them clouds we seen over the mountains so put the buggy inside the barn. Don't want no wet seat tomorrow and that buggy's good enough to steal in these times."

Joshua's eyes gleamed, shining like the gold hidden in the carriage. "Been sleepin' out all the years I was campaignin', Unk. I'll take Red to the barn and we'll bed down there after supper."

They fed well on the country fare of the inn, greens and sweet potatoes and less welcome mutton, rank from a ram, but seasoned with pepper and spices to ease the smell. Wiley drifted to bed when dark fell and Josh forked some hay next to the buggy in the barn. He tied a cord to Red and a wheel, then checked his pistol. When he was satisfied, the trooper burrowed down into the fragrant hay. Red curled next to his knee and snored beside him.

According to the innkeeper, a voluble talker when he

brought their breakfast the next day, the Union area of Monroe County had provided a goodly force for the Confederates. Concentrated in Captain Bryan's Company, McLaughlin's Battalion, they had served with the Virginia Field Artillery. Now the county was in West Virginia, he stated proudly, seceded from those rebel rascals in Virginia. The Searle family, particularly, mostly local farmers but with one branch running a small store in the village, had sent several sons off to war with Bryan.

Their server flaunted his own Union leanings with a sidelong glance and quiet laughter. Wiley let him ramble, restraining the angry Josh with a grip on the youth's arm.

"Lousy Rebs," the innkeeper said. He spit and openly gloated. "Don't know what good that'll do 'em now." The Searle family split, he went on, and two of the boys had gone with the Union. His tale described a familiar pattern, boys shooting at their kin, with one Searle killed. Now the remnants of the rebel company were back from their combats, few indeed after the slaughter by both hot metal and disease.

With the inn gossip buttressing his plan, Wiley drifted to the local store to meet the Searle men and recruit a volunteer.

His action angered Joshua. He pushed on his uncle as they walked. "Goddamn it, Unk, they ain't no need for nobody else on this deal. We're enough to kill Shaw an' his kin."

Impassive, Wiley brushed aside Joshua's protests. "I got to have a spy, Josh. Somebody to drift in quiet like and work with Shaw. We know ever'thing he does then."

His explanation silenced but did not satisfy the muttering veteran. "Ain't no need," he insisted. "We buy oursel's some he'p when we git thar."

Wiley ignored him and fell into conversation with the storekeeper while buying a flask of gunpowder from the store's small supply. With little stock on the shelves and a good bunch of hangers-on, it was apparent that those Searles' fortunes were low. When Wiley casually mentioned that he was in business as well as a preacher, one of the loungers moved over. He was a sturdily built, erect, military type, about five ten, with blue eyes and straight black hair. Contrary to the other loungers, he sported long sideburns but a shining clean jaw. And like the rest, he was dressed in faded rebel uniform remnants.

"Name's Charlie Searle," he said. "You lookin' for any help?"

Wiley sized him up, his eyes narrowed. He waited, leaving the burden on the young Confederate to make another move.

The young man shifted nervously but did not drop his bold eyes from those of the preacher. "Charles Henry Searle, late of Bryan's Artillery. Ain't but twenty but I can cypher and read and write. Good with farmin', horses or any stock, an' willin' to work."

"How do you feel about a Virginian who rode with the Union?" Wiley asked. Might as well get it out on the table, he thought.

The face in front of his hardened and a sneer curled the boy's lips. "If he ain't my brother, John, he's no better than a cow flop. I'd kill him in a minute if he crossed me."

Joshua struck his hands together and Wiley smiled. He had his man. He glanced at all the attentive men in the room, piqued by the turn of their conversation. "Let's talk private," he said, heading for the door.

Two days later, with Wiley rested and Red healed, they rode out toward Charleston, West Virginia, where Charlie told them he had to appear in June and give his parole to the Union forces.

* * *

It was a windy, rainy Wednesday when Abel House, the banker, came to visit at Greenbottom. Lutetia Shaw received him cordially, this cousin of her husband Claude and banker in Gallipolis. He doffed his dripping raincoat and hat in the vestry, then took her hands in his and made his greetings. Letty recalled her first meeting with him in that very hall. She had been recently married and he had waited on her, tall and spare in his tongue-tied shyness. Now she felt like giggling at the bald pate that bent toward her and shined in the light. Both double chin and potbelly attested to his growing prosperity and bulk, and he was a little hunchbacked. All those ledgers probably. She put aside her recollections and led him into the parlor, her long skirts swishing on the hardwood floor during her graceful pacing. Her maid followed behind and waited on her mistress's orders.

"Coffee, Ruby, if you please."

"Yessum, Miz Letty," the maid answered.

Letty settled her small, plump frame primly in her own chair and House sank into a cushioned one opposite. He sighed in pleasure at its softness and stretched his long legs to their fullest.

"Good to get out of that buggy," he said.

"You been gone long from Gallipolis?"

"A week. Started seeing folks down by the Big Sandy and worked up the river road."

Letty and he exchanged small talk about her children and the times until the coffee arrived and was poured.

"Not real beans, Abel," she said, with a wry smile, "just the chickory still."

He sipped the liquid gratefully, pale and sweet with its cream and honey. "Best we got in Gallipolis, Letty. Coffee beans are too costly to use." A cookie on the tray enticed him and he tried a bite with the next sip.

She waited, her hands in her lap after their pleasantries. He came to the point quickly but in a roundabout way.

"Claude due back soon?"

"Can't say, Abel. When he was here for those few days last month, he said he had to get his friends and bring them up, the ones that saved his life." Her rosy face clouded. "Don't know what we'll do with more nigras. Money mighty scarce."

Abel nodded. "It's what I'm here about, Letty." He took another swallow and coughed, daubing his lips with his napkin. "Bank's in a tight just now. Need for Claude to give me back as much of that loan as he can."

Her hands flew to the enameled brooch on her breast

and her face paled. "We chance losing this place?"

His voice gentled and comforted her. "Only if it comes to the worst, Letty." He prodded her. "Can you sell off anything?"

A whisper fearfully asked. "How much do you need?"

"If you could give me three hundred on account, I can get by. Callin' everybody's notes and most are helpin'."

Letty's face cleared. "We'll sell the best five of the milk cows," she said firmly. "Had an offer just last week for them. That'll tide us over."

"Who asked?"

"Captain Jones, on the Evangaline. He wanted to sell them down river in Indiana. Said he could make a good profit." She paused. "He'll be back from Gallipolis next week and I'll signal him in to our landing."

Abel nodded. The river boats plied a thriving, increasing trade between Pittsburgh and Cincinnati. But loss of the productive cows troubled him, a good revenue source for the family in deals with the river traders.

"It'll cut into your butter and cheese sales won't it?" He nibbled on another cookie. "Can you get by?"

"We'll still have seven milkers, and two heifers are coming fresh next month." Letty thought for a moment and counted on her fingers. "We can get enough together to pay off your loan on time. Then the corn in the fall should make a thousand bushels. About seventy acres was all we could plant without Claude here."

"No tobacco?"

"No," Letty replied. "Don't have the hands to work the patch. Only other crop we have is the garden."

Their business settled, Abel's questions shifted to Letty's support. Satisfied at last, he finished another hot coffee and cookie and took his leave, refusing to stay overnight. "Got to see Parker Kitts up by Spencer's store," he told her, "then stop at Catletts. Put the same deal to them as to you."

Letty's face wrinkled up and she twisted her fingers together. "The bank isn't going under is it?"

"No, Letty," he replied. "Now don't you worry, your place

is safe."

House wished Claude well on his rescue mission and received Letty's note to deliver to Captain Jones. With his rain clothing restored in the hall, the banker was brusque as usual and gone without long farewells, a busy man about his tasks. When he had driven out of the lane and onto the northern river road, Letty instructed Isaiah to set the signal at the landing on the Ohio River.

5

Jubal Peavey's headache fussed him something fierce, a throbbing that echoed in his skull. It pounded hard when he rolled off his cornshucks mattress that rainy morning of House's visit. He stretched and swallowed and tasted his tongue a few times. Its sourness and cottony feeling added to the discomfort of the pain in his gut from the white lightning he had drunk the night before. Jubal staggered over to the pail and downed a dipper of tepid water, then sprayed a great mouthful into the fireplace. Drops ran down his tangled beard and dripped onto his wrinkled shirt. Hitching up his baggy pants, he next slipped his feet into his shoes and faced the day.

"Hank," he yelled, "roll out."

When no life stirred, Jubal hobbled into the abutting room and beat on the frame of his grandson's bunk with his cane. Its hardwood clatter was enough to wake the dead.

Hank's tousled head came up off the pillow and sank right back down. He grasped it in both hands and groaned. "God a'mighty, Gramps," he said, "what you want now?" Hank sat up on the edge of the bed and made sucking, flapping noises as he cleared his mouth and held his head.

"Need cold warter, boy. Damned skull 'bout ter split off m'body."

"Ain't no more'n mine, I 'spect," Hank said. "Damn but that whiskey whar good." He stretched and yawned and massaged his face. “Better dip your top in the creek instead o’ that ol’ water bucket. Lots colder.”

The youth went outside after pulling on his pants. His large white feet slapped in a drum beat when he crossed the porch and went down the steps. A worn but rocky path stretched from the flat stone landing to the creek bank south of the house. Hank picked his way, avoiding hurts, to a gravelly place that afforded access to a clear, deep pool. He edged down on his knees and dipped his top half into the water, submerging his head and bony shoulders. A few dunks and swings wet and cleansed him as he gurgled, blew air and spit. When he had rubbed his hair and the stubble on his face to his satisfaction, he cleared his mouth and rose out of the way. His bushy hair dripped and the top of his dirty gray longjohns was soaked.

Peavey rested on his cane, his sunken mouth silent but forbidding. “Ain’t never liked no bath thet way,” he said sourly. “Jest look at yourself. Wet all over an’ ye ain’t fit for nothin’.”

“Clears m’ head, Gramps,” Hank said cheerfully. “you orter try it.” He whipped more drops off his hair and stubbled chin and felt his chest. “This’ll dry soon enough outa the drizzle.”

With his grandson out of the way, Jubal knelt down, groaning as his knees bent, and splashed a little of the creek water over his face. It was barely enough to wet his beard but straightened the strands when he combed it with his fingers. Peavey had brought the dipper and drank several large drafts of the liquid, sighing in pleasure when he tossed the last of a partial refill. His next steps were toward the house.

“Got things to do, boy. Git on up thar and fix me some bacon and cornbread. Couple o’ them eggs help too.”

“Why can’t we git us a cook, Gramps?” Hank’s complaining increased. “Hate that damned chore! Since Grandma died you ain’t done nothin’ but put things on me. An’ I can’t cook; you know that.”

“Have to pay the niggers now, boy. Ain’t none fer free so ye’ll jest have to do it.” Peavey grumbled on. “Money we got hid is goin’ to fox ol’ Claude, ain’t payin’ no nigger.”

They were back out on the porch, resting in their chairs, when Abel House turned into the Shaw lane. Hank bent forward and rested his chin on the porch rail, riveting his eyes on the creaking buggy. Old Peavey squinted, trying to make out the driver.

"It's that banker from Gallipolis, Gramps." Hank leaned back, his chair protesting the wracking. "Member how he dunned us fer that little piece o' change?"

Jubal spit over the rail of the porch and growled, "You'd a'thunk we was tryin' to rob him, way he carried on." His injured tone continued. "We promised him the money fer the loan. Warn't no paper needed."

Hank laughed. "Had to fetch the sheriff ter git it outen us when he started pushin', but ol' Bandie warn't much taken with the idee."

"Maybe so, but I hold thet agin him an' that fool banker." Gramps rocked a few times. "Knowed Tom Bandie all his life. He orten to have run fer sheriff. Puts him agin all his friends." His lips tightened and he squinted along his raised cane as if it were a rifle barrel. "Pow, pow," he said, then passed his judgement. "We git even fer thet. Ain't no folks crowd the Peaveys." They watched in silence a while later when House drove toward Point Pleasant on the river road.

Jubal stroked his beard as the rig receded and passed from view, his chair rockers squeaking stridently on the weathered boards. "You still beddin' that yaller girl over to Shaws?"

"Whenever I want, Gramps. Josie mighty hot an' she allus come a'runnin'."

"You jest slip along quiet like next day or so an' find out what thet banker was a'doin'. Mayhaps there's somethin' where we kin take a slice outen ol' Claude." He chuckled. "Thet banker too, if the ground lays right."

* * *

Far to the south that week, Claude had found a two hour visit long enough to settle his score at Blackshear's. An even fatter Granny Pearl fed Claude and his partners, but could not help them find Henrietta and Delcy. The women had never come back to the plantation since their flight, nor had they sent her any word. Claude pressed her but Granny absolutely refused to leave.

"Got my family all 'roun', Claude. "Jist cain't go off fum my chil'ren and grandbabies."

Claude nodded. "Understand, Granny. But we're leavin' you something to help with your living."

Hannibal added, "Dat's right, Granny." He ran out to the carriage and came in with a pistol, rifle and their trappings. His sack of treasure added to his burden.

Granny Pearl asked, "What you got dere?" when he laid them before the group.

Hannibal swelled up, pompous. "Took em off de bandits up de trail. Leave de guns fer pertection or tradin'." He jounced the sack up and down. "Got plenty money fer Granny."

"Dat all belong Claude, don't it?" Granny Mandy asked. "He de Massa."

An angry Claude confronted her, his face a thundercloud. "You're all free, Granny, FREE," he said vehemently. "I'm not a Massa any more. Hannibal took these from those rebels. It's as much his as mine."

Claude's outburst cowed her and she trembled as she shrank away from him. "Ain't meanin' no harm, Claude," she said. "Can't get rid o' de notion you own what we got."

Her fear burst on Claude like a thunderbolt; the realization that he had frightened her wracked him. He grasped her in a big hug and said softly, "You're free, Granny. Not I nor anyone else is going to take what's yours, or Hannibal's and Hester's."

Her face lightened and she smiled. "Me an' Hester sit here an' watch while Hannibal give Pearl some o' dat. Gotter git used ter havin' tings."

She and the other women mumbled to each other, their heads together as they looked on, absorbed in the clink of the coins when Claude counted the hard money. Hannibal bent over close. He inspected all the separated coins and asked about their value, his first lesson in numbers and money. Claude set aside the worthless Confederate bills to keep for sentimental reminders of his service and traumas. A little over fifty dollars of pennies through Spanish silver dollars remained, added to by three one dollar gold pieces.

"We got a ways to go an' others to see," Claude said. "We'll give you ten dollars, Granny, for helpin' us." He counted out a selection of silver and copper coins and handed the pile to Hannibal who passed them to her.

Granny Pearl took the money casually in her fat hand and jingled the coins, then dropped them into a small empty crock. When the rattle stopped, she reached down another container from a shelf and poured the first full. "It's de salt," she said. "Ain't nobody likely ter look under dat."

The travelers left her to her family with their blessings and Claude's promise to help if she needed it. Pearl laughingly refused his invitation for her to visit Greenbottom.

"Ain't no reason fer no old nigger like me ter move way up dere, Claude." She squinted her eyes and winked at Granny Mandy. "You got Mandy an' she got de second sight. She 'bout all de he'p you an' Hannibal need."

Granny Mandy preened at the compliment, her head nodding. "Claude right thick headed an' Hannibal don' pay no mind ter de spirits," she said. "I'se gwine look over 'em bof."

With their farewells done, they made the Chattahoochee River and crossed by early afternoon, an easy passage on a new flatboat at the ferry. Coal Mountain lay but a short few miles north, along a hard trace with little rutting. There they sought out their quarry, the church of the Right Reverend Rodney Duckworth. Lying just beyond the village, a spruced up, steepled white structure faced them. It was a peaceful setting, wooded and quiet except for the bird calls and their squeaking carriage. As they rumbled into the churchyard, Hannibal whispered to Claude and pointed to the numerous new mounds of reddish clay that populated the cemetery, expanded since their November escape. Piano music was pouring out into the air when they stopped and tied off the team.

Duckworth's playing crashed into discord at their footfalls on the board floor of the church. He was his nattily dressed but bald-headed self. Thinner than when they had escaped with his help, a gaunt face belied a small potbelly. Claude strode forward with his hand out and the advancing preacher took it with a smile and instant recognition.

"So you made it, Lieutenant," he said. "The Lord moves in mysterious ways."

"He surely does, preacher," Claude answered. He made way for the Negro. "Hannibal's here too." He looked for the women but they had settled into a rear pew.

Hannibal laughingly joshed the minister as he shook Duckworth's hand. "Ain't movin' in no coffin dis time, preacher. Dat 'bout finish me off. We got us a real kerriage out dere."

Duckworth held his sides and roared with merriment. His cheeks were rosy when he caught his breath and turned serious. "That hearse took thirty seven of you folks to freedom, Hannibal. It did its job." He reflected a moment on his spiritual message. "The Lord says, 'Ask and thou shall receive,' remember? Your prayers for help were answered."

Recollections used up the rest of the afternoon and they stayed the night in Duckworth's forest cabin. This time Hannibal sorted out ten dollars from the hoard, a gift that brought a few tears to Duckworth's eyes. The preacher wiped them with a white linen cloth and blew his nose, unable to speak for a moment.

"I'm mighty grateful, Hannibal," he said haltingly. "Hasn't been much hard money around these parts lately. I can use this right nicely."

Claude reached into the sack and fished out a gold piece. Its yellow brightness contrasted to the silver and the coppers. "We ain't got many, Reverend," he said, "but I want you to have one."

The preacher's pleased grin radiated his thanks. "First gold I've seen in months, Claude." Duckworth turned the piece to gleam in the light. He stored it carefully in a vest pocket, separated from the marred and tarnished coins. "This time the Lord giveth rather than taketh away."

When the tales were done and the fire died down, the party slept in peace, their dreams protected by the rich prayer that Duckworth blessed them with.

* * *

Ashley Pickens' disgust permeated her disdainful censure of her husband. "You mean you're going into business with that factor in Charleston?" Her failure to repeat his partner's name told all to Rance, a disapproval that carried a heavy burden. "You'll be nothing but a merchant, a dirty trader. Don't you have a shred of pride left?"

"At least it'll bring in money, my dear," Rance replied. He calmly added, "We need that for all those new gowns you been pinin' after."

Smoothing out her faded dress, Ashley lifted and fluffed out the skirt. A few patches showed and a ragged hem needed mending. "Well look at this old thing," she said bitterly, "it's about time I got some, wouldn't you think?"

"Soon as Pinck sells those few cotton bales we had hid out, I'll give you half that money. You can buy whatever it'll pay for."

The promise did nothing to mollify his wife. She denigrated their long-time friend in spiteful tones. "Pinckney Middleton ain't on his high and mighty no more, is he? He always acted like he was better than us, he and Rose too."

Rance sighed and gently said, "Now you know that isn't true, Ashley."

Ashley stamped her foot and her formerly beautiful but faded face contorted into a devil's mask as her temper soared out of control. "He did so," she shouted at him.

His mouth fell open when she swore, something he could not recall in all their years together. She had been so prim and proper a lady, with a cultivated, soft inflection, but she now raged like the troopers he had commanded. “And she’s a damned cat, a mean, underhanded bitch, always purring but lording it over everybody like she’s a queen.” She could not speak for a second, strangling on the words. “Pinckney knows my family’s been in South Carolina longer than either one of theirs.” Her lips quivered as her angry facade crumbled and tears ran down her face. “Now you’re in with him,” she sobbed. “How could you do this to me? You were a gentleman, one of the gentry. Now you’re going to be nothing but a damned merchant.”

Her wails increased and she cried uncontrollably. Weakness overcame her and she sank into her cushions. But she struck out at him when he went to comfort her and drove him off with a contemptuous, “Get away from me.”

It was too much of a goad for the planter. Swearing, he grabbed the coil of hair on top of her head and dragged the weeping woman up out of her chair. Holding her at arm’s length, he slapped her back and forth across the face until she crumpled against him and and sobbed, “Don’t, Rance, I’ll be good. Please don’t hit me any more.”

He thrust her out again where he could stare into her eyes. With a grim, intimidating scowl, he laid down the law. “Times are gone, Ashley, when we were rich. We got this house and the land and almost nothing else. I’ll do what I must to restore us, trader or no.” He shook her and pulled her close, glaring at her scared, tearful face. “I’m going in with Pinck and Claude Shaw up on the Ohio. We’ve a few ideas on some crops and manufactures that we can send to Claude for sale along the river, and others that Pinck can send overseas. They’ll help us all.”

“But you don’t have any money,” Ashley wailed. “How’ll you get started?”

He held her tight and stroked her trembling body. “None of us got money, Ashley. I’ll grow a big garden and peddle the extra in town and in Charleston. Plant a little cotton if I can manage it.” His spirits soared with his move to action and his voice calmed and grew more powerful and assured. “Hunt skins this first bad year. Lots of deer around and skins are worth a dollar. Jed and Bub will help. Those scamps are the best yet in the woods."

Ashley sagged in his embrace, her first surrender since her castigation and rejection of him days before. He hugged and coddled her, his voice dropping to a whisper as he crooned a message of love. Ashley's body slowly relaxed and melded with his as she accepted his overtures for a new beginning, a resumption of their love and marriage. When he took her hand and drew her toward the door, she went willingly, following him on the steps to the bedrooms upstairs.

Unseen by the couple, Aunty Susan peered from an alcove in the hall where she had listened to the argument and Ashley's surrender. Her eyes gleamed and she chuckled at Rance's sudden militance and violent behavior. Aunty hugged herself when they went up the winding staircase, muttering, "Dat's de right way, Massa Rance. Dat woman need beatin' some to mek her mind." The old servant waited until she heard the bed squeak. With quiet restored in the parlor, she went into the room and tidied up, straightening the pillows and shawls, readying the furnishings for Rance and her mistress.

* * *

Ian McLellan turned into the lane of the rambling white house. Its two-story frame with wrap-around porch fronted the Ohio River on a sloping, grassed headland, a white landmark to the steamers that plied the waters between towns. The prominent house supplemented a lighted navigation beacon on the dropoff below. His fertile farm lay adjacent to Crown City but the small community was encroaching on his property as the buildings multiplied and grew along the road toward Gallipolis. With a long freight landing, Crown City was developing into a major trading center. But it was not the steamers that concerned Ian this day. Medium in height and with a thatch of red hair, his rolling, drunken staggers thrust his chunky body from side to side while he aimed at the house. When he stumbled at a little step in the front path leading to the porch, he stopped and squinted with one blurry eye, its crevice overshadowed by a bushy eyebrow.

"Damn house is movin' again," he muttered. He reeled over to a maple and held on while he closed his eyes. It did not relieve his dizziness nor his fevered brow. Unable to go farther, he called out, "Joe, Joe, where are you, boy?"

A lad of about fourteen ran around the side of the house after his third yell. Without a sound he took his father's right arm and put it over his shoulders. Propped up by his son, Ian assayed a few more steps. His bulk and faltering equilibrium overcame the strength of the slender boy and they both crashed to the ground.

Ian rolled over on his back and hoorawed. "Ain't that a sight, boy. You can't even brace me up." He rolled around holding his sides and laughing. But when Joe stood over him, he squinted at the boy and looked up anxiously. "You ain't hurt, are you?"

"No, Pa," Joe replied. He brushed dirt and bits of grass off his clothes, then reached for his fallen father. "Lemme help you up."

A few staggering lurches later took them to the porch and its five stone steps. With Joe's help, Ian made it to the top and stood on the gray painted floor boards, swaying as the boy tried to steady his muscular frame. The drunken farmer breathed deeply and collected himself, making ready to enter the house. Resignation changed his grinning jollity into a cloudy frown. His gentle, quiet voice did not surprise Joe, used to it and his father's earlier, raspy commands when he was drunk.

"Recken your Ma'll give me hail columbia, boy."

"You got it comin', Pa." Joe grasped his father when Ian suddenly sagged and bent over sideways. The boy's meager strength and pulls restored his heavy father to full height. A few pushes started Ian slowly toward the door. When he hesitated, Joe struck him in the back.

"Ma's waitin' in the parlor," the boy said, "so's best you git on in there." Tears trickled down his cheeks and his lips quivered. "She ain't going to like your gettin' lickered up agin no matter how sorrowful you are."

He wiped his nose on his sleeve, then angrily jerked his father's arm to offset a little lurch as Ian took a tiny step. "She asked Garrett at the store not to sell you no more whiskey, so how'd you get it? Your credit ain't no good nowhere."

Ian chuckled. "Ol' Garrett ain't like his brother, Claude. He'll sell to anybody if the coin is there, and I had one."

"When Captain Shaw gits back from the war, he'll cut you off, Pa, just like Ma asked."

Joe propelled his father the few steps to the door where they swayed together while the boy tried to steady him. The youth clutched Ian and the door handle, then spoke his mind to his drunken father before letting the man enter. His lecture rushed out in a torrent of words.

"We orta move over to Greenbottom, Pa. Captain Shaw gave you that job and watched over your pay. He made sure Ma got some then. He can use you on the plantation and raftin', and he'll probably get another river boat. You're good on those."

"Could be, boy," Ian replied. "But first I got to go see your Ma." He drew himself up to his full height and walked through the front door, slamming it behind him.

When his mother's gentle tones rose over Ian's loud lamentations, Joe scurried around the side of the house. He headed for the river and his lookout at the light on the point. A seat of soft grass awaited him, one he had piled up for comfort in the days he spent there. A short hour later a familiar sight came down river, the Mary Anne towboat pushing four barge loads of coal. Joe jumped up and down and hollered at the craft when it passed the light. The pilot whistled twice, his steam whistle hidden by a cloud of condensation. A slight echo reverberated off the West Virginia hills.

"Halloo, halloo," Joe shouted.

"Hiyah, Joe," the call came back, faint from the distance. A wave from the pilot accompanied the message. The tow boat's stern wheel threw spume as it drew away.

"When I grow up," Joe said aloud, "I'll be the best engineer yet on those boats." His agitation overcame him and he shouted into the wind, "You hear me, river? I'm a'comin'."

6

A few days of hard travel, with another rainy morning burdened by lowering, damp clouds and mists, took Claude and his companions through the foothill area of the Appalachians. A short stop at Nelson's renewed their friendship with Aunty Mittie. The dumpy figure, with her freckled face and reddish gray hair was as feisty as ever, her combative Ashanti blood coming to the fore when they entered the cabin.

"Ain't heard nuttin' 'bout dose Minns since you went thoo, Claude. Dey back down country?"

Hannibal chortled, "Dey dead, Aunty."

Aunty Mittie rolled her eyes upward and raised her hands to the sky. "Praise de Lawd," she intoned. "Dey ain't gwine bother dis chile no mo'."

The travelers stayed overnight with the amiable woman, sharing their food and their wealth. Hannibal's ten dollars in coin went into a hole between wall logs, safe from prying eyes and thieves. The party left her as before, a helpful figure on her doorstep, waving with her grandchildren until lost from sight.

Later in the day, the carriage rolled past the Talking Rock Creek battleground where the two Minns had faced Duckworth and the escaped slaves tried to kill the mountaineers. The preacher had closed his eyes and shuddered when he told Claude and his companions of the battle and blood. Covey, his old driver, had forced him onto the seat and had driven away at a gallop. They had not stopped for five miles, though Henrietta and Delcy in the coffins had protested violently from the pounding of the rough road. When Claude told Hannibal to hold up, two skeletons showed in the high green grass next to the path, undisturbed since the killing. Nodded over by some brown eyed susans, a few wild flowers served as markers for their last resting place.

"Dishere's de meadow de Reverend tol' us about," Hannibal said. "We 'bout ter where we turn west on de road ter Granny Eva's. You want ter go on?"

Hester's frightened cries intruded. "Dey's dead," she wailed. "Git along! De spirits git us, we stay here."

Granny Mandy chimed in. "Ain't good place, Claude. Seein' more troubles iffen we stop."

Hannibal dug the graves while Claude sat with the two women and held their hands, his reassurances keeping them quiet. Two hours later they were off to Mary's. Miss Mary was not at the farm near Blaine's when they rolled into the farmyard. The carriage rocked back and forth on the forest lane approaching the house. It was as Claude remembered, a quiet, peaceful farm, fertile and productive. But the owner was new and sent them on with little concealed contempt that a white man would be associated with Negroes. He had bought the farm from Mary, he told them, and wanted no nigger-lovers about.

A long, sloppy trace faced them from the bridge over Talking Rock Creek to Granny Eva's past Carters, discolored water in the ruts rich with a clay burden. Globs of yellow-red earth glued themselves to the carriage wheels as they slipped and slid along the rutted road. Worn out from jouncing and the strenuous pull over a long traverse, both man and beast welcomed the evening stop at the Granny Eva's cabin, one of a few occupied on the abandoned plantation. Claude wondered at the grown-up grounds and the open front door of the big house. Loose shutters flapped back and forth and banged against the siding, eerie slaps that added to the gloomy dirge of wind in the surrounding trees. A glum Granny Eva greeted Claude and the Negroes in front of her cabin, her fat right hand holding her protective club.

Little Rosemary peeked from behind her skirts. Massive still in height and girth, the solemn negress no longer carried herself regally. Lines creased her face and her shoulders drooped, in keeping with the sad cast to her jaw.

After a cheerful greeting and the women were unloaded, Hannibal said, “I’se tek keer of the horses,” and drove off toward the barn.

“See if there’s any grain,” Claude shouted after him. “They need a good feed and watering.”

He introduced the grannies, a standoff of two ancient women that dissolved into hugs and muttered greetings. A shy Hester helped Granny Mandy into the cabin, silent for once. She and Mandy took stools at the side when Granny Eva and Rosemary sat down in the lone rocking chair, its back and seat draped with a cushioned deer skin and colorful crochet.

“What happened around here, Granny,” Claude asked. “Everything’s grown up and don’t see nobody.”

“Massa an’ his boys all kilt in de war,” Granny said, “an’ Miz Clementine jist pine away.”

Taking Claude to the door, she aimed her staff at a grove of dark green cedars on a small, bordering knoll. A few tombstones poked up above the weeds. “She in de graveyard, yonder.” Her big frame quivered and tears ran down her cheeks. “Dat Kunnel a good massa, an’ his sons kin’.” Her sobs grew into a stream of tears and wild crying. Rosemary’s shrieks added to the din. “Ain’t got nobody tek care o’ dis ol nigger.”

Claude reached his arms around the massive body and patted her head and back. “I’m here, Granny,” he said soothingly. “We’ll take you and Rosemary with us up to Greenbottom. Ain’t no reason for you to stay here.”

His stroking gentled the woman, her shudders and sobs ending with a resolute, “Go wid yuh, Claude, me an’ Rosemary. Ain’t got nothin’ here.”

Hannibal cheered everyone when he carried in meat and cornmeal from the carriage boot, a gift that brought a welcome glint to Granny Eva’s eyes. She and Mandy set to the supper task, while Hester played with Rosemary. A soft, fateful footfall disturbed the peace in the cabin. Projecting her bulging belly before her, Elsie waddled in the door.

"Howdy, Claude," she said to the staring planter.

He gaped at her, speechless. A red flush ran up his neck and spread over his startled face as the young negress came closer. Claude felt rooted to the floor, unable to either breathe or to escape. A child, he thought. Is it mine? His mind raced over the wild doings of the party in the tobacco barn during his November escape, and his falling from grace. He shrank from the thought of his transgression. God almighty, what will happen next?

Eva extended a cheerful greeting to Elsie, then roared at the planter, "You gitten yerself a boy, Claude, way Elsie's stickin' out. Boys allus hang out front."

* * *

Osprey's Landing hummed with activity on a bright Thursday late in the month, about two weeks after Rance's first visit. Pinckney Middleton's wharf on the Cooper River held two battered wooden scows end on, with kedge anchors out to protect against the strong currents from the river flow and tidal reverse. The dull colored water, stained with its brown tannic acid and fine dark silt from the salt marshes, boiled through the piling of the wharf and past the ends of the vessels. Roiling waves gurgled around the restrictions as the flow tried to tear the vessels away from the landing. But tight, surging ropes, dipping now and then into the water, bound the barges securely, though squeaks from their protesting, worn timbers holding the cleats presaged failure and escape.

Pinckney Middleton hobbled about on his cane, favoring his healed but sore hip wound while he inspected loading of the cotton bales. Sweat-stained Negro laborers moved their heavy weights, with a stiffleg used to hoist them aboard. Middleton's Scot overseer, Henry MacLaughlin, always erect and aggressive when under the planter's gaze, cursed at the men as he had in slavery days while urging on the work. His choleric face matched the red of his hair peeking from under a plaid cap. But freedom for the Negroes had exacted a price; MacLaughlin lacked a long leather whip to spur them with. Even so, cursing and a former slave driver gave him control. Big Wes, a massive, black Negro whose loyalty was bought with bribes, overcame any independence of the workers. Big Wes reacted when the overseer cursed, battering men with his fists while he moved among them, issuing threats from which they cowered. He intimidated by size and punishment, a huge, remorseless battering ram who would kill any person who did not submit. To further cow the men, a long machete hung from his wide leather belt.

Rance Pickens mopped his sweaty brow and moved to the shade of a magnolia from his perch on a barrel on the wharf. His two wagons had already driven out of the lane, heading back upcountry with Jed and Bub driving the teams. Rance fanned himself and waited on Pinckney to join him. When half the bales were aboard, Middleton stomped up the slope on his bad leg and sought the magnolia and his partner's company.

"Right good number of bales you gathered up," Rance observed. "With your twenty one and those from the Youngs and Pendletons added to mine, we got two hundred eighteen." Pinckney contentedly puffed on his thin, black cigar, a round stub that projected from a drooping brown mustache hiding his lips.

"Yankees didn't burn 'em all when they went through from Georgia," Rance said. "Everybody had bales hid out." He used his handkerchief again, wiping his face. "What are they worth?"

Middleton stared absentmindly for a few moments. "Cotton real high right now, according to Captain Crain. Figure fifty seven hundred for the lot." At his friend's stir and lightening face, Pinckney flicked the cigar ash and jammed the stub in the corner of his mouth. "Your part'll be five hundred seventeen, the price less handling and factoring."

"That English barque ready to take them?" Rance asked.

"The Seasprite?" Middleton puffed on his cigar and blew

out a cloud of smoke. "Captain Crain's waiting. He was right anxious for the cotton when I negotiated with him. He'll pay gold tomorrow when the bales are on board. Says the English mills are having trouble getting cotton right now and he'll take all we can round up."

Rance gasped in surprise. "Paying gold? Not on account in London like we used to do, with drawing rights?"

"He's anxious, Rance. His company's looking to get a jump on the others now that the war's over. And we ain't the only ones scratching around. Ransom is barging him over about a hundred bales from Georgia. Gettin' here on Saturday."

"Roger's moving cotton? I thought he was too tore up."

Pinckney's cheek muscles corded and crinkles developed around suddenly frosty eyes. "Those Yankees burned his place. Left him destitute. He ain't much able but it's that or Sallie and the children will starve. He doesn't have any kin or credit left."

The doleful recital struck Rance forcefully. At least he had his health and his plantation house and a few of the Negroes to help. His resolve increased to expand his search for goods.

"Any more ships coming?" he asked.

"Their next is the Seaspirit. It's due this August."

"They want anything else?"

"Tobacco, if there's any around. Turpentine too." Pinckney puffed away and bragged a trifle. "See those small barrels? I'm sending some honey which he'll sell for me. Got onto a big hoard of crocks last month and bought it all. Ran it into the barrels." A chuckle of satisfaction escaped. "Ended up with eighty three pounds of beeswax as a dividend. Now that'll yield a handy profit."

Rance's head reeled with renewed hope. "I'll make a sweep upcountry with my wagons and the coin you pay me. Buy whatever I can find and fetch it down."

"We can use deer hides for the islands. They're always looking for fine leather."

Rance nodded. "I figure to put Jed and Bub to hunting this winter, soon's the cold weather comes. Hides spoil too easy right now and the fawns are still small."

The two friends watched from their vantage point while the overseer drove the crew. Silent, each dealt with his thoughts as the rest of the loading was completed. With MacLaughlin in charge, the barges cast off and headed downsteam, their rowboats attached. The strong current would deliver them to the Seasprite within three hours, with transfer of the cargo to follow.

A day later, Pinckney collected his payment from the Captain and delivered Pickens' share. He gave the planter five hundred dollars more to trade with, an amount that surprised Rance.

"You want me to buy whatever I can?"

"Cotton, tobacco, honey, leather, turpentine, chestnuts," Middleton said. "The nuts sell good in the islands. See what else you can find. I'll try it out." He drew on his cigar. "What's Claude Shaw doing?"

"He won't be back up to Ohio until next month from what he wrote me. Once he's there, we'll strike some deals."

"He still have his store on the Ohio?" Middleton asked.

Rance nodded. "Store's still there, an' his plantation, neither doin' much, from what he says. He plans to get a riverboat like he had before the war. With those three, we ought to be able to trade." He reflected a moment. "The railroads'll soon be all over the country and we'll have faster transfers. We can use the wagons and barges for farm work, no long hauls."

Pickens' curiosity about their West Virginia partner drove him on. "You known Claude long?"

"About fifteen years." Middleton blew out a little ring of bluish smoke and watched it float away. "We traded a bunch of things, particularly rum. He sold a lot of the dark Jamaican for me." He chuckled, his upset growing into laughter. "Didn't realize he'd take my gold to buy his freedom at Sorghum, or forge my name to a pass. Helped him escape." A rueful grin and a shrug replaced the mirth. "Guess I'd have done the same if I was in his shoes. An officer's obliged to escape. Claude's a brave man and absolutely honest."

They parted after a fine lunch presided over by Rose, mistress of the plantation. Rance kissed her hand in farewell, a flowery, gracious courtesy that brought a glow to her cheeks. His mood was jubilant as he rode off but he had taken the precaution of purchasing a new Colt revolver for a belt gun to add to his derringer, horse pistol and rifle. With over a thousand in gold on him and his chance for a new start, he resolved not to submit to any robber.

* * *

Hank Peavey's dalliance with Josie led to a sweaty coupling in the barn. He rode her hard in the hayrick while she moaned and wiggled and gasped, "Dat good, Hank. Push it in. Ain't gittin' dere yet."

His motion grew fast and furious when she grasped his buttocks and pulled him closer. She lifted her legs higher into the air and raised her ample brown bottom, ignoring all but her pleasure. A swish and loud slap cut through their trance and a red welt sprang out on Hank's white skin. Another strike left a parallel hurt before he could react.

"Ow," he howled.

A third welt arose from a sting of the flailing quirt as he rolled off Josie. He clambered to his feet and faced a furious Letty. Hank hopped about and tried to pull up his pants while his left arm warded off her blows. Josie scrambled to one side and ran out of the barn.

Letty's scornful, "You worthless, no-good loafer," was but the least of a continuing diatribe as she whipped him, until he, his pants belted, seized the quirt and yanked it from her. She pulled a pocket pistol when he threatened her with the leather.

"Don't you come at me, you, ---, you, --," she sputtered, finally flinging a contemptuous, "you Peavey," at him.

He whitened at the slur. Using his name as an insult was a monumental degradation no Peavey, not even a worthless one, could undergo without taking revenge. Hank flicked the quirt and drew it through his left hand, separating the strands of the tip. Tightened muscles converted his tanned face into an evil, contorted mask, slitted eyes under bushy eyebrows at once threatening even as he backed away from her pistol.

"You don't scare me, you Shaw bitch," he said. "I'll take the whip to you, miz high and mighty, next time I ketch you."

Letty paled, then her round face flushed red. "How dare you," she gasped. She leveled the pistol, her small hand unsteady. The barrel wobbled but fastened on his middle when she gripped it with her other hand. She faced him resolutely and cocked the piece. "Now you get before I shoot you."

Peavey cursed and tossed the whip into the hay between her feet. His vicious smile and piercing eyes carried the hate of the white commoner for the successful, the failure for the man of property. "I'll be back," he said. "Come over here any time I want and take thet Josie."

"You do," she said sternly, "and you'll answer to Captain Shaw. Now git!" She fired a bullet between his feet.

He jumped into the air and yelled, "Quit thet; ain't no need o' gunplay."

Letty waved him out of the barn with the gun barrel. He slowly backed away as she advanced on him with a determined step. Josie waited at the side when he left the barn but slunk off toward the big house instead of going with him. At another shot from Letty, Hank ran headlong toward the road and Peavey property on the hills beyond. Jubal, far distant on their porch, shook his cane at the scene, his shouts unintelligible to Letty.

"Any trouble, Ma?" Claudius said from his post on the lane. Her skinny, sandy-haired son held a shotgun at the ready. The eldest boy, his four sisters were lined up on the mansion's porch, with his little brother Garrett peering from the protection of their skirts.

His mother lowered the pistol and put it back in her pocket.

"No, boy," she said, "but your father's got to talk to Jubal when he gets back. Can't give that thievin' Hank free run of this place. He'll steal everything we got left."

"I'll watch, Ma." The raggedly dressed teen was following Hank's ascent of the Peavey porch. "Old Peavey's givin' him what for, looks like. Shoutin' and hittin' him with his cane."

"About time," Letty said. "That boy never was much good after he went off to war." She sighed. "Landsakes, the trouble that war has brought. Hank was a good boy, growing up. Now he only works hard when Jubal rides him. It was the war that made him bad. Lost all his respect for people or their things."

A motion caught her eye as Josie went for the steps. "Come here," she yelled. "Yes, you, Josie," she commanded, when the Negro hesitated.

The scolding did nothing but bring "Yes'um," and "No'um," from the down-turned face of the pretty negress, a light colored girl blooming into full womanhood. She ran into the house when Letty sent her to the kitchen.

With her brood safely back inside, Letty settled into her rocking chair. Relaxation brought on a trembling she had not anticipated and an exhaustion from the danger and excitement. She closed her eyes and rocked a few times, crooning a hymn, but a hard place in her apron bumped when she shifted on the quilted pad to relieve an ache. Conscious of the pistol, she took it out and laid it on the stand beside her. The shining, blue-black metal fascinated her, a tool Claude had insisted she carry while he was gone. He had been so thorough in teaching her how to load and fire it. Today it had saved her from harm. Letty caressed the cold metal when she picked it up and held it against her cheek. She could almost feel the presence of Claude, far off in the south but soon due home. His image was with her when she carefully cleaned the weapon and reloaded it, ready for Hank Peavey or any other threat to her family.

Jubal Peavey's dingy black buggy creaked down the Greenbottom lane the next morning, greeted by Claudius' shouts. His anxious cries rousted out his mother. After a glance from the living room window, Letty waited on the porch with her hand on her pocket pistol while the ancient vehicle approached the wide graveled circle at the entrance. Subdued chirks and Hank's slaps with the reins guided the bony red horse to a stop before the steps. A groan escaped Peavey when he climbed down from the buggy with his grandson's help. He and Hank lined up on the large stones of the bottom landing and faced Letty's stern, disapproving face. Garrett and her daughters peeked out of the door behind her but Claudius had retreated inside, only to show at the corner of the house with a menacing shotgun.

Peavey doffed his dusty hat and bowed slightly to Letty. "Ain't meanin' to disturb yuh, Miz Letty, but I brought Hank over to 'pologize. What he done an' said jest ain't fitten', not with a lady. I done beat him good with my cane."

"You afraid Claude will kill him?" Letty said.

Hank's lanky body jerked as if struck. He straightened up, rigidly erect, and his blazing eyes met Letty's cold gaze. Little flecks of light showed in his slitted eyes and the corners crinkled at his prominent cheekbones. Knotted jaw muscles compressed his lips as he struggled to reply. "Ain't skeered o' Claude or no damned Yankee," he said.

"Hush, boy." Peavey struck his cane against Hank's tensed body and raised it for another blow. "Now you 'pologize like I tol' yuh."

At his grandfather's reprimand, all the fight went out of Hank. He doffed his hat and mumbled, "I'm sorry, Miz Letty, fer what I did and said. It were the whiskey talkin'. I take it all back."

Letty softened as she gazed down at the youth, a man in size and years but still only a boy to her, one she had seen grow up and had fed more than once. She couldn't fault him for chasing that spicy Josie, a real trial now that she had blossomed. But he had changed, due to that damnable war, she thought, a boy who had gone off innocent and unspoiled, now an embittered, battle-hardened soldier. He had fought in many skirmishes from the local gossip of the mountains and his painful wounds that sent him home in sixty four hadn't helped. Well, he'd make a good hand if he would work, a strong man, but only if he gave up drink and had the resolution of old Peavey.

Her mind settled on an offer but she braced the grandfather first. "Jubal, you reckon Hank will work if I offer him a job? He was a good boy once when he helped us before the war."

Jubal Peavey's wrinkled face shrank further into a shrewd, calculating cast. His mind leaped back to Hank's tales from Josie and the coming sale of the milk cows to Captain Jones. It was a godsend, Hank on Greenbottom land, a chance to steal the cows at his leisure and drive them clean away before discovery. Those damned Shaws would pay for those niggers he had lost. He glanced around at Claudius, alert with the shotgun. Could git him too; lot of accidents happen around stock. A kick in the head with a horseshoe would fix him.

His absent-minded delay stretched Letty's patience to exhaustion. Her sharp, "Well, will he work or not?" flung down the gauntlet to both of the Peaveys.

"He will, Miz Letty," Peavey said firmly. "Hank'll be over termorrow mornin' at sunup."

"Gramps," Hank squalled, "don't want to work fer no woman."

"Sober?" Letty asked Peavey, ignoring Hank. "And no thievin'? Have I got your word?"

"Yessum, Miz Letty" Jubal replied. "He won't get no drink ternight." He lied again. "Lern't that stealin' in the Army ter stay alive. Bad!" Peavey shook his head violently. "He won't steal nothin'. Iffen he does, you'll git it back and he'll git a beatin'. Jest can't hev thet."

Jubal struck Hank's shoulders with the cane when he protested. But when the buggy rolled up the lane, the two were in a quiet conversation, their heads close together.

Claudius ran alongside until they were clear. He was puffing when he returned to his mother. "I don' trust 'em, Ma," he said. "From their whisperin', they ain't up to no good."

"I'll take Jubal Peavey's word, boy," Letty told him. "We got along before the war and we can again. Better he's a friend than an enemy. Hold's grudges real bad."

Claudius shook his head and said, "Hank ain't no good no

more."

"We'll see," his mother responded. "I pray you're wrong." She shooed the children into the entrance while Claudius sauntered off toward the corner of the house and the cellar door.

7

Rains on the timbered slopes of the Allegheny Mountains set the loose rock tumbling and clay banks a'trembling over the muddy trace from Union to the west. Trees stuck up out of earth slides at odd angles, scattered jackstraws with leafy or needled tops. An occasional errant rock bounded down and bounced on the rocky trail, its crackling splits adding to the gentler music of the gurgling runoff. Little streams of water ran everywhere, each carrying its burden of mud for the creeks below. Travel was a soggy mess, a hazard for Wiley Minns and his nephew, but the preacher took no heed.

"Mighty wet an' soft," Joshua said, as he guided his horse around a half-buried boulder. A quick finger rubbed along his hat brim showered off the raindrops. Crimping reshaped the soggy felt to send the flow away from his eyes.

"When the clouds are hangin' like this," Charles Searle added, "it's likely to rain fer a week," . The young mountaineer leaned out of the buggy and checked the wheels. They were bouncing over rocks and sinking in a foot in the soft places. "Purty hard on your rig."

Wiley chirked at the teams and slapped his reins up and down on their backs. "Don't matter none," he said, "we're goin' on. Never git there holin' up."

Joshua reined his mount around at the sound of another bounding cobble, this rock as large as his head. The animal shied when the missile swished past and crashed into the treetops below the trail.

The rock's fall startled and deterred the preacher. He tightened the reins and halted the buggy. His horses reared and nickered nervously when the slope above slid downward a foot. Its trees took on a more perilous slant and a slimy, oozing toe encroached onto the trail. A little whining sound emanated from the earth as it ruptured and split, its joints inviting the water that lubricated its failures. A pine tree snapped with a bang and its green top fell close to the trail.

Another sudden lurch of the slope decided Minns. "It's comin' down," he shouted. "Let's git out of here." His whip and "giddap," together with his wet, flapping reins, spurred the animals into rapid flight.

The buggy creaked and groaned at the pounding it took from the rocks in the trail. Even with the damp, Minns' horses shod hooves struck sparks, instantly extinguished by the wet mist. Wiley was nursing the buggy around a tight curve when a loosened boulder chanced the hillside above and struck the right rear wheel, instead of bounding on past. The violent weather had claimed the buggy as its victim and stopped the preacher in his tracks. He and Charles piled out of the rig and gathered at the broken member. With unbiblical color, Wiley damned the boulder and buggy to hell. Not only had the spokes splintered into bits, but the big rock had bent the wheel rim and axle on the carriage itself. Minns stamped around the half-turned-over vehicle, raging at the mist, the rain, the torrent cascading down the hillside, the ill-luck. He persisted until Searle castigated him.

"You ain't soundin' much like a preacher, Minns," Charles said quietly, from his station near the damage. His wet face wrinkled in disappointment and his reproof, "Ain't s'posed to bandy the Lord's name aroun' like that," caused an instant cessation of the preacher's ranting.

"You're right, Charlie." Minns turned his face up to the sky piously and folded his hands. "I ask the Lord's forgiveness." A flying cluster of pine needles with its cone struck him in the face as he prayed. With a mumbled epithet, he wiped the fragments off his rain-slick skin. "The good Lord done chastised me, boys, an' I deserved it. Time we stop the shenanigans and looked after the carriage."

Wiley reached into the boot of the vehicle and came up with an axe. "Let's go, boys," he said, and headed uphill for a grove of arrow-straight regrowth. "Need one o' them hickory saplin's."

Once the woodsman, Charles, had cut and trimmed the skid, the three pried up the rig and and bound the hickory pole to the frame. Wiley cursed the rain silently as he jounced up and down in the buggy, testing the skid. It bowed and sprang back but did not split.

"Jerry Clum can fix the wheel," Charles said. "He's only 'bout five mile on."

Minns shrugged and settled onto the passenger's side of the padded leather seat. "You know these mountains better'n me," he said. "Take us on in."

With a springy jouncing of his passenger, Charles nursed the leaning buggy into the yard of Clum's blacksmith's shop at Connover's Tavern near Wolf Creek. A deep gash in the soil commemorated their path, rapidly smoothed over by the running water with its mud burden. The water still flowed, though the heavy rain had eased to dewy mists.

After "Howdys," the burly blacksmith ignored the shadowing Wiley and walked around the rig in silence. Probing the wrecked wheel, he felt of the tire iron at its sharp bend, then picked out and tossed aside some of the shattered wood that rode beside the skid. Wiley was bouncing around, bursting to talk by the time the blacksmith pulled at the hickory. The latter put his massive weight into a back and forth shaking until the rig squeaked.

"Well, can you fix it?" Minns asked crossly.

The rough-hewn, bearded man turned and stepped toward the preacher, his pale gray eyes narrowed under black eyebrows that ran into his hair. A callused hand sought his leather apron and pulled a pair of tongs from a loop. "Ain't no need fer fussin'," he said quietly. Then he raised the tongs and uttered a warning. "Don't take kindly to no pushin'."

Wiley hastily backed away with his hands up and sought amends. "Ain't meanin' no offense. It's jest thet we got to git on to Charleston, soon's we can."

"Not on thet, you ain't," Clum answered. "Tire iron's cracked and needin' weldin' in the charcoal. Got ter git a whole new set of wood spokes and half the rim. Then shrink on the iron."

"How long?"

"Bout two weeks." The blacksmith gestured to a little house and barn across the trace. A chiseled plank sign on the barn door advertised woodworking. "Banks kin make the hub an' spokes an' rim fittin's and I fix the iron but we's both purty busy." His piggy eyes tightened as he slyly peered at the flushing face of the preacher.

"Ain't nowhere you kin buy a wheel ner nuther buggy. It's this one er walk."

Wiley's devious mind decoded the covetous message in the blacksmith's proposal. He had connived enough to sense an opportunity to strike a quicker deal. His offer played on Clum's cupidity.

"Five dollars gold more'n the regular price git it done any faster?"

"Need two fer Ol' Banks too," Clum instantly replied. "Fer thet, he'll set aside those other timbers he's a'makin'. Pay the coin an' we'll do 'er in five days."

"Done." Wiley fumbled in his belt pouch and fished out three gold pieces. Clum's eyes flashed at the sight. He eagerly took them into his horny palm but inspected the coins closely before jingling them together. A smile followed.

"Ain't seed no gold last three year. You pay the rest in coin?"

"Yes," Wiley said. "When the buggy's ready."

Clum nodded respectfully, "We'll try to make it four days, Reverend." The blacksmith dropped the gold into his pouch and spit a brown stream onto his charcoal forge, where it sputtered and sizzled. “Take your traps to the tavern. Kin git lodgin’ there an’ Miz Calway sets a purty good table.”

“We ain’t got that much to spare,” Wiley said. “We eat there but bunk in your hayloft, if that suits.”

Clum shrugged. “Suit yersel’s” he said, “but don’ ’low no smokin’ ’roun’ the hay.” He waited on a confirming nod, then turned to the broken wheel.

Minns grunted. The deal struck left him free to guard the buggy and its hidden cargo of gold, while resting in a dry, sleepy haven nearby. “You boys settle in,” he told his companions, “while I go visit Miz Calway an’ find out ’bout supper.” Little streams of water flew from his clothes as he splashed off toward the tavern.

Charles Searle’s troubled stare followed Minns until he disappeared in the tavern door. Charles’ conscience bothered him, he a religious boy before the war, observing all the kowtowing to the preachers. Those hardshell Baptists just didn’t break the commandments, according to his parents’ teachings, but Wiley Minns had uttered swear words of the most evil sort. Searle worried about Wiley and his duplicity and shystering, more fitting to a snake oil medicine man than a preacher. Seasoned by war, he had seen his share of sutlers and their cheating ways. Wiley reminded him of something he thought he was done with - dishonesty, but beyond that, scheming tricks. Was he right in going off with the man to ruin some renegade southerner turned Yankee? It was a bother to worry over. He said his nightly prayers in the dark of the haybarn at bedtime but his sleep was fitful, broken up by dreams of Satan and his works.

* * *

Ian McLellan staggered on the deck of the ferry leaving Proctorsville, Ohio, and grasped at a rope to keep from falling. His strong grip and knotted arm muscles straightened him up but his next step lurched to the right. Only the hard timber of the rail kept him from disappearing over the side of the swift paddle-wheeler on its journey to the West Virginia shore.

In the pilot house, Enoch Kitts fingered his cigar from his mouth and roundly cursed the deckhand. “Damn Ian, anyway. Fool drink’ll kill ’im one o’ these days.”

His elderly helmsman, Omer, peered over the sill of the pilothouse windows. Wrinkled, long-fingered hands grasped the wheel tightly as he rotated it and steered the vessel across the Ohio’s strong current. Omer gauged the drift, then swung the helm two spokes counterclockwise, aiming upstream, above the landing on the West Virginia shore. With his course set to quarter the river’s flow, he took the time to spit into the nearby crock and squinted at the foredeck. “He ain’t so bad today, Enoch.” His mournful bass aimed a shot at the real culprit. “Garrett ought not sell Ian no spirits. He knows Claude’s dead agin it.”

Disgust clouded Enoch’s hawkish face. "That Garrett wants only one thing - money. He’d sell ice to old Nick hisself if it’d make him a copper.”

“Well Ian is one good hand when he’s sober,” Omer said stoutly. He squinted at their travel across the swift, turbid current and adjusted the wheel a trifle. “Claude kept him workin’ steady nigh on three year ’fore he went off to war. He’ll git Ian off the lightnin’ when he gits back.”

Ian’s equilibrium occupied their gaze for the next few minutes as the ferry progressed against the strong pull down-stream. The mate turned deckhand worked in full view around the cargo below on the foredeck, gradually accelerating his pace at straightening his lines and clearing the deck of tangles and encum-brances. He had the side exit open for the landing and offloading by the time the vessel approached the shore.

“He sure kin work when he sets to it,” Enoch admitted. “Strong as he is, we can git along with just him an’ only one of Claude’s niggers.”

“They ain’t his no more,” Omer reminded him. “They’s all free and workin’ fer wages.”

“True, but they still got to have a job and we can pick

the best." The rotund Captain sighed regretfully. "Ain't likely to git that Isaiah though. Nor Hannibal. They's too close to Claude. He treats them 'most like white folks."

The ferry's paddlewheel slowed as the vessel slid in toward the floating landing next to the steep bank, Omer silently wrestling the wheel. A plume of steam blew away when he whistled once to alert all on the road above that the ferry was landing. Separation of boat and dock slowly disappeared as he pointed the bow upstream to avoid a crash. With hardly a bump, the helmsman made his landing and Ian threw the bow line to the waiting Negro on the float. A few turns of the line around a sturdy pile bollard snubbed it tight and the ferry drifted solidly against the dock, held by the pressure of the current and the spring line. A breast line below the rail exit finished the mooring.

Ian's release of the chain gate at the side opening and his call to the freighters brought a swarm of men from the interior of the ferry and helpers from the shore. Above the landing a group of wagons and people waited on the offloading, their turn and trip to Ohio to follow. Two light buggies left first, then the heavily laden wagons, each shift from vessel to float rocking the two up and down. A particularly heavy load rolled the ferry with its side springing up quickly when the wheels shifted to the float. This more difficult discharge of freight wagons was proceeding rapidly under the mate's direction when a scream and splash drew all to the side of the ferry.

"My baby, my baby," a woman on the upper deck shrieked. "Save her," she cried, and crumpled to the deck. Men in her party looked to the woman, but only one bent over the rail to check the floundering girl, then removed his coat as if to jump after her.

The thrashing child screamed when she came up and bumped along the hull, drifting downstream toward the slowly rotating paddles at the stern. Without a word, Ian ran along the side and jumped into the water nearby. He seized the sinking girl and raised her above the surface, her piteous cries now interspersed with coughing. Floating her on his chest, the deckhand braced against the ferry and pushed off violently, coasting his body toward shore. He and the victim were seized by men knee-deep in the water and dragged ashore to safety.

"Ian ain't no coward," Omer said in the pilothouse. "That took some doin', with that wheel a'goin'."

Enoch nodded and reset his cap over his thinning hair. "I'd best be down to see to Miz Wilkes and Maybelle," he said resignedly. "I done told that woman a hundert times not to let that child sit on the rail. Maybe this'll cure her." Tossing his cigar remnant into the crock, he headed for the door.

A few minutes of sobbing and hugs and warnings from Enoch settled down Mrs. Wilkes and the wet child. When the passengers dispersed, the Captain sought out Ian on the foredeck, busy loading freight and passengers for the trip to Ohio.

"Mighty fine thing you did," he said.

Ian shrugged, his wet shirt emphasizing his muscular body. "Weren't nothin'," he said. "Ain't gonna let no child drown." He chuckled. "Scairt that Maybelle somethin' fierce. Mayhaps she won't ride that rail no more."

"Her mama says so." A point nagged at Enoch, one that had to be said. "You're a hero, Ian. Ever'body knows you can't swim. Took real courage to do that."

"Wasn't nothin' special," Ian replied, and went back to his work.

* * *

Fine weather in South Carolina had blessed Jess Ebert and his son Jobe. They had bought the old mule with the gold from Claude and had started on the plowing. Now, just a few weeks later, some garden truck in the plot near their cabin was sprouting out green and their cleanup of fields was making the farm ready for production. Five deer hides cured on the wall of the barn and a tendril of odorous gray rose from the smokehouse roof. A few pigs squealed in a pen behind the barn. Jess Ebert's limping step had turned springy and he whistled as he worked the mule.

He reined in the animal and wrapped the leathers around a plow handle when Jobe approached at noon. The boy carried an aromatic wood platter and a gourd.

"You feelin' purty good? " Jobe asked.

"Mighty pert, since Claude give us that loan. It'll be our savin'."

Jobe held out the platter. Ebert took a piece of corncake and speared a large chunk of fried pork with his belt knife. They sat on unplowed weeds and fed hugely from the simple fare on the platter between them, washing it down with water from the gourd. A grunt and belch topped off Ebert's meal and he lay back with his hands under his head and stared at the sky. "Life mighty good, son."

"We owe Captain Shaw somethin' fierce, Pa," Jobe replied. "I ain't fergittin' this."

Ebert raised up on his elbows and nodded. "Ain't jest money we owe, boy. He was a damned Yankee yet he he'ped us. He give us hope." Ebert shook his head. "Hard to believe."

"He's a farmer first," Jobe said feelingly. "That's why. You see him take thet handful of loam and feel of it? He knowed we got a good place."

"Could be," Ebert said. "We pay him the money but if he needs some other he'p we do thet too. 'count o' him, we's a family agin', with a chance." He spit and wiped his mouth with the back of his hand. "Yer mother's eyes are sparklin'. She's gittin' the house fixed real nice an we're a'ready makin' somethin'. Can't fault thet."

"You want any more, Pa?"

"No boy," Ebert said. The farmer took a swig of water and went back to the plowing while his son carried the platter to his mother.

* * *

Hank Peavey stole Letty's cows from the small pasture next to her barn the night before Captain Jones and the Evangeline were to return. He led them through the early morning hours in a cold, driving rain, quartering over the soft, grassy ground to the narrow creek that passed their house, a flow fed hugely from the Peavey valley beyond. It was an easy if wet walk up the swollen, cloudy flow to Peavey's holding pen about a quarter mile off the river road. Hank abandoned the stock there willingly, wet through from the raindrops. He shivered and cut for the house along the sloping path, familiar steps he had taken a thousand times before.

Jubal Peavey sat in front of the fireplace when his grandson entered, its flickering flames casting shadows on the far wall. He drew his scarf tighter against the wet, chill wind through the door. "You git 'em?" he asked.

"Five, Gramps." At his grandfather's raised eyebrows he hastily explained. "Fetched all but Sally. That damned Jersey got too much wild cow in her. Run through the fence where a tree fell an' I ain't got no time to ketch her."

With his grandpa silenced and staring into the fire, Hank stripped off to his underwear and wrung out the worst of the water onto the stone hearth before the blaze. He crouched in front to dry and steamed until his shivering stopped. A more comfortable seat at the side left his now only damp but odorous clothes hanging in front of the fire.

Jubal Peavey sniffed and exploded with a curse and a complaint. "My God, boy, I ain't takin' too many baths but you jest plain stink. Whyn't you run on out and warsh yourself an' those things in the creek?"

Hank laughed. "Can't stand a little scent, Gramps? You orta smell troops after a hard march an' a battle. Got the blood too then an' all those dead men."

"Git on out, boy." Peavey's stick rose for a blow which Hank easily evaded. "You git yersel' warshed up."

"It's too cold," Hank whined, delaying before the fire. "With them spring flows that creek's even worse'n the rain, and it's cold enough."

Peavey rose from his chair and flailed about with his cane, repeatedly striking the youth across the shoulders. Hank seized his clothes and ran out of the door barefooted. Only his shoes steamed before the fire. Old Peavey shook his head and pushed them to one side with his cane. "Leather'll shrink hard," he said. "Thet boy ain't got no common sense."

Hank was clean, even shaved and with his hair slicked down, a model of better Peavey manhood when they took to their porch chairs in midmorning. A dry and pleasant day with the storm long past, the scattered clouds and soft breezes that blew in from the southwest made for good sitting weather. Languishing with Jubal and making small talk passed their time, not long after interrupted by the sound and plume of Captain Jones' whistle. The tall stacks of the river steamer showed over the trees bordering the river and flashes of the white superstructure allowed glimpses as the boat approached the Shaw landing. Faint shouts accompanied the mooring and the lane to the river soon was graced with the figures of two men. Easily recognizable was the Captain, in white and with a cap. The other sported a wide-brimmed felt hat and gambler's grays and blacks, his frock coat set off by a colorful vest. Four hands followed, led by a mate in rough clothes and cap.

"Miz Letty didn't find no cows this morning," Hank said. "I saw 'em stirrin' aroun' but they couldn't find nothin'. Isaiah was runnin' all over, lookin' fer tracks." He chuckled. "Ain't none with thet rain."

"Them cows hid good?"

"In the holding pen, Gramps. I jest got too wet an' cold to move 'em on up the valley."

Jubal swore. "You ain't never learned, boy. You got to git them animals clean over the ridge. Isaiah'll find 'em fer sure."

His grandpa's gloom did little to disturb Hank but the old man didn't realize that his fears were nothing like the sheer anguish he had caused in Greenbottom. When Captain Jones and the gambler arrived, Letty interrupted her crying to let them into the parlor. They cleaned their boots on the scraper's iron then entered soft-footedly, taking care of the polished plank floor.

At the sight of the gambler, Kittie Mae ran to him with a shriek of joy and hugged him tight around the waist. He picked up the slight girl and whirled around. Her skirts flew out as he asked, "How's my little girl?" and squeezed her tight.

Kittie giggled and said, "More, more."

Letty smiled through her tears and daubed her eyes. "Worth is a real joy to that child," she told Captain Jones. "Hasn't been here but twice since she met him on your boat but she's really taken."

"You're right, Letty," Jones said. "Worth Fauquier is a real gentleman and loves children, even if he is a hard man. "He spoke softly, in a tone inaudible to the gambler. "He's quiet 'bout this an' I ain't never told you nor Claude. He don't like nobody to know but he used to have a big place down around Petersburg, with lots of nigras. Rich. War took his whole family and the land too. Nothin' left but his courtliness now." He laughed. "And the best with cards and a gun. He's killed several men down around Cincinnati."

Letty's renewed sniffling brought him back to the present. The gambler and Kittie Mae were waltzing on the hardwood floor, his jollities interrupted by the girl's laughter. Kittie Mae's sisters quietly watched from the side and young Claudius looked on from his post behind his mother, his face at once disgusted and bored.

"Now what's wrong, Letty," Jones asked sympathetically.

"It's the cows, Cal." She broke down and bawled, resting her face against his chest. He put his arms around her and patted her back but it did not stop her crying. "They're gone, Cal, stolen. All 'cept the old Jersey. Somebody took them last night."

"They're gone?" Jones exclaimed. "Who did it?"

Kittie Mae stiffened at the exchange and Worth Fauquier, overhearing, immediately drifted over to the pair, with the girl clinging to his left arm. The gambler's lips set in a grim line as he asked, "You know who, Miz Letty? We'll go get them."

Letty turned her wet, reddened eyes toward Fauquier. "It's probably those Peavey's, Worth. Nobody else around here could have taken them." She flared up, enraged, her tears erased. "Old

Jubal promised me Hank wouldn't do no more thievin' but I 'spect he's got 'em hid out."

Worth put aside the girl and his face took on a hawk-like set. As the gambler straightened up, he seemed somehow to bulk larger than his slim, elegant figure, filling out clothes that before had simply fitted him. It was as if he had tightened a bowstring, Letty thought, as she looked into the cold, slitted eyes of the man. A shiver ran over her and she asked his help.

"I was fixing to brace Old Jubal when the boat whistled." She pulled her pocket pistol. "Claude gave me this and I know how to shoot it."

Jones took the gun from her and laid it on a small table. "You won't need that if it comes to shooting," he said. "Worth and I will handle any trouble."

"That's right, Miz Letty," Worth added, and flipped open his coat flaps. A pistol belt showed around his middle and his vest pockets bulged. He hitched up his belt and adjusted it, then eased his pistol out of its sheath in a smooth, flowing draw. Reholstered instantly, the gambler next felt of his vest pockets and said, "I'm ready, Cal."

Collecting Isaiah and his crew on the way, Cal Jones and Worth bracketed Letty as they marched up the lane and over the river road to Peavey's, picking their way around the puddles. Kittie Mae and the smaller children remained on the Shaw steps but Claudius sneaked behind the party with his shotgun. Old Jubal greeted them from his porch but Hank came down into the yard where the party had stopped and faced them with an insolent grin.

"I'd invite ye in, Miz Letty," Jubal said, "but I ain't got that many chairs."

"Don't matter, Jubal," Letty said. "We're here for the cows Hank stole last night."

Hank ran forward with an oath and shook a threatening fist. "Damn you, Letty, I ain't takin' none o' thet. I ain't no thief."

Fauquier paled and sprang between Letty and the mountaineer even as his hand sought his vest. He cocked his derringer during a lightning fast draw and extended his arm. The weapon's shiny black barrel glinted in the sun from its perch at the end of Hank's sharp nose.

The gambler's soft but brittle order would have forced even a gunman to retreat. "Apologize to Miz Letty or you'll rest in hell tonight."

"He'll take it back," Jubal yelled. "Don't kill the boy; he ain't a'meanin' it."

Peavey stumped toward the steps to the yard. Rebel eye stared at rebel eye while righteous rage battled with the hate of the mountaineer for the plantation owner. A probe with the derringer settled the matter. Its sharp end tore the skin from the tip of Hank's nose and blood flowed down his chin.

"I 'pologize, Miz Letty," Hank said sullenly, but his eyes conveyed a different message.

"Where are my cows?"

Hank's emphatic, "I ain't got 'em," was contradicted by a faint lowing up the valley. Two other cows chimed in.

"That's Maude," Letty cried. "He's holdin' 'em in the pen up the creek."

Isaiah and the boat crew returned with the milk cows in about twenty minutes, a time of silent condemnation by Letty, while Jubal unsuccessfully tried to patch things up.

"You're both liars," she retorted, when he persisted. "Stay off my land from now on." Her anger increased when she saw the cows' distended udders and intermittent squirts of milk from their teats. "You didn't even milk them," she complained, "just let them suffer. Have you no decency?"

Peavey and his grandson stayed in the yard until the cows and attendants had retreated to the Shaw land. Back on the porch, the old man was still lambasting Hank when Captain Jones and Worth made ready to leave with the hands and the cows, after the animals had been milked.

"Here's the other sixty dollars in gold, Letty," Captain Jones told her in the parlor.""I paid the $300 to Abel as you asked." He fished out the receipt and handed it to her.

"I appreciate the help, Cal, and thank you kindly. Claude

will be pleased." Letty's forehead wrinkled and her face grew solemn. Fauquier and Kittie Mae were hunched over a spread of cards on the big table.

"Kit wants to go to Cincinnati, Cal, like she did a few months ago."

"We got room, Letty, at no cost." Jones took her hand and patted it. "You don't need to worry. Worth says she's just like his younger daughter." He whispered, "She was killed by a cannon shot that knocked down their house during one of the big Petersburg battles." His voice boomed out again and carried to the table. "Worth will shoot anybody bothers Kittie Mae."

The gambler looked up at that. His steely eyes and set jaw promised even more as he nodded and added, "True. No need to worry, Miz Letty. She's safe with me."

Kittie Mae left with the river party when they departed down the lane to the landing, her valise carried by a deckhand and herself in the care of Worth Fauquier. Letty knew he would treat the girl as his daughter. They had bonded instantly when they first had met. Her worry at the beginning, that the girl was enamored of an older man, had proved false. Then had come the realization that Worth, the gentleman, was a second father, enjoying the love of the girl as she matured. But the whistle when the river boat left Shaw's Landing brought a twinge and a doubt that she would rest well until the girl was safely back.

8

In the weeks since the cotton sale, Rance Pickens had scoured the countryside for skins and other trades, his spirits most lifted when he found four hogsheads of fine tobacco hidden at Widow Peak's. He had paid her a fair price for the redolent, cured leaf but a twinge of conscience bothered him when he thought of the big profit he expected. Should he have given more to the widow? No! After all, he had to do the freighting and pay Pinckney for storing and factoring the leaf. He settled on asking quadruple his outlay at his friend's warehouse. The amount amazed him when he thought of the desperate straits they had been in. In just a few trades he had gotten a good stake to start over. Even as he walked his horse toward home, half-dozing while his mind concentrated on his problems, Jed and Bub were freighting the tobacco to Charleston. It would end up in the pipes of the English, probably by shipment when the Seasprite returned.

With the two Negroes working for wages and keep, he felt like a man again, equal to anything, ready to reclaim the overgrown fields of his plantation. When the Negroes came back he'd round up a few of his old hands and start on the eastern fields, grubbing out the saplings and weeds. It wouldn't do to just leave farming to Old Ben, young Chancy and the vegetable garden, though their crops were growing fast and the family would soon start eating out of the patch. Vegetables would be wonderful, he mused, some fresh things beyond picking ramps and dandelion leaves. So far they'd made out with mostly meat and cornbread but his mouth watered for some good greens and potatoes and cabbage. As he walked his horse along, another unrelated thought struck him. Ashley's blossoming was the best of all, rejuvenated, loving, attentive since his return from Charleston with the cotton money. His wife had been overjoyed at the three hundred dollars he gave her from his first trades. She had clutched the coins in a tight grip and worked the metal together to feel its weight, then had come right to him after, clutching him around the body and crying. "Oh, Rance, I never thought I'd get anything again. This'll buy some pretties for me and Nancy."

"Don't forget Aunty Susan in your buyin'," he reminded her. "She needs some new things and you must pay her wages we agreed to. Keep and a dollar a month, hard money."

Ashley grimaced at Rance's reminder. When he squeezed her arm, she nodded and said, "I'll do it, Rance. It just seems so wrong, givin' nigras money."

Rance shook her lightly, but his sharp reply brooked no interference. "Pay her," he ordered. "The nigras are free now."

Dismissing the reverie, his heart lifted on this latest, yet another return to a loving family from his trading circuit. Within a mile he reined his mount into the lane to his home. Once the animal was turned out into the pasture, he ran up the porch steps with a light heart and greeted his wife in the parlor with a squeeze and a kiss. Her new flowered dress and rosy cheeks, set ablaze with a little of the foreign rouge, added to her coy smile.

"Go along, Rance," she said, blushing. He felt of her smooth, supple body, unbound with any stays in the privacy of their home. It bent willingly toward him, inviting his caresses, but her cupidity became more powerful than her desire. She pulled away from him and asked, "Did you make some trades?"

When he told her of the tobacco and sweet potatoes he had bought, she clapped her hands. "Maybe being a merchant isn't so bad as I thought, Rance."

He laughed and seized her, holding her in a tighter grip. "The coin we make will carry us back into farming, Ash. I'm startin' on the east fields next. We'll do it all."

She diverted his attention and roving hands, though she had responded to him and pressed her body close. "A messenger came yesterday with a letter from Pinckney," she said. "It's on the table."

He looked up in wonder a few minutes later, the paper dangling from his left hand. "He wants us to go up to Greenbottom later this summer and talk to Claude about the river trade in rum. You up to it?"

Ashley's sunny face turned sour, but it cleared when she saw his frown. "I'll go, Rance," she said. "I might not like the man but if he adds to your trade I will be civil to him and his folks."

He nodded and took her in his arms again. She joined tightly with his aroused body. "Now let's go up to the bedroom," he said. "It's been too long."

* * *

Claude had stopped at Wood Stephens' place below Dalton, Georgia, after visiting Granny Eva at Carters. The carriage was full now that the huge Eva and bulging Elsie had joined the others. Claude's conscience bothered him and its niggling voice demanded that he provide for his future son, black or white. He could not leave the radiant Elsie, whose gaze sought him out at every encounter. She held on as the carriage rocked in the ruts, her protruding stomach misshapen but somehow beautiful and a magnet for his eyes. God, he thought, have I got myself in a pickle!

Clarke Stephens saw them first when the carriage turned into the yard, and yelled, "It's Claude, Ma." His slight limp did little to deter his run to the side of the vehicle.

A day of happy visiting restored the travelers to full vigor, erasing their tiredness from the constant jouncing on the rutted roads. Clarke's mother, Belle, fattened them with her rich cooking, from meats to biscuits to vegetables to sweets, the latter from the honey of the bee tree and the pumpkin pie and whipped cream.

It was a jolly time, but one of tears when Wood Stephens said the final blessing before their departure.

"These are our friends, Oh Lord, Yankee, black and white alike. I used to think we was all different, but we ain't, Lord, and we can live in peace. These folks saved our son. We ask thy blessing on them in their travel and through life and that we may always be together in peace and in spirit. Bless this food to our bodies and us to thy service. Amen."

A chorus of amens echoed around the crowded table, where Yankee, Rebel, black and white broke bread together.

Claude stood above Athey Minns' grave a day later, his mind churning. Someone had buried the corpse hanging from the spear point and the yellow clay mound already was partially obscured with leaves. It had only been seven months since the fight and Minns' killing but his shuddering returned when he recalled his desperate dispair. Athey had been so close to shooting him when Hester ran the hunter through with the heartpine spike. He shook himself into the present, banishing the terrifying past. Hester was not there to inspect the site of her triumph and a grave. She had refused to accompany them, remaining with the other women in the carriage on the road to Dalton. The sidehill beckoned Claude after a trembling prayer. Hannibal ran down the slope ahead of him and soon located Gabe's and Jared's burial place. It was sunken and the cross had fallen in.

"Ain't right, Claude," Hannibal said. "Gabe a good man and deserve a marker."

"The Minnses too," the planter replied. "We'll go on into Dalton and get a stonecutter there."

Another day of search and bargaining arranged for the stones and identified the graves to the carver. When the man stood beside each, Claude handed him the inscriptions and bound him to the contract. "We'll be by in the fall," Claude told him, "to visit the graves."

"Ain't no worry," the stonecutter answered. "They'll be set in a month."

Hannibal hugged the planter hard when they were out

of the man's shop. "Carvin' de stone as Gabe Shaw mighty fine, Claude. Gabe shore 'ppreciate dat."

"He was a good friend," Claude answered. "He laid down his life for us. Least I could do."

Two weeks beyond their Dalton stop, Claude and his party arrived at Shaw's Landing, completing the journey to Greenbottom by buggy, railroad and river steamer from Cincinnati.

It was Wednesday next, after a joyous, tumultuous welcome, with Letty in tears when she hugged him and his crying children surrounding him, that Letty summoned Claude into the library.

His heart flipflopped when he faced her solemn face, a countenance that he had only seen once before, when he had been too friendly with a flirt on the steamboat off Rockport. Silence occupied their settling into facing chairs. Claude waited for the explosion, expected since she had closed the sliding doors to the hall. This was to be close combat, he thought, and could only be about Elsie. The young Negro had waddled into quarters with Granny Eva and Mandy, but Letty's sharp eyes had seized on the obvious. Got to admit it right out, he concluded. Best if she gets it directly from me.

"Elsie says she's carryin' my child, Letty."

His straight out admission startled her. Letty recoiled and went white. Her eyes closed, followed an instant later by streams of tears on her cheeks. She snatched a hankerchief out of her bodice and sobbed, bent over like an old lady as her small, plump body at once shuddered and was overcome by waves of trembling. "How could you do that," she wailed. "She ain't nothing but a nigra."

"It was while I was on the run," he replied gently. Her muffled "No, no," tore at him. "That's no excuse, Letty," he added, miserable at the admission. "We just came together in the night and I just had to, being gone so long."

She sat up straight in her chair and choked back the sobs. Scrubbed with her handkerchief, her cheeks tightened and her eyes narrowed. "You fixin' to bed her more?"

"Never again, Letty," he said. "I ask your forgiveness." He placed his hand on the Bible on the coffee table. "I promise that you are the only one."

"That infernal war did more'n kill men, Claude," she said. "It damned people and I hope you aren't damned with them." When he started to interrupt, she added, "Now you be quiet. We'll pray together each day for your salvation." Letty struggled for a moment but her innate fairness won out. "Meantime you'll take care of that woman and her child same as my uncle did with his three youngun's with Kate. He raised and educated them just like my cousins." She waggled a finger at him. "And if it's yours you'll give it your name."

"Agreed," he said humbly.

She surprised him by taking his hand on the way out of the parlor. He pulled her close to him and bent down to kiss her. "I love you, Letty," he said. "You ain't got no reason to worry."

* * *

The Reverend Wiley Minns and his nephew settled into a boarding house in Point Pleasant, West Virginia, while they waited on Charles Searle to join them. At Charleston the Reb had found Union officials not ready to issue paroles to Confederates. Minns had handed him a few gold coins and told him to follow whenever he had his clearance by federal forces.

A night to remember adapted the two Minns thoroughly to the river town. Wiley, minus his religious trappings, took Joshua on a round of taverns, buying drinks and asking about Claude. His money secured singularly little useful information other than that Greenbottom lay west on the Ohio River and Shaw hadn't been around for years. Joshua walked the stumbling Wiley back to the boarding house while his uncle complained of a monumental headache, slurring all his words.

"Got to fin' out all 'bout Claude Shaw now," he mumbled. "Talk to the bankers termorrow."

"Yes, Unk," Joshua said, patient with his drunken uncle. He tumbled Wiley into bed and pulled the boots off the already snoring figure. Looking down on the supine man, he chuckled. "You shore ain't got no head for licker." A few minutes later his own snores added to the din.

* * *

Flowers overflowed the parlor of Greenbottom on the tenth of July, Letty's decorations for the wedding. Their fragrance enhanced the scent of new-mown grass that entered the windows. Gentle breezes drove its sweet perfume all through the house. Two lines of chairs filled with guests, white and black, left a center aisle for the waltz of the bride to be. The pleasantries of arriving friends joined with piano music, and added to the hum of soft laughter and subdued conversation.

All eyes shifted to the front of the room when the minister held up his Bible. As if on signal, Claude and Hannibal stepped from a recessed arch and stood at attention to his left. Hannibal was magnificent in his black broadcloth suit, his big frame barbered and polished into an upright statue of virile, well-turned-out manhood. A Captain of the 7th Ohio Cavalry sided him. Claude wiggled in his bright, new uniform with its polished brass. A scratchy collar itched him, but he forced himself back to attention after easing his neck.

"Different fum de war," Hannibal said. His whisper came out of the corner of his mouth.

"Don't think of that," Claude replied. "Lee surrendered more'n three months ago and we're back safe. That's all that matters."

The Negro wriggled his shoulders and fanned his face. "I'se kinda hot."

"You're just nervous. It won't take long."

Hannibal's fright amused Claude. Here was a man who had faced bullets and blades but his nervousness at the religious ceremony still plagued him. The planter seized the Negro's bulging biceps and squeezed them hard while he murmured his reassurances.

"I'll be right here with you. Just do it like we rehearsed."

Granny Mandy chattered away with other ancients in the front row of chairs, prominently settled in the place of honor at the end. Granny Eva and a fat Elsie sat in the row behind her. Though each sported a colorful turban above flowered prints, they were silent and composed, leaving the talking to Mandy and her friends. Hester's granny was resplendent in a red taffeta dress with many rustling folds, its beauty complemented by a flamboyant silk bandanna that captured most of her white hair. Even her stick was new, a carved hickory staff with a cat's head on the knob. Granny's sage wisdom dominated the others. But they crowded even closer when she bent over to pass along a morsel of gossip, then nodded their heads and laughed at her juicy tale. Giggling interspersed with whispers when they put their heads together and traded stories.

As hostess to the wedding, Letty circulated at the rear of the room and greeted everyone. Claude's gaze fixed on his wife from his position by the preacher. Lovely, he thought. Her well-turned-out figure showed handsomely in a light gray dress with flounces, the one he liked so well. She seated some last minute arrivals and motioned to him that Hester was ready.

The pianist struck up the introduction at the cue while Claude went to the main hall to escort Hester. He circled her in delight when she whirled on the polished floor for his inspection. The beautiful young woman wore a magnificent white dress as his and Letty's gift, the two together creating a statuesque figure. Claude offered her his arm after the pirouette. Lightly and with graceful steps, she accommodated to his measured, booted stride. Hester drew envious as well as admiring glances when they paced down the aisle to the strains of the wedding march. Two small Negro girls strewed flowers before them, blossoms gathered from the blooming fields. Hannibal greeted his love with a broad smile and a protective hug when she joined him. As soon as the group settled to his liking, the preacher commenced the marriage service.

"Who gives this bride in marriage?"

Granny Mandy struggled up, braced by her stick. "I'se her Granny, Mandy Pickens fum down ter Columbia. I gives her ter Hannibal."

The wedding ended quickly under the preacher's practiced litany, all the well-known terms and promises rapidly fulfilled. A cheering audience and Granny's waving cane celebrated his presentation of the married couple. Claude joined at Hannibal's side as they went into the dining room for the reception and sampling of the cake. Merrymakers already were busy at the amply laden table.

"Come into the library, Hannibal," Claude said, "soon's you can. We need to get straight on the land."

Hannibal joined the others about thirty minutes later. He stood transfixed after he entered, gazing in awe at the walls lined with books. But the decoration that took his eye was the polished rifle on deer antlers over the fireplace. A powder horn and fat leather pouch hung from the rack at the butt end.

"It's Minns' rifle," Claude said, when Hannibal reached up and gently rubbed the piece. "Now come meet the folks."

Introductions finished, Claude and his old friends were all business while Hannibal looked on. Judge Jesse Marvin and Records Clerk Archie Wolf from the land office completed Claude's deeding of his Little Seven Mile Creek farm to Hannibal Shaw. It took only a few minutes after Hannibal signed his name, a proud accomplishment taught to him by Hester.

"The deed settled to your satisfaction, Judge?" Claude asked the white-haired, portly jurist.

"It's Hannibal's property, Claude, free and clear. Just needs recording."

"I'll do that Monday, Claude." Archie's nasal voice continued. "It'll be in the land records as in the name of Hannibal Shaw."

"You'll see that Hannibal gets the deed?"

"I'll handle that," the Judge said. He puffed on his

cigar, then blew out a smoke ring. "Archie's right around the corner. I'm going out to Seven Mile next week on a legal matter and can drop it off."

Abel House had been waiting quietly while the land transaction proceeded to its conclusion. Dressed in his confidence building blue serge that identified his banker status and intimidated borrowers, he fitted snugly into the close-knit group. His control over money and credit established his influence among the visitors as well as the local residents along the Ohio River.

He coughed and said, "You mentioned some farm things and credit, Claude?"

Claude nodded. "I've already given Hannibal and Hester a cow and mule." He paused, his face thoughtful. "And a wagon and farming tools. He's got a garden planted and Letty helped Hester with the house." The planter's brow furrowed. "He may need some other things and I want to help him get started."

Rising to his feet, Claude walked over to the racked rifle and took down the small but heavy sack. It clinked when he pulled the drawstring open. He poured out some coins and held them out to the banker.

"Here's four hundred and seventy eight dollars in gold and silver, Abel." At their exclamations and shocked faces he explained. "Took it off a reb who tried to kill me. He stilled and sold whiskey. Hester killed him when he was about to shoot me. She saved my life. The coins belong to her and to Hannibal."

Abel jingled the treasure while he sorted and counted the collection. Handing some to Hannibal, he put the rest in his coat pocket and said, "I'll bank four hundred for you, Hannibal, on interest. Keep the others for things you need from the store."

The silent Negro turned the coins in his palm and clinked them together. While the others watched, fascinated, he held them up to the sunlight at the window, letting the rays reflect off the yellow surfaces as he turned the coins in his palm. It was money that was his, his first, beyond that they had given away in Carolina and Georgia. He was mystified, Claude thought, unused to the practice of buying and selling, of owning property, of being a free man. He spoke gently to his friend.

"Keep the deed safe, Hannibal. Don't give or sell it to anyone before you talk to me. And I and the Judge and Abel and Archie'll help you. You just ask. You understand?"

Hannibal nodded, his face twisting. He could not speak. Instead, he joined Claude and hugged him.

Claude asked, "Abel, Archie, they saved my life. Help them and I'm in your debt."

"We will, Claude." Judge Marvin's loud reassurance was reinforced by nods of agreement from the others.

"There's one other thing, Jesse, the emancipation."

The Judge puffed out a smoke ring. "Lincoln was crafty, Claude. He made the Proclamation apply only to the rebelling states. Hester and Granny Mandy are automatically free."

"But what about Hannibal?"

"Got the manumission papers right here," the Judge said. He picked up a document from the side table holding his traveling case. "This'll set Hannibal free."

The manumission paper, witnessed by all present, went into Hannibal's pocket. Its presentation was accompanied by warnings from Judge Marvin to keep it safe with the deed.

They concluded their business and stubbed out their cigars when Letty called to them. She bustled in, her nose wrinkling and arms waving at the clouds of blue smoke that drifted in the faint breeze through the library windows.

"Land sakes," she said, "you'll suffocate in here." Her friends rose and bowed, laughing sheepishly as she coughed and fanned herself and gently reminded them of Hannibal's new family.

"It's time they went on to Seven Mile, Claude. Hester and Elsie and their grannies are already in the buggy, waitin' on Hannibal."

It was the free man who answered. "We be right dere, Miz Letty."

Hannibal grasped each of the men's hands in turn, his expressive eyes and awkward thanks accolades for their work.

Each, in turn, pledged his help. Neither he nor Claude could speak to each other, their embraces replacing the inadequate handshake.

Only the planter stood in the drive when Hannibal descended the steps after he took his leave of Letty. The rest of Claude's friends waved from the porch. Negroes clustered in the shade of the large maple and buckeye trees and fanned themselves. They jollied Hester with ribaldry amid laughter and the wave of Granny Eva's huge stick. The women's bright dresses and bandannas projected above the jet black of the vehicle, their sprays of colorful flowers in the buggy. Hannibal arrived unnoticed by the Negroes but he was not to leave unheralded. A fat bluetick hound barked and rushed out of his bed under a shrub, his stub tail wagging.

Hannibal bent down and patted the old dog's head as Blue snuffled at his pants; then his fingers scratched the itchy spots behind the hound's ears. He laughed when he ran his hand along the plump, sleek sides of the animal. "Old Blue mighty fat, Claude."

"Letty makes sure he gets good baits. He'll always have a home here."

One last pat and Hannibal shooed Blue back to the side. The buggy screeched when it sagged under the weight of his step up. Dust rose from the lane as Hannibal and Hester left the waving crowd and started off on their new life of freedom.

9

"Oh! Oh! Owwwwwww! Elsie's long, drawn out howl and arched back brought a pat from Granny Eva and a "shush" from Granny Mandy. "Cain't be dat bad," the old woman grumbled. "Ain't but a little t'ing, belly you got showin'." Elsie screamed again and Hannibal ran into the bedroom, a gun in his hand.

"Git outen here," Eva thundered. "Dishere's woman's work."

Hannibal backed away from the middle of the night party of women at the bed, just in time to block the door to Hester. She pushed him aside.

"You men ain't got no sense," she said, grinning at him. "We git 'er through it. Whyn't you git on out ter de barn?"

Even there he could hear the squalls, interrupted at last by a baby's thin wail, new life snuffing out Elsie's screams. Quiet rumbles came from the house. Picking up his blanket, he ambled back to his new home and sidled into the room.

Hester held up a small, squalling bundle. "Right pert boy," she said. "Got six toes! Plenty to skedaddle wid."

Bringing in the big Bible Letty had given them and her writing desk, Hester laid them on a small table near the window. She opened the Bible to the family chronicles page with a flourish and entered the birth in a carefully traced inscription.

"Today, August 20, 1865, our Elsie bore a strong boy,

named Douglass Hannibal Shaw, after his father and her saviors."

Hannibal winced when she read it aloud. "Shaw? It ain't right you blame Claude. He don' have but one chance an' he pretty pore den."

Eva laughed and Mandy giggled. "Claude got 'nough," Eva said, "way dat Elsie fox him inter de shed on de Saugy last winter."

"Well, I ain't believin' it," Hannibal insisted.

The three women laughed uproariously until Elsie raised her sweat streaked head from her pillow and quietly interrupted. "Douglass de man," she said. "He de onliest one 'roun' wid six toes . Most'a his kin got 'em." She went on. "You keep dis quiet now. Miz Letty got atter Claude cuz he tinks he de man." She laughed. "I tells her right quick. Nobody else."

"Miz Letty keep 'im hoppin', a'right, iffen he tinks it his young'n." Mandy went on. "Woman need little stick. Good one fer Miz Letty iffen Claude don' know."

Hannibal's outrage washed over them. "You ain't tellin' Claude?" He sputtered and cursed, "Well, I tell him directly we git together."

Hester stuck her face up to him and fussed. "You do dat and I ain't letting you in my bed no mo'. You hear me?"

He backed away from the three hostile women, Granny Eva with her cane raised, the knob end threatening a great blow. "It best fer now, Hannibal," she said. "Claude learn when Miz Letty reckon it time."

He went away grumbling while they bathed Elsie and the baby and restored peaceful quiet to the house.

* * *

A month later, Elsie's baby was fat and shining when Letty came to visit late in the afternoon, the sun already close to the western mountain top. She slid from the sidesaddle at the tin roofed porch and tied off the horse to the hitching rail at one side. Morning glories ran up trellises on the knobbed cedar posts, blooming with purple and white flutes. Hester came out as Letty stomped up the steps, shaking the dust off her skirt. A wet apron and whitened spots on Hester's arms attested to her baking.

"More biscuits?" Letty asked as they hugged. With a final shake of her skirts, she headed into the house over the unpainted, creaking porch. The young Negro followed close on her heels, chattering all the way.

"I tells you, Miz Letty," Hester said impatiently, "dat man eat mo' biscuits than you kin count. Ever since he bought dat white flour, he ain't been a'lookin' at no cornbread. White biscuits, butter and honey jest glide down his th'oat. Gittin' dat money fum Claude done ruined 'im."

Letty laughed and walked over to Douglass's rocker crib, while waving to Eva and Granny in their rocking chairs. She bent and hugged Elsie in her chair. The girl was knitting while gently rocking the crib with her foot. Elsie put down her needles and reached along the crib, straightening the baby's clothes.

"Ain't he a right good beauty, Miz Letty?"

"Sure is," Letty replied. She reached down and stroked the baby's chubby arms. "Plenty fat, too." She glanced at Elsie's full bosom. "You're givin' him lots o' milk." Douglass waved his hands at her and grinned and cooed his pleasure.

When Letty straightened up, she said, absently, "Hannibal isn't spending all your money, is he?"

"No," Hester said, "but I done told him he jest got to keep it safe. He like a kid with a new puppy. Cain't seem to git 'nough o' going in to see Mistah Park at de sto' and fishin' out his purse like he's important."

"Dat right, Miz Letty," Elsie said. "Hannibal puffed up like some big ol' rooster."

Letty laughed. "Hannibal is important to Clay Park. He's a customer with money." She frowned. "Hannibal will get over it, Hester. But you got to hide the rest if you have to. Don't want to start takin' any out of Abel's bank. Save, always save some against the bad year."

"I keeps tellin' him, Miss Letty,.but he won't listen." Tears flowed down Hester's cheeks as she softly sobbed. Douglass squalled, adding to the tumult. A quick feel and Elsie changed him, restoring quiet in the house.

Eva and Mandy chimed in from their squeaking chairs, a puff of smoke floating lazily from Mandy's pipe. "Hannibal listen to Claude," they told Letty. "Ain't no one other'n Claude."

The women's gloom lightened when Hannibal walked in, wiping his forehead with a red bandanna. "Mighty hot," he said, "but the corn lookin' good now after dose rains. Make some coin this year on dat and de chesnuts. Lot's 'round."

At the mention of coin, Hester burst into tears. Granny Mandy creakily rose from her chair and put her arms around her granddaughter. Her croon started as Hannibal, transfixed, looked at each in turn. Mandy stroked the hair of the crying woman.

"It be awright, chile. Miz Letty and Claude fix tings. Jest smile fer ol' Granny."

Hester perked up and Hannibal burst out, "What did I do now?"

It was not the time to mince words, Letty thought. "You need to stop your wild spending, Hannibal. Hester's worried sick 'bout you and all the coin you're tradin' at old man Parks store. You need to save some and not spend it all. Times might get bad. Claude'll tell you the same thing."

"I got me plenty," Hannibal boasted. "Crop comin' in and de bank holdin' de rest. Ain't spendin' much."

"You're not figuring on having any children?" Letty asked.

Hannibal's mouth fell open and his speech deserted him.

"You know Hester's carrying your child, don't you?" Letty struck again when the stricken man stared at her, "Well, don't you?" At the silence, her gaze switched from Hannibal to Hester and back again. "You mean Hester hasn't told you?"

Hannibal's frozen figure relaxed and he took Hester into his arms. He held her close and stroked her back. "You 'spectin'?" he said in a low, tender voice. "Got our chile?"

She nodded against him. He pressed her tight, then held her out at arm's length, a broad smile exposing his gleaming white teeth. "I git me a boy?"

Hester pouted. "Land sakes, Hannibal. You knows I can't tell."

Granny Mandy blew a puff and stuck her cane into his side. "Jist one boy dis time, Hannibal. Seen it in de dream. You git yer boy and two mo'."

Hannibal struck his chest and yelled, "Yoo haw!" He struck his chest even harder and jumped high into the air, the floor resounding when he hit. "I got me a son comin'!" He took Hester by the arm and forced her away from the other women and into their bedroom, dragging her over her protests. Her cries gradually faded into giggles as the shadows lengthened.

"Recken he done tamed her," Eva said. "Give her what she want."

Mandy and Letty laughed, but Elsie began sniffling. She burst out crying when Letty bent over and hugged her.

"What's wrong?" Letty asked.

"It me, Miz Letty. I ain't done right." Her sobs interrupted her tale of the tobacco barn on the Saugy. "I'se sorry, Miz Letty. I done tol' you lies 'bout Claude and dis chile." She launched into an impassioned recital, impossible to interrupt. The words spilled out in a torrent.

"I'se wanted to come north and tol' Claude a lie. Claude went to sleep in the 'baccy barn last November." Her picque surfaced in bitter recrimination. "I'se hot fer him and he don' even want me he so tired. Jest 'bout died." A twisted, angry grin passed fleetingly. "I done got even wid 'im. Stripped off his pants and tol' him we done it when he woke up."

At Letty's severe frown, Elsie wailed. Letty patted her as the negress ran on. "Claude, he don' 'member nuthin' when day come. He even tired den. I try him agin but he jest shove me 'way." Her voice rose and shrilled out, "He ack jest like a little boy, hung 'is head, shamed he wid me. I jist let him tink he cover me, but he 'shamed. Den he hol' his head in 'is hands and cried, 'Letty, Letty....my God what will Letty think?'" Her spite flamed, "He don' know de truth an' I doan tell 'im."

Letty's heart quickened when she thought of Claude and his secret misery, even as he had confessed to her. He had not been unfaithful! Maybe at the start he was tempted, when he was fevered up by Elsie's voluptuous charms, easy to see. God said, 'Thou shalt not commit adultery,' and Claude had not, though he had lusted after the buxom negress. Oh, but he's afraid I'll never forgive him, she thought. She hugged herself, confident of her magnaminity in his absolution, and relishing a delicious revelation. Claude would be so contrite and she would forgive him and get herself another boy as a reward.

Elsie cried bitterly and Eva and Mandy interceded. "Miz Letty," Mandy said softly, "Cain't you forgive dat flighty gal? Elsie ain't got much sense 'bout men but she tell de truth."

"Dat right, Miz Letty," Eva chimed in. "Iffen she say Claude don', he don'. She allus a good gal. An' Douglass do have six toes."

Letty settled the matter. "I forgive you, Elsie," she said. She embraced the weeping girl. "Now you just smile and raise young Douglass up right. Claude and I will help you."

With joy in her heart, Letty swore the women to secrecy. "Don't you tell Claude! I want to crowd him a little for some fixin's we need. He don't feel too good about this right now and he's about to fall all over himself lovin' me. Gives me anything I want."

"Need little somethin'," Mandy said, "ter keep dose men heelin'. Dis he'p you wid Claude." She thoughtfully puffed away. "My man uster come a'runnin' when I mad, bowin' and treat'n me nice like. Took some doin' but woman jest got ter mek her man want ter pleasure her."

"Mandy say it right," Eva said. "Claude ain't so bad. My fust man chased ever' gal 'roun'. I tek my club ter him an' run 'im off. Claude right good man. Cain't see him doin' nuthin' ter hurt you."

"Well Claude will be Godfather to Douglass," Letty said, "and I his Godmother." She took a small coin from her purse and gave it to Elsie. "Keep this for him as our first gift."

The girl rubbed the coin and passed it to the other women before it disappeared into Elsie's possibles sack. Peace reigned when the women hugged their goodbyes on the porch and Letty mounted her horse. It was twilight, with a mixture of orange and bluish rays showing in the western sky over the blackening ridges.

"Ain't you skeered, Miz Letty," Eva said. "Gittin' on full dark 'for' you git home."

Letty ran her gaze over the squat house and porch and smiled. "I love this place," she said, "our Little Seven Mile house. Claude and I lived here three years after we were married. Claudius was born here and I know everyone around." She reined in the restive horse. "Nobody'll hurt me and Jack has been over the road hundreds of times."

Eva shook her club. "Ain't all dat neighborly now, Miz Letty. Some low-lifes here since de wah. You be keerful."

Letty raised her quirt in salute and turned Jack toward the lane. Shots down the valley startled Jack and she reined him back to the house. A door slammed inside and Hannibal ran out with a shotgun in his hands and a pistol jammed into his waistband. He was barefoot, with only his pants on.

"You awright?" he said huskily. At their nods, Hannibal listened a moment, very alert and still.

At a rustle in the night sounds he tensed and seized Jack's reins. Swinging Letty down bodily from her side saddle over her outraged protests, he shooed her and the Negro women into the house. "Be quiet and git!" he ordered. A few minutes later he came back. "Turned Jack loose in de pasture, Miz Letty. You stayin' de night."

Erect, indignant, Letty faced him and said angrily, "I didn't like that one bit, Hannibal. Haulin' me off Jack like I'm a sack of meal. Ain't no danger."

He shook his head. "Dey been night riders here 'bouts, Miz Letty. Bothered us some."

Her hands flew to her breast and her face paled. "You haven't been hurt?"

"No," he said,"but dey come back. Saw dey boot prints out

by de barn. I watch close."

His face twisted and lamplight reflected off the dent in his cheekbone. "I kill 'em, dey try to harm Hester, or de rest. Now you eat wid de women whilst I circle."

Hannibal went into the kitchen, returning with a peeled potato and a hunk of meat. He was chewing the potato to bits when he left the house with his shotgun and two pistols stuck into his waistband.

Late that night, Letty fell asleep on a pallet on the sitting room floor. Hannibal had not come back and her weariness had overcome her curiosity. She had refused to take Hester's or Elsie's bed and left the Grannies to their own little cabin. Two loud blasts and a wild scream up the hollow startled her into wakefulness at break of dawn. Dark gloom and a cool wind faced Letty when she rushed onto the porch, the night broken by a little paling over the eastern mountains. A night hawk called and a bird rustled by. Startled, she sought her pocket and pulled out her pistol. With an unseen menace in the unknown, her shivering fear drove her to flee back into the house. There she found Hester lighting the lamps.

"What's going on, Hester?" Letty demanded, as she pocketed her pistol. "Those were from a shotgun. Was it Hannibal?"

"Recken so, Miz Letty," Hester said. "Hannibal done chased men 'way twicet before. Dey come sneakin' 'roun'."

Elsie burst out crying in the bedroom, "I'se scairt, Miz Letty." Her baby wailed. The bed rattled, followed by cooing sounds and rustling of her covers. A sucking sound replaced the wail.

"You stay there with that child," Letty ordered. "No one's going to bother you."

But she trembled and looked about, surveying the flimsy walls and open windows and door. Open because of the heat, the house was completely vulnerable to any sneak who wanted to enter, only deterred by Hannibal's vigilance. Landsakes, she thought, he had to sleep and work. The idea of cruel outlaws harassing her friends stuck in her throat and her anger rose.

She boiled over at Hester.

"Why didn't Hannibal tell Claude he's having trouble," she snapped.

"Ain't wantin' to stir up things, Miz Letty."

Letty listened with increasing rage as Hester told her of their problems. Hannibal had made a big garden and they were eating well, but his work on crops had been curtailed due to a few shots from the woods. One of his shoats was killed and butchered in his woodlot. He felt the rounds near him were not meant to kill but to warn him off from making a go of the farm. He had not told Claude of the harassment because he did not want to bother his friend.

"Claude's going to be mighty mad," Letty said. "Not at Hannibal," she hastily added, when Hester shrank back.

The girl relaxed and her breath escaped in a whoosh. "Mighty glad o' dat. Hannibal ain't wantin' ter vex Claude."

At full daylight, Hannibal returned, his great bulk silently beside them before Letty knew it. She shied away in alarm, then fussed. "How'd you do that? Scarin' us so?"

He laughed. "Easy, Miz Letty, barefoot." His humor passed into a few sniffs at the meat Hester was frying. "Dat 'bout ready?"

At the table he told them of his encounter between huge bites. "Onliest one man dis time, Miz Letty. He circle 'roun' fum de creek road, real quiet. Come ter de edge o' de woodlot, den jest squatted dere, watchin'."

"You know who it was?"

"Too dark ter tell," Hannibal said. An edgy nervous tremor crept into his voice. "But he'd been waitin' fer you on de road, Miz Letty. Ain't up ter no good, way he sneakin' along."

"What'd you do?"

"Run in on him squallin' like de bobcat and fired twicet. Scairt 'im bad. He skedaddled right up de holler." Hannibal roared and rocked back on his protesting chair legs. "He run head on inter de big hickory at de turn. Knocked 'im flat. I screeched agin and he got!" He chortled and bent again to his food, rapidly shoveling in a train of meat and eggs.

Letty looked at the man with fondness. He was worried about me ... and Hester and Elsie and the Grannies too, she thought. Will I ever learn to trust him as my friend? When she thought of the intruder she grew icy cold and trembled. Just have to tell Claude. No reason they should suffer so. Claude would make it right.

"How are your studies coming?" she asked, diverting them from the night's anxiety.

"Just fine, Miz Letty," Hester answered, careful with her pronunciation. She poured Hannibal another cup of coffee and shoved a few more hot biscuits onto his plate. "I'se helping him with his writing lessons and he reads the Bible aloud every evenin'."

Hannibal reached over to the sideboard and picked up a small version of the large family volume. "Reverend Creadey gave me the little one ter practice wid." He haltingly read a small passage.

"Your diction is better," Letty said, "and your's too, Hester. Keep practicing saying the whole word. Take your time."

All the Negroes sounded better to Letty. They also were very clean and neatly dressed compared to her first sight. Lord's sakes, she thought, they don't smell. That lecturing I gave them on cleanliness helped! And the recipe for the soft soap I showed Hester. She made a whole barrel.

"I'se...," Hannibal hesitated and spoke very carefully. "I'm going to be a preacher, Miz Letty."

She beamed at him. "That was wonderfully said, Hannibal, just perfect."

A blush would have shown on a white cheek but he was just as pleased, his smile a reward. "All our folks have started a church, Miz Letty. You and Claude are invited."

"We'll be happy to come, Hannibal, and will help if we can."

The early morning flew by, with Hannibal reading an even longer passage to Letty's approving cluck and rapt attention.

When Elsie fed Douglass for the second time, the sun was high and Letty took her leave. Jack was hale and frisky after a night's rest. He pranced down the lane on his way to Greenbottom.

A week later a party of armed men turned into the Seven Mile farm just after sunup. "Halloo," Claude shouted in a blast loud enough to awake the house. "Where are you, Hannibal?" Dogs ran out barking, their din adding to roosters crowing and the sound of steel horseshoes on the stony lane.

All of the Negroes greeted them from the porch of the house, the horses milling about the yard until Claude ordered, "Dismount!" The six men swung down in unison, a relic of the war and their service. A few wore remnants of federal trooper uniforms and each carried the cavalry carbine in addition to a sawed off, double barreled shotgun swung from a saddle thong.

Hannibal clattered down the steps and embraced Claude, his grin adding to his, "Welcome, Claude, you folks et?"

"We're not here for that," Claude said. "But yes, we have been fed." With that he introduced Henry Hull, his cousin, and the other four troopers. Little nods identified each name, "Howdys" sufficing. The men touched their hats to the women, and then looked intently at Claude.

He braced Hannibal straight out. "Letty told me of your troubles, Hannibal. Now I want to hear the whole truth about your bothering".... Claude's intense rasp turned angry...."we fought a war for freedom and I just don't intend to stand for anyone crowding you." The others nodded and surrounded them.

Hannibal shifted uneasily and glanced about. "It ain't been much. Jest one shoat taken and stealin' around some at night. Ain't skeered. Run 'em off each time."

"That's not the question! No reason for anybody to bother you, night or day. You suspicion who it is?"

When Hannibal hesitated, Claude sharply ordered, "You tell me and the boys, right now!"

Henry's low, calm voice added, "Claude's right, Hannibal. We ain't toleratin' any night riders around here. We need to know."

Claude dragged the information out of Hannibal slowly, the Negro's reluctance increasing the band's exasperation. But finally they had two names, one of those Hank Peavey. When they were done, the troopers all went up to the hollow and inspected the tracks, a few plainly showing in a muddy place. One heel was worn on the inside rather than the outside.

"I know that one, Claude," a trooper said. "It's that Seely boy, like Hannibal suspicioned, the one with the broke ankle when he was a kid."

Claude nodded. "Time to go then. We'll start at the head of the creek and work down. Warn everybody off."

In a long day of riding, the band progressed from the Logans at the divide down to the Ohio River bottoms, moving northeast along the foothills. The Seelys faced him truculently when he warned off their son, identified by his limp and heel print. Claude's men sat in their saddles in a wide semicircle around the group, their weapons covering everyone.

"Now Terry," Claude said to the father, "we been neighbors more years than I can count, but I won't tolerate Absalom sneakin' around Hannibal's place, fixin' to cause mischief."

"I ain't never been there," the boy protested. He shook his fist at Claude. "You're lyin'."

Henry interceded before Claude could take offense. "We seen the tracks, Terry, all of us. Ab was layin' out behind Hannibal's barn."

At the confirmation, Ab's mother covered her face with her apron and ran into their house. Her sobs resounded into the yard. Seely tensed as his florid Irish face reddened. Abruptly, he motioned to Ab to get behind his stiffened frame. Seely ignored Henry but his forceful reply, eyeball to eyeball, settled the issue with Claude.

"Ain't gonna be no more trouble from here, Claude. Ab been running with that"... he strangled and spit out phlegm contemptuously, then wiped his mouth on his sleeve..."that Peavey, but he ain't any more."

He whirled, grabbed Absalom by the shirt and dragged him

around to face the riders. "Now you apologize to Captain Shaw and these men fer all the trouble you caused. And you promise it's ended."

Ab squirmed but his father's tightening grip produced a weak, "I'm sorry." Another squeeze and a hard blow to the head brought, "I promise."

Seely manhandled the boy to his front and looked him full in the face. Ab's gaze fell before his father's cold eyes and clenched jaw. But Seely grabbed his hair, twisted his head up and forced him to stare into his eyes. "You done promised, boy," he spit out. "It's our honor now and a Seely's word gotta be good. You break your word and your mother's heart and I'll hunt you down myself." He flung the boy away from him. "Now you git on into the house and comfort your mama."

They parted silently, the troopers trailing away and Terry heading for the house after Ab. All the way to Greenbottom, the patrol visited neighbors and passed the word to leave the Negroes alone, or make Claude an enemy. At the Greenbottom lane, they split up.

"Thanks, boys," Claude said. "I'll warn Hank Peavey myself."

"You need any help, Captain," a trooper replied, "you jest send Isaiah."

A wave answered. Letty had not told him of Hank's curses or threats but it had come to him from his friend Cal Jones. Two days later, Claude strapped on his pistol and made the last stop. He visited the Peaveys, extracted another apology, and made Hank grovel, on threat of death.

10

The sycamore tops were crisping when the early fall came on, with the walnut trees dropping leaves and green-cased nuts, and the black locusts flying brown whisps that whistled under sharp winds. It was time for planning the timbering and the spring rafting to the sawmills downstream. Corn still covered the fields, drying into the hard yellow ears that would be harvested after a cold spell and freeze. Peace invested the land but Greenbottom bustled with its master back.

Claude looked up from the desk in his side office when Searle's steps sounded at the door. The little room opened into Greenbottom's basement through the brick foundation, a convenient addition where Shaw could do his trading deals and get to the house without going outside. Their greetings finished, Claude got down to business.

"Those timber contracts let, Charles? Winter be here 'fore you know it, " Claude went on, while Searle felt in his pockets. "Timber's best cut early. Floats better in the spring."

Charles Searle took his pipe from his mouth and blew out a blue gray circle. "All set, Captain. Those three Jones brothers near Fraziers agreed to cut poplar. Two hundred logs for us. And old Grist beyond the Peaveys, he's fixing to fetch another hundred. Plus about fifty chestnut. Make up a right nice raft."

"River'll boom, come March," Claude said. "Take 'em all the way to New Orleans if needed .... unless those Cincinnati mills want the lot. Made us a good deal before."

Searle puffed a few times before replying. Claude waited, used to the ex-rebel's careful manner of thought before talk, even though a very young man. He had debated hiring such a youngster but had liked Searle's steady, unflinching eyes.

"Didn't realize Grist had so many kin. He's roundin' up about twenty men and boys to help."

"All those Grist men have big families," Claude replied. "Now what were the terms?"

"Wouldn't sell outright this year," Searle replied. He held out the papers from his search. "Didn't sign. Want to work on shares. You get fifty percent for rafting and factoring. That suit you?"

Claude could have whooped for joy when he took the unsigned contracts. He wouldn't have to put up any money for the timber! Just finance the raft and sell it down river, then split the proceeds. A wide grin and his "Agreed" sealed the bargain.

"I'll circle back tomorrow, Captain, and tell 'em. Ask for the logs at your landin' by March first. That satisfy you?"

Claude nodded.

A few puffs and Searle dropped his bombshell. "Wiley Minns snoopin' around. Offerin' to outbid anything you offer ... and to pay gold."

Claude swore through clenched teeth. His right fist pounded the desk as he spoke. It jumped up and down and rattled from the forceful blows. "You tell Jones and Grist that we been tradin' together for fifteen years. I always treated them fairly and will now. They got my word, which is more than they'll get with Minns."

Searle laughed. "Ain't seen you so het up before, Captain. It becomes you." He puffed again. "I'll tell 'em," he went on. "They'll stay with you. Last thing Grist said was that you was 'fair' as he put it. Seems to like you powerful good."

"His son and I soldiered together. Saved his life one time." Claude's droll needle took aim at the Confederate. "Big reb fixin' to shoot him until I killed the man."

Charles shrugged, unmoved by the Union tale of killing his compatriot. "That's good enough," he said. "Men's as been in battle got a bond can't be broke."

When Searle's footsteps died away, Claude sat at his desk and fumed, his thoughts going back to his enemy. Would he never be rid of those damned Minnses? And that sneaky Wiley. Where is he getting all that gold? He went into the house, troubled, seeking the calming solace of Letty.

* * *

Charles Searle pulled off his boots and wiggled his toes before the banked fire in his little cabin. Sinking into a leather covered hickory chair, he puffed away at his pipe, his eyes thoughtful. Reckon Shaw's not the traitor Minns made him out to be, he thought. We hit it off just fine and those timber cutters think the world of him. A feeling of unease, of shame ran over him. Why spy on Claude for Minns?

"You git on down the river, Charles," Wiley had told him in Minns' tavern in Point Pleasant. "Shaw's lookin' for hands to do raftin' and handle stock. You're good at that from what you say." His face hardened and his eyes flashed in the candle light. "Lemme know what he's doin'."

He had taken the gold pieces from Minns' hand but now he fished out the two coins remaining and let them reflect in the firelight. Was he a Judas? Or a Judas goat? One used by Minns to lead the unsuspecting Claude to a slaughter? Fitful dreams chased him in his dozing before the fire. Sighing, he finally set aside his pipe and sought his bed. But his mother's voice reproached him in his tossing sleep.

When Searle rose the next morning, his body mocked him. "God, I'm tired," he said, a strong man made weak by his doubts.

* * *

Claude's angry bellow scorched the staggering man picking at the wagon tongue. "Dammit, Ian, you're drunk again!"

"Ain't not," Ian protested. He grabbed the wagon bed and pulled himself up. "Jest had a little."

Claude held the swaying man erect, the raw whiskey fumes strong about him. He searched the back of McLellan's overalls, easily discovering the small bottle. It held but a swallow more. Claude tossed it against a rock. Rank fumes boiled up after the crashing of glass.

"Now why'd you do that?" Ian slurred out plaintively. "Ain't like I drunk a hull quart. It was jest a little."

"That's the trouble," Claude said. "You're a drunk, Ian, can't stand any."

He walked McLellan away from the wagon and laid him down on the thick pasture grass. The cool October breeze of Indian Summer blew leaves across the prone man from the fence row trees. A snore sounded from the bedded man, comfortable in his grass nest. Claude looked down on his old friend, a pitying twist to his face.

"What can I do with you, Ian?" he whispered. "Poor Mary Jane ... and Joe and his brothers. How they must suffer." He dropped on his knees beside the prone man and prayed to the God that had saved him in battle. "Oh Lord, Ian is a good man, but Satan's got him, just as the rebs had me. Bring him safely home Lord, as you did me. And relieve him of his terrible thirst."

His thoughts crystallized with the revelation to cut Ian off from the store and to counter his brother's avarice for selling anything to anyone with money. Dammit, Garrett would sell no more whiskey to Ian! Of that he was sure. Hard to get it through his thick head but he'd pounded sense into his brother when they were boys and he'd do it again if needed. No more whiskey for Ian, no matter how much money he had. And he'd ask all the neighbors to cut him off. He could make it work! But he'd need to keep Ian too busy to get away to drink. I'll talk to Mary Jane, he resolved. We can do it together. And Preacher Creadey. He'll drag Ian to his mother's grave. Make him swear off the bottle kneeling on the mound. A shadow crossed Claude's face as he recalled Joe's last whispers, a message that turned him hot with rage and cold as ice in his resolve.

"That last gold piece of Pa's came from Preacher Minns."

"What for?" Claude had asked.

"Tried to git him to sell him that piece o' land above your landin' at Crown City. Pa told him to go to hell. Minns jest laughed and tossed the coin down. Said there'd be more if he changed his mind."

"So Ian took it?"

"Pa looked a long time," Joe said. His head dropped and he choked a little before the tears started. "Picked it up and went straight for your store." He cried openly, a wild sobbing. "Can't you get your brother to tell him no?"

Claude had taken the boy in his arms and hugged him. "We'll do it, Joe. Ian is too good a man for whiskey to beat him." He had consoled the boy and later called on Mary Jane. God would help them, for his sleeping friend deserved better than a whiskey fog, and slavery to that damned Minns' coins. Comforted, he covered McLellan with a horse blanket and left him in the pasture, resolved to deal unforgivingly with his brother and Wiley Minns.

Three days later, Claude was working in his office when Ian knocked on the door jamb. Erect, with a clean face and in faded but pressed overalls, he was the ruddy picture of health, strong and ready in the early morning light.

"Claude?" Ian said hesitantly.

"You sober?"

Ian's temper flared. "Can't you see that, Claude? Man takes a few swallows and you insult him."

"Good reason, with you lying in the pasture grass, snoring, stinking of whiskey. Where's your pride, Ian? You used to be an upright man." His squint took in the suddenly lowered head and the trembling hand that went over McLellan's eyes, brushing away moisture.

"It's jest hard, Claude," Ian mumbled. He reached in his

back pocket for a bandana, wiped his face and then blew his nose. A paroxym of crying convulsed him.

"Reverend Creadey come to see us yestiday. Prayed with me and Mary Jane then took me across the river to mama's grave." He straightened up and faced Claude, his eyes reddened and unable to continue.

"I hope he beat some sense into your head," Claude said. "Prayin' don't seem to help."

Unheeding, McLellan sobbed and continued, in his own world of memories. "Mound 'bout grassed over, thick. Needs cuttin', it's growed so much. That manure, I guess. Git the scythe up there Saturday."

"So what did the Reverend do?" Claude asked.

The question finally penetrated Ian's ramblings. "Made me kneel on my own mama's grave and pray to the good Lord." He cried openly, the tears running down his face. "Got mama's stain on my knees. Never come out."

The abject sobbing gave way to shudders and he fell to his knees. Fascinated, Claude could not tear himself away from the man, even in his final degradation.

"Old Creadey knelt right there with me and put his arm around my shoulder while he prayed for my soul. We both pressed so hard on mama I couldn't stand it. I throwed him off."

"You didn't!" Claude's roar brought Letty to the basement opening, her hands wet. Claude waved her away.

Her face whitened at the sight of the weeping McLellan, then softened. With a little compassionate clucking, she rushed in and cradled Ian's head against her warm body, rocking back and forth as she crooned to him and stroked his hair. "Going to be all right, Ian, the Lord will help. Just you cry it all out and you'll be all right."

When Claude reached to take the man, she shook her head. "Git, Claude," she whispered. "Ian and I'll take this to the Lord right here. Go get yourself some coffee."

A shaken but erect Ian faced Claude when he reentered the office an hour later. His face clean but eyes reddened, Letty stood at McLellan's side with her arm around his waist. The two braced for the onslaught but Letty's jutting chin warned Claude off. He went right to the work to be done.

"I offer you wages, Ian, to boss that timber cutting gang up on the ridge. Same as before the war. You do the work, no whiskey." His harsh tone flayed the man. "You swore on your mother's grave, Ian, and I'm holdin' you to it."

Letty's gentle voice broke the tension. "Ian gave his word to me and to the Lord, didn't you, Ian?"

A resolute man faced them both, the shudders gone and back straight. Looking Claude straight in the eyes, Ian held out his hand and accepted the challenge. "I'll cut your timber, Claude, and you got my word. I'm off whiskey for life."

Their strong grips sealed the bargain.

"You bring Mary Jane and your boys to visit," Letty said. "We haven't talked tatting for a long time." She giggled. "And I think that Joe is a little sweet on Kittie Mae. They were holding hands last time."

"I thank you, Miss Letty," Ian replied. "I'll tell Mary Jane and she'll send word. You folks are the best friends I got and I'll do you both proud."

* * *

"Lookee here, Josh," Minns said exultantly. He held out the note and handed it off. "Charles is in thick with Shaw."

Joshua, leaning against the fireplace mantel, spit a brown stream into the tavern fire. A slow scan of the paper and he said, "Wouldn't have thunk that Shaw would take him right off."

"Well, you know Charles, strong, with that trusting, open face, always reading his Bible nights. He'd set right with Shaw."

His nephew shook his head, his face clouded. "It don't figure. Why was Shaw so eager to take him on? Think maybe he suspects?"

"He can't," Minns said. He went on. "Remember I tol' Charles to go direct from Charleston when he got his parole?

That paper probably set him in with Shaw."

Joshua swore mightly. "Damn it , Unk, it war too easy. Smells too high." He paced back and forth, his brow furrowed. Another stream went into the fire. "Next time that Charles comes in I'll have a little set-to with him. I'll git the truth."

"Don't you scare him off, boy. Charles was mighty uneasy on the trail. We want him on our side, not Claude's."

Joshua laughed. "Ain't fixin' to run 'im off, Unk. But if he's crossin' us, I'll put 'im in the river."

His uncle raised his fist and Joshua shied away. "Don't do that boy! Charles will help us." Minns took a pull from a bottle on the floor beside his chair. "You drift on down to old man Peavey's. Talk to him about Shaw's timber. Must be some way we kin git at it."

"I'll do thet while you're over to Eureka. You still wantin' that land above Shaw's Landing, I take it, from what you said." A smile crossed Joshua's face. "Gives me plenty of time. Git at that little nigger gal at Shaw's. Hank'll fetch 'er for me."

Wiley sighed. "You ain't gettin' in Heaven that way."

"No, Unk, I recken I ain't." Josh laughed. "It sure is some fun goin' when Josie's around."

* * *

Jobe danced around the pile of scraped and dried skins, then bent to pull out several edges. "How many we got, Pa?"

Ebert spit and wiped his lips with his hand. His wiry beard carried brown streaks from the corners of his mouth. "Twelve, Jobe," he said. "Makes over fifty with those others we sold. Right smart money at four bits a hide."

"You recken we kin go up to see Captain Shaw this year?"

"Anxious, are ye, now that it's gittin' cooler?"

"Jest wondering 'bout that old Ohio River. Hannibal said it's most a mile acrost. You recken anythin' is that big?"

"You sure it ain't them Shaw gals?" Ebert jollied the boy. "Hannibal said thet one, Kittie, right purty. An' she ain't old."

Jobe blushed and dropped his eyes. “Want to pay our owin’s, Pa. I ain’t of a mind to be beholden to no man, not even Captain Shaw.”

Ebert patted his son affectionately. “Thet’s a good lesson to learn, Jobe. Don’t owe nobody. Keep your land safe that way.”

“How much we got, Pa? Enough for what he lent us?”

“Not yet. Time we got the new plow and those purties an’ cloth fer your Ma, only left nineteen dollars. We’ll git more of them hogs from the swamp soon’s it gits colder. Some fer sellin’ instid o’ jest eatin’.”

“Long as they’s not ear notched,” Jobe reminded him. The boy picked up several hides. Taking them into the barn, he climbed the ladder and began a stack in the loft, his cheery whistle carrying into the yard. Jobe’s three trips moved the skins while his father forked some hay into the mule’s stall.

“Jobe?”

The boy turned obediently. “Yes, Pa?”

“You recken you kin git up a load of turnips fer sale termorrow? An’ some of them termaters and carrots?”

“Be easy, Pa. Turnips are right fer harvest, rest little past prime. But I kin find plenty.” He picked up a digging fork and set it beside the barn door. “I’ll git ’em together an’ take ’em in early. Sell the whole lot a’fore noon.” Jobe perked up. “We orta git same as last time, Pa, ’bout four dollars for all those turnips.” He laughed. “The others won’t bring much but Missus Raney sure will like pawin’ over ’em.”

“We keep on savin’ in the can, boy. Git the rest o’ Claude’s money when the sweet taters dug and the corn shucked. We eat good this winter." Ebert set his pitchfork aside and sniffed. “Now let’s git to the house. Ma’s got some tasty meat cookin’.”

An hour later, fed to fullness, Ebert slouched before the fire and broached the trip north. “Fixin’ to go see Captain Shaw late November, Matty. That suit you fer travelin’?”

A pleased grin covered his wife’s face. “You’re takin’ me and the girls?”

“Sure am. Right proud of your gittin’ this cabin up, Matty.”

He went to her and gave her a hug and kiss.

She blushed and wiped her hands on her apron when he persisted. “Go ’long now,” she said, her face wrinkled, somber. “You got Shaw’s money?”

“Will have by then, after we harvest. Plenty fer travelin’ too. Git to stay in some o’ them inns.”

“But who will look after the farm?”

“Jack Vance. I done him that turn last month killin’ them wild dogs after his sow. He never fergits a favor, all the years I’ve knowed him.” He sprang his surprise. “Jack told me he’d do it right off, when I asked.”

Her delighted laugh rang out. “I’ll be ready. And I’ll do you proud with those fine folks. That new material will make up nice fer the girls an’ me.” She looked her husband up and down. “I’m askin’ you to get some new clothes too. Don’t want them folks thinkin’ we’re nothin’.”

Jess nodded thoughtfully.“Yer right, Matty. Me and Jobe’ll match you. Can’t be lookin' like no white-trash at Greenbottom.”

* * *

Jubal Peavey rousted his grandson as soon as the door slammed. Awaking from his doze in the chair before the fire, he called, “Whar you been, Hank?”

“None o’ your damn business, Gramps,” came the surly reply. Hank poked at the glowing embers and threw on some oak billets, complaining. “I’d think you’d at least keep the fire up.”

Jubal glanced at the mantel clock which struck quarter after two at that moment. “Ain’t keepin’ awake fer you, boy. You git wet?”

“Rain ain’t come on yet, Gramps.” Hank yawned and stretched. “God, I’m tired.”

“Wouldn’t be, iffen you’d quit this ridin’ with Minns.”

Hank shook his head and lay down before the revived blaze. “Me an’ Wiley and Joshua got some things goin’. Can’t stop now.”

Jubal bent over and seized the boy's shoulder. "I'm fear'd fer you, Hank. Heard they was a robbery down below Burlington, an' two nigras kilt. Those damned abolitionists 'll hang you if ye're caught."

"I don't know nuthin' 'bout those," Hank replied. He shifted away from Jubal's grasping hand. "Now lemme alone. Soak up some o' this heat fer the sore spots."

Old Peavey spoke softly, almost in a trembling whisper. "Where you ridin', boy? You an' Joshua and them rowdies from the tavern?"

Hank just shook his head. His snores interrupted Peavey's question, "Why, boy?"

Jubal sighed and leaned back in his chair with his cane over his knees. His hard face sagged into wrinkled leather and his shoulders slumped as he prayed to the God of his mother. "Oh, Lord. I done failed and this boy's goin' wild. Thet damned war an' Minns' gold done ruined him. Help him, Lord to see the way. And me, Lord, to git him straight." His visage hardened and he rose from the chair. After a last pitying glance at the boy, he covered Hank with his shawl and sought his bed.

"That no good Wiley gonna git us all kilt," he grumbled as he hobbled away. "Kill that bastard m'self iffen he don't let Hank alone."

11

Wiley Minns settled into the caned chair at the rough plank table, resting his fat bulk with a sigh. He stretched his feet out to the fireplace, wiggling his toes, freed of the muddy boots discarded at his side.

"Mighty good, Josh, to git back here." Minns pulled a fat cigar from his inner coat pocket and bit off the end. He ran it under his nose, sniffing, then rolled it between his palms and wet it with his mouth. "Those Yanks over the river," he went on, "want more'n I plan to pay."

Joshua reached a splinter into the crackling fire and transferred a light to his uncle. A few puffs started the cigar, its glowing end and redolent smell bringing a satisfied, "Ah," from Minns. He sat and smoked a bit, until the cigar had a half inch of ash, before gesturing to his nephew.

"Ain't likely they'll sell," Josh said. "Heard the old man's some kind of kin to Shaw. Claude'll find out real quick you're askin' and buy it hisself if need be."

Charles Searle took in the conversation with unease. He had recently come back up the river road to Point Pleasant from Greenbottom to look for a mount, his conversation with Claude uppermost in his mind. "Got to have a sturdy horse, Claude, all those trails 'round those timber tracts. Probably a mule'd be better. Eat less too."

What had Claude said? Nothing about him workin' and

not lettin' him off. Just, "See Letty's cousin, Jedediah Haines at the head of the Guyan River. He's got the best mules." Then Claude had written and handed him a note. "Give him this and tell him you're workin' for me. He'll sell reasonable."

Yet here he was meeting with Wiley instead, and him talkin' of doing Claude dirt, buyin' land in Ohio that would shadow Claude's landing at Crown City. His gorge rose as he flayed himself. Was this what mama raised me for? To be a cheat? Eating Claude's salt and stabbing him? A worm of an idea slithered into his consciousness and exploded into a light. He would help Claude! Go along with that snake Wiley but protect Claude. It was only right. Satisfied, he brought his mug of hard cider to the table and sat across from the Minnses.

"You plannin' any more land deals, Wiley?" he asked.

"Not afore I get all the pieces on that point above Crown City landing," Minns said. "Been lookin' at some bottom by old Jubal Peavey's place. Made an offer for it, and to Jubal too for his homeplace." He puffed a moment and cleared his throat. "Derned old reprobates are catankercus, won't sell." He laughed scornfully. "Jubal said his family been there since the Revolution and Hank would own it some day."

"They got a graveyard up the hollow, Wiley." Searle counted on his fingers, silent. "Maybe ten graves, some with old stones. Old Jubal is right that they been there a long time."

"Don't matter," Minns replied. His bile spilled over. "We own that land we can get to that nigger Hannibal over the ridges and drive cattle up the holler to that growed up woods road."

The quiet Josh spat into the fire. "You think Shaw's neighbors won't tell, Unk? They's mighty close."

"All but that Seely," Wiley replied. "Since Claude run his kid off of Hannibal's place, he's been mighty sore. Told me he's gettin' even when he can chance it. Don't like no damned Yankee pushin' on him."

"He won't do nothin'," Josh said scornfully. "Jest talk!"

Searle's heart leaped. What an opportunity to warn Claude! It would help him get close to the family, passing on that rumor, picked up from idle talk. Charles diverted their interests to their past plan for him to run the Bull's Head tavern and adjacent factoring at the river landing. "What about the Bull's Head, Wiley? Since Claude took me on, I can't be here at Point Pleasant any more. Got to keep busy at that timbering."

Puffs answered, Wiley at last stirring. "Josh'll have to do that. We'll hire Melton for the bar." An afterthought struck him. "He okay with you, Josh? Melly don' seem to be no drinker."

His nephew nodded. "We been gettin' on and he's temperance." He laughed. "Dead set agin drinkin' it hisself but he likes that bar money." He reached for a cigar Wiley offered. "I kin get Fran Gates to run your warehouse and help with the factoring. Both o' those boys right thinkin' men, southern."

"In the war?" Wiley asked.

"Melly shot once an' drags that foot, but it don't keep him from ridin'. Fran one of Bryan's Artillery but never touched, not even in all that Virginia fighting." He sighed and felt his thigh, shifting in his seat. "Some men just ain't meant to be kilt in battle."

"Well, that's it," Wiley said. "Warehouse be done by January so we'll need Melly right away for the bar and to get the hands ready. You decide what to pay him and Fran."

Searle got up from the table. "I'm turning in. Got to get that mule tomorrow and be back to Greenbottom in two days. Claude's expecting me."

"You ain't told me nothing," Wiley said. "What's that derned Shaw doin'."

Charles eased back down onto a bench. "Contracting for timber and planning on a little trading of the crops. Not much harvested this year. Mostly grown up, him gone to the war." He added, "Hannibal just scrapin' by but he's working hard."

Josh flared up and shook his balled fist. "I'm killin' that damned nigger one o' these nights, Unk. Goes agin my grain, him ownin' land."

Wiley slammed his palm flat down on the table, rattling all the mugs. "You leave that nigger alone, boy! We ain't touchin' none o' them 'til we bust Shaw. That was the plan."

A thundercloud faced him, Josh tensed and ready to argue. Wiley's face swelled, grew apopleptic. His protruding eyes were cold and his command brittle as his right hand slid into a coat pocket. "You leave him be, boy!"

His nephew shrank back, recoiling from his Wiley's threat. "Okay, Unk," he said bitterly, "but you just 'member now that I wanted to finish him. That nigger ain't goin' be nothin' but trouble fer us."

Searle puffed on his pipe throughout the dustup. He kept his peace, inscrutable, until Minns interrupted his smoke.

"You go on back to Shaw," Minns told him. "Send me a note any time, here to the Bull's Head."

"I'll do that," Charles said. "You goin' down the river again?"

"Yep." Wiley drew a little map with some cider spilled on the planked table. "They's a piece just above the Big Sandy Shaw was lookin' to buy before the war. May still want it. I got a promise for gold." He laughed. "Shaw'll be mighty put out he finds I own the landin' he wanted. Shut down his Big Sandy River bargin' fer the next year."

Josh smiled. "Won't take long for you to break 'im, Unk. Once he's on the run, I'll see all of them over my sights."

* * *

Jubal Peavey started up out of his doze in the rocking chair on his porch. He drew his shawl close around his boney shoulders and rose to meet Wiley Minns at the steps. Wiley's light buggy shrieked at the fat man's exit, its joints protesting the violent shaking. Joshua tied off the reins on the brake handle and followed his uncle.

"Howdy, boys," Peavey said, his right hand waving.

"Howdy," Minns answered. "You got room for us tonight? We got to talk."

Peavey nodded. He sidled back to his chair and sat down

with a relieved sigh as the two Minns settled in alongside him.

Wiley coughed and cleared his throat. "How's your whiskey?" he asked. "Man needs a swaller after that long ride from Point Pleasant."

"Hank ain't brought none from the still lately," Peavey replied, "but they's a little jug settin' on the mantel."

Without a word, Joshua rose and swiftly recovered the earthenware jug. It passed around twice before Minns belched and wiped his mouth with his sleeve.

"Powerful good," he said.

"We use stillin's like my grandpa taught me," Peavey said. "Put apples in with the corn." He took a swig and smacked his lips. "Mighty tasty."

Minns turned Peavey's glow into gall. "Didn't you tell me Shaw stole your slaves back last year?"

A mortal blow would not have staggered Peavey more. "That son of a bitch sure did," he said. Jubal swung his stick at the porch railing, splintering it in two pieces. While he pounded with the remnant, he cursed Shaw, damning him to hell and perdition.

Pushing, Wiley laconically observed, "I didn't see many niggers there when we come through first time. Couldn't have had yours."

"It war that damned Shaw boy," Jubal sputtered. "Claudius ain't no better'n his daddy and learnt that abolition from Preacher Creadey."

"You don't like Creadey?" Joshua asked.

"He's always preachin' the good book but when it comes to makin' the niggers equal I ain't holdin' with him."

Minns chided him. "Lincoln and the war made the nigras equal, Jubal. Ain't you learned that yet?"

Choler colored Peavey's face, his sputtering unintelligible to the Minns. He swung the jug up to his lips and took a swig. "Takes all the whiskey I can drink," he said thickly, "afore I kin talk 'bout that."

Joshua whittled some shavings from the stick he had picked up from beside the chair. His added to a growing pile that testified to other whittlers who had jawed with Peavey. “Ain’t you plannin’ on gittin’ coin for those niggers?” He tweaked the old man scornfully. “Seems like the Peaveys ain’t much to put up with Shaw takin’ your property.”

Old Jubal rose from his chair and towered over the younger Minns. He pushed back his frayed and rusty black coat, revealing a hostered handgun on his belt. “Men been kilt fer less than what you jest said, boy. You want to take that back?”

Wiley scurried between them and grabbed Peavey’s right arm. “He ain’t intendin’ no harm, Jubal. We take it back.” He kicked Joshua. “Do it boy!” he ordered.

“Didn’t mean it,” Joshua said as he rose and backed away. “Just seein’ how much you valued those niggers.”

Old Peavey halfway drew his piece. “Ain’t the niggers, boy, I’m fussed with jest now. Don’t take kindly to no insults.”

Wiley gripped Peavey’s arm tightly and forced the weapon back into its holster. “Let it go, Jubal. Boy ain’t got no sense to say that. Lost it in the war, probably.” He swung Peavey back down into his chair. “He took it back, so let’s talk how we git back at Shaw.”

“I can help you,” Joshua said, regaining his seat. “Be glad to git that boy and fetch ’im to you. Or beat ’im good.”

“I want coin for them niggers,” Peavey said. “Ketchin’ Claudius do nothin’ but rile Claude. He ain’t to be trifled with; kill me and Hank too.”

“But that would get the law on him,” Wiley said. “He’d go to jail or git hung.”

Peavey snorted derisively. “With that Bandie lookin’ on? They’s kin. Bandie won’t sheriff Claude.”

Minns jumped at that revelation, of Claude and Sheriff Bandie being kin. He pressed the old man on the slave stealing. “What happened, Jubal?”

Jubal sputtered and spit. “Claudius took ’em one night those bucks wasn’t chained up, rowed across the river and drifted down to Burlington. I seen ’em at the stone courthouse there but that fool Sheriff Love just laughed at me. Said they was free men." He mumbled and took another large gulp of the whiskey, his voice unsteady and bitter when he ran on. "Told those abolitionists in Burlington and they run me out of town. It's all that Claudius's fault," he whined. Peavey's head nodded and sank to his chest. "Shore would like to see that boy have an accident," he drunkenly mumbled. Loud snores followed.

Minns shook his head. "Nothin' more out o' him tonight, boy. Let's git some sleep." He took a shawl from another chair and threw it over Peavey. "He might as well keep warm. Tomorrow we'll see if we can scheme somethin' with him."

The morning brought mist and a hint of rain. Old Peavey groaned as he sought his chair at the breakfast table. He took a swig of Joshua's black coffee, coughing as it went down. "My God!" he said. "Don' recken I better drink no more o' that damned whiskey. Head 'bout killin' me."

The two Minns bent to their plates, forking in eggs and potatoes along with greasy bacon. "Better have some," Joshua said, pointing with his fork. "Mighty good."

Peavey grimaced and took another gulp of coffee. "I pass, boy. Gotta git rid of these shakes fust." He rose and took a jug from the sideboard. His temper improved after a short swig and a swallow of coffee. But he got down only one bite of egg.

Wiley finished his plate and rocked back in his chair. He fished a cigar out of his pocket and lighted up, puffing contentedly before he spoke. "Ain't finished with Claude, Jubal. We got to conjure more afore me and Josh head for the Big Sandy."

"Just so's you work on that Claudius," Jubal growled. "He needs a good whuppin'."

"Josh'll do that when we get back," Minns said. "We got more important things just now." He turned to his offer for Peavey's land. "You ain't ready to sell?"

Peavey glared at him. "Go to hell, Wiley. This place ain't fer sale."

Wiley's unctuous tone lapped over Jubal, soothing him. "Just lookin' for ways to get at Shaw, Jubal. Need land or his notes. He owe on any hereby?"

Peavey's back strightened and his eyes gleamed. "He bought that Taylor piece next to him," he said, then dabbled at his plate. "Recken it was sixty one, when Hank went in the war."

"Taylor take a note?" Wiley asked.

Peavey ignored him. "Heard that Shaw paid too much. Lookin' to make big crops with the gov'mint needin' corn and taters." He bent toward them, his voice dropping. "'fore Taylor left, he bought some o' my whiskey to take with him. Headin' fer Ioway, he said. Told me Shaw laid off his note with Abel House at the bank."

Joshua interrupted. "That the other cousin o' his'n?"

"Yep. Old Claude got lots o' kin." Peavey's smouldering anger came out as he told them of the incident with the cows and Letty. "Abel ain't the smartest in the world. Had two loans go bad on him last year, I heard. Most went broke hisself."

"You think maybe House can be persuaded to sell Claude's notes?" Wiley asked. "I can offer gold."

Peavey laughed. "Gold'll buy most anythin' 'round here. People ain't got much hard money. Like it better than that paper," he said scornfully. "Can't figure why the gov'mint printin' money. Gold's better."

"Easier to carry around," Minns said. "And they can make as much as they want."

"Well, you git Claude's notes," Peavey said, "then ask fer gold and you'll have him. He don't have no gold for what he owes."

Another plateful of eggs and meat satisfied Joshua. At midmorning, the Minns harnessed up their team and headed along the river road toward the Big Sandy and Kentucky.

* * *

The rider stopped by in the late afternoon, calling out to Letty in the yard as he turned into the circle in front of Greenbottom manse. "Got some mail for you folks, Miz Letty."

Letty smiled at their youthful visitor after he pulled up.

Claudius walked to one side, appraising the horse. The rider's red hair stuck up wildly from under a woolen cap and freckles patterned his ruddy face. "You got time to step down, Anse?" she said. "Got some hot coffee in the kitchen. Claudius'll take care of your horse."

"No ma'am," Anse replied, shifting his lanky body around in the saddle. "Been to Point Pleasant two days and time I got on home." He reached in his right saddle bag and brought out a packet. "Was to the post office and Jake asked me to fetch this if I was comin' by. Happy to do it."

"Well, we surely appreciate the kindness,' Letty replied, as she took the packet. "Next hog killin' we'll have somethin' for your Ma."

"Thank you, Miz Letty. Ma can use it. Pretty hard since Pa kilt in the war an' me goin' on the river with Captain Jones." He eyed the sun. "Leavin' again termorrer so I better git on and do my chores."

The boy wheeled in the lane and waved from the river road, spurring his horse into a trot. Letty looked at the mail idly as she went toward the house. A thick brown envelope with a South Carolina return address picqued her curiosity.

Claudius danced around. "Who's it from, Ma?" he said.

"The Pickens, son. I'll just take this to your father." Diverting her steps, she passed around the south side of the house to Claude's office in the western wing. Claude leaned back in his chair when she and the boy entered.

"So who was here?" he said. "I heard a horse."

"Anse brought this from Jake," Letty said, handing him the packet. "Looks like a letter from Rance Pickens."

Claude's face creased into a pleased grin. "Great!" he said. He tore the envelope open and scanned the handwritten pages. "Coming in November, he says, if convenient." He strode around and squeezed his wife. "Ask him over Thanksgiving, Letty?"

She leaned against him, receiving a hug and a kiss to the top of her hair. "You know it's all right, Claude." She glanced slyly at her son. "And Claudius will be glad. They got a daughter. Tell him they're all welcome."

The boy reddened and hung his head. "Ah, Ma," he blurted out, "I ain't interested in no girl."

Claude and Letty laughed and his mother hugged him tight. "You will be soon enough," his father said. "And they're good stock. Make you a fine wife."

Claudius ran out of the room to their laughter. "I'll send off a letter quick," Claude said. "Ask them to stay a month. We can take passage on the Evangeline and do a little trading in Portsmouth and Cincinnati."

"Can we get away that long? Crops be needing work about then, to get everything in."

"I'll leave Isaiah in charge. He's developing into a fine overseer. Can ask Hannibal to look in on him while we're gone." His face clouded. "And Henry, in case those Minns act up."

Letty pressed against him and squeezed his body. "Remember our first trip, Claude," she whispered. She turned her face up to his. "Left Rockport on our honeymoon, coming up to Crown City."

He tightened his grip and kissed her gently. "It will be like then, Letty. Just you and me. Granny Eva can come over and look after the children." They hugged and kissed, quiet.

Claude's letter brought a quick response from Captain Pickens. They would arrive November 15 for a month's stay. A week after, Pinckney Middleton sent word that Captain Pickens would act as his agent in selling rum along the river. Claude planned stops at settlements between, and to lay in a supply for the store at Crown City.

Kittie Mae was ecstatic when she heared of the excursion. "Can I go, Pa?" she pleaded. "Worth promised to show me some more card games." When he hesitated, "Please, Pa?"

Claude laughed. "No reason why not, Kittie Mae. I'll send Cal Jones a message to pick us up just after Thanksgiving, the way I figure."

Kittie Mae danced off singing. Her skipping steps on the hardwood floor were a fitting complement to her joyous song.

"She'll marry that man if we're not careful," Letty warned. "Soon as she's old enough."

Claude shook his head emphatically. "I had a long talk with Worth on his last visit. He's sees his dead daughter in her. Worth is acting like he's her father, Letty, and he'll treat her that way."

"Well, you watch out," Letty warned. "I don't want Kittie Mae running off with a gambler."

12

Rance and Ashley Pickens arrived with their daughter, Nancy, by carriage from Point Pleasant the afternoon of November 15. A stack of trunks, strapped tight, filled the platform behind the passenger compartment. Isaiah hallooed the house and pulled the team to a stop in the circle before the front steps. He jumped down from the driver's seat and hastened to open the side door of the carriage. The dry, sunny day held a hint of weather, presaged by a brisk breeze and high cirrus clouds to the west. Claude met Rance at the foot of the steps, hastening forward, while Letty waited on the porch and touched up her hair and dress. Old Blue showed around the corner of the house barking but Claude shooed him off. The fat dog slipped under a bush and stretched out on his belly with his eyes fixed on the tableau. His tail wagged from side to side in a continuous greeting.

"Welcome, Rance," Claude said jovially. "How was the trip?"

Rance stretched and stamped on his bad leg. "Reckon those trains need improvin'." He moved to one side as Isaiah helped his wife from the carriage. "Mighty hard seats and lots of jouncing but the river boat to Point Pleasant was easy. Wouldn't mind more of that river travel."

Claude nodded and moved forward to greet Ashley and the girl following her. "We're glad you could come, Mrs. Pickens." He glanced at the girl standing just behind. "And your pretty daughter. Letty's been looking forward to your visit."

Ashley stretched out her hand but her eyes held no warmth. "It's good to be out of that carriage, Captain Shaw. We do appreciate your hospitality." With a slight hesitation, she said, "My daughter, Nancy."

Claude nodded to the girl. He formally took Ashley's hand and escorted her up the steps. "You folks be careful," he warned. "We still got a few loose stones to reset. War and the winters left some damage."

"We have more, Captain," Ashley sharply retorted. "Those Yankees of Sherman weren't kind when they came by Columbia."

Claude struggled to maintain his composure, his face flushing. "I understand, Miz Pickens," he said gently. "It was the war and men get fevered up when they're winning."

His random shot struck home and her cheeks tightened, with her mouth a grim line. Letty smoothed over the difficulty with a surrounding hug and a, "Welcome, Ashley. Welcome Nancy. We have a warm room for you to rest. Trips always are tiring."

While the men visited at the steps, looking over the slope of fields to the river, Letty issued the orders. "Bring the trunks up to Miss Ashley's room quickly, Isaiah."

"Yessum," he answered.

Two house servants with Isaiah made short work of the trunks, delivering them to a corner of the big bedroom. Ashley and her daughter sat on a lounge while they worked, Ashley's gaze taking in the fine plaster work and the oil paintings of ancestors gracing the white walls. A large bed centered on one side. When all the baggage was stacked, she and Letty turned to the unpacking.

Ashley shook her head and uttered a little embarassed laugh. "Didn't realize we had so much; do you have a maid to help?"

"Not since the freedom," Letty said, "just two Negro girls to help around the house, and Aunty Isobel, our cook." She sighed, but then cheerfully said, "It really doesn't matter. You and

I can do it. We've plenty of room and Nancy can stay with our girls. She and Kittie Mae are about the same age."

"Can I, Mama?" Nancy asked. "It'll be fun to have a Yankee friend." She giggled. "I can tell all the girls at Miss Mabel's Academy when I get back."

"Yes, dear," her mother said, "just sort out your trunk. Missus Shaw'll show you the way and get a house boy to move it."

A step sounded at the door, with a clatter of heels on the hardwood planking. "Here's Kittie Mae now," Letty said. She introduced the girls with a hug around each.

Without waiting for a servant, the robust Kittie Mae seized one end of Nancy's trunk and hefted it. The box tilted off the floor. "Why, it's not heavy, Nancy," she said, setting it back down. "Take the other end and we'll just mosey along. Got a good soft bed for you and plenty of room for your things in my dresser."

"But where will my dresses go?" Nancy asked.

"In my wardrobe." Kittie Mae surveyed her new acquaintance. "I'll bet your things are beautiful. Lil and I have been looking in Harper's. We've been wild to get the patterns." Her enthusiasm drove her forward to feel Nancy's lace as she inspected the girl's traveling attire. "That's fetching. You must have some of the new styles."

Nancy colored and smoothed her ruffled skirt. "It's just an old house dress," she said disparagingly, though with a triumphant little smile. "We been making new but the best material is mighty scarce in Columbia right now." Her eyes gleamed and she asked excitedly, "Do you really have a new Harper's?"

At Kittie Mae's nod, Nancy said, "Then let's go!"

She seized the other end of the trunk and they hoisted it together. The girls chatted vivaciously as they maneuvered the bulky trunk out the door. Their voices faded down the hall. A shut door reduced their chatter to a murmur and occasional faint laugh.

A smile softened her mother's face. "I haven't seen that

child so happy in years," she said. "They'll make good friends. She's been needing to meet someone new."

"Kittie Mae will introduce her to a lot of girls. And a few boys too," Letty added slyly, glancing at her guest. "She have a beau?"

Ashley laughed, a deep welling, hearty explosion that loosened her stays. "Great heavens, no! The child's hardly thirteen. Boys will come later."

"Well, she's pretty, and she'll draw the boys." Letty chuckled. "Imagine Claudius will come smooping around, but he's shy yet. Likes guns and fishing."

"Claudius?"

"Our oldest son; named after Claude. He turned fourteen in July."

"It'll be interesting," Ashley said. "Now let's get on with the unpacking." But she went over and looked out the window first, then impatiently exclaimed, "I swan, Letty, Rance is down by the barns with Claude, looking over those horses. Sometimes I don't think he gives a fig for us, just animals."

Letty's laughs pealed out, while she held her sides. "Men are all alike, Ashley, particularly in farming. A new barn is better than a house."

A moment later, Ashley chimed in. "You surely are right on that. Rance is itching to build a warehouse for trading at Columbia." Her pride surfaced in a compliment. "You'd never think he once did only planting. The ideas that man has."

The two women gossiped freely about their families as they slowly emptied the chests into the dressers and wardrobes. When the trunks were empty, Isaiah and his hands moved them out of the room and the women settled into the easy chairs.

"Would you like to rest, Ashley?" Letty asked. "You must be worn out from the trip."

A bright glint in Ashley's eyes refuted the notion. "I'd rather talk about our families, Letty. Rance is bound and determined to partner with Claude." Her face turned hard. "Can we all get along?"was her harsh challenge. "Yankee and southerner in business together after trying to kill each other?"

"Claude trusts Rance, likes him," Letty said quietly. "Told me more than once he's a gentleman who will keep his word. Claude and I are willing." She waited but Ashley did not reply. "I take it you don't like Claude? Is that it?"

"Yes!" Ashley stridently replied. "We lost so much in the war, it just don't seem right." She sobbed. "We just about lost everything, and six of my cousins and my only brother were killed. Two we don't even know where they lie." Her hands covered her face while tears flowed. "I can't right now."

Letty rushed to the stricken woman. She cuddled Ashley's head and crooned, "Don't fuss yourself, Ashley. Some of our kin are gone too. It's best just to pray for them to ease the pain."

"But Claude was one of those who...." She could not go on, sobbing against Letty's breast.

Letty pulled her out of the chair and thrust her to arms length. She shook Ashley hard. "Now you listen, Ashley," she ordered. "Our kin are also in the ground. But the good Lord says, 'Vengeance is mine,' so it's time to forgive and forget."

A strangled wail broke from Ashley's mouth. "I can't!"

When the lament continued, Letty slapped Ashley hard on the cheek. "You stop that, right now, Ashley Pickens! You're a good woman, strong as I am, and moping around in what's past isn't right. Look to the future, woman! Your children need a strong guide, not some weakly, grieving ghost."

Fury colored Ashley's cheeks, her outrage visible in a tense body and balled fists. Letty gripped her guest's shoulders tightly until she crumpled slightly and reached for her handkerchief. After a few sniffs and a daubing of eyes, an erect, proud woman faced Letty, composed when she spoke. "You're right, of course. We Pickens can't ever be less than strong and I thank you for the reminder."

"We buried the hatchet on the war," Letty said, "and don't hate anyone." She held out her hand. "Let's be friends, Ashley, all of us. You'll learn to appreciate Claude. He's the finest man I know, and this business with Rance and Pinckney Middleton will prosper."

Instead of taking her hand, Ashley gave Letty a big hug. "We'll start, Letty. It'll be our secret about Claude. Please don't tell him," she pleaded. At Letty's nod, she said, "I will try to like him."

* * *

The bottom land attracted Rance when he and Claude finished admiring the horses. The planter led the Carolinian along the lane to the big bottom, only partly cultivated. Thistle and small cedars dotted the rest among the weeds and grass grown to waist high. At a little swale, Rance stooped down and grasped a handful of loose soil from an old corn row. He squeezed and rolled it in his hand, dribbling bits of the loam until it all was gone. Slapping his hands together to clean them, Rance delivered his opinion.

"It's wonderful, Claude." He swung his body around to gaze over the sweep to the river. "No steep slopes and with this fine growing land, you'll be rich."

"Backs up my trading," Claude replied. "But you're right. The bottom is our fortune."

Rance turned up the lane. "Let's get on back." He laughed sheepishly. "Ashley'll wonder where we've got to. She always did say I loved the land more'n her and Nancy."

"It's the land that never leaves us," Claude said, striding alongside him. "A man with land can always make it if he applies himself. When my greatgrandaddy John came from Ireland in the seventeen sixties he was a peasant with nothing. My grandpa Robert started us in Virginia, my pa, Enoch, lies in the graveyard on the knoll. I'll never let this land go."

Two days later, on a clear breezy day, the Shaws and Pickens took a carriage to Little Seven Mile, leaving the girls to their own amusement. A fast team delivered them to Hannibal and Hester's farm in early afternoon. Isaiah hallooed the house when they came up from the creek bottom road, a yell that brought Hannibal flying out of his barn.

"Hello! Hello!" he yelled and took hold of the right horse's harness. He and Isaiah gentled the team to an easy halt. Hannibal ran around to the carriage door and opened it. "Welcome, Claude, Letty," he said with a big smile. "An' you too, Captain, Miz Pickens. Heard you was at Greenbottom."

When the four were on the ground, he sent Isaiah to stable the horses and led the party up the steps to the waiting Hester, flanked by Granny Mandy and Granny Eva. Rance and Ashley blanched silently and exchanged looks when Claude and Letty hugged the Negroes and they engaged in familiar first name pleasantries. But the two Carolinians were not forgotten. Hester approached them with a smile and outstretched hands, the hands of equality.

"It's good to see you both, Captain. And you, Miz Ashley. Welcome to our place."

Ashley's womanly instincts overtook her years of owner-servant breeding and she hugged Hester. "I see you're expecting, child. Do you feel well?"

"No trouble so far, Miz Ashley," Hester replied. "An' I got Granny Mandy and Eva ter help."

Mandy pushed forward and faced the Pickens, propped up by her cane. Her chiseled old lines softened as she inspected Rance. "You lookin' well, boy," she said. "You 'bout as fat as you was when I use' ter sneak you dose cracklin's an' cornbread."

Rance's roaring laughter echoed from the surrounding hills. He took the old, spare figure in his arms and swung her in a circle. "Mama didn't like that at all, Granny. But they surely were tasty."

"Membered, boy," Granny replied. "Me an' Eva done made a big bait fer you an' Miz Ashley. An' Hester been cookin' all morning...ham, sweet taters, greens." She rolled her eyes, "scrumptious."

Rance put her down gently and picked up her fallen cane. "Could we go in," he asked. "Would you please fetch the big trunk, Hannibal? Isaiah has it in the boot."

When the trunk rested before Ashley in the living room, all

eyes shifted to it and silence replaced the happy gossip. "Captain Pickens and I brought you something, Hester," Ashley said. She glanced at the others. "And Hannibal and Granny Mandy. We have plenty for you too, Granny Eva."

Yielding up bolts of colorful cloth and needles and thread, lace, and buttons, the cornucopia overflowed with happiness for the women. Following were kitchen knives, dippers and forks. A copper kettle and a large cast iron skillet came next. At sight of the latter, Granny Mandy's eyes gleamed.

"Jest what we need, Miz Ashley," she said. "We ain' had but a small one ter do with. Dat heavy skillet fry lots o' meat an' de best bread."

Ashley smiled. "There's a few more things in the the other trunk in the boot but they can wait. Some guns and knives for Hannibal. And a few packets of seeds from Europe that Rance got for Hannibal and Captain Shaw."

"Empty 'em now, Miz Pickens," Hannibal asked, "so's you can take de trunks back?

"No," Ashley said. "You keep them for Hester to store things in. She'll need something to get together baby clothes."

Effusive thanks poured from the Negroes. The afternoon rapidly slipped away into darkness as Hannibal spoke eloquently of becoming a learned preacher. At supper, Hester continued with Hannibal's dream.

"Would you say the blessing," she asked.

"Our Father," he began. "We are met here together, black and white, in freedom and in friendship. Remove our old wounds, our hates. Let us all live in equality and in peace, helping one another. And we ask you to bless this food to our bodies and us to thy service, Amen."

In the carriage the next day, after a night spent sleeping in soft beds in Hannibal's new outlying cabin, the visitors ruminated on the Negroes.

"That new cabin for Mandy and Eva was mighty nice," Letty said. "Hannibal surely has been busy."

"His two Negro hands helped," Rance added. He laughed.

"Hannibal a land owner and boss. Who would have thought that in sixty one!"

Claude chuckled. "Times have changed, Rance." He rolled and braced himself at a jolt in their passage. "Hannibal's a fine, honest, hard-working man. He and Hester will be a credit to your family and mine."

Ashley stirred in her seat, wincing. "Well I'm glad Hester has Mandy and Eva there," she said. "That girl's having trouble but Mandy will see her through the birth."

A moment of quiet ensued, relegated to thoughts. "Hester and I made up, Rance," Ashley finally offered. "And Granny Mandy. You and Letty were right. It's time to go on, let the war and the past be forgotten."

Rance's smile and delighted exclamation, "Letty told you too?" settled the differences between them. They gazed at each other fondly, each oblivious to the Shaws. Letty's hand slid over and took Claude's. She squeezed his fingers and was answered as they rode on, swaying in the carriage, the silence broken only by Isaiah's encouragement of the team.

Miles later, Ashley stirred into a firm talkativeness. "I'm going to help Hester with her school, Rance. Letty and I together. She and Hannibal been practicing on their English with Letty's help."

"I noticed that," Rance said. "Mighty fine."

Ashley went on. "We can get the books and slates and things like that. Hannibal will build a schoolhouse and go on with his preaching. My goodness, if the Negroes are to be part of us, they need learning."

Letty nodded. "There must be ten children closeby that will come, some white." She put her hand over Claude's mouth when he made to interrupt. "Claude has a cousin that teaches and will help. Polly always was a strong abolitionist; started a school in Burlington for the runaways years ago."

"What about the ones down home?" Rance asked.

Ashley's conversion shined through. "We'll just have to do the same there. No reason we shouldn't." Her firm voice took a combative edge, warning him off. "I'll see to it!"

Rance hoorawed. "When Ashley talks like that, Claude, I stay out of the way. She means it."

His wife blushed but Letty stoutly said, "She's right, Rance. The old times are gone. Ashley and I will help the Negroes. It's only right."

After return to Greenbottom, Rance and Claude talked in the library while the women visited and quilted. The exacting work was a surprise to Ashley who had done fine needlework but not quilting, leaving that to Granny Mandy and others. Unlike the women, the men's transactions were strictly business.

"Five hundred gallons of that new darker rum should be enough," Claude said. "You say it's the best?"

"Seems so. Pinck's been selling it to taverns around the low country and it goes well."

"Half down when I send the order and the rest on arrival here? Draft on the Gallipolis Bank, not coin?"

"That will do nicely," Rance replied. "Pinck has to pay the ship's captain on offloading, so we keep up our cash."

With their business settled, Claude casually shifted to the Minnses. "You know a Wiley Minns, Rance? And Athey's son Joshua?"

The Confederate started and leaned forward in his chair. "Why do you ask?" he said, his lips a thin line. "Those two up here?"

"They are," Claude said. "And they're aiming to make trouble for me. Reason, of course, is that we killed Athey and his sons in the escape. Is Wiley a blowhard or serious?"

"Serious as a canebrake rattler," Rance replied. "Don't trust them and watch your back." His contemptuous put down answered Claude's next question. "Wiley is a no-good, conniving, jackleg preacher. Always involved in shady deals and with the courage of a cornered rat. His nephew, Josh, is different. A wounded veteran, cited for bravery in several campaigns." Rance shook his head. "They aren't to be trifled with."

Claude sighed. "My God, won't this war ever be over!"

"Not as long as those two are rousting you. Can you find a way to kill them?.....Legally?"

Rance's matter-of-factness shocked Claude. "No!" he exclaimed. But the idea intrigued him. Maybe he could provoke a confrontation. Or the next time they caused trouble for Hannibal, maybe they could just be shot? What could he do other than sit at the bullseye, waiting? And what about Letty and his children? Wiley and Joshua wouldn't hesitate to kill them all.

Rance broke into his meditation. "Kill them, Claude. First chance you get."

Claude slowly nodded, his silence an agreement. Their business finished, they spent the rest of that day gunning along the river. Crossing over the next day, they visited Claude's store in Crown City.

"My brother, Garrett," Claude said, in introduction.

Ian McLellan came over as the three spoke of the dark rum and its consignment to the store and river taverns. "Howdy, Claude," he said, nodding to the visitor.

"Ian works on my logging," Claude said. "He's first rate at timbering and rafting. His family there," he added, motioning to Mary Jane, Joe and his two brothers, "are fine people, salt of the earth."

Ian fidgeted and his cheeks reddened. "Aw, Claude, you don't have to pass no compliments." His pride rose to the occasion. "But you are right about Mary Jane and the boys."

"Joe's interested in Kittie Mae," Claude said casually. "Can he come over, Ian? Stay with Claudius a bit?" He added the sweetener. "Captain Pickens' daughter is visiting Kittie Mae. Right pretty girl."

"I'll fetch Joe tomorrow, Claude, when I head back to the mountain. He'll like some huntin' with Claudius."

Pleasantries and business swiftly finished the visit to the store. A cruise across the river to Shaw's Landing took them back to Greenbottom and the company of the ladies.

"When is the Evangeline due," Letty asked at dinner.

"Three days hence," Claude replied. "Long enough for Rance and me to get two good bucks."

Letty chuckled and Ashley laughed. Letty waved her finger at Claude. "Is guns all you think of? I would have thought you both got your fill in that old war."

"Not Rance," Ashley said. "He always loves the hunt."

Claude shuddered, the image of Wiley Minns intruding. Hunt! I may have to hunt him yet, just like the buck! The shadow remained with him all the way through that pleasant evening.

13

"Lookee, Josh," Hank said, from his crouch on the knoll. "It's Elsie, the nigger that birthed Claude's new buck."

Joshua spit a brown stream from his seat against a hickory sapling.

"You recken it's true, that Shaw covered her?"

"Josie swears she heard Letty give Claude hail columbia for it. He's got a nigger son."

"Well I ain't thinkin' 'bout that just now. Lookit her down there, hanging that wash. Mighty prime an' I ain't had none lately." Joshua whistled softly. "I just think I'll mosey down and visit her a bit."

Hank nervously peered about and shifted his rifle. "You ain't seen Hannibal have you?" He squirmed around for a look at the trail down the creek bottom. "Don't seem like nobody there but her."

"I been watchin' since dawn, while you come over from our camp. Them old grannies and their Rosemary brat are up the creek a piece birthin' that Logan gal. Saw Logan yestiday an' he said they was comin'." Joshua spit again. "Ain't seen Hester. Hannibal and his hands rode out fust light. Long gone."

An explosive, pleased, "Ah!" escaped Peavey. "We can do her easy."

They took a circuitous route to circle down the backslope and came upon the house from the barnyard. Joshua leaned his rifle against the mitered logs and ran around the corner to the clothes line, intercepting Elsie with her mouth full of clothes-pins. He choked her before she could cry out but the strong young woman twisted and jabbed her captor in the stomach, doubling him over. When she sprang free, Hank ran at her.

Elsie screamed, a loud terrified wail that set the dogs barking. A big black and tan rushed around the house growling. Joshua pulled his belt gun and shot the dog when it lunged. The loud report scared off the pack, which kept up its protest at a respectful distance.

"Watch the rest of 'em," Minns shouted and ran after Elsie.

The girl had gathered her skirts in her hands and was making for the new cabin. Joshua overtook her at the door and fell on top of her into the room. They thudded down next to a massive hanging basket. A patchwork quilt hung over its edge, a colorful ornament with a crosshatched pattern of woven honeysuckle vine. Her outstretched hand fell short of the basket and the supporting rawhide thong up to a rafter. The Carolinian grabbed her by the neck and dragged her to a stand beside the basket.

"Now you be quiet," he said, "or I'll put my knife to it."

Douglass's fat sleeping face peeped from the covers in the basket, oblivious to the peril. Elsie relaxed against the grip of her attacker. She pushed the basket slightly, setting it to swinging.

"Don' hurt my baby!" she implored weakly. "Please don't! I do what you want."

Joshua cuffed her alongside the head. "Jest so's you know it, bitch." He looked around the spacious room which contained only chairs and tables and a large fireplace. "Where's yore bed? You mean you niggers got a separate room fer sleepin'?"

Elsie flared up, flaying him. "We got more'n you white-trash 'cause we work fer what we got. Don' lay around like you drunks,.....er steal."

Flaming passion colored his face, his fury expressed in blows to both of her cheeks. His raised hand stopped when a step sounded outside. Casting her aside roughly, he drew his pistol and slipped to one side of the door, backing up against the wall with his arm bent close to his body and pistol aimed at the ceiling.

"Josh? Where are you, Josh?"

Hank stepped over the sill as he spoke, only to recoil away from Joshua's aimed weapon. "God almighty!" he said, "it's only me. Why'er yuh so edgy?"

"Thought you might be that damned Hannibal," Joshua said. "He ain't to be trifled with. Silent as an Injun in the woods." He bitterly complained. "Wanted ter kill the bastard but Unk said not 'til Claude's ruint." He shook his head mournfully. "That nigger's too good with guns and trackin' ter suit me. Be the death o' Unk, he ain't keerful."

"Well, he ain't 'round," Hank said, "I done circled the hull place." He sidled over to Elsie and grabbed a breast with his left hand, drawing a crying protest. His other fingers slipped down the neck of her dress. A quick yank tore the fabric loose from her frame, exposing the brown skin of her bosom, breasts bulging and with distended nipples.

Joshua holstered his pistol with a quick flip and pushed Hank aside. "I ain't lettin' you go first, man."

Hank opened his mouth but shut it quickly and moved away at Minns' scowl and silent menace. "You jest wait your turn," Joshua said.

He twisted Elsie's arm until tears ran down her cheeks. "Show me where the bed is bitch, the one you an' Shaw use." She sobbed and moved into the bedroom fronting the creek road. A slam of the door and Hank was left alone.

Loud creaks and Elsie's cries woke Douglass. Increased shrieks from his mother answered his impatient wails. Hank swung the basket more violently but its motion only generated a terrified lament. Slowing the swinging to a gentle arc reduced the protests but a howl broke from the baby when Hank stuck his bony, mustachioed face close above Douglass's head. The baby's frightful screams transfixed the man. He absently pushed the rawhide thong to and fro while thuds and invective in the bedroom testified to a damaging fight. A final thunk and the floor shook. A moment later, the bedroom door opened. Stark naked, Elsie ran from the doorway and picked up Douglass. Ignoring Hank, she cooed to the baby and quieted him even as she moved to a table in the far corner of the room. Elsie began to change Douglass as he gurgled contentedly.

Hank switched his open-mouthed gaze first to the negress, then to the open bedroom door and its silent interior. He drew his belt gun and eased over to it with slow, cautious steps. "My God!" he said when he stepped inside.

Joshua lay naked on the floor, face down. Holstering his gun, Hank turned over his friend. A big purpling bruise on the forehead and the adjacent bent poker testified to the reason for Joshua's unconsciousness. Hank checked Minns quickly. "Breathin' a'right," he said. "He ain't hurt much. Just an achin' head when he wakes up." Hank chuckled, his glee growing into laughter. "Recken he deserved to go first!"

Peavey led a still groggy Joshua out of the bedroom ten minutes later. Elsie rocked in a chair with Douglass at her breast. Her naked glory mocked Hank, inaccessible this time.

"We ain't takin' this, nigger," Hank said, as he supported Minns and shuffled past her chair. "Josh will kill you sure."

Elsie's hate rubbed salt into his wound. "He didn't git what he come fer and he ain't gonna." She spit on the passing Joshua. "Tell 'im next time he come, I kill 'im."

* * *

When Hannibal returned late that afternoon, he pulled up at the sight of the strange tracks and Elsie's scattered wash beside the dead hound. Slipping out of his saddle, he yelled, "Take care of the horses, Lew." A quick read of the scuffed dirt and he followed the tracks to the grannies' cabin, his revolver at the ready. He found Elsie in the living room, clothed but asleep in the rocking chair, with Douglass in her arms. She waked with a start and a small scream when his foot hit the doorstep and ran into the bedroom. The slammed door brought Hannibal to a skidding stop, his gaze at once darting around the room.

"What you feered for, Elsie?" he said loudly.

The bedroom door opened slowly and Elsie peeped past the edge. At sight of him, she smiled and came into the room. Douglass grumbled when she shifted the child in her arms but she crooned and patted him into silence. "We done had dat Hank and Minns here," she said calmly. "Run 'em off."

Hannibal stiffened and strode over to her. He took the girl in his arms and cuddled her. "You ain't hurt?" he asked.

She broke down and began wailing, spouting out bits of the story as her tears cascaded down her cheeks. "Dat damned Minns figure he tek me ter bed," she said. "Say he kill Douglass iffen I don't." Her wails increased.

Hannibal exploded angrily. "You mean Wiley Minns come 'round here? And Joshua?"

"Not de ol' Minns," she burst out. "It was dat Joshua, de mean one. He come wid Hank Peavey."

Hannibal cursed but continued his cuddling while Elsie gradually quieted. When she was beyond sniffling, he guided her into a seat and went to search the farm, particularly his barn. Five dried deerskins were missing from the pile he had stacked for sale. His fists balled up as he stood over the last of the laboriously gathered skins. It was money they had taken, money for his family, money he could use at the store.

"You see any harm around the pigs or cows?" he asked, when his Negro hand came into the barn.

Lew shook his head. "Ain't none o' 'em missin'." He picked up a pail. "Fixin' ter slop de hogs and go on wid de milkin'. Dat all right?"

Hannibal nodded while he thought over the situation. He and his folks had better conjure on the raid, for that is what it was. Plus the attempted rape. Women weren't safe. Property wasn't safe. Needed to leave a hand close every day with a rifle and belt gun. His mind settled, he joined the hand to finish the chores, his last task hanging the rest of Elsie's wash on the line.

When Grannies Eva and Mandy arrived with Hester

and Rosemary about seven that evening, he gathered them around a table set with cold pork, butter, cornbread and left over vegetables. Coffee perked and a hot steaming cup was soon poured for each, with Rosemary's heavily sweetened and mostly milk. Silence prevailed as the adults blessed their evening meal and selected from the offering.

Mandy sat in her cushioned chair, her lined face inscrutable. A sip of coffee preceded her reach for a bit of bread and meat and a cooked sweet potato. "Why you so quiet, Hannibal? You ain't said nothin' since we come back."

Elsie broke down, telling them of the attack on her and the farm in a trembling voice. She finished with, "Dey say dey kill Hannibal an' de rest o' us iffen he tell Claude." She clutched Douglass tightly to her bosom. "I'se scairt."

A chill settled over the group, with silence its dividend. All chewed in abstract isolation, worrying thoughts their only companions.

Eva first broke the dismal climate with a decisive, "Gotter tell Claude. He's de onliest one can stop dose trash."

Enraged, Hannibal shook his balled right fist in the air and shouted, "No we ain't! I'se a free man! Ain't no slave no more, nor you and you and you," he roared, pointing to each. "Past time for de white man to take care o' me. I do it myself."

"Dat's right," Granny Mandy said. "Hannibal say it right. Nigger want freedom, he got ter fight fer it hisself. Claude done tol' 'em once. Dey don't mind Claude so we do it."

"But dat Hank and Joshua ain't lettin' up," Eva observed. "Can't kill 'em. Git hung fer sure."

"We Injun 'em," Hannibal said grimly, "if we need to. Leave 'em in the woods."

Mandy nodded, a hard edge to her voice. "Boy right. Tek keer o' oursel'es."

"You know de woods, Hannibal," Elsie said, "but dat don' he'p me. What you figure fer me?"

All eyes fixed on the big man as he leaned over the table, spearing another piece of pork for his plate. He sliced a square of hard cornbread then split and liberally buttered it before inserting the meat. After the first huge bite of his sandwich, he offered his counsel.

"'Vengeance is mine,' the Lord said, but ain't no angels 'round to perteck us from dose men. An' Claude mean well but he can't be here. So we do it oursel'es."

"You don't recken dat Hank an' Joshua pay no attention to Claude's warnin'?" Eva asked.

"Too mean," Granny Mandy answered. "We git de other niggers in de valley ter hep. Keep a watch and run 'em off."

"There's ten o' our men hereabouts," Hannibal said, "an' lots o' boys. They kin keep 'em sighted. An' the men's mostly armed."

Elsie's tremulous, "What if dat Joshua come in agin?" brought reassurance from Hannibal.

"Got me a quiet place over the ridge only I knows about. Hide 'em good."

Eva waved her stick and struck the floor a resounding blow with the knobbed end. "De women an' younguns hep," she said forcefully. "I trail up an' down de creek wid Rosemary next few days, tells 'em. Dey all watch an' send word, jest like in de wah in Jawga."

Hannibal settled the self-help defense. "I ride over an' warn off Peavey. He can tell Minns." The powerful Negro pounded his breast as he pronounced judgement. "Ain't Claude this time. It's me! They come in peace or they git buried."

* * *

Cal Jones and the Evangeline moored at Shaw's Landing on November 30 to pick up the families for the journey down river. He had whistled for the stop on the brisk, clear day. Claude and Rance met him at the landing. The river flowed deep and clear as the river boat swung its bow upstream and put out its lines. Two men ran the bow line to a large sycamore upstream and tied it off. Current forced the tethered boat against the landing and hands swiftly secured the breast line and let down the planked brow.

"Mighty fine landing," Rance observed. "Haven't seen better on the Congaree down home."

"Cal Jones is the best Captain on the Ohio," Claude said. "He's been boatin' all his life. Knows the river like no other." He added an afterthought. "Got one o' my cousins on the wheel too, Shawn. Good man."

Kittie Mae and Nancy Pickens ran over the brow ahead of their elders' more sedate saunter. On deck, Kittie Mae jumped into the arms of a waiting, gray-clad Worth Fauquier, who swung her around. His severe habit was broken by a gaudy vest and black string tie. A sweeping gray planter's hat with a feather topped a pale, mustachioed face. Nancy stepped to one side as the two jollied each other.

"You're more beautiful than ever," Worth told the girl. He hefted her. "And bigger," he added.

Kittie giggled and he squeezed her harder. "Aw, Worth, you just say that," she gasped out. But she reddened a little and held on to his arm after he put her down. "Meet my friend from South Carolina, Nancy Pickens."

Worth swept off his hat. He bowed to Nancy and took her outstretched hand, bending and kissing it. "I am honored," he said. "A friend of Kittie Mae's is a friend of mine."

Nancy curtsied and inclined her head with a smile. "I would not have expected such courtesy from a Yankee, sir."

A sad mask passed fleetingly over Fauquier's face. "I am a Virginian, Miss Nancy. But even with Yankees I have found courteous treatment to be a constant."

Nancy drew back at the mild rebuke. Kittie Mae walked her to the upper-deck ladder as Claude and Rance approached Fauquier and Cal Jones, who had joined the gambler. Introductions quickly finished, Jones refused to visit Greenbottom.

"We lost a day upriver, Claude," he said, "and the water stage is just right. Ain't time for visitin', much as I'd like to. Letty always sets such a fine table."

"Well then, on the way back?"

"Yes," Jones said. "I'll plan on it."

Letty, Ashley and all their trunks were loaded in a busy hour, along with two of Letty's Negro maids to help the women. A large store of her cheese and butter rounded out Letty's baggage, for sale to merchants. Kittie Mae and Nancy watched from the upper deck as the boat swung into the stream. The fields and timbered slopes passed rapidly as the paddles pushed it forward in the strong current.

"Do you like it?" Kittie Mae asked her friend.

"It's so fast!" Nancy said. "The Ohio is big!"

Kittie Mae laughed. "It's fun to go down, but slow coming back." She tossed a chip from her pocket into the stream. It floated behind. "See," she said, "this boat is fast. We'll be in Cincinnati before you know it."

In the days of stops for freighting and trading, Letty disposed of her merchandise, amazing Ashley. "I didn't realize that you traded too," she said.

"Surely do," Letty told her. "Did it all during the war to get some hard money. Cal helped me. And when Claude was in that prison, it scared me bad. Many a night I wanted to cry and give up. But I never did. Traded to keep going."

Ashley slowly nodded her head. "Rance terrified me too," she said. A note of pride crept into her voice. "He always was leading those charges, finally got shot bad and came home. I was mighty thankful." She shook off her nostalgia. "No reason I can't do the same as you back in Carolina." She was reflective for a moment. "Always looked down on trading. Rance told me different. You and he are right."

The women clasped each other in a quiet embrace, tears conquering. They purged their thoughts to one another, cementing a permanent bond.

* * *

Hank Peavey came in the house after the Evangeline

whistled. "They done pulled away from the landin'," he said. "Headin' down river."

Old Jubal looked up from his bowl of soup. "You heard from Josie how long they be gone?"

Hank walked over to the fireplace and spit a brown stream into the fire. A crackle and flicker of flame answered. "She said they's tradin' downstream fer three weeks. That Pickens feller takin' orders for rum, pinetar, and such."

Old Peavey wiped his mouth with his sleeve after another spoonful of soup. "With only Claudius there, mayhaps we kin catch 'im nappin'."

"You want me to burn the house, Gramps?"

Peavey exploded. "No, by God! They'd have that damn Bandie sheriffin' us right off."

He bent to his soup for a few more swallows. A piece of cornbread went down his gullet with more soup while Hank dished up his own serving. Jubal's uncertainty and thoughtful mien continued as he slowly sipped his soup. Through Jubal's hesitation, Hank noisily downed a bowl. The old man's decisive order came just as Hank belched.

Ignoring the distraction, Jubal said, "You go fetch Wiley and Josh next few days, boy, while I study on my plan."

Hank listened between spoonsful. After washing up the dishes, he and Peavey spent the evening playing checkers and roaring at each other about cheating.

* * *

Claude's forty dollar loan to Jess Abert had slipped his mind when a letter arrived from the farmer after their return from Cincinnati. The wrinkled envelope was smudged and dirty from many travels when he slit it open with his knife.

"Look here, Letty," he said. "Remember that farmer I told you of, Jess Abert?"

"The one you lent the forty dollars?"

Claude nodded and scanned the sheet quickly. "Listen

to this."

> 'Dear Claud, Jobe is heppin me with this, since I dont tek much to writin. We was plannin on comin up ter your place this fall to fetch thet loan but a fire burnt out my barn. Kilt our ol mule and a farrowing sow. We got ter use the money we saved ter rebuild and git new stock. I aint fergot, Claud, how you hepped us. Weuns, me and Jobe and the Missus will be up when we kin git the money tergether. Maybe next year. Made good money with taters and termaters like you said an gittin other hard coin with deer hides. Aint got no debt now thanks ter you.
>
> Your friend. Jess Abert.'

"He's an honest man." Letty said. "When you answer, invite him and his family to come any time."

"I'll do that," Claude replied. "I just hope he's not here when Hank or the Minnses cause trouble. Jess struck me as an impatient man, and he'd back me in a minute. But my fight isn't his no matter how beholden he feels."

His wife nodded and sidled against him, putting her arms around his waist. "I prayed last night about them and their hate," she said. "Then I had a dream and they faded away. The Lord is on our side, Claude. Don't you worry none, for I am at peace. They will not hurt us."

Letty's equanimity was shaken a few days later when Preacher Creadey stopped by Greenbottom. He left his horse hitched to the rail and came in for an afternoon's cup of tea with cookies. His small talk finally shifted into his concerns.

"You see Ian about every day, Miz Letty?"

"Yes," she replied. "He's been around the past week working with Claude. Going back to the timbering next Monday."

"Smelled any whiskey?" he said casually. "Heard maybe he was drinking again." His long face turned even more sorrowful. "And even after I made him swear on his mother's grave."

"It's not true!" Letty burst out. "He's been livin' in the

house here. He's sober." She chuckled. "I told Isaiah to watch him and tell me. Isaiah says Ian prays aloud as he works. Over and over, he says, 'Deliver me from demon rum, Lord. I will not fall from your graces.'"

Creadey's face cleared and he raised his eyes heavenward. "Thanks be to the Lord. I didn't want to believe it when Wiley Minns told me."

Letty's hands flew to her mouth and she gasped. "Minns said that? You know he's sworn to hurt Claude for killing his brother down in Georgia?"

"I do," Creadey replied. "He's the snake in Eden, Miz Letty, a fallen angel." His mournful voice continued, "And he calls himelf a man of the cloth. It pains me to say it."

"He's bad, pastor."

Creadey nodded. "Him and those two boys, Hank and Joshua. You tell Claude to watch his back. They are the ambushing kind I saw in the war. Won't face him man to man."

Letty sobbed and grasped one of Creadey's bony hands. "Will you help us, pastor?"

Creadey's flushing face took on a glow. "It will be my aim, Miz Letty, to listen, to spread the word, to help. Folks I preach to ain't puttin' up with no snakes in Eden and those three are surely that."

One more cup of tea finished Creadey's visit. His last remarks reassured her. "Now don't you worry none, Miz Letty; the Lord will provide."

14

Preacher Creadey paced back and forth in front of the fireplace in the Shaws' parlor, his eager tenseness evident in his forceful, blunt peroration. "I'm telling you, Claude, that Hannibal has the gift, the burning eye."

Claude laughed, only to be silenced by Letty's frown. The preacher's angry face and a jabbing forefinger skewered him, taking him aback.

"Don't you take the Lord's work in vain," Creadey thundered. His craggy face tightened. "Hannibal has the gift! I swear to our Lord and Savior that when he prays my soul is uplifted. The Lord has touched him."

"He has no education, pastor," Claude said. "How's he going to study the Bible? Little bit of reading he knows won't be much."

Letty rose from her chair and marched over to Claude. She faced him while Creadey held up the tails of his swallowtail coat and warmed his bottom before the fire. "Now you listen to me, Claude Shaw." Her bosom rose and fell animatedly. She struggled with a rosy face and quivering lips, unable to speak.

He shrank back from her preemptory tone, one he knew so well. She's riled up, he thought. When she got that glint in her eye, he could expect some free and unwanted advice, and not a little clawing. The storm broke over him as he expected.

"Don't close your eyes to a true miracle," Letty said, after chewing on him. "Preacher Creadey is right! Hannibal's got a glow about him when he talks of the Bible. He reads it all the time, the one I loaned him. Haven't you noticed?"

"Can't believe he'll learn that much so quick. An education don't come easy."

Creadey quickly interceded. "We fought that abolition fight, Claude, hard. And you know I was at the front in battle. Got shot twice doing same's you did. This is but another battle, but it is for souls, free with the Lord."

"Who will teach him the language and the theology?"

Letty fussed impatiently. "Oh ye of little faith! Haven't you any faith at all, Claude?" Her irritation scourged him. "All the while Preacher Creadey and I have been teaching Hannibal to read and write, you just passed us by. Hannibal gets lessons every Sunday afternoon and reads from our library and the reverend's."

"If you think that much of him," Claude said reluctantly, "I'll help. But he's got to make that farm pay. A Negro can't rely on preaching for a living."

"He'll do that," Creadey said. "I told him he must farm, but to tithe to the Lord." He ruminated a moment. "I tell you, Claude, he'll be a great minister some day. You just got to help."

Claude surrendered gracefully. "Man needs his own library if he's to be a preacher. Can't do it with borrowed books."

Letty clapped her palms together and kissed him. Creadey wrung both of Claude's hands hard when he left, a tear in his eye.

"Thank, you, brother," he said. "The Lord will bless you."

* * *

"They been back," Hannibal said gloomily, when he entered the kitchen. "Took the mule this time, and just when we're in the middle of spring plowing."

Hester rinsed her hands in clear water and dried them on her apron. She clasped him around the body and put her head on his chest. Nearby their baby slept in a rocker crib. "Don't you worry none, love. Claude will he'p if you just tell him. He won't put up wid no such foolishment."

His body stiffened and he thrust her away. "I ain't asking nobody to fight my fight, gal. War's over a year back and they don't know it." He reached for his rifle in the deer hoof rack over the stone fireplace, a Spencer carbine bought from a Union soldier. A swing of the loading lever exposed the round from the barrel, then he reinserted it, ready to fire.

Hannibal gathered up his campaign belt from a crude halltree, a heavy burden hung with a holstered gun and bowie knife on the opposite sides of several pouches. After strapping it around his waist, he made a check of his loads and slid the revolver back into the holster. A quick draw and return evidenced the slick fit of weapon to leather. A large bag on a shoulder strap came next, clanking when he dropped it to the floor beside the fireplace.

"You fixin' to go off right now?"

A nod answered Hester as he went into the shed pantry and its copious storage. He was struggling into his dark brown greatcoat with all its pockets when he came out. She had his meat ready and his canteen filled. Opening the oven of her new stove, she took out a brown circle of cornbread, warm and aromatic. It went into his shoulder bag, along with the meat and water. A wistful glance passed between them before he swung the strap over his shoulder and swept her up into his arms.

"I be back in two, three days gal. Ain't no Minns or Peavey take our stock."

Hester's hands brushed his cheeks and she kissed him tenderly. "I'se worried, Hannibal. What I do you don' come back?"

A chuckle broke her fears. "You think I git kilt by those trash? Ain't none of them kin beat me in de woods! I'll Injun 'em, they come after me."

With a last tender embrace and kiss, he left her in the kitchen and struck up the hollow toward the ridge. She ran to the porch and waved as he entered the trees. He shook his rifle in the air in answer. Hester could bear it no longer. She snatched up her baby and ran to the granny cabin, sobbing wildly and calling for Granny Mandy. An hour later she still rested in the arms of Granny Eva, soothed by the old black woman's crooning, while her little one napped on the couch with Granny Mandy.

* * *

The track of the bent shoe was easy to follow, denting the soft clay in the wooded creek bottom and its start at the ridge. Hannibal soon stripped his coat and bundled it on his back, sweating in the warming May day. He searched the hardwood cover constantly with his eyes while he slipped from one copse to another. The far side of the first ridge was bare, stumps and a few gray boulders protruding from the newly sprouted pasture grass. Hannibal took note of a cluster of paw paw bushes for fall collection of fruit. "Be mighty nice after frost," he murmured. Movement to the south around the greening hill revealed a small herd of Jersey heifers. The farm buildings lay beyond, in a grove of poplar and willow trees just west of the creek in the hollow. A quick flight across the open land led him to the next wooded slope. Primal hardwoods, massive columns in nature's cathedral, rose above the forest mulch, yeasty from the damp. He could not pass those immense virgin trees without wonder and a humbling of soul. Hannibal stopped at a six foot diameter oak and knelt before its black bark. Raising his eyes to the fair blue sky with its light clouds, he folded his hands over his heart and prayed.

"Oh, Lord God of All, the black as well as white. Give us peace in this land, peace as quiet as these wonderful trees. Help this lamb, Lord. And bless those Peavey's and Minns in spite of their orneriness. Give them religion, Lord, for by all's holy, I don't want to kill 'em."

Five ridges east he discovered the rail corral with his mule. Hidden in a little swale surrounded by white pine and laurel thickets, he would have gone by except for the rumblings of the mule's belly and the smell of droppings. When he broke out on the north side, he found it up on the high ground, behind the Peavey buildings that bordered the river road. Mighty fine hideout, he thought. Just the place for thieves. Squatting in the bushes above the stock pen, he ate corn bread and meat and watched for an hour, debating rescue of the mule.

The sight of Hank Peavey on the narrow path from the house galvanized Hannibal. He half-rose from his seat and aimed his Spencer before shaking his head and scurrying to a more secure cover. Hank was followed singly by two men, roughly dressed, each cradling a cap and ball rifle. A broad-brimmed black campaign hat covered one head, a coonskin the other. Their talk, indistinct at first, grew intelligible when they approached the corral. Hank set his rifle aside and leaned his arms over the top rail as he extolled the virtues of the animal.

"Best plowing mule I ever seen, Cappy." Rolling his chaw, he spit a brown stream into the enclosure and continued on the mule's merits. "He ain't ornery a'tall."

Cappy laughed. "You jest foolin' me as usual, Hank? He any better'n thet broke down mare you sold me? Damned hoss quit afore me an' Lije ever got to the Big Sandy."

He swung his tall body over the top rail and entered the pen, after depositing his rifle against a crooked log. Walking close around the mule, he continued his criticism. As he passed by the mule's rump, it lashed out with a hind hoof. Cappy jumped clear and swore. "Ain't ornery? You'd best take a club to 'im."

Lije picked up a split-off piece of fence rail. "Here's your pole, Cap," he said, and tossed it into the chewed up dirt in the corral. "Give 'im a piece o' this."

"Hold on!" Hank said, when Cappy waved the chunk. Hank's ominous tone chilled their banter. "Don't you hit my mule! You orta hev sense enough not to walk aroun' his back." His scorn continued. "All mules kick."

"Hell," Lije said. "Cain't you take nothin', Hank? We was jest funnin'." His words were light but he backed off a few steps and readied his rifle.

Cappy ignored Hank and made a closer inspection of

the mule. When he pried at its mouth to look at its teeth, the animal tried to bite him. He struck the mule hard with his fist and grabbed the halter, violently jerking its head sideways. The animal followed docilely as he walked it around the pen. Observing from his hideout, Hannibal chuckled. Just like that fool mule, he thought. Trouble one minute, ready for work the next. But he was a good mule.

"Well, Hank," Lije said, "how much you askin'."

"I got a debt comin' due er I'd take 'im to Gallipolis fer tradin'." Hank swung up to sit on the top rail while Cappy trailed the mule around. "You an' me been tradin' last ten year, I recken. Fer you, two hundred rock bottom, cash today."

The two mountaineers hooted and Lije slapped his gunstock, laughing. "Give you fifty gold," he said.

Cappy protested vehemently, "He ain't wuth it, Lije. Offer 'im forty tops."

Outraged comments on each side filled the air as the three men jockeyed their positions, engaged in their trading sport. They struck a deal at $75 gold, with $40 paid on the spot.

"You ain't gittin' 'im 'til I see the rest o' that coin," Hank warned.

"Don' want 'im now," Cappy said. "We got a buyer comin' through down to Logan. Wagon train boss from Missouri. Pay the rest when we come by." He squinted at the sky and a droll grin softened his dour face. "Satiday after next. Dark o' the moon, jest like last time. Ain't wantin' no folks watchin'."

Hank nodded. "Any time you want, long as you got the coin."

Cappy swung over the creaking rail fence and picked up his rifle. He hitched up his pants as if readying to move on. "You keep 'im here?"

Hank shook his head. "Plenty o' grass comin' on along the ridge. I jest turn 'im out in the high pasture. He'll stick close to the grass and the spring. Nobody see 'im."

Desultory talk persisted while Lije turned from the two and relieved himself. Belting up his pants, he glanced furtively around, then softly asked, "You got any good horses in mind?"

The casual question shocked Hannibal. Here was an open admission of a horsethief ring, operating not just for the mule but one of long standing. Claude would surely be put out. He stole closer through the densely green thicket, worming his way on his belly to just a few feet from the unsuspecting thieves.

Hank spit out his chaw and folded a few new leaves into his mouth. He chewed and rounded the mass. Cappy and Lije waited patiently for their accomplice to make up his mind.

"Claude Shaw bought two matched draft horses last month," Hank said, "along with a heavy wagon. Fixin' to go inter the freightin' business." Bitterness tinged his anger. "He ain't never paid gramps fer them slaves Claudius run off to Ohio back in the war. Weren't neighborly to steal a man's niggers."

It was a tale Hannibal had never heard. Claudius had freed some slaves that Peavey owned? And Claude never said a word? His love for the Shaws bloomed, his heart expanding into a song. Reality sobered him, concentrated his attention on the thieves. What would Hank do, consumed so by hate?

He and Hank's two silent partners waited for Peavey's verdict. "Easy to steal when the moon's dark," Hank said. "Burn his barn too. Josh Minns'll he'p me. You bring two hundred more in gold, we get 'em fer you and throw in the rest fer the mule."

"Done," Lije said. "Take 'em all on your word. Be back during the black dark."

Their procession down the path went slowly. Lije slipped on a slick wet spot, drawing ridicule from the others at his flop on the stones in the well-worn path. Angry swearing floated up to Hannibal, secure in his hideout. He lay there for another hour before moving, waiting until the two visitors rode away from the Peavey house and Hank was inside. Hannibal sneaked his mule over the ridge to the east, directly opposite to his route home. He left plenty of tracks down to a large creek, waded the mule for a mile and left on a rocky spot that bordered the creek trail. Ain't no way they follow, he thought. They'll think the mule broke down those rails. His disgust with Hank's shoddy fencing had led to a perfect escape, with rotten rails kicked to pieces in a bushy corner. He rode the mule in a twenty mile circle, camping out one night, until he struck the headwaters of Little Seven Mile Creek. The last of the meat and cornbread took the edge off his ravenous hunger while he rode the remaining few miles.

Hester hurried out of the cabin at the sound of his hail and the mule's hoof beats, meeting the running Hannibal on the porch. She grabbed him around the chest and squeezed hard. A sniff and she thrust him away. "You been layin' out too long fer me to love," she said. "Go down ter the crik an' git rid of that stink!"

Ignoring her protest, Hannibal set aside his weapons. He swung her up against him just as Aunty Eva came out the door, drying her hands on her flowered apron. She chuckled at the struggling Hester in Hannibal's bear hug, a wild resistance that grew weaker until Hester said, "I love you so."

"I'se hear all dat, Hester," Eva said. "Man can't keep clean when he's out pertectin' you." She punched the limp Hester in the back, interrupting a long kiss. "Got water on stove heatin' an' washtub ready fer de youngun. We scrub Hannibal 'stead."

"No you ain't," Hester retorted. "Ain't nobody touchin' dis man but me. Now you git!"

Granny Eva burst into laughter. She recovered her staff and stomped one-legged down the steps, favoring her left leg. Limping across the yard, she joined Granny Mandy in their porch swing. Amiable chatter drifted across to the lovers until they went into the house.

"Ain't like Hannibal," Granny Mandy said. "He done left the mule tied to dat hitchrail." Her hail brought one of the hands who took the mule to the barn. A few swings later, Granny Eva answered her. "Man ain't thinkin' o' no mule when he got Hester. She makin' sure right now he don't fergit it."

* * *

Claude's fury at the story of the mule and Peavey's plan to steal his new draft horses alarmed Hannibal.

"Don't Claude," he counseled. "Man just got to be forgiving forever."

"Forgiving, hell. I'll shoot them down if they come by." Shaw paced back and forth in his office, his face drawn and his head down, a caged lion penned by emotion and his creed. When his head lifted his jaw was set. "Henry and I and some of the boys'll be here when they come."

"Get Sheriff Bandie," Hannibal said gently. "Let the law catch 'em."

Claude resumed his pacing back and forth across the room. He took a minute this time while the Negro waited. "You think that'll cure 'em?"

"Sho' will, Claude, 'specially when they stand before Judge Marvin. He already warned Wiley Minns once about troublin' you."

Shaw gave in to the argument with ill grace. "Shootin's better," he growled, "but I will get Bandie ... and Henry and the boys. We'll catch them all in the act."

"You're doin' right, Claude. Man got to live by the law. The Bible says 'Thou shalt not kill.' Ain't you killed enough boys in the war?"

As Hannibal's last comment sank in, Claude cringed. Killing boys! He had promised Wood Stephens in his Georgia escape that he would kill no more. But these aren't boys, he thought. They're thieves, all grown men. No matter, his conscience nagged him. They're people you've known since boyhood, friends once. Now they steal, just like they learned in the war. Would you kill them for a horse? His mind turned to the Negro, threatened, his stock run off.

"You be all right, Hannibal?" he asked. "I can arrange for some of the boys to drop by every day. We got plenty live in easy riding distance and they're all strong for law and order."

A warrior showed through the calm of the budding minister. "Done talk to the Lord in the woods, Claude. He say I can walk without fear." His eyes took on a magnetic glow. "Got a ministry to serve, Claude. Preacher Creadey and Letty and Hester are teaching me reading, writing and speaking proper. Read the Bible fer the faith. Built the log church along the creek for baptizing." A deep breath and a hopeful look followed his long speech. "First service next Sunday. Will you come by?"

Claude's heart soared at Hannibal's simple faith. "Gladly," he said, "and with Letty and the children."

That Sunday not only the Shaw family settled on the benches among the blacks but also Henry and several of the 7th Ohio, all with their rifles and sidearms. Hannibal commenced his first sermon with, "Do unto others as you would have others do unto you." A rambling delivery with hesitant pronunciation followed but the powerful voice brought many "Hallelujahs!" After the service, their happy picnic was marred by a few ringing shots in the woods.

* * *

After Claude's friends drifted in to Greenbottom that Saturday afternoon, coming along the river in skiffs rather than in plain sight on the river road, Sheriff Bandie laid down the law in their meeting behind the house.

"Ain't goin'a be no lynchin' boys," Bandie said. "Nor wastin' Judge Marvin's time." He puffed on his pipe and blew out a cloud of smoke. "Judge said to just surround 'em, warn Minns and the Peaveys and send those no-count Jeters packin'."

The group stirred and angry mutterings erupted. Henry protested. "Don't seem right we can't git justice, Sheriff. Been three hosses stole hereabouts last month er so. Hannibal heard 'em says they's stealin'."

Nods and muttering supported him. The group shifted around and a few felt lovingly of their guns and coils of rope. Bandie's fat face reddened and he turned on Henry in a fury. "Damn it, Henry, ain't you got enough of killin'?" He sputtered for a moment. "Judge ain't quibblin' but he's right. We warn 'em this time and send 'em packin'. Tell all the folks in the county. It'll finish that gang."

His uncompromising stand quieted the men. Long past a meal on the lawn, he led the group to the Peavey house in full dark, surrounding the home and the saddled horses at the hitch rail. Clumping up the stairs onto the creaking porch, Bandie met Jubal Peavey at the door and crowded in past him. He, Claude, and Hannibal confronted the four men rising from their chairs around the table. The Sheriff brushed his coat behind his belt gun and faced the men foursquare while Claude and Hannibal separated and raised their rifles. Jubal Peavey shuffled around the posse, squawking loudly at the intrusion.

"Ain't no need fer no trouble, Sheriff. Aint' doin' nuthin'."

Bandie didn't even look at Peavey. His eyes bored into Hank's and he issued his judgement. "Hank," he said bitingly, "You and Minns ain't keepin' good company with those Jeters." He waved down their protests. "Now we know you stole Hannibal's mule." He laughed at their open mouths. "It ain't up in thet high pasture no more."

Hank backed away from the table and slid closer to a rifle standing against the wall. His smouldering face threatened as he said, "Thet nigger's a liar."

"I done seen the tracks," Sheriff Bandie said calmly, "so I know you and the Jeters had 'im. Your boot tracks are all over and they're on Jubal's land around the corral." He shook his head. "Mighty shoddy fence. Busted down in the corner."

Jubal cursed his grandson as he strode up and down wringing his hands. "Ain't you got no sense a'tall, boy. You an' them goin'a git hung."

Bandie went on mercilessly. "You're fixin' to steal Claude's draft hosses tonight too," he said. "Take 'em all to Logan to sell fer wagon trains."

The four men froze, rigidly silent, their faces a study in fear and amazement. The Jeters broke first. "Ain't so, Sheriff," Cappy whined. "Jest visitin' Hank here, playin' a little cards." He fished out a deck and commenced shuffling them.

Josh and Hank shifted nervously and glanced at one another when Henry called, "You need any help, Sheriff? Me an' the others come on in if you want."

Bandie ignored him. His severe tone laid down the law. "We know you been stealin' hosses but Judge Marvin appreciates you boys all been in the war. He allows eighteen sixty six ain't no more war times, with its foragin', and you boys got to accept that."

Lige lunged toward his rifle and the Sheriff pulled and aimed his pistol. "Hold up there," Bandie shouted. The cowed thieves bunched back together. "Judge says to warn you off and tell folks all along the river. Next time it's a bullet or the rope."

The tension was broken by Jubal. He gathered up the Jeter's weapons and threw them out the front door. They clattered on the porch boards and bounced on down the steps. "Git," he shouted at the Logan men. "You come here agin', I shoot you myself."

When Bandie nodded, Cappy and Lije ran out of the room. Scuffling noises outside were followed by curses from Henry and his patrol. Rapidly diminishing hoofbeats faded into the night.

The Sheriff turned his attention to Jubal. "You got anything to say?"

"I ain't no thief!"

"I know you ain't," Bandie replied. "We been friends nigh on to forty year. But we can't allow no thievin' by Hank here." His voice turned into a pleading softness. "My God, Jubal, I done knowed Hank since he was a baby. I don't want to hev to hang 'im or shoot 'im."

Joshua Minns and Hank settled back down into their chairs and Hank's face took on a contemptuous smirk.

"Ain't got the guts?" Hank said insolently.

Old Jubal backhanded his grandson with all his strength, a blow that started the blood spurting. Hank's hands flew to his face, rapidly crimsoned by his mashed nose. He jumped up screaming wildly, aiming for his rifle against the wall.

"I'll kill you, Gramps," he shrieked. Yelling oaths, he struggled with Claude and Hannibal, fighting off their clutching fingers with wild madness. At the Sheriff's call, Henry and two men ran in and tackled the gyrating threesome, striking a blow that sent the entire mob crashing to the floor. Hank bit, kicked, swung his fists, cursing all the while. Their strength conquered his body but not his hate, his mouth spewing threats. When they finally hauled him to his feet before Bandie, he was gasping but unbowed. His scorn cast fire on Joshua, settled quietly in a chair under the watchful eyes of their captors.

"Why ain't you he'pin'?" he yelled. Veins bulged in his neck and his face corded as he surged against his captors and screamed wildly, "You yeller bastard!"

Sheriff Bandie answered. "He ain't wantin' to git shot, boy." Grabbing a shirt hanging on the back of a chair, he dipped it into the water bucket beside the fireplace and wiped off Hank's face while the man strained aginst the tight grips on his arms. Reddish drops flew as Bandie both cooled and cleaned Hank's hurts. His calm voice quieted the struggling man.

"I ain't wantin' to hurt you, son. You an' me done fished together when you was a boy and ate a lot of sidemeat and cornbread at this very table. Yore daddy and I was raised close, hunted and fished, camped together." His melancholy deepened. "But he got kilt at Cedar Creek an' now they's only Jubal and me to guide you."

"Don't want none of you ner him neither," Hank spit out. His gasps and protest resumed. "Only want ter be left alone."

Bandie went on remorselessly. "Can't do no more stealin', boy. Ain't no war no more." He brushed his fingers across his eyes and blew his nose on a bandanna. "You and Jubal got a good farm here. Make money if you work your land and tend them hogs turned out to the mast."

Henry started and stepped back when Minns rose to his feet. A pistol appeared in Henry's hand as if by magic. "Where you goin'?" he said. "Sheriff ain't finished yet."

Joshua's sidling walk to one side took him toward the door. He ignored Henry's pistol, his eyes fixed on Sheriff Bandie. "You fixin' to arrest me now?" he asked. "If you ain't, I'm leavin'."

"Git," Bandie said. "You tell Wiley 'bout this." Henry stopped Minns at the Sheriff's motion. "You tell him we ain't puttin' up with no Minns' shenanigans, no kind, no way."

"I'll tell him," Joshua said coolly. "But I ain't sure he figures on you tellin' him what to do." Turning on his heel he walked out before Bandie could answer.

An hour later, after the posse had left, Hank sat by the fire, warming his feet and holding a cloth to his nose, all the while complaining. "You ain't needin' ter hit me so hard."

"Fer yer own good, boy," Peavey replied. "Had ter git that Bandie off yer back."

"I know," Hank said resignedly. He blew coagulated blood from his nose into a reddened cloth. "I ain't holdin' it agin you." He settled into a quiet that lasted until they both went to bed.

* * *

The September day sweltered, a hot sky adding to a moist air that suffocated. Hester's baby cried and cried until she took it up and cuddled it to her breast. Rocking and crooning settled the little child into sleep, sweat beading its brow. Hester's toes kept up the beat even as she dozed in the oak chair, gradually wetting her own dress with the small exertion.

A door slammed across the yard and loud voices woke her. She clutched her son to her breast, alarmed until she saw Granny Eva hurrying to her with her cane and limp. Barking dogs chased after Elsie and a strange Negro man followed along behind. Granny settled into the other rocker with a thud after clumping up the creaking steps.

Eva waggled her stick at Elsie and the man, stopped at the foot of the steps. "Com'on up, Elsie," she ordered. "If you fixin' ter leave, you orta 'least tell Hester why. Been eatin' Hannibal's bread long 'nough."

The two sidled up the steps and tiptoed to Hester's

chair. Elsie spoke in a whisper while bent over the baby. "Dis here's Tandy Russell, Hester."

The small, roly-poly negro flashed a huge grin with white teeth in a dark skin. He doffed an old derby hat, brown with dust. "Howdy, Hester. Elsie mighty sweet on you. Say your cookin' de best."

"You fixin' on settin' up?" Hester asked.

Elsie stiffened, combative. "So what if we is?"

Hester's stern face cowed the girl, who shrank back against Tandy. Eva chuckled at the sight of the two hens faced off against each other, Hester in a silent rage, Elsie trying to hide behind the bulk of her man.

"Hannibal ain't gwine like you two goin' 'thout marryin'." Granny said.

"Exactly," Hester seconded. "Man needs a wife, not no woman." She fixed on Elsie. "All Hannibal an' Claude done fer you, you ain't goin' less Preacher Creadey tie de knot. Keep dat Tandy from leavin' you."

Tandy scowled. He faced up to Hester, almost as tall as she, and upbraided her. "I'se got job, woman. Don't want no other than Elsie. I marry her any time you say."

A tense two hours of argument later, Hannibal returned and sorted out the controversy. Retrieving his Bible, he married the two on the porch in front of Eva, Hester and God, intoning the simple religious service that Reverend Creadey had taught him. On conclusion, he blessed his first couple joined together, leaving the hugs and kisses and tears to the women.

"Wait," he said, and went into the house, while Elsie collected some things from the granny cabin. A few minutes later Hannibal reemerged with a sheet of paper, a marriage certificate provided by the Reverend Creadey. Elsie cried when she saw the beautiful scrollwork and engravings and the flowing handwriting Hannibal had labored over.

"Dis really say we married?" she asked.

"Sho' do," Hannibal said. He read it off to her and to Tandy, pointing out the meaning. Hannibal handed it over to Elsie, saying, "You frame this and keep it in the living room of your house in Gallipolis. It tells ever'one Tandy Russell and Elsie Shaw is man and wife."

Tandy fidgeted about the porch. "Ain't got no money ter pay wid, Hannibal." He held out his hand and gripped Hannibal's tightly. Looking the minister in the eye, he said, "I he'p wid your harvest when you want."

Hannibal nodded. "Thank you, brother; I'll send word. But Elsie ain't goin' off without a present." He held out a $5 gold piece removed from his Bible. "Save this," he said, "for a tight time."

Elsie's tears gushed as she took the piece and thanked him. From her embrace, Hannibal fixed his piercing gaze on Tandy. "Those Peavey's and Minns likely try to do dirt to Claude and to me. You keep an eye on 'em in Gallipolis for me? Send word?"

Tandy smiled and nodded. "Sho' do dat, Hannibal." He whipped out a long-bladed knife from a sheath at his back and swung it around in the air. "I a good fighter, too. He'p if dey come on you."

Elsie and her new husband took Hannibal's buggy and a hand with them when they left Little Seven Mile for Gallipolis. They went with Eva's shouts and Hester's blessings and a quilt of Granny Mandy's. But Hannibal just waved and smiled silently, reassured by having a spy to help him against the Minns and their allies.

* * *

Granny Mandy and Eva were on their porch smoking their pipes when Claude and Letty came to visit the next Sunday afternoon. Their quiet time extended to a swinging somnolence, only occasional grunts and shifts extending their earlier agreement to help the young folks as their children were born.

"Dey ain't got much common sense when it come to chil'ren," Mandy said.

Eva laughed. "Sho' different fum my day. Hester even got

a stove. Make all dat washin' easier wid de hot water."

They lapsed into silence and dozed as the sun dropped toward the tops of the western hills. Leaves on the walnuts had turned, acompanying the browning of the sycamores and black locusts. It was a time before the cold slid into the fall, Indian Summer weather. Sight of a buggy up the creek road revived them and they sat up. Eva waved as it turned into the lane and came on to the main house.

"Halloo, Grannies," Claude hollered as Letty waved her handkerchief.

He had hardly tied off the team and gotten settled with the women on the porch of Hannibal's house when two silent riders galloped into the lane. Hank and Joshua slid off their horses and faced the group. With his belt gun showing, Claude placed himself at the top of the steps.

"You got business here?" he gruffly asked.

Stony faces stared back, silent until Joshua opened up. "You didn't have no call ter sick Sheriff Bandie on us last May, Shaw." His injured tone deepened into hate. "Me an' Hank been up an' down the river the whole of the last two months. Ever'body thinks we's thieves. Won't do no business tradin', ner anythin' else."

"Maybe you ought to try honest work," Claude said, "and your uncle too."

Joshua turned red and quivered, his right hand inching toward his coat pocket. He sputtered and shook but his hand remained exposed when Claude drew his pistol and pointed it at him. Their stand-off shifted at the sound of another buggy. Hannibal jumped down even before it stopped rolling. He dragged a double barreled shotgun from the seat and cocked it as he strode off to the side of the visitors.

"You needin' any help, Claude?" he said politely. The two big bores of the shotgun swung back and forth between Hank and Joshua.

"No," Claude replied. "They are just leaving." He waved them to their horses. "Now boys," he said coldly, "you leave Hannibal and his folks alone. If you come after me or him, you'll fight the whole Seventh Ohio. Just you remember that."

Hannibal gestured with the shotgun. Only malevolent glances were returned as the men mounted and rode out. They went at a walk to the road, then spurred into a gallop with a screeching rebel yell and shouted threats.

"We goin'a have to kill 'em," Claude said. His face clouded. "Wonder why they waited all this time to brace me?"

"Dey said dey ain't got no work ner nothing," Eva replied. "You de the reason nobody trade wid 'em."

Letty paled and her voice trembled. "You reckon they mean it?"

A soothing preacher's voice answered her. "They won't cause no harm, Letty. They know they git kilt."

A gloomy Claude shook his head. "I see black times, Hannibal." He trembled and his voice quivered but then hardened into a threat. "They come after any of us, we fight."

Hannibal shook his head. "I hope they don't," he said. His shoulders shook with a big sigh. "I don't want to kill again. The war was enough and the Holy Bible says, 'Thou shalt not kill.' Can't be no minister and be killin' folks."

* * *

"You git all that gold in the bank?" Joshua asked.

Wiley Minns took a long pull at his tankard. He wiped the foam from his moustache and belched. "Put another thousand in the Valley Bank and a thousand here." He laughed. "You should'a seen Abel House's eyes when I dribbled that gold onto his desk. Gleamed like a deer's in a jacklight."

"How about the other bank in Point Pleasant?" Joshua asked. "Old Cranker want yer money jest as bad?"

Minns swung around on his bench and furtively inspected the clientele of his tavern. A few men played cards at a table near the door and another clutched his tankard and snored on a corner bench. The dim light from the gimballed hanging lamps shone on the smoky air like fog, with edges and corners blurred into indistinct shapes. A slide around to Joshua brought his head close to his nephew's.

"Jet Cranker ain't honest," he whispered. "He and me goin'a do a few deals."

Joshua laughed. "I swear, Unk," he said. "I don' know how you figure 'em out. Git some help ever'where we go."

Minns tapped his head with his forefinger. "After all thet Bible study, boy, an' wrestlin' with the congregation and old Satan, it jest is easy. Fear of going to hell allus handy for folks, he'p me good."

"But Cranker is a banker," Joshua protested. "He don' do right fer his neighbors, they tar and feather 'im."

Wiley shook his head. "You're wrong, boy. Bankers steal more than any other. An' old Jet ain't no different."

Joshua hollered at the barmaid for another tankard for the two. He tossed her a coin when she set two foaming containers before them and took the others. A quick swig preceded a relaxed belch, "God," he said, "that's good."

"Don't you use the Lord's name in vain, boy," Wiley said. "It ain't right."

Joshua chuckled at the sudden change in his uncle. "You preachin', Unk?" he asked slyly. When Wiley raised his mug instead, Joshua rocked back in his seat and laughed.

"What's wrong with a little humility?" Wiley said witheringly.

"Unk," Joshua said solemnly, "you got more gall than a turkey cock. Here you was tellin' me yestiday about buyin' that land bordering Shaw down river so's to crowd 'im. Now you're preachin' agin." He chortled. "Humble ain't your strong suit. When the Lord handed out snake oil he gave you plenty."

Wiley's evil grin bared his teeth. "It just goes to show, boy, that there's more than one way to skin a cat. Old Jet 'bout fell over when I offered fifteen hundred for that last little piece at the spit. Couldn't sign the papers fast enough. He don' know it's jest the right place for a landin'."

"A landin'?" Joshua asked.

"Yep," Minns replied. "Finally got all of thet hooking point into the river. My landin' there'll block the Evangeline right good when it heads for Shaw's. Drive it onto the shoal without he's extra careful."

Joshua nodded and slowly smiled. "Who you fixin' to manage the place?"

"Fred Baukey," Wiley said. He took in another swallow. "He'll do anything I want if I flash enough coin."

A few swallows later, Joshua whispered, "You git thet end of the road piece over by Crown City?"

"No, but I ain't stoppin' there. Two more handy to Shaw's business I been prospectin'. And some of them men around there ain't too fond of Shaw."

"Why not?"

"He ain't givin' 'em credit like afore the war. Seems he ain't got the cash to carry 'em." His face lightened and a grin bared his large incisors. "Just waitin' to take a bite out of 'im. Those neighbors will help for a few coins. Gold gits 'em all."

Joshua laughed uproariously. "You're an old fox, Unk." He winked. "If you ain't the most weasely man I ever met. You're even better'n some of them foragers in the war."

His uncle smiled and leaned back, patting his ample stomach. "Got the gift, boy. Man got a gift, even for weaselin' ways, he better use it."

A hard-eyed Joshua stared at him, his face chiseled in stone. Anger tinged his reply. "I just want to kill 'im fer Pa and the boys, ... git even."

"You will," Wiley replied. "You got my word on it."

* * *

Claude's smile deepened as he read the name to Letty. "It's a letter from Clarke Stephens," he said. "Wonder how he's been?"

Tearing open the envelope, he read the rough handwriting. "His leg don't hurt anymore," he told Letty. "Just a little limp.

Letty's "Thank the Lord," and hands clasped as in prayer echoed his "Wonderful!" Claude went on, "He wants to come visit next spring."

"Invite him," Letty urged. "Kittie Mae needs to see some good boys now. He and the Abert's son would fit right nice."

"Done," Claude said, smiling. "But don't you forget Joe. He and Kittie Mae been playing together since they were little."

15

Hank Peavey leaned over the plank table in the Bull's Head Tavern, his rank whiskey breaths rolling over Wiley Minns. The fat man grimaced and shied back.

"Ain't you had enough of that, Hank? You smell like a rotten whiskey barrel."

Hank laughed and belched, an aroma of sour stomach repelling Wiley.

"Damn you, Hank," Minns said, "you ain't worth nothin' when you're drunked up like this." A whine crept in. "We got to plan, boy. Can't spend all our days in this tavern."

Joshua swept the mugs away from the drunken Peavey. The barmaid screeched and jumped at the shattering clatter. Joshua hauled Hank to his feet and propelled him to the door. Hank wrestled against the hard grip, swore, tried to kick and yanked back but his powerful bouncer just lifted and dragged his feet along. Throwing Hank out the door, Joshua paused but a moment. With his uncle egging him on, he seized Hank and partly dragged, but mostly walked him down the clayey slope to the river. A mighty splash followed, one drowned out by the cheers of the patrons lined up along the shore.

"Good riddance!" Lennie shouted.

"River'll make him smell better," said another, before pulling on his tankard.

They drifted back up to the tavern, joshing, while Hank

waded out of the river. He shook his tangled mane and sat down. Pulling off his boots amid a running invective, he dumped the water out of both and laid back on the sloping ground.

"Ow!" he hollered. Sitting up, he reached behind him and pulled up a stone. Throwing it into the river, he lay back down, with Wiley and Joshua standing over him.

"You know, Wiley," he said reflectively, "old Josh there ain't much of a rough an' tumble." He chuckled. "I git on my feet, I do the same to him." Tickled, he laughed, then howled, rolling around.

Wiley nudged him with a boot toe. "You sober enough to plan, boy?"

"Sure be," Hank answered. With a roll and a crouch, he jumped at Joshua and tackled him in the middle. They yelled and struggled and strained while Lennie and the boys ran out and whooped up the new fight. It ended with both in the river. Dripping, they stood knee-deep in the water and shook hands. When both rejoined Wiley, their faces were peaceful, with clear eyes ready for serious work.

A night later, the plan was ready. Lennie and the boys had joined them at Wiley's invitation when Charles Searle strode in. At a snap of his fingers, the barmaid brought a mug of beer to his seat at the table.

"Took some doin', Wiley, but I'm here." At Minns' puzzled look, he added, "Been sent to contract that stand of poplar up on Paw Paw Crik. Jest passin' through and figured to report in."

"How's Shaw doin'," Wiley asked.

"Overextended, I figure."

Minns' eyes gleamed and he struck his beefy fist into his left palm. A loud splat preceded, "about to git 'im this time."

Joshua coughed and spit. "Ain't too sure, Unk. Thet damned Shaw got nine lives, jest like a cat. Knowed ever'thing we done afore."

Wiley looked furtively about. Except for the barmaid, no one was near except an old Negro swamper with his broom. Wiley bent closer and kept his voice soft. "We take over his loans, ever'place we can." He swigged some beer and belched. "Best we buy that timber too, before Charles gits there."

The group fell silent, it's attention settled on the beer and Minns' plan to directly interfere with Shaw's timbering. Searle broke the silence.

"Claude be mighty mad," he said. "Won't stand fer that,"....he frowned..., "How you figuring on delayin' me? I'm up on a good hoss and plan to start at daylight."

Minns laughed. "Accidents happen, Charles. Might even find your hoss done hurt a leg in the stall, all those loose poles."

"No!" Searle boomed out as he jumped off the bench. "You ain't doin' no hurt to Paint." He paced to the fire and faced them with his coat drawn back, his pistol exposed.

Minns stiffened, the angry young Confederate an immediate threat to his person and his plans. He raised both hands palm out. "Ain't goin'a do it, Charles," he said calmly, unctuously adding, "I swear boy, you sure are touchy. We ain't even got to the real part yet and you're ready to shoot me jest fer talkin'."

An hour of sharp rejoinder finally settled the matter. "I'll go down the river to Burlington," Minns said. "Heard from Jubal's friend there that Claude's got some notes at the bank."

"Lots o' niggers at Burlington," Hank said. "Hannibal there couple months back, preachin'. You be careful they don' hear .... jest like tellin' 'im."

"Where they mostly from?" Minns asked, "Kentucky?"

"All over," Hank told him. "Big underground railroad stop before the war." He swore, bitterness crumpling his face. "That damned Claudius took our Peavey niggers there in sixty four. Freed 'em!"

Minns dismissed the irritation with a wave of his hand. "Don't matter now. I'll buy all Shaw's paper I can get, but private like. Heard the banker there could use some coin right now. He's short."

"Where you gittin' this from, Unk?" Joshua asked.

Wiley's mouth and cheeks twisted into a sneaky grin. "Never you mind boy...but I tell you one thing...nothin' like a gold coin to open mouths."

Josh laughed and Hank slapped his thigh. They rocked back on the bench so hard it tipped over and spilled them and their beer onto the floor. The two lay flat, laughing hard as the barmaid walked over and picked up the mugs.

"You boys had enough?" she asked.

"Two more!" they shouted together.

Once on the upright seat, Hank swigged and spoke. "You know, Wiley, Hannibal takin' a wagonload of truck to Gallipolis soon. Me an' Josh'll drift down with the boys and try them again. Ain't likely Claude'll be handy this time."

Josh nodded and glanced at Lennie and his friends. "You got horses, boys?"

"Sure do," Lennie replied, seconded by the others.

"But what about the timber?" Searle interjected.

"I'll send Lennie to see Trumbull," Minns explained. "Give 'im the contract and gold coin fer it. How much is the timber worth?"

"Twenty two hundred on the stump," Searle said. "Claude cruised that piece hisself. You got that much handy?"

Minns laughed. "You ain't never done much business, have you boy?" He chuckled. "I'll offer him twelve hundred cash. When those gold coins flash and clink in his hand, he'll take it."

Searle shook his head. "Doubt thet. Claude talked to old man Trumbull right smart. I was there when he done it. Trumbull's cagy and he warn't agreein' to no less. Stubborn!"

"You watch, boy," Minns replied.

He laboriously wrote out the contract while the others talked and refilled their mugs. When Lennie had the contract in his pocket and his instructions memorized, Minns opened his money belt and counted out sixty gold pieces, stilling their chatter. Sharp intakes of breath shattered the deep quiet as the men stared covetously at the glinting coins.

Minns crashing blow to the table broke the spell. "You better come back, Lennie," he said ominously, "with that signed contract. You don't, I'll send Josh for you. He never loses a trail."

"I'll be back," Lennie said, but he trembled when he pocketed the heavy packet of coins Wiley Minns handed him and glanced at the frowning Joshua.

"Git," Minns ordered. "Charles ain't leavin' 'til morning but you're goin' now. You'll meet him coming back."

Searle's heart flipflopped. By golly, it had worked! Claude was right. Let Minns have that poplar. No way to git it to the river in time and Trumbull will be in Claude's debt for the sale. He exulted, rememberin' Trumbull's laugh when Claude hatched the plan with him. Old Minns, the connivin' sucker, didn't know Claude and Trumbull had soldiered together. Payin' a good six hundred more than it was worth! Wait 'til I tell Claude!

Charles stretched and yawned. "I got to git on early, Wiley." He drained his mug and rose from the bench. "Turnin' in."

"Don't start too soon, boy," Minns said.

Searle grinned. "I won't," he promised.

Another hour of whispering settled the raiding plan with Hank and Josh. They would drop down to Hannibal's place in a few days with the tavern boys.

* * *

Hannibal and his family were visiting Claude and Letty when the Peavey's with their cohorts and Joshua Minns rode from Point Pleasant to burn out the Negroes. Searles had arrived a day earlier, having met Lennie and turned back from his ride to Trumbull's.

"Ain't no use," Lennie had told him at the steep trail junction turning into sharp vee of the Paw Paw Creek hollow. "Trumbull snapped up that gold, jest like Wiley said." He slapped his pocket. "Got the signed contract right here."

"I'll be gittin' back to see Shaw, then," Searles had replied. "He'll be mighty disappointed."

Lennie chortled. "Don' matter. Wiley owns that poplar stand. And they's some big walnuts mixed in along the creek," he said with satisfaction. "Shaw cain't do nuthin'."

Searle had nodded and had ridden hard for Greenbottom. He had passed no one on the river road and the track of Hank's horse's bent off shoe had not speckled the trail. Arriving with a lathered horse, Claude had met him at the Greenbottom barn. With the steaming animal relegated to a hand for a cooling walk and rubdown, Claude and Searles had sauntered off into the fields to insure that Letty didn't hear.

"Minns took the bait," Searle reported, once they were well into the lane to the river. "Bought it for twelve hundred gold."

Claude roared with laughter. His joy brought tears to his eyes, wiped quickly with the back of a hand. "Bill 'll be mighty happy with all that coin."

Searle chuckled but then turned serious. "Wiley be hoppin' mad when he sees them sharp slopes. Won't take him long to figure there won't be enough flood water in that crik in the spring to float all the logs. High but don't last."

"Can't matter then," Claude said. "Too late."

He pulled out a cigar and handed it to Charles. After they both had lighted up and puffed to glowing ends, he leaned against a fence rail and blew out a smoke puff. "Minns wants to raft up wirh anybody in the spring, he'll have to drag 'em to the river through all that snow and ice." Another puff and a chuckle later, "I can hear 'im swearin'."

"Didn't see Trumbull, Captain, but he sent me a message by that old swamper in the Bull's Head. Said he'd be down this winter to talk about a coal seam he found after a slide."

Claude whistled. "That's good news if it's any size."

"He said it'd mostly average four feet. Good long seam an' easy to bring a spur or lane to."

Silence greeted Searle's staggering announcement of the great riches underground. Ever practical, Claude said, "It'll make our fortunes, Charles. I'll help Bill with the financing and will give you a share of mine. Money'll help you get that farm you been talkin' 'bout."

Searle let out an "Aw, Claude," and choked up. He wrung

the merchant's strong hand and got out an, "I'm in your debt."

Their locked stares and grips solidified the bond. The intense moment eased when Searle cautioned, "You better git it tied up with Trumbull afore Wiley hears. He'll be after the mineral too."

"I'll go up next week. Take Judge Marvin with me and get the paper done." Claude puffed a few times, in deep thought. "Good time to ask Bill down and to bring his family. His girl's right pretty and about Claudius's age."

"How'll you do the freight'n?"

"Wagon or a spur to barges on the river. You can handle all the freight business. We can set up a hauling company. Go havers."

Searle nodded but his face wore a grim set. "Appreciate that, Captain. I'll do my best." He fidgeted a moment. "They's something else....serious."

"What's that?"

"Josh and Hank and the tavern boys....you know that shiftless Lennie and the friends he runs with...they'll be on their way to Hannibal's again."

Claude swore and struck a post with his fist. He paced around, puffing furiously, muttering, "Bastards didn't learn nothin' the first time." His head swiveled to his lieutenant, "Minns with 'em?"

"No. He's goin' to Burlington to buy up your notes with the banker there. Said the bank needed coin or it'd go under."

A wolfish, triumphant grin distorted Claude's face. "Hallelujah!" he cried. "Old Wiley heard that story I planted." He laughed. "It's not true. The Burlington bank's solid as a rock."

"Ain't you worried 'bout your paper?" Searle asked.

"No! Old Wiley's been suckered. He don't know that Cal bought up the notes and signed them over to me. They're against a new steamboat we're building next year, if we can finance it. Minns got a hard trip for nothin'."

"Good" and a grin preceded a fine smoke ring from Searle. "Now what about Hank?"

"I'll send Isaiah for Henry and the boys. Plan on six days out." After a few more exchanges they hurried toward the house.

* * *

Hannibal rode with Claude, Henry, and his twelve troopers of the 7th Ohio when they headed for Little Seven Mile. Hester had wailed but Hannibal was adamant. She and the rest of the women would stay at Greenbottom while the men settled the issue. He insisted on a prayer before leaving. His sonorous voice rolled out over the heavily armed force, calling on his God for success in their mission. But he did not forget his ministry. A last part of the prayer asked his God for forgivness on Hank and his wayward friends, and to lead them into righteous ways.

The troopers were hidden around the buildings and sheds at Little Seven Mile when Josh and Hank rode in. A burnished sun showed through the brassy haze that presaged a storm. Only three tavern rowdys accompanied the raiders that afternoon, with its oppressive, ominous sky. Uncaring about the weather warning, the raiders' first act was to hooraw the homestead, firing into the buildings as they wheeled and turned their horses. Beyond the crowing of a lone rooster, deep silence was their only answer.

Hank's drunken shout, "Ain't nobody hyar?" was followed by more pistol shots into Hannibal's porch.

Silence reigned as the five men bunched. "Where'd you git that popskull, Hank?" one complained, reeling in the saddle. "My head's 'bout to split open."

"Good whiskey, boys," Hank replied. "You cain't swaller thet, you ain't much o' no man."

His scornful tone was answered by another raider spurring for the creek. When the man slid out of the saddle, he flopped on the bank and dunked his head. A moment of submersion was followed by vomiting and swearing and more soaking in the creek. When he raised and shook his head like a dog, scattering droplets from his long hair and beard, he screeched at Hank, "You lyin' bastard! Thet's the worst likker I ever drunk!"

Hank instantly pulled his other belt pistol and fired at the man. His bullet missed the rump and legs, the only parts visible as the raider again dipped his head in the creek.

Interruption of Hank's deliberate aim came from Joshua. He spurred his horse against Hank's and grabbed his gun hand. "Ain't gitten nothin' done this way. Let's burn the buildings and move on. Kill any niggers as run out."

They were bunched when Claude and Hannibal stalked to a stop in front of the group. Hank laughed at the two, both armed, and spit out, "Well lookee here, the two nigger brothers."

With a running jump, Claude seized Hank and wrested him from the saddle. As they thrashed about on the ground, Joshua and the raiders drew off, aiming their pistols but watching Hannibal. Their heads swiveled when clicks sounded and Claude's troopers surrounded the mounted men.

"Now you jest sit there proper," Henry said. Picking out two troopers, he ordered, "Fred, you and Cab fetch the other one from the crik."

Two men obediently split off and herded the sick man to the group. He reeled in his saddle, alternately holding his head and cursing Hank.

Peavey flailed away but he was no match for the enraged Claude, a madman damning Hank's soul to hell even as he pounded and choked him into submission. When Peavey lay on the ground unconscious, Claude rose and unsteadily faced the others, his chest heaving. His shirt scattered in tatters about his feet, with red spots and abrasions on his muscular white frame and tanned face testifying to the severity of the fight.

"Get a bucket of water, Hannibal," he said.

When Hannnibal brought it, he threw it over Hank's body and head. Peavey choked and spit as he rolled around and sat up. Another bucket revived him to full alert, erect and covered with mud.

Claude stuck his face next to Peavey's, his words biting. "You ain't livin' this time, Hank. We're goin' to hang you right here."

"You can't do thet!" Hank screamed. "You an' me been friends, neighbors." He stared a long moment into Claude's menacing scowl. "It ain't legal," he shouted frantically. "You can't!"

"Take all their guns, boys," Henry said.

With the raiders disarmed and surrounded, Henry's men pulled thongs from their kits and bound the raiders' hands behind them. Working in silence, they herded the five toward the large walnuts bordering the creek. A few minutes later all five sat their horses with nooses around their necks and ropes over large tree limbs.

Claude's brusk, "You got anything to say before we hang you?" created pandemonium.

Piteous cries and lamentations broke from the tavern rowdies, and a din of protests. Hank just spit while Joshua's contempt bathed them all. "You ain't never seen no dyin'?" he asked. "Men only die once. Don't matter how or when your time comes."

"I'll bless them," Hannibal said, "before we do it. Even the fallen deserve no less."

Hoofbeats sounded up the creek road, growing louder as they arrived at the hogback with the pine thicket. The horsemen came into view just as Hannibal got to "Our Father,.." Sheriff Bandie and two deputies trotted their mounts along the rutted road, coming by Hannibal's little church, and pulled up at the grim scene.

"What's goin' on?" he demanded in a severe voice. "You got a lynch mob here?"

Claude shook his head. "Just keepin' some skunks from killin' Hannibal and burning out his place. Heard they was comin' and got here first with Henry and his boys." He rubbed his bare chest. "Hank here and I set to a bit before they gave up."

The Sheriff looked at him suspiciously, meantime having his ears filled with complaints by the raiders. "You willing to swear out a warrant, Hannibal?" He glanced at the complaining raiders. "They come to kill you and burn you out?"

Hannibal nodded. "I will do that, but it grieves my heart to do so, even though we warned 'em once. I was praying for these boys' souls and their conversion from their evil ways when you come up."

"I saw your Bible open," Bandie said gently.

"Him an' Claude was goin'a hang us," Joshua said scornfully. "Ask that hypocrite about that. Him openin' thet Bible don' mean nothin'."

Sheriff Bandie turned red, his anger explosive. "You shedup, you no-good tramp. I fought on your side but I ain't puttin' up with no lies. Hannibal's a minister an' preaches the Gospel. I heard 'im myself."

With Hannibal remaining at his farm, Bandie took the five raiders into custody and herded them down the creek to the river road. Claude and the troopers flanked as an escort. They stopped by Jubal Peavey's, waking the old man.

Jubal wrung his hands at the sight of the bound men. "My God, boy, you in more trouble?"

"'bout to git hung," Hank replied, "hadn't been fer Sheriff Bandie driftin' by. Claude an' his boys fixin' to do us."

"Why? How come your face so swole?"

Claude pushed forward, his bare top a revolting sight. Peavey stared, his mouth open. He cringed at the planter's clipped words.

"They were fixin' to kill Hannibal and burn all the Little Seven Mile farm, Jubal. We warned you and the others once." He sighed. "Can't have them roaming with killin' on their minds. I'm swearing out a complaint."

"They'll be in jail 'til they see Judge Marvin," Bandie told Peavey. "You want a lawyer for Hank, you scout one up."

Old Jubal's jaw hardened and he straightened up. Pointing a long bony arm and finger at Hank, he intoned, "You done it this time, boy, after I warned you. You git outen this yourself." Turning on his heel he went back into the house.

The force split up, with Claude to Greenbottom and the troopers heading home, carrying all the raiders' arms. "I'll see you day after tomorrow," Claude said to Bandie. "Draw up the warrant and complaint."

The Sheriff nodded and led his party up the river road.

Three days later, they were smiling when Claude sat in the straight chair next to Bandie's desk and finished signing the documents against the raiders.

"I swear, Seph," Claude told him. "I didn't think you'd get there on time. Thought I'd have to hang 'em."

"Good thing Hannibal came up with the prayer. Took Claudius a piece to find me an' fetch me down the road."

Claude burst into laughter and wiped his eyes. "That was a caution, wasn't it. He's one smart minister."

"You be careful," Bandie warned. He leaned over and spoke in a low voice. "Wiley is gettin' powerful friends 'long as he pays gold. Been spreadin' it around ever since he come here."

A nod and Claude said, "You know I got friends all around, Seph. They been warnin' me." His somber face fit the next piece of evidence disclosed. "Josh is the mean one. He wants to kill me now but Minns won't hear of it. Keep track of him for all our sakes."

"I'll do that, Claude. Put out a caution' ever'where, more than your boys of the Seventh Ohio."

A quick handshake finished the visit, with Bandie seeing Claude to his horse, his belt gun prominently in view and a deputy off to the side with a shotgun.

* * *

The Negroes went back to Little Seven Mile two days later when Hannibal came with the wagon. Hester rushed into the lane at the squeaking and threw herself into his arms when he stepped down.

Wailing, she said, "You all right, Hannibal? I worried sick." She caressed his stubbly cheek, and pulled his lips down to hers.

He held her close while she sobbed. "No reason to worry,"

he said gently. “Lord done come to me again in a vision last night. I ain’t never gonna be kilt.” His face took on a glow as he raised his gaze to the sky.

On the porch, Letty nudged Claude and whispered. “You see that! He’s blessed, just like Preacher Creadey told you.”

“I gave him a new six shot Colt,” Claude replied. “I also praise the Lord but a bullet may be necessary.”

Letty’s sharp intake of breath accompanied Hannibal’s, “Lord told me I’m to be a fine preacher, he’pin’, bringing the word. Ain’t no trouble to touch us.”

Hester squeezed him adoringly. “Let’s go home, love. No reason to bother Letty no more.”

The party and their traps were soon in the wagon. Claudius accompanied them with a belt gun and rifle when they rolled down the river road toward Little Seven Mile. He had insisted on going, his young face serious as he faced down Letty’s fears.

“Don’t hold with those Minns, Ma. Nor Hank. I freed those Peavey slaves and I’m growed enough to help Hannibal. I’ll be back when they’re safe home.”

He waved to his parents before disappearing around the sharp sidehill at the bend. Letty clutched Claude and wept.

“Don’t you worry, Letty,” Claude told her. “He’s comin’ on a man.” But his heart trembled at the danger to his older boy.

16

An unusually warm winter brought rain instead of snow before Christmas. Claude stamped in one night from his carriage, leaving Isaiah to take the team to the barn. Flinging his coat onto the halltree, he doffed his campaign hat with its dripping wide brim as Letty's tapping heels grew closer.

"My heavens, Claude." she said with a grimace, "you're trackin' in all that mud and water." She called to the maid to bring a mop and pulled a small rug away, leaving his boots on the bare hardwood. Inspecting him, her distaste produced a sharp order. "You get right back onto the porch and take off those boots! No reason to have all that mud in here."

He sheepishly walked through the doorway and cleaned his boots on the scraper. A pull at each liberated his feet, his one-legged, unbalanced stance drawing a giggle. Claude threw the boots down next to the wall and and stepped over the threshold, pleading, "Get me a towel. Don't want to stand in the wet and catch pneumonia."

Letty tossed him the tiny rug instead. "Use this. It needs washin' and sprucing up."

The rug provided a stepping stone to another farther on. By then the maid had a mop at work, cleaning the stains.

"When you're done, Jennie," Lettie said, "take Captain Shaw's boots down to the kitchen for drying. Tell Isaiah to have them polished up when they're dry."

"Yessum," the maid replied.

Greenbottom, festively decorated and enjoying the on-rushing Christmas Season, was a mecca for a host of visitors following the heavy rains. Abel House and Judge Marvin called the week after and stayed the night in the guest cabin Claude had erected the second year after his return from the War. It fronted on the side lawn, a low, shingled dwelling under the shade of a towering poplar, with a wide porch with rocking chairs. Claude had struck the massive trunk with his hand when the site was chosen, saying, "It's been here two hundred years, I recken. With those roots and overhang should shield the cabin good."

"You're right, Claude," Ian McLellan had said. "Now get Hannibal and Preacher Creadey to bless the site before we start. Don't like to build less'n it be bless't."

His friend's cryptic reluctance took Claude by surpise. Why? It was a side of Ian he had never known, the reformed alcoholic. But then, why not a blessing? It won't hurt and maybe it will help Ian with the Negro builders. They had been deeply silent when he showed them the plans. Claude had everyone to the gathering for the blessing on a Sunday afternoon in mid-summer, with Letty and Hester in the front rank of the hangers-on. The tree over them rustled quietly under a light breeze.

"Good to see you, Jubal," he had told Peavey when the old man's curiosity made him hobble over to the crowd.

Jubal's eyes swiveled, swiftly surveying the site. "You ever know the history of this tree, Claude?"

"Heard rumors only," Claude said. "Some Indian troubles."

"My grandaddy tol' me." Jubal shifted his cud. The crowd closed in to hear the tale, one more for which Peavey was famous. "His pa was the fust man in this bottom. Saw the hull thing."

"Well, get on with it, man," Claude prompted impatiently, when Peavey stopped and reflected.

Jubal spit a brown marker onto the corrugated bark of the poplar. "Party o' Injuns camped right hyar, right under this tree. Had a white man, hands thonged tight. They burnt 'im right hyar.

Tied him to a post with a few feet of rawhide tether and built a fire in a circle around the post. Roasted him alive."

Creadey's right hand flew up and covered his eyes. "Merciful God in Heaven," he cried. "May the Lord bless him and give him a peaceful rest."

"How do you know all this?" Claude asked.

Peavey shrugged unconcernedly. "My greatgrandaddy was hid out in the brush over there by the creek. Didn't dare to move. Took 'im two days to die, the slow way they done it." He marked the tree again. "Spirits 'round about. Some nights afore you come an' built Greenbottom I used to hear screams. Give me the shakes."

"Well, we ain't heard nothing," Claude said testily.

"Dat ain't so, Captain," Isaiah said. "When you decide on the cabin, de folks stirred up. Says deys hants. Don' want ter come down de path dis way." He shook his head violently and other Negroes shifted and murmured. "Skeery."

Preacher Creadey broke in. "You need this site bless't, Claude. Send that poor soul on to heaven. Relieve his torment."

"You saying he's still here?" Claude asked.

Peavey nodded. "His soul is still roamin', Claude. Best be an ordained minister do the blessing. And Hannibal should pray too," he generously added.

Hannibal's sharp intake of breath overcame the silence. "You recken to need me, Preacher Creadey?"

"Amen, amen," rose enthusiastically from the bordering Negroes, along with muttered encouragement. A slight increase in the breeze added its sighing to the exhortation.

But Hester was more bold. "Those Injuns not white, were they?" At Creadey's nod, she said, "Hannibal ain't neither. An' he got the gift to talk to hants. Seen him out prayin' in de moonlight right often. They's somethin' aroun' ever'time."

With that endorsement, Hannibal took a small Bible from his coat pocket and opened it to the Twenty Third Psalm. He sidled over to Creadey who also was searching his volume. "Shall we pray," the minister said.

With a solemn, sonorous enunciation, he and Hannibal read from the Psalms and each blessed the site. Invoking the Lord's name they beseeched Jesus to forgive the Indians and to take the tortured man's spirit to his bosom and give him rest. As they intoned the ritual a cloud drifted by. A shower wet the grass, drops sparkling in the sunlight that peeped past the drifting shadow. A few leaves planed down upon them and a small branch fell.

"It's de Lord cryin'," Josie shrieked, upsetting Creadey.

"Hush, girl," he said. He wiped tiny drops from his whiskers. "The Lord has heard our prayers. Hannibal and he knelt, followed by the others. "Bless this site," they repeated together. "Let there be only good done here."

"I promise that'll be so," Claude said.

The sturdy cabin went up fast under Ian McLellan's driving force. His skilled Negro carpenters laid huge locust joists on the stone foundation and set hand-hewn stringers across them. It was an easy matter to run up the walls and cedar shingled roof, laying a puncheon floor to resound to hard bootheels. But the unpainted cabin, with its several rooms and broad shady porch was well suited to Claude's idea of a guest house. Really, he thought, as he strode through the finished house with Ian and the Negro foreman, it's stronger built than Greenbottom, and handier. He inhaled deeply, conscious of the clean odor of fresh lumber and paint only in the kitchen. Claude chuckled; Letty had been so insistent about that! Probably cooler too, he thought. Have to bring Letty out here some in summers when the haze is bad. He thumped on several timbers and stamped on the floor.

"Solid as a rock," he said. Surveying the interior, he said, "Finished right smart, too. Fine trim work. You men did yourself proud."

Ian spit into the fireplace and nodded. The Negro foreman, Lucas, puffed up with a big smile. "It be a purty house, Captain. I'se happy you like it."

Taking them up to the Greenbottom library, Claude paid the men off. He rummaged in a cabinet and gave them each a box of cigars, plus two more boxes for the crew. "Little present," he said pleasantly, "that I been savin' just for this. Good Havanas."

Lucas beamed. "De men take to dese, Captain." He smelled the tobacco and closed his eyes. "Sweet," he intoned. "Ain't like dose leaves dey raise demselves. All de bitter gone."

With their business settled and the men ushered out, Claude settled back into a large, soft chair to smoke and reflect. The new house pleased him but a picture of the tortured man intervened. Somehow the figure of Wiley Minns kept substituting in his vision. Dozing, he watched Wiley run around the pole screaming, the Indians' fire curling his skin. When a door slammed he woke with a start, trembling. "God almighty, Claude," he said aloud, "get that hate out of your mind. It ain't right." At Letty's call, he hastily threw his cigar into the fireplace and rushed out of the room.

* * *

Abel House and Judge Marvin sat with Claude and Hannibal in the library for hours during their visit before heading for a good night's rest in the new guest house. The heady days of 1865 and the end of the War were long past, replaced by hard, strenuous efforts to recoup fortunes missed during military service. Wiley Minns and the crime he stimulated with the Peaveys and the tavern boys were the Judge's first concern.

"Warned 'em once more," he grumbled. "They come up again and I'll look to the state pen to calm them down. Won't stand for any more stealing or fighting."

"You think they got the warning last time?" Hannibal asked. "Seemed mighty peaceful after that last Seven Mile raid."

"I hope so," the Judge replied. "Let 'em cool off a month in jail before lettin' them go." He shook his head, his mournful voice continuing. "Used to fish with Hank when he was little, just like the sheriff did. Boy knew all the best holes for channel cats." He sighed. "Sure do hate penning a soldier." He struck the armrest a blow. "Damned war done ruined a lot of good men."

Abel waved away the smoke from his cigar. "It's Wiley's

gold that's doin' it. He's payin' for the devilment."

Claude sat up in his chair, alert after a lethargic slump from a heavy dinner and warm fire. "I been thinkin' about that devil. He's getting mighty tiresome and I just want to be let alone."

"He still blames you for his brother's death," Judge Marvin said. "Came to me long ago, like I told you. Complained about you killin' Athey. Said he was a civilian and you had no right, him not being in the Army."

Claude exploded, his furious leap from the chair and tense, quivering body facing the Judge. He could barely get the words out. "That bastard shot at me! Hit me! Hester killed him to save my life."

Abel House soothed the outraged man. "Minns ain't thinkin', Claude. He knows the truth. But you're his target, not Hester."

Silence reined for a few minutes, puffs of smoke coming from the cigars in rapid succession. The haze deepened until Claude crossed to a window and raised it. A little cross-draft to the fireplace lightened the burden.

"That gold's changing some of your friends." Abel puffed and continued. "The Bramers and Harts been saying Minns is a fair man. He traded with 'em just last week. Took all their potatoes for a good price. Paid in coin."

The Judge spoke the question none of the men could answer. "Where did he git all that gold?"

Abel House shook his head. "Don't rightly know, but ain't no preacher that rich." He speculated a bit, his guess close to the truth. "Joshua said his father was a stiller. Imagine he got all the gold together down in the Carolinas."

"That's the truth," Hannibal added. "Black folks aroun' Columbia say Athey rich...not take anything but coin for his stillin's."

Nods confirmed the conclusion. "Makes sense," Claude said. "Whiskey market always there. Prisoners paid good money for it and plenty in the camps."

The banker summed up Minns' thrust."He's always around

trading, Claude. Those farmers across the river are ready to listen when they see the yellow shine. They tell me he always bad-mouths you and .... here he looked at Hannibal ..., "... his nigger friend."

Hannibal sat impassive, his eyes closed, but Claude trembled and turned red. The planter's jaw set and a knot rose on it. "That bastard better never say that around me. Hannibal is my dear friend."

House hastily apologized. "I didn't mean nothing, Hannibal, and I'm sorry. Just repeatin' what the men tell me."

"It don't matter, Abel," Hannibal said. "Lots wuss said about me before. I forgive Minns and pray for his soul."

A few minutes later, Judge Marvin held everyone spellbound with his tales of Wiley and his plans. Perhaps the Carolinian would run for political office! Many Confederates were solidly behind him. Imagine, a preacher in office!

"You be careful of him," the Judge warned Claude. "He's jest like a weasel, sneaky. Always looking at legal twists, how to git power." He puffed. "He ain't been here more'n two years yet, but I ain't never seen a man so envious or crafty."

"Thought he had learned better," Hannibal said. "Didn't get nowhere with that suit against Claude." He snorted disgustedly. "Claimin' we stole those weapons in that raid. He near got laughed out of the courthouse."

The Judge's accompanying chuckle turned serious. "If Bandie hadn't told me about it, I might have let it go to trial. He was so mad, he sputtered."

"I didn't know that," Claude said thoughtfully.

"Yep," the Judge replied, "Throwed the case out on his confidences. Warned Old Peavey and Minns again about the law and night ridin'."

Abel House broke in. "Minns complained to me about you, Judge. Said he couldn't get no justice. I told him to quit stirring up trouble along the river, but I don't think he paid me no mind."

The puffs increased in tempo and size as each settled

his thoughts. A slight breeze rustled the curtains at the open window, its noise broken by a growl outside and then frenzied barking. Claude ran to the window and stuck his head out just in time to see a dark figure run off into the bushes followed by Blue in full cry. The dog's song persisted for a minute or two and then ceased. Soon after the dog's snuffle and turning sounded as he bedded down close to the house wall.

"Somebody listening to us," he told the others solemnly. His cheeks flushed and his jaw muscles tightened. "That damned Minns'll get 'em all killed yet."

"Maybe it was Hank," the Judge said. "You remember those Negroes Claudius set free at Burlington?"

Claude nodded.

"Well, Jubal still holds that agin you. You pay him for them, maybe he'll be more kindly disposed."

"So that's it," Claude said. "I'll settle with him this season. Maybe then he won't help the Minns no more."

When their cigars and desultory talk were finished, the library was left to the clearing breezes and the sound of Blue's loud snores.

* * *

Jubal showed up at the Christmas Eve party, reasonably well dressed and civil when he came to call at Greenbottom. After filling his cup with punch, Claude steered the old man into the library and pulled the sliding door shut. He motioned to an easy chair and took one opposite when Peavey sat down.

"We got an old sore between us, Jubal," Claude said. "Needs to be cleaned up." He took a sip and peered closely at the gaunt, aging man.

Peavey set his drink aside on a small, starkly simple black walnut table. His hand caressed the shining wood with its glossy patina. Jubal's face softened and he spoke gently. "You 'member this piece, Claude? I done made it myself thirty year ago. Kept it 'til my Sally died. Give it to you when you was married to Letty."

"I do," Claude answered, startled. What was the old devil getting at?

"Allus before, we was friends." Peavey took a sip and coughed. His bitter, "Thet is 'til Claudius stole them slaves o' mine," brought an instant response.

"That's why we're here, Jubal, to get that settled." Claude shifted his rump into a better contour. "Claudius felt mighty strong 'bout abolition. Always after me to free my slaves. He couldn't stand seeing the hands treated like animals."

"Well why didn't you?"

"Thought I couldn't afford to pay wages," Claude said. "Kept 'em on until the war and President Lincoln said no more." He shook his head and sighed. "I was wrong. Should have done it long ago."

Peavey's eyes gleamed and he perked up. "You fixin' to settle?"

Claude nodded, thoughtful. "How much you figure they were worth?"

With the prospect of being paid, Jubal's voice shifted to his trader's whine. "All prime, worth five hundred each. They was the best niggers I ever owned."

"Dammit, Jubal," Claude said testily, "you know that ain't so. I saw all those men before I left for the war. Three of them was stove up and one of those was over sixty."

Jubal sharpened his tone. "Don't matter none," he growled. "Claudius stole my property and Bandie wouldn't do nothin' about it."

Claude scowled and waved his hand. "We'll settle now," he said shortly. He leaned forward and stared long into Peavey's eyes. "I offer two hundred in gold and that hundred acres of bottom land where your west branch comes out. You and Hank always wanted that."

"Done," Peavey instantly said, surprising Claude. "Best land around for corn." His grimness disappeared and his voice softened. "Maybe git Hank ter settle down. He allus wanted thet piece."

They wrote the paper together, ironing out the words and meets and bounds to satisfy both. Calling in Judge Marvin, Preacher Creadey, and two other friends from the party as witnesses, Claude read the agreement aloud. He and Jubal signed the document and obtained the witness signatures. Ten clinking gold double eagles sealed the bargain, with Peavey jingling them in his hand.

"I'll get this recorded next week," Claude said. "It's your land. May you and Hank use it well."

Judge Marvin stirred in his chair. "Hank better be a farmer from now on," he warned Jubal bluntly. "No more of this runnin' wild or savaging Hannibal and his family." He jabbed his finger at Jubal like a sword. "That bottom is the best around. No reason Hank can't make a good livin' with it and the other land you own."

Peavey bristled. "Don't you go tellin' us Peavey's what to do."

Claude got between the two ruffled men. He spoke his ultimatum with finality. "He'll either stop or be killed if he attempts to bother them further, Jubal. Ain't no more to be said."

Jubal swore softly and stomped out without another word, thundering leather heels giving his reply. Hank waited outside with the carriage. His loud censure of his Grandpa Jubal carried to all the men in the house, upbraiding him for crawling to Shaw.

Shaking his head, Claude said mournfully, "I was hopin' this would settle it."

"Let us pray for an end to violence and hate," Creadey said, kneeling down. "I'll visit Hank and read with him of the return of the prodigal son. Take him to his mama's grave for prayer. He allus loved his mama."

The men knelt together while Creadey asked the Lord for peace, and for help to set Hank on the path of righteousness.

* * *

Colorful finery covered both Granny Eva and Granny

Mandy at the Greenbottom festivities, Mandy in her brilliant red dress and Eva with a rainbow hued turban. They sat in chairs at the side of the ballroom, chatting with Hester, who again was pregnant but barely showing.

"Mighty fine folks," Mandy said. "Treatin' us jest like quality."

Eva belched, covering her mouth too late to suppress the sound. Hester giggled and Mandy shushed them both.

"Don' act like no fiel' han'," she said severely. "We's wid de white folks now and got ter act proper."

Eva covered her mouth again, only a tortured apology coming out. "Cain't hold in ever'thin', Mandy. Them taters an' turnips an' ham somethin' scrumptious."

Some of Claude's cavalry troops came in with their wives. Henry steered his wife over to the sitting Negroes and made their courtesies, bowing low. Others nodded to the Negro grannies and Hester.

Mandy chuckled. "Recken dey don' quite know how ter treat wid us yet. Claude and Letty powerful friends but de others ain't so sure."

"Isaiah say some of 'em badmouthin' Claude when dey ain't 'roun'," Eva said, a thought confirmed instantly by Hester.

"You right," she said. "Some white folks around ain't sure about our families bein' together." She leaned over and whispered, "Dey think Claude the father of Elsie's child."

Mandy nodded. "Jest got ter bear de blame right now. De good Lord sort out all dis white an' black hatefulness. Ain't no reason fer it. We all de same to de Lord."

Their next visitor was the Right Reverend Absalom Creadey, his tall, spare frame showing the beginnings of a protruding belly. His bulging neck with its goiter was ignored by all, an affliction of many older citizens. Creadey's black, funereal frock coat and tight trousers were worthy complements to a pasty cadaverous face and thin, whitening hair. But his mind was brilliant.

"Ladies," he said cheerfully. "The Lord bless you for

coming. We need more of us together." He looked around. "Where's Hannibal?"

"He be here directly," Hester told him.

When Hannibal entered the door from the hall, Creadey made his excuses and hastened over to the big Negro, resplendent in black broadcloth.

"Dey look jest like a scarecrow an' a hawk," Mandy observed.

Hester smiled. "He my man all right. The best."

When Hannibal joined them he was ecstatic. He carried two more small religious tracts and an invitation to preach at Creadey's church in Greenbottom.

Claude circulated among the guests, stopping to pay court to the old Negro women. When he drifted back to Judge Marvin, he thought of the bountiful crops and the timber harvest underway. The year was finishing out on a high note. He couldn't help thinking, though, of the evils working unseen, Wiley Minns and Joshua undermining his and Hannibal's futures. Carriage noises in the lane and creaks when a heavy bulk descended preceded a tremendous thumping on the front door knocker.

When the door was swung wide by Isaiah, Sheriff Bandie led Wiley and Joshua Minns into the hall. "Where's Claude?" Bandie asked, before Letty could welcome them.

All chatter stopped in the assembly. Claude hastened to the Sheriff, followed by Judge Marvin and the other guests. After desultory greetings and an invitation to join the celebrations, Bandie declined.

"Here on business, Claude," he said. With both Minns grinning behind him, Bandie presented a subpoena. When Claude glanced at it, the Sheriff said, "Orders you to appear in Judge Allen's court, Claude, to show cause why you shouldn't be tried for fraud, for cheatin' Minns here on the timber deal with Trumbull."

"They're grown men, Sheriff," Claude said, repressing his rage. "Minns bought it from Trumbull, not me."

"You cheated us," Wiley bellowed, shaking his fist in fury.

"Weren't the amount you said you cruised."

Judge Marvin stepped forward. "Ever'body be quiet," he ordered. "Claude'll be there, Sheriff," he said formally, though they had known each other all their lives. "Your job is done. Take these Minns and git."

Departure removed the persons but not the irritations. Henry was particularly vocal, threatening reprisals from 7th Cavalry men. With the cheer dampened by Wiley's visit, the party broke up early, leaving Claude and Letty facing the fire in adjacent chairs in the library.

"Thought it was to finish fine, Letty," he said bitterly, "but that damned Wiley had to spoil it all."

She reached out for his hand and squeezed it. "Hush," she said. "The good Lord will watch over you."

* * *

Their Christmas Day dinner was a celebration after Hannibal's love and forgiveness message, powerfully voiced at Creadey's Greenbottom church. Presents to Claude and Letty and their children completed Hannibal's and Hester's day. Letty offered the two a massive, new Bible with footnotes, for scriptures and the family record.

Two days later, Cal Jones called on Claude, arriving by carriage from Point Pleasant rather than by the Evangeline. It was a cold day but not raw or snowy, one for greatcoats and no boots. He shucked the outerwear in the hall, attended by Isaiah, and was shown into the living room with its pleasant fire. Letty and Claude hurried in a moment later, Letty drying her hands on her apron. Jones' serious mien stopped her effusive greeting of a dear friend. After slight pleasantries, his uncomfortable stare disconcerted her.

"What's wrong, Cal?" she asked.

"It's men's business, Miz Letty," he said. "Not that I object to your stayin'," he added apologetically, "but Claude and me got to talk private like."

She nodded and headed for the hall, closing the sliding

doors behind her. Cal waved away the cigar Claude held out and took a seat. He spoke softly to his friend, "You wanted a boat next year, Claude, with me partners. You still plannin' on it?"

Claude nodded. He puffed on his cigar and said, "Gettin' good money for the crops and Ian sawing lots of timber. This mild weather holds, he ought to put together two big rafts for down river mills."

"You thought of buyin' the Evangeline? She's a fine boat that you've rode for years."

Shaw laughed. "She's over twenty five years old, Cal! Needs lots of work. You told me so yourself." His grin changed to a frown when Jones did not smile. "You trying to unload that broken down old boat on me?"

A twinkle in Jones' eyes and twitching lips alerted Claude. "Well," his friend said, stoking his mustache, "what if you was to offer to buy the Evangeline for four thousand cash and debt, come summer, after you sell the timber? You recken Minns might hear of it and make a better offer?" A grin followed his sly look.

Claude drummed his fingers on a chair arm, then chortled and bent forward in his seat, wiping the tears from his eyes. "You sneaky old son of a gun! You offerin' me a way to snooker Minns again? He's already takin me to court for the Trumbull deal."

"Wiley took to that right sharp, didn't he? Snapped it up like a bass on a frog."

Claude roared. "Got me a subpoena on that one but Judge Marvin says it'll never go to trial. He'll talk to Judge Allen." He drew on his cigar and exhaled a blue cloud, slowly calculating the possibilities. "Recken I might if you'll take a note."

"Why?" Jones asked. "You said you'd have plenty of money comin' in. Coin is always better."

"We'll put all my profits into Abel's bank. Give you forty percent stake up to four thousand for the Evangeline. Use that and a loan to buy a new boat in Cincinnati."

"Ah," Jones said, settling back into the cushions. "Mighty steep price but that's what'll hook Wiley. It's fine with me." A worrying thought surfaced. "How much you figure on takin' in this year? Enough for a boat?"

Claude puffed a few moments. "If the mild winter holds and that dark rum from Captain Pickens sells like it did last year, Letty and I'll bank about nine thousand over expenses."

Jones whistled. "God almighty, Claude, you're rich!"

His friend shook his head. "Got a few notes due in Ohio on the store and that new landing." He cleared his throat. "But we're doing well. In a few years we'll get back to as much business as before the war."

"I'll shake on that forty percent in the new boat, Claude. Plenty good ones layin' idle at Cincinnati. When we're ready we'll go down together and get one cheap."

Silence led to Claude's suggestion. "Drop the word to your new pilot quiet-like about selling the Evangeline and my offer of four thousand. Charles Searle says he drinks in the Bull's Head in Point Pleasant. Minns will hear."

Jones chuckled. "I'll do that, Claude."

"Sell to Minns as high as you can get. Keep all over four thousand for yourself and put that in our account."

With their business settled, they settled in with a taste of the latest rum, watered and flavored with lime juice. Limes were a new present from Captain Pickens, sent for trial and sale with the rum.

* * *

Letty sat in the adjacent chair tatting while Claude flipped the pages of the newspapers. A warm fire crackled in the living room fireplace before their outstretched toes. On that cold clear night, its bright flicker added to the yellow lamplight.

"Did you hear what Claudius and Joe McLellan did?" Claude said offhandedly.

"They bedeviling Isaiah again?" Letty replied, never missing her rhythm. "He tells me those boys are just full of tricks."

Claude shook his head. "Not this time. They went to see Worth Fauquier about a family matter."

His words took a moment to sink in, her careful tatting uninterrupted until Letty froze. “What do you mean,” she demanded, staring.

“Joe’s fixing to marry Kittie Mae when they’re old enough,” he said matter of factly. “He and Claudius warned off Worth.”

Letty crimsoned and stammered, “What on earth do those boys think? That Worth would take Kittie Mae?"

“Worth told me about it. He was laughing so hard he could barely get it out. Said those boys were dead serious.” Claude stretched and wiggled his toes at the fire. “Told me again Kittie Mae reminds him of his daughter and he loves her. But marry? Never!”

Letty relaxed and giggled. “What those boys won’t think of!” She paused and grew pensive. “You reckon Joe is free of that whiskey thirst? Don’t want Kittie Mae with no drunk like Ian was.”

It was a challenge that Claude could assure her on, he thought. A sense of satisfaction suffused his being. “Joe came to me after and asked for Kittie Mae, young as he is. He swore he’ll be a teetotaller all his life. Had enough of his pa’s drinkin’ and his mother crying.”

She resumed her tatting, her fingers nimble. “Ian showed up sheepish like and thanked me for being sober. Said it was me that did it. He hasn’t had a drink since.”

“That why he gave you that fine walnut vase?” When she nodded he added, “How’s Mary Jane doing in their new house in Greenbottom?”

“It looks just marvelous,” Letty said enthusiastically. “She’s been sewing and had Joe help her with the decorations.” Her hands fell into her lap. “I do hope they’ll be happy this time.”

Claude’s summation reassured her. “Ian is cured, Letty. I gave him a share in the timber if he stays sober but it ain’t needed. He’s swore off for good. Prays all the time.”

They chatted amiably for a few minutes until tatting and the newspaper interrupted. When Letty resumed, Claude moved to the writing desk to answer letters from Pickens and Abert. Always business, he thought, but Rance and Middleton had made him richer by their friendship and sale of the dark rum. Maybe he and Letty and Kittie Mae could visit in the spring, when everything was in bloom in South Carolina. And Jess Abert, he knew, would come when he could. He renewed his invitations, sealed the letters, and resumed his reading. The fire was dull coals when he and Letty extinguished the lamps and padded off to bed.

17

"He's mighty pretty," Hannibal said, gingerly taking the tiny bundle from Granny Mandy. He cradled his new son in his arms and rocked him back and forth, murmuring endearments. The baby squalled and squirmed violently, its arms and legs working.

Granny Mandy hastily took the infant from the big man, cooing and cuddling. Its upset cries instantly diminished.

Hester sat up in bed and reached out her arms. "He hungry, that's all. Ain't but two days old. Ain't no wonder Mark don't know his daddy yet."

Mandy handed over the child who fastened himself to a nipple and began to suck. His little body relaxed in his mother's arms and familiar smells and he slurped as he fed.

The bed in the farmhouse was attended by Mandy with Eva in the kitchen cooking. She called to Hannibal from the stove, her voice following the enticing aromas of hot bacon and eggs. "Got yer breakfast, Hannibal." When he did not answer she jangled her frying pan and hollered, "What you doing, boy? Dishere food git cold you don' come on." Grumbling and complaint issued through the door until he took himself away from the side of the bed.

"Don' you know to come when I'se calls?" she fussed. She raised her knobkerry, but giggled as it went up into the air. "You want I give you more ob de stick?"

Hannibal laughed and grabbed her around the waist. He kissed and squeezed and whirled her. "Not even your hot biscuits keep me from my son," he said proudly. "Got me Mark now to go wid Matthew. Gonna have Matthew, Mark, Luke, and John afore we's done."

Granny threw him away and punched him in the belly with the knobby end of her stick. "You better ask Hester 'bout dat." She dished up the hot food and set the steaming platters on the kitchen table, followed by a pan of hot biscuits from the oven. "Man don' tink o' nothin' but hisself," she grumbled. She called to Mandy and joined Hannibal at the table.

Bub hurried through the back door at the same time as Granny Mandy entered from the bedroom. He sniffed and said, "Mighty temptin', Granny. I'se heard yer hollering an' came a'runnin'."

"You get all those chores done?" Hannibal asked.

"Sho' did," Bub said, and reached for the plate of bacon. He shoveled pieces onto his plate and set the bacon platter aside. "Like it here, Hannibal. Don' miss Jed or t'others a'tall."

Mandy tweaked him about his manners. "In dis house we wait on de blessin'."

Bub jerked his reaching arm back, leaving the plate of eggs in place. He said, "I'se sorry, Hannibal," and bowed his head.

His education and his status got another jolt from Eva. "Man o' de house gits de fust servin', boy. Ain't no mo' reachin' like you done."

The young Negro's bowed head bounced up and down. "I sorry," he said humbly.

After Hannibal's sonorous blessing, Eva served him a large plate of select bits, placing them before him. She picked out a particularly large biscuit and set the honey and blackberry jelly in easy reach. With those honors done, she passed the platters and biscuits to Bub before she and Granny Mandy served themselves. The young man watched the service intently.

"Dis your fust breakfast wid us," Granny Mandy said, "since you come up from de Carolinas. You pay 'ttention, now you livin' wid us. Make you inter a gent'man."

Hannibal interrupted more lessons from the old grannies, but his bluntness was the same. "Got a fine farm here. Corn and taters and pumpkins all in and garden feedin' us good." He threw down the gauntlet. "Can't do it all 'thout work, Bub. Expect you to work, study with Hester, learn to read and write. You don' want to be a farm hand all your life." He thumped the table. "Make your Granny Mandy proud. Save your money. Own your own farm."

The old woman swelled up, sitting straighter in her chair. "You listen ter Hannibal, boy. We all he'p yer, but you gotta work hard."

"I do it," Bub said. "Jed stay wid Captain Pickens but he never be nothin' but foreman. I tol' him I want more. He got mad. Tol' me to git ter work or git. I come up here."

Mandy laughed, but her lips trembled and her eyes spouted tears. "I declare, boy, but you are a sight." She sobbed and wiped her eyes. "You was de shiftless one o' you two boys when you was growin' up." Her crying stopped and she eyed him suspiciously. "You sho' you fixin' to work hard,...tell de trut,...back Hannibal?"

Bub fixed his eyes on Hannibal. "You got a Bible here?" he asked. When Hannibal assented, Bub said, "I swear on dat holy book, you fetch it in."

Hannibal entered Bub's oath on a leaf of the family Bible after he swore solemnly to fulfill his Granny's and Hannibal's rules and expectations. It rested there in a clear hand, faded but legible as the years passed.

* * *

By Christmas season, Hannibal's relation with Reverend Creadey had flowered and flourished to the point of his assisting frequently in the Greenbottom church services. His own Little Seven Mile Church attracted Negroes living within a few miles, plus budding friends up the valley.

"Those white folks closeby are mighty accommodating," Hannibal told Creadey, "lettin' me preach to 'em."

The pastor stroked his goiter and kneaded the growing mass. "Don't make no never mind that you're black, Hannibal. God loves us all." He sighed. "That terrible war was for nothing. We could have got along, black and white, if we had just tried."

"Too many hotheads," Hannibal replied. "You weren't down in South Carolina." He frowned and shook his head. "Bad! Wiley Minns is a good example. Don't want to forget. Kill Claude and me if he can."

The Reverend Creadey shuddered. "Heard that from Charles Searle on the sly. Botherin' him and he wanted to pray on it." He started and put his hand over his mouth. "Should not have said that, Hannibal. It was a confidence."

His friend put up his hand, palm out. "We been knowin' that for a long time, me and Claude. Don't you worry none."

They resumed their planning for a gala Christmas program, black and white bent together in friendship over their notepapers.

* * *

Hester fussed around Granny Mandy's chair, while Eva rocked nearby. "You feelin' poorly, Granny?" Hester asked.

"Ain't much fer workin' terday, gal. Got a mite o' de slows." But Mandy chuckled and her eyes gleamed as she glanced up at her granddaughter, shrewd in gathering attention. Her parchment covered hand stroked the young mother's arm, and settled on her fingers with a light grip.

Eva stirred from a doze. "Don' you worry none 'bout Mandy, Hester. She doin' right fine in her porch chair. Allus visitin' wid de folks comin' by."

A clip clop sounded up the creek road and the younger Sproul boy rode past. Granny Mandy raised her stick at him and he waved his hat and shouted back. "Ma be by later, Granny. The baby's ailin'."

"What I tells you, Hester," Granny Eva said. "Mandy de bestes doctor 'roun' hereabouts. Doctors ever'one dat come by or sends fer her."

Hester stroked Mandy's hair and tucked the shawl around her granny's shoulders. The old woman perked up and rocked lightly. Floor boards squeaked under the onslaught of the oak rockers, clashing with Eva's crooning.

Stopping her lullaby, Eva said, "Yer granny got mo' stories dan de white folks ever heard. Dey comes fer her folktales much as de doctorin'."

Mandy perked up and raised her stick. "Ain't so," She protested. "Dey knows I'se got de best yarbs 'roun', an' dat I goes anytime ter he'p."

Hester patted her back. "I knows that, Granny. Ain't nobody got the gift like you. White folks call it wisdom."

A spate of desultory visiting passed before faint sounds of a buggy carried to them, slowly bouncing across the rocks of the creek road. Loud knocks resounded when its wheels struck the eroded flat ledge at the sharp turn by the outcrop.

"'spect dat's Miz Sproul wid Andy," Eva said. "Come ter you dis time, Mandy."

Granny Mandy nodded. "Go ter 'em any time." She tucked her shawl tighter and rocked a heavier stroke that the floorboards loudly protested. "Good she come terday, though. Feelin' right poorly."

Granny's knowledge of natural medicines and herbs had endeared her to the surrounding people for she cured many and never refused to go to a sick person, or to doctor the ill. Many among the mountain people were her friends, strong, reliant settlers who appreciated her knowledge and giving nature. Old men and their wives, white and black, dropped by and visited, rocking away as they swapped stories. They brought her little money, but presented soft treats she could gum down; things she could feed her grandchildren.

An hour later, Mrs. Sproul was ready to leave with Andy, his cough reduced by an oily, sweet concoction made up from Granny's chests and containers. The mountain woman had brought a jar of honey in return, her offering to the medicine woman.

"You come by first o' the week, Granny?" she asked, before climbing into the buggy.

Granny leaned on her cane on the porch. "I do dat, Miz Sproul. You keep Andy warm by de fire an' give 'im de yarbs like I'se tol' you. He sweat it out 'bout two days."

Miz Sproul nodded and handed Andy up to her daughter. She swung up to the buggy seat with an agile step and untied the reins from the brake handle. Leaning over, her lined face quivered and a tear dribbled down her cheek. "We'uns in your debt again," she said. "Ain't got no money but somethin' you want done we be here to he'p."

Granny's back straightened and a glow suffused her being. "Doin' de Lord's work, Miz Sproul, 'nough reward. You tek good care dat little one."

Tears flowed down Miz Sproul's cheeks as she nodded and said "Giddap," waving her whip as the horse trotted out of the yard.

* * *

Eva nudged Granny Mandy dozing in her chair. "You fixin' ter work on dat quilt terday?"

Starting up, Mandy rubbed her eyes and yawned. A stretch like a cat followed smacking of her lips. "Recken we better git at it," she said. Her belly grumbled when she stirred. "Go ter de outhouse fust."

With Eva's help, she completed her detour, them moved from the porch to a seat at the quilting frame. Her friend steadied Mandy as she shuffled, Eva's body strong and her eyes bright.

"You purty steady yet," she said.

"Cain't do much," Mandy replied. She sighed and wiped her eyes. "Gonna love Hester's babies long as I'se able, Eva. De good Lord ain't gonna tek me yet."

Eva soothed her upset. "You's too good at doctorin' an' lovin' fer Him ter want yer, gal." Her gentle voice bathed Mandy in a tide of love. “I he’ps yer all yer want. Kin git de young Sproul gal ter come by too. Miz Sproul promised fer when I’se gone.”

“She mighty handy,” Mandy agreed. “Big, too..strong!” She laughed, her sides shaking. “I ain’t bigger’n a minute now. She toss me ’roun’ like a pillow.”

Eva nodded and bent to her pattern of stitches. “Git to it, Mandy,” she said. “Dat drummer offered five dollars gold fer dis one and de pillows when dey done. He be by next month. We’uns hev some coin fer de chil’rens’ presunts.”

A big bag of cloth scraps rested by Mandy’s chair. She reached in and pulled out some colorful lace, a thin strand several yards long. “Look at dis,” she said, holding it against the edge of the quilt. “Preacher Creadey’s wife give it ter me. Mek fine border on dishere side.”

Steps on the porch interrupted their chat. Hester came into the room with her two boys. Mandy struggled up and took the older boy into her arms. “Matthew,” she cooed, “ain’t you de handsome one.”

The little boy smiled and felt his granny’s hair, running it between his fingers before caressing her face.

“I declare,” Mandy said jovially, “he gwine be a real lady’s man, Hester.”

“I’ve got to run over to the store and meet Hannibal, Granny. Bring back his new plow while he goes on to see Claude. Can I leave them?”

Eva took baby Mark. “You knows we do dat, Hester,” she said frostily. “Dese boys jest our joy. You tek long as you like.” Happy laughter and clapping hands filled the cabin when Hester tiptoed out.

“They ain’t cryin’,” she told herself, when she had gotten off the porch. Climbing into the buggy, she headed out the lane.

* * *

The corn waved in the sunlight, stirred by a gentle breeze

from the west. Its dark green, offset with tawny tassels, spread across all the bottom, inviting admiration from the men rocking on Peavey's porch.

"Mighty fine crop comin'," Jubal said. "Don't believe I ever seen a better. Layin' fallow all those years really he'ped it."

"Figure I got eighty acres in," Hank said in a satisfied tone. "Those others growed up in too much bresh."

Old Peavey nodded and spat a brown stream. "Soon as you git some money together from the crop, you kin hire those Johnson boys. Clear the rest."

Silence claimed them, the rockers squeaking on the rickety porch boards. Jubal shifted his cud. "You settlin' down right nice, boy. Ain't had no fight last six months."

"Don' intend ter be shiftless all my life." Hank squirmed in the caned seat and scratched a bite. "The last time Judge Marvin fussed us, he warn't funnin'. I ain't aimin' ter go to the state pen fer nothin'."

Old Jubal slapped him on the back and said, "Praise the Lord! You come ter your senses!"

Hank grinned. "Fooled you, did I? When I git me some coin, I think I'll 'set up'. That orta please you, good grub from my woman."

"'bout time you done it," Jubal said. "Time I was twenty four like you, I already got two kids, yer pa an' yer aunt Hilda."

Hank stirred, his restless energy taking him from the chair. He paced the porch, his hard heels drumming like the grouse in the woods. "Still thinkin' o' the deal down ter Logan. The Jeters an' Josh might come aroun' this fall. Lots o' ideas."

"You stay clear o' them damn Jeters!" Jubal said sharply. "They're shiftless bastards." He swore. "They ain't nothin' but thieves. Gonna git hung."

His grandson tensed and shook his head. "Ain't doin' it. That corn crop'll be mighty good but one deal will make me an' the boys mor'n it's worth." He shouted down Peavey when the latter berated him, so Jubal shifted his tack.

"Claude paid up on those slaves,"he said. "Been treat'n me

right neighborly ever since. I ain't doin' him no more dirt." He rousted the silent Hank. "You work that piece of bottom, boy. Make you rich, iffen you try."

"Take too long," Hank replied, "with too much sweat. Somethin' comes by looks good, I'm going with Josh and the boys from Logan."

* * *

"I swear, Unk, but you're gitten fatter'n a boar hog."

Joshua's comment stirred Wiley to a raging fury. He rose from his bench and threw his mug of beer into his nephew's face across the table, castigating him. "You lazy son of a bitch. I ain't taking that kind of talk, even if you are my blood." His derringer appeared next, pointed straight at Joshua's chest.

The latter instantly backed off, retreating with his hands up, palms out in front of him. "Now hold on, Unk, you knowed I was only funnin'."

Wiley trembled, his derringer wobbling at the end of an extended arm. With Joshua now more than five yards away on the stone floor and still backing, Wiley's shot was much less certain. "You carryin' that Colt?" he asked.

In answer, Joshua whipped out his belt gun and leveled it at Wiley, sighting along the barrel. "You ain't got a chance, Unk," he purred in a silky voice. "This distance, you can't hit nothin' with that derringer, even if you fire both barrels." His eyes flashed as he laughed scornfully. "Ain't even got it cocked! Gonna shoot a man, you better do it quick, not fiddle around like that."

Wiley's arm dropped and he put the little weapon back in his vest pocket. He slumped back onto the bench. "Sit down, Josh. Ain't thinking right."

"You bet," Joshua said. "Shaw's been gitten to you, ever since that sorry timber deal. Onliest thing, you didn't lose on the Catfish here." He looked around the small tavern with it's cadre of drinkers and two barmaids. "Make money on this one, just like the Bull's Head."

Minns grunted. He belched and beckoned to a barmaid who brought a new beer. With a satisfied smirk, he said, "Best thing 'bout this deal was those bugeyes when we paid in gold."

"Jasper's still got plenty, Unk. Whiskey business good in Carolina an' Jasper's sellin' it better'n we ever did. They was three bags in the stash when I visited. Ma give me those two you got an' said she wanted to visit." He stuck in another dig. "You wern't hardly knowin' I was back, you was so drunk."

Joshua took out a gold coin and flipped it up and down on the planks. Its yellow flash and clinks fascinated the swamper, who was mopping up Wiley's beer. The latter raised the mug to his lips but set it back down untouched. He swirled it around in a wet spot on the planks before speaking.

"You're right, boy." Minns said. "Man can't do no business iffen he's a drunk. I'll do without." His face took on a shrewd leer. "I'm takin' your gold over to Abel. Flash it in the bank before gitten the deposit box." He sipped from the mug absentmindedly. "You do the same. Don't spend much but show it along the river. Tell ever'one Minns pays in gold."

His nephew stopped him when he raised the tankard again. "No more, Unk," Joshua said sharply.

Wiley slid the beer aside. "Let's decide on their visit," he said. "You think she really wants to come?"

Joshua shook his head. "Jasper mostly," he said. "To see the country and to git Red, but talkin' bloodthirsty." He sighed. "Boy ain't never kilt no one. Ain't no time ter start."

Wiley nodded. Their silent reverie was broken by his, "We'll have 'em next spring, early. Write yer mother and tell Jasper he ain't to cause no trouble." He thought a moment. "He can have Red back. That hound ain't been no use to us, jest underfoot."

"I'll do that, Unk." Hank's face hardened. "Don't need Jasper, you ever git tired o' chasin' Shaw. Ain't broke 'im yet. I'm killin' him and that damned nigger, soon's you say."

* * *

"Travelin' on those cars mighty pleasant," Jess Abert said, when Claude met him in Gallipolis. He had swung down from the step with a smile and outstretched hand, then helped his wife, Matty, alight. His children, Jobe and his little sister, skipped closely behind.

Claude's eyes crinkled at the corners. "Sure different from the war," he allowed, "no saddle sores or sore feet." When Abert chuckled, he said, "Never seen so much rain as down in Tennessee, and sittin' in a wet saddle the whole time. The railroad has made it easy."

Jess nodded. "Seems like it were forever rainin'." He introduced his wife, who curtsied. Irrepressible Jobe shook hands like a man, and swung up his sister for Claude to hold for an embrace and a closer look.

Hours later they were ensconced in Greenbottom, the ladies chatting and Jess and Claude roaming the farm. Jobe tagged along, poking into the corners of the barn and outbuildings. After several expressions of wonderment at the size of Greenbottom and its fertility, Jess got down to business. "That crate I brung," he said, hesitantly, "got sixty prime deer hides in it. Ain't been able to git 'nough hard money for the debt but offer them in trade." He glanced at Claude, his face fearful. "It ain't exactly right; I do whatever you want."

A few steps of thoughts led to Claude's reply. "Prime hides bringin' a dollar fifty from the eastern buyers, Jess. That's more than enough. Ninety dollars is too much though." He walked on.

Jobe was all ears. He ran around in front and halted. "I shot some o' them bucks," he said. "Can I ship you more hides on commission? Plenty 'roun' our place."

They had stopped at a fence corner, the rails stacked into a crossed pattern. Three inclined braces served as footrests as they talked. A crisp, light breeze pushed fleecy clouds across the blue sky.

Claude stretched and took a deep breath. "Pretty day to be

alive," he said. His eyes twinkled. "And to talk business with an enterprising young man. I was raftin' on this river at fifteen, Jobe. Not too early for you to get started."

Jess laughed. "He's all-fired hot to make money, Claude. Jobe's the trader of the family. Been hawkin' our crops ever'where. Doin' good."

"Tell you what," Claude replied. "We'll take those hides to Gallipolis and sell them. You give me forty dollars for the loan and I'll call it square." He clapped Jess on his muscular shoulder, now clad in a respectable suit for the trip. "Use a little of the other to put Jobe in business."

"Will you sell my hides?" Jobe asked.

"That I will, lad," Claude replied. "Charge you ten percent for factoring, plus warehousin', same as anywhere else." He shook hands with the boy. "We got a contract now, Jobe. Man shakes, it's a deal. Man's word gotta be good."

The boy straightened and stood taller. "No need to worry, Captain," he said. "Pa taught me good."

Jess had watched the interchange in silence. His troubled face revealed doubts. "You ain't makin' anythin' on our deal, Claude. Thet ain't right."

The planter shook his head. "Repayment's all I want, Jess. My reward is seein' you and your family doin' well." He chuckled. "Besides, Jobe's gonna send me lots of business."

"That's right, Captain," Jobe said in all seriousness. "I'll be a trader with you."

Two days later they sold the hides at a Gallipolis warehouse specializing in skins. With the auctioneer's and warehouse fees deducted, Jess held eighty four dollars in his hands. He counted out Claude's debt and gave ten dollars to Jobe, who clutched it tightly in his pocket.

"Thirty four dollars left," Jess said. "I'm mighty grateful." He stiffened into an erect posture and his face shined with confidence. "Kin git me another plow fer this spring's turnin'. An' buy the wife and sister some pretties."

The party left in haste to do their shopping before their

river steamer was to leave for Cincinnati. A short cruise for Jobe's pleasure would be just right, Claude had thought when he bought passage. The steamer would drop them off at Greenbottom's landing. Claude spotted Minns during their shopping before his enemy was aware they were nearby.

"Minns," Claude said pleasantly, though the hair rose on the back of his neck. "How are you?"

His hopes for a peaceful encounter were dashed by Wiley's reaction. "You cheated me on that timber deal," Minns growled, resurrecting the past.

He motioned and the six roughnecks with him split to surround Claude and his friends. Minns had never seen Jess, the Confederate with much experience in battle. Instantly alert to the danger threatening, Jess moved off to one side and bared his belt gun, a long barreled Colt revolver. Jobe sidled the other way and closed Minns, producing a derringer. Minns alternately turned red and paled pasty white as the silent threat escalated. His men gauged the grim ex-Confederate and backed off.

"We ain't gittin' shot," one said. "Beatin's one thing; you ain't payin' enough fer gunplay."

Minns' fear turned to rage as his purpose was exposed and he acknowledged defeat. He swore great oaths, while still standing his ground. But it was only bluster until he gave up and took his unwholesome crew back toward the river front.

"He a Carolinian?" Jess asked quietly.

"Yes," Claude replied. "When Hannibal and I escaped in sixty four, his brother Athey and two of Athey's sons chased us. They all got killed." Downcast, he said sadly, "Minns has lots of gold. Come up here to bust me, then kill me and Hannibal both."

Jess nodded. "Understand, Claude. You need help, you jest send word." He spat. "They ain't nothin' but low-down white-trash. Same as down our way." His jaw line tightened. "Scare 'em off.......or kill 'em."

* * *

Ian had taken two log rafts down the Ohio in the early March flood, with Joe McLellan as a hand helping the three Trumbulls. Claude waited anxiously for their return, his worry assuaged one May morning. With Joe following at his heels, Ian strode into the office unannounced. The whistle of the steamboat at the landing and going on upriver had warned the planter of a visitor. On entry, Ian did a little jig, jumping and clicking his heels and stomping them on the plank floor. Claude grinned and waited on the Celtic celebration from a stance beside his desk.

"Done made a pile, Claude," Ian said. He searched his pouch and proudly laid a draft in Claude's outstretched hand. The planter tossed it onto the desk and advanced on Ian.

"I don't want that right this minute," Claude said impatiently. "I want to shake and tell you and Joe how glad I am that you're back safe." He clutched and hugged them before he stepped back and said, "How much?"

"Seventy one hundred, net," Ian replied proudly. "Those New Orleans mills offered top price."

Claude whistled, then his face sobered. "I thought you'd sell at Cincinnati. What happened?"

Impatient at his father's slow search for words, Joe said, "They got the stingies, Captain. Ain't payin' hardly nothin'."

"Quiet, Joe," Ian said. "Lots o' rafts hit the waterfront together, Claude. I cut right out and struck for New Orleans when I seen the others. More'n those mills could saw in six months."

With the draft back in his hand, Claude held it up and admired it for a few moments. "You paid off the Trumbulls and Joe?" he asked.

Ian nodded and reached for his pouch. "Got forty seven dollars left o' that money you give me for expenses."

"Keep it as an advance on your share, Ian." Claude searched a desk drawer for a moment and pulled out a ledger. Flipping to a page, he said, "Accordin' to our agreement, you get ten percent, seven hundred ten dollars. I'll pay the rest, soon as I deposit this with Abel."

"We'll be at the farm, Claude," Ian replied. "Joe and me

got a big garden to plant. Be ready to work in three weeks, you want something."

The planter nodded and made a ledger entry. He sent them off with high humor, excitedly running to the house to show Letty the draft. Golly, he thought, I can square my debt with Abel and have two thousand left over! He and Letty celebrated that evening with a toddy before dinner, toasting each other and their success. Within a week Claude had settled his business with his banker cousin. Abel beamed when Claude left with the money for Ian and $20 in gold as a bonus for Joe.

The shiney double eagle will fire up the boy, Claude thought, trotting his horse on the road home. Keep him workin' hard for betterment. He chuckled. With Joe so interested in Kittie Mae, he'd better make sure his future son-in-law was a worker with means. He passed a small pile of saw logs on the way, dumped by the road for transport to a mill. It spurred his thoughts, and recalled his purchase of barn boards a year before. With the country growing, there would be a big market for lumber. Claude mulled over the thought, only half-attentive to his homeward bound horse. I'll use a thousand of that profit to set up a sawmill, he thought. Set Ian to running it with Joe as helper. His new business venture disappeared from his mind as his horse nickered and he turned into his lane. Home, he thought, inspecting Greenbottom as he drew closer to the house. A girl's voice pealed, answered by the deep chuckle of Worth Fauquier.

* * *

The gambler leaped forward when Claude dismounted and handed his reins to a stable hand. His face alight, he said simply, "How fine to see you, Claude."

The irrepressible Kittie Mae was more joyous. Running at her father, skirts flying, she jumped at him and embraced him warmly with her arms around his neck and her legs drawn up to the rear.

"You're heavy," he roared, clasping her tightly and swinging her in a tight circle. “How did the cruise go?”

“Oh, Pa,” she gushed, “You should’a seen those gamblers when I beat them.” She kissed him and slipped away from him. “They were so mad.”

Letty sidled up for a kiss and a swift hug. “She can’t get over it, Claude. A girl only and gamblin’,” she said disapprovingly. “Winning.” Her matronly instincts overcame her rush of words and she added. “You and Worth come on into the sitting room. We can talk.”

When they entered the parlor, Kittie Mae scurried in front of them and took her little rocker off to the side of her parents. “Kittie Mae!” Letty said, frowning, “where are your manners?”

The girl grinned impishly at Worth and her father. Bowing her head, she said, “I’m sorry.”

The two men looked at her lovingly, Claude with a perplexed grin and Worth with admiration. In the next few minutes the gambler related the facts about the trip and Kittie Mae’s gambling. “She’s a natural,” he said. “Keeps the card count, seems to have a sixth sense on bluffing, knows all the games now.” He pulled a small pouch from a coat pocket. “Here’s the money she won.”

Claude fielded the tossed sack and counted out seventy seven dollars into a pile on the occasional table in front of Letty. She clinked them a time or two and then said, “Keep them all, child, for your hope chest. A wife should have some money of her own.”

The girl blushed and dropped her eyes. She glanced shyly at Worth but he was direct, and gentle in reply to her question. “I’m not the one, Kittie Mae, as I told your father.” Letty jumped as Worth continued. “You’ll meet a fine young man when you’re older, ready for marrying. Maybe Joe? Or Jobe? Or that Trumbull boy?”

Kittie Mae turned even redder and said, “Oh, Worth, how you carry on.” With Letty shocked into silence, Kittie Mae boldly stated, “Don’t want any one not like you, Worth. You’re just like another daddy, like Pa here.”

"Take care of her, Worth," Letty said. "She will go on the steamers. We both want her to be a lady."

"As do I," Worth stated grimly. "She won't come to no harm and I will do my best for her." He grinned. "After all, I do have some experience with girls." A cast swept over his face, a mask dropping before them. "Long ago," he said in a somber tone.

* * *

Hannibal's journey to Gallipolis took him near Elsie's place. She ran into the big, erect man on a downtown street, him mulling over a display of merchandise in a store window. Giving him a hug, she asked, "You in town long, Hannibal?"

He shook his head and set down his small valise. "Just overnight, Elsie. Need a heavy new suit for my preachin'."

She squealed and clapped her hands. "Got just the feather bed for you. Ain't no reason you payin' good money to that drafty old hotel down the street."

"Don't want to impose, Elsie," he said.

The silent Tandy Russell butted in from his stance nearby. "You ain't never fussin' us, Hannibal Shaw," he said huffily. "We'uns tek you any time.... Less'n you got de uppities," he added.

"Hush yo' mouf," Elsie said. "Hannibal de finest man 'roun'," adding, "atter you, o' course."

Tandy was not to be intimidated, his voice hoarsely challenging. "You comin' wid us er not?"

The Reverend Hannibal Shaw gave in with a chuckle. "I deserved that, Tandy. Just ain't thinking right. I accept with pleasure."

Tandy's tense stance eased and he took Elsie's arm. "We steer you to de right sto'," he said bitterly, adding, "dishere one's a Yankee, ain't interested in no black folks trade."

Hours later, over pumpkin pie, Tandy got to the important news for Hannibal. He edged around the matter until Elsie jabbed him.

"Tell de man, Tandy, same's you tell me."

Hannibal bent forward, his pie forgotten as Tandy related Minns' plans. "Minns payin' two o' dem warehouse hands ter let him onter Claude's shipments."

Hannibal nodded. "Know who they are?"

"Them Whistler boys," Elsie said disgustedly. "Atter Claude he'p dey mama and give 'em a job.' She grumbled, then spat out, "Ain't right, bitin' de hand as he'ped 'em!"

"Dey's mo'," Tandy said. "Dey whisperin' dat Minns pay gol' fer saltin' all Claude's rum kegs. Give 'em one little piece. De gol' glint in der eyes."

Hannibal whistled and a chill ran through him. "That's mighty bad." He laid his fork down, the pie forgotten. "How you know this?"

Elsie's bitter tongue dripped scorn. "Dey ain' got no sense. Braggin' to other boys. One o' 'em right obliged to Tandy and tol' 'im."

Tandy finished restoking his pipe and blew a smoke ring. "I'se keepin' close watch on 'em, Hannibal. Dey ain't 'greed yet ter take Minns' gol'." He puffed away. "Der mama tol' 'em no an' dey right scairt o' her. She religious. Don't hold wid devilment."

"Claude will be here next week," Hannibal said. "I'll tell him." He absently cut and chewed a forkful of pie. "You take me to their mama tomorrow," he said decisively, "then to the warehouse."

"What you goin'a do?" Elsie asked.

"Put the fear of the good Lord into her and those shiftless boys," he thundered. "The Holy Bible got enough cautions to stamp out all evil." The dishes rattled as his agitated body bumped the table. One fell and broke but Elsie just nodded.

Tandy laughed. "Eat your pie, Hannibal. We git dat suit termorrer and hogtie dose boys." Silence while working on the pie was followed with, "Claude needs good crew, Hannibal. Cain't jest depend on me."

Hannibal nodded. "Claude won't put up with no criminals.

He'll get it straight."

* * *

The messenger arrived just before dinner time. He pulled at his cap when he dismounted before Letty in the front yard. "Miz Letty," he said, "is Captain Shaw about?"

"He's down to the barn, Enoch," she answered. "Come in and have some coffee while I send Isaiah for him."

She led the way into the parlor and settled their guest. "How's Mrs. Kitts?" she asked, while they waited on Claude and the coffee.

"Right pert, Miz Letty," he replied. "Edna's rattlin' around in that big old house now that Louise is married." He sighed mournfully. "Missin' our baby girl."

She nodded. "We have that to go through."

They were chatting and laughing when Claude entered. Enoch bounded out of his chair. The two men shook hands cordially, old friends in the war and before.

"How long you been with Cal?" Claude asked.

"About five year now."

"Ferry at Proctorville shut down?... haven't heard anything."

"No," Enoch explained. "He offered to sell last week an' I grabbed it. Was tellin' Letty. Me an' Edna's movin' to Point Pleasant. Family growed and gone. Two livin' there so we're fixin' to see our grandbabies more."

Claude nodded. "Understand," he said quietly. "but who will run the ferry?"

"Charles Palmer," Enoch said. "He went in havers."

Kitts glanced uncertainly at Letty. "Could we talk private, Claude? Got some news from Captain Jones."

Letty waved at his embarrassment and went out of the parlor, pulling shut the double sliding doors.

"What is it, Enoch?" Claude asked.

"Minns bought the Evangeline, Claude. Paid the whole

five thousand."

"No!" Claude expostulated. "He really went that high?"

"Yep! An' paid in gold! Cal said to tell you it all worked, whatever that means."

Claude chuckled and waved his hand. "Just a little understanding we had." He whistled. "Well, I'm happy for Cal. Gives him a good stake for a new boat."

His guest fidgeted. "There's more, Claude, an' it ain't good."

"Can't put it off, Enoch," Claude said gently, but gloom settled over him. Would his troubles go on forever?

Enoch drew a deep breath. "Evangeline left Gallipolis last night, like usual, but with Minns' crew. Boiler blew up a mile below the city an' it burned on that bar at the first bend."

The loss staggered Claude. Not the Evangeline, he thought, a boat he and Letty had ridden for years. It was a mainstay on the river, always helpful to him, and to the settlers and merchants. That it would be no more was a disaster, even if Minns' boat. Cynical thought intruded. His and Cal's new boat would have it even better. He reproached himself for an evil idea, even as it recurred. Minns was always trying to hurt him, but now the shoe was on the other foot and Minns was suffering.

"Anybody hurt?" Claude asked.

"One man lost into the river and two with broken bones," Kitts said, "but the rest were saved."

"Thank God the loss was so small."

"That ain't all, Claude. Minns is ragin' and blamin' you an' Cal. Threatened you both."

Claude's heart sank as he asked, knowing the answer. "Cal recken' he means it?"

"Cal's actin' brave but he's scairt. Sheriff Bandie warned Minns and that mean lookin' nephew of his to shut up and be peaceful." He was quiet a minute. "That Joshua give me the shudders, Claude. Never felt such evil as when he looked at me. Like Old Nick hisself. You be careful."

18

Old Peavey stiffened when Joshua stomped onto his porch, squeaking boards protesting the impact of hard leather. Jubal slammed the front door behind him as he walked out and confronted the visitor. Sticking out his jaw, he half-shouted, "What you want, Josh? Wiley got some more devilment planned?"

"Shut up, old man," Joshua said, dismissing Peavey with a contemptuous wave. "My business is with Hank." He swiveled around, inspecting the premises. "He 'round?"

Jubal shook his head. "He's down in the bottom workin' the corn." He scornfully added, "Honest sweatin' for a change, more'n you be doin'."

Joshua turned on his heel and left the porch, clumping down the front steps. Jubal shook his fist at the retreating back. "You leave Hank 'lone," he yelled. "You trash ain't bringin' him no good."

An enraged man spun on his heels and leveled a pistol. A loud click and it was cocked, aimed straight at Jubal. Joshua's right eye stared along the sights, directly into Peavey's, a rock-hard face outlined beneath. Silence was broken by loud breathing and Minns' relaxation. His pistol tipped up, clicking as he uncocked the piece. A swift, smooth motion restored the weapon to its holster.

"If you was to kill me," Peavey said calmly, "Hank put

you down fer sure. Him and me got our troubles but blood's blood. You think 'bout thet."

He left Josh in the yard and stalked back into the house. Jubal rocked at the window, his rifle ready, until Minns rode away. With his horse tethered at some thick, moist grass in the cornfield lane, Joshua hallooed down Hank. They perched on a windfall, its two foot oak trunk providing a comfortable seat. Hank had wiped his sweaty brow with a red-checkered bandanna and whipped off his soaked shirt before straddling the oak. A bilious white, hairy chest aired in the breeze rustling the corn. When settled, Hank slapped the blackened, corrugated bark.

"Good fer oak splits or the fire," he said. "Purty big though, fer workin' up."

"Ain't here to talk about no oak tree," Josh grumbled. "Wiley wants us to visit Hannibal agin." He grimaced and sniffed. "Ain't you tired o' all thet sweatin'? You jest downright stink."

Hank laughed. "Been so long you was sweatin' you done forgot? How many times you run in the war and was worse'n this?"

A slow grin lightened Josh's face. "You got me there, Hank! Down to Franklin, I must'a run two mile. Couldn't hardly breathe." He laughed as the thought overtook him but it snuffed out, his grin hardening into a drawn, stretched skin as he gloomily reminisced. "Warn't no fun all them men killed. My cousin too. Him an' me shared many a campfire."

Ignoring the war, his friend packed a corncob pipe and lit it, the smoke curling about his head in the light breeze. "Why does Wiley want to git at Hannibal again? Seems like Sheriff Bandie tol' us plain to leave 'im be."

Josh pulled his jackknife from his pocket and pried open its biggest blade. He began working on the log, carving a big "J" into the corrugated bark. "Wiley don't put no stock in that. He figured the sheriff was just tryin' to scare us off."

"That's crazy, Josh," Hank said. "I been knowin' Bandie all my life. He don't back down ner do no funnin' 'bout the law."

"Well, Wiley thinks different. You in or out?"

Hank shook his head. "I got to think on this and talk to Gramps. It ain't no hurryin' matter, the way I see it." He puffed away at his pipe before rising and picking up his axe. "You come back next week this time and I tell you straight out. I got to see Gramps fust."

A week later, Josh and Hank looked over Hannibal's cornfield in the late Sunday afternoon. They had come over the ridges instead of riding, with Josh complaining the last mile.

Hank laughed at him. "You ain't done much walkin' lately, hev you Josh?"

"Why should I when Unk's got all them good horses? Don't see why you had to come by the ridges. We could of hid out up the road and saved them blisters." Josh took off his boots and soaked his feet in a trickle of water. He inspected his heels and slapped a sheet of loose tobacco over each before pulling on his socks. With his boots restored he rose to his feet. "You ready?" he asked. "They's gone agin so we can do this quick."

When the two men sneaked along the side of Hannibal's barn, snores stopped them. "It's thet hand from Carolina," Hank whispered. "We git him fust."

A pistol butt to the head immobilized the sleeping Bub. Hank bound his hands and feet with rawhide thongs and gagged him as well. Bub's bandanna covered the Negro's eyes. With a grunt, Hank rolled Bub into a pile of hay and forked hay over him.

"He don' bother us now and we kin git on with the cows and pigs. We git the pigs fust."

Turning the pigs and cows into the cornfield was a few minutes of herding. The pigs fell to work breaking down stalks and eating the ears. Hank shooed three cows farther into the rows, laughing as the green corn fell before them.

"Don' recken they'll hev so much meal this fall." He swore and said, "jest ain't right thet niggers hev all this crop."

"Reason why is they work harder'n you," Joshua said. "An' they allus was good farm hands. Knowed more 'bout corn than any white man."

Hank took a step toward Josh and raised his clenched fist.

"Don' you go tellin' me 'bout no niggers. Me and Jubal had plenty afore the war. Growed good crops."

Joshua knocked him down with a roundhouse swing. They fought silently, rolling and tumbling and taking prodigious blows. Exhaustion stopped the fight. They lay in the down corn, dirty, blowing, but again friends.

"It war a good tussle," Joshua said. "You got plenty in thet swing."

His opponent rolled over and got to his knees. Hank wiped his face and blew his nose, flipping off the bloody mucus. "Ain' so bad yerself, Josh." He rose up and staggered toward the horse trough. Sticking his head under water, he scrubbed off and swung his head to clear his head. Droplets showered around him.

"Let's git on back, done enough here."

They eased up the eastern hill, sticking to the hard ground and the leafy places.

"Ain' goin' to find us this time," Joshua said. He glanced at the sky. "Rain comin' on an' we ain' left nary a trace."

* * *

When Hannibal and his brood returned from church, the lowing of the milk cows echoed though the drizzle. He swung down with a hasty step.

"Bub ain't milked yet," he said. "Git after him right quick once you in the house." When he had handed down the last child and granny, he headed for the barn.

"Bub," he yelled, "where are you." He broke into a run at the silence and disappeared into the structure. Hay dust sifted down when the loft's floor boards rattled. "You up there, Bub?"

The banging intensified. Hannibal pulled his pistol and slowly climbed the ladder, raising his head inch by inch into the loft. Before him hay heaved and muffled cries added to the banging. Sheathing his weapon, Hannibal exhumed Bub from the stored hay and freed his bonds.

"Damn!" Bub said, sitting up and feeling his head. He

pressed gingerly, groaning at the lump. His fingertips were red when he wiped his hands together.

Hannibal grabbed Bub when he fell over sideways and retched. "What happened to you?"

"Doan know," Bub mumbled "Tekin' little nap 'fore milkin' time an' wake up like dis." He felt his head. "Hurt bad."

Hannibal eased the injured hand down the ladder and carried him to Granny Mandy's, hollering on the way. The old woman had the door open and bent over Bub's head when Hannibal laid him on the couch.

"Easy, boy," she said as her fingers explored the bleeding bump. "It 'bout dried up. Poultice mek it well an' little bark put you to sleep. Well come mornin'."

She busied herself with her medicine kit as Hannibal questioned Bub.

"Don' see nobody, Hannibal," Bub insisted. "Sleepin' and wake up in de loft." He shied away from Granny's hands. "Dat hurt!"

"Be still, boy," she said, dressing the lump. "Dishere mek it well."

Hannibal broke in, "Hank again, probably. Or those tavern rats Minns hired. We'll see, come light. Tracks bound to show."

But the rain had removed all traces when daylight broke. Hannibal circled repeatedly and found tracks of neither horse nor man. He joined the others in the house and sat in council with a cup of coffee warming his damp frame. Granny Mandy's somber face confronted him, confirming his gloomy thoughts.

"An acre of the family corn gone," he said, "and two more acres trampled, before I got the cows and pigs out. Be short on meal this winter." He swore feelingly and instantly bowed his head and said, "Oh Lord, forgive me for taking thy name in vain."

"Lord lookin' atter us," Granny Mandy stoutly added. "Bub be well an' we git by wid de money fum de quiltin' Eva and I done make. Got ten. Sell 'em all in de city."

Hannibal nodded. "I ain't expecting you to spend your

money, Granny, but I accept gladly." He drained his cup. "It's best now I go see Claude. After all these months, I thought those devils had settled down."

* * *

The planter rounded up Sheriff Bandie visiting at Point Pleasant, outside the court, but he had little to offer.

"No tracks, you say?"

"No," Hannibal said. "Rain washed out everything."

"Well, then, I can't do nothin'." Bandie drew on his pipe stem and blew out some smoke. "But I will go with you and Claude again to see Jubal." His face wrinkled as he puffed. "This is the last time. They been warned enough. You either catch them in a crime or fergit it."

His face took on a set, inscrutable cast, open to the point of guile before his casual, "Can't keep a man from defending his home. Man gits shot dead invadin' ain't got no standin' with me, nor in court. Ain't likely be any trouble with the law." Bandie stared into Hannibal's eyes. "You take care of it yourself."

He's telling me to kill them, Hannibal thought. A chill ran over him and he shrank at the implication. Kill another man? He just couldn't, not ever again. Then Hester's tearful face intruded and he shivered, the chill shaking his resolve. He would do it. The Lord would understand. Thou shalt not kill did not keep him from saving himself and his loved ones from being killed. He would do what he must.

Hannibal nodded at Bandie's determined stare and picked up the gauntlet. "I will do that, Sheriff. Ain't no raiders hurt my family, nor me."

Patient and silent, Claude added his convictions. "Only way. Hannibal and I and the boys will take care of the trouble next time, if it comes to us. But we will not provoke it."

The following Tuesday, a vacant court date, Bandie and Claude paid a last visit to Jubal Peavey, accompanied by Hannibal and Henry. The latter had been vociferous about the inconvenience.

"Whyn't we hang 'em at the crik, Claude. Would'a saved all this ridin'. Man's got his own work to do without bracing Hank and Jubal all these times. We done too much talkin' already."

"Trying to be peaceful, Henry," Claude explained patiently. "But I won't ask you again, unless it's to settle the matter."

"Right," Henry replied. "We'll put those bastards under where they belong."

"Now Henry," Bandie said mildly, "I ain't never heard you say thet. You just make sure you folks are lawful in whatever you do."

Henry opened his mouth but Claude intervened. "It will be settled, Henry. Hannibal and I already figured that."

A stiff breeze caused their faces to roughen when they cantered into Peavey's yard. Jubal and Hank came onto the porch at their hail.

"What you want now?" Jubal growled. His flushed face and Hank's stagger testified to a few swallows of corn spirits. "You come peaceful?"

"No, Jubal," Claude replied. "Hank and Joshua turned Hannibal's cows and pigs into his corn. Leave them short on meal this winter."

"It ain't true!" Hank shouted.

A calm, erect Preacher of the Gospel faced Hank. In a resonant voice, Hannibal said calmly, "I forgive you, Hank. As the Bible says, 'Love thine enemies.' Though I can't understand why you hate me so, I still love you, Hank, as a human being."

Hank staggered as if struck. He paled and choked on his words, stumbling over, "You damned nigger. I ain't got no use fer you or that nigger-lovin' Claude."

Henry raised his rifle, only to be crowded away by Bandie. "Hold on, Henry. We ain't here fer gunplay."

When they again faced the Peavey's, both Hank and Jubal had their pistols aimed. Jubal said, "You lookin' fer trouble, Sheriff, we give it to you."

"Holster your weapons, Jubal," Bandie said quietly. He moved his horse between the two groups. "Now this is the last time I warn you." His icy voice continued, battering them. "You keep the peace or I'll end up hanging you all."

He gestured to Claude, who led Henry and Hannibal out to the road. Bandie tarried a minute with the Peaveys, Hank's loud protests carrying to the waiting men over the Sheriff's low drone. When Bandie joined them he had but few words to say. "I ain't interfering no more, Claude. Go home and keep the peace."

* * *

Wiley chuckled when Hank told him and Joshua of the confrontation. He raised his tankard and toasted Hank.

"Jest what we need, boy."

"Why, Wiley?" Hank asked in a low tone. He leaned over the boards of the Bull's Head's table. "You fixin' to raid agin'?"

The preacher shook his head. "Only in court, boy. We take Claude and his cousin Henry to court fer threatening you and Jubal." He took another swig. "An' thet Hannibal too," he added. "Sali will claw 'em right good."

Hank said, "Don' know 'im."

"Best lawyer fer us," Wiley whispered. "Come in here a while back and hit me up. Ain't got no scruples. Likes that yeller gold."

Their complaint came before Judge Croft, an old slouch of a man with a white beard and a known taste for corn whiskey. Jubal had sent on two gallons to his chambers before they appeared in court. The jugs sat on a table before the bench when they arrived, a prod to Jubal. He fidgeted in his seat, his brow wrinkled. When they were all seated after the case was called, Judge Croft began the proceedings.

"This your whiskey, Jubal?" he said icily.

"Yes, your honor," Peavey replied.

"Ain't your counsel told you 'bout bribery? Leaving those two jugs in my office ain't exactly legal."

Sali Hudler rose and faced the bench, sweeping back his frock coat. "No error intended, your honor," he said in an unctuous voice. "Jubal just sharing some of his new stock with his friends. Said he's been knowin' you since you was a kid."

"Hudler," Judge Croft said, "I been in these mountains a long time and sendin' whiskey to a courthouse ain't done among friends. Old Jubal there fit me more'n once when we was kids. Was a fair man 'til the war made him start lyin'."

Hank rose out of his seat but Hudler waved him down. "Apologize for the mistake," he said. "We'll take the whiskey with us when we go." He went forward and moved the jugs to a place behind his chair.

"I read your complaint," Croft said, when Hudler again faced him. "You got any more to add to that pile you sent me? Ain't never seen so many papers on a two-bit argument."

His hostile attitude persisted as the counsels proceeded, culminating when he banged his gavel down so hard that a chip flew off the implement and arched to a spot before the bench.

"I done heard enough of this drivel to gag me," he said, "old as I am. Jubal," he said, "you and Hank come forward. You too, Claude, and bring Hannibal." When they were assembled he settled the case.

Pointing his gavel at all of them he said, "You folks keep the peace. And if you got any two-bit differences, then fight it out with fists like we always done. But don't you come in here wasting my time again with this kind of frivolous suit." He looked past them to Sali Hudler, "You hear that, Hudler? You ain't getting off to a good start here."

"Yes, your honor," Hudler replied.

Croft stared at Peavey and castigated him. "Jubal," he said, "I been hearing things about you and Hank that I don't like." Peavey cursed. "Shut up," the judge said harshly. "Bandie told me all about that horse stealing and Hank's night riding. Now you take your damned whiskey and you and Hank obey the law."

He banged his gavel and announced in a loud voice, "Case

dismissed."

Hank went out muttering curses. Hudler picked up the jugs and his folders and followed them.

At his office later, he listened to their fury. "Never was able ter beat that damned Croft," Jubal muttered. "He'd pick up a stick er somethin'; never fit fair." He shook his head and his tone dropped to a hoarse whisper, "Ain't fair him bein' thick with Shaw. I figure I'll lay fer him some night."

"No you ain't," Hank answered. "If they's any fightin', it's my rifle will do the job."

Hudler banged on his desk with an ornamental gavel. "Shut up!" he shouted. "You two ain't making sense. You kill old Croft and you'll hang."

Their murderous looks silenced him. "Man don't crawl ter nobody," Jubal said. "Gonna be blood spilt afore this is done."

* * *

Ian McLellan knocked his pipe against the fireplace lintel and took his knife to the bowl. When he began reloading tobacco he spoke softly. "You know Wiley Minns is tryin' to buy the Butler place, Claude?"

"Where did you hear that?"

"Drivin' through Point Pleasant. Had to fix my harness and two o' those tavern loafers were talkin in a stall next to the blacksmith. Weren't quiet at all."

"That point above Crown City ain't too much use, Ian. Waterfront got a lot of shoal."

"Said he was plannin' a wharf and Butler controls the road access from Crown City."

"I'll look into it," Claude said. It troubled him as he recalled the waterfront. With the Butler farm to round out his other purchases, Wiley would have all the land upstream, including the entire point. With it, he could block the approach to the Shaw Landing even without the added benefit of the shoal. Behind was plenty of deep water and it was shielded from the current.

On his visit to his brother and the store in Crown City that Saturday, he ran into Butler. "Jim," he said cordially. "How is your crop this year?

"Don't matter, Claude," Butler said. "Sold out. Me and the Missus movin' to Athens to be close to Amy."

"Mind tellin' me who bought your farm?

"Wiley Minns." Butler hesitated and his face turned reddish as he averted his eyes. "Paid in gold, Claude. You know how long since I seen that much gold?"

"I wish you well, Jim," Claude replied. "Man gets gold and a fair price is doing right by his family. Can't fault you for that."

"Knowed you wanted the land too, Claude, but Minns come by jest as I had a debt."

Claude nodded. He shook Butler's hand. "Our families been friends a long time. Take good care of yourself."

On his journey back across the river, he thought of the looming hazard to his wharf and business. Old Minns foxed me this time, he concluded. Got to be more careful or he'll squeeze me out of here. A riposte to the challenge eluded him even as he faced Letty and told her of the potential damage to his river access.

19

The winter of 1867-1868 brought heavy snows in the mountains and bitter cold. The Ohio River froze over in January, cold enough to drive teams across the ice. With river traffic suspended, Captain Cal Jones came to Greenbottom to stay a few days and collect a deer and turkey in his annual hunting trip with Claude.

At their drinks before the fire in the living room of the guest cabin, that cold day of his arrival, Jones was direct as his usual habit. "Joshua been gatherin' up low-lifes, Claude. Sorry lookin' trash; steal anythin' probably." He shook his head. "Men mostly honest afore the war. Foragin' changed them."

"Had word from Elsie and Tandy just yesterday," Claude replied. "Same as you said. I sent word back to Tandy to watch the warehouse."

"He ain't but one man, Claude, even if he works there. Can't be there all the time." Jones gloomily sipped at his glass. "And that night guard Padgett hired ain't much, probably sleepin', or even takin' a bribe."

Claude nodded, silenced for the moment. They both stared into the fire, somnolent in the heat after a day in the cold. "Turnin' in," he said, "'bout to go to sleep in my chair."

Jones stirred and laughed, then drained his glass. "That's for sure right." He stood up and accompanied Claude to the door. "Lookin' for that big buck tomorrow."

"Breakfast at break of day," Claude reminded him. "I'll tell Isaiah to call you early."

He passed out into the cold night, stars glittering above. Wind whistled in the trees and clouds scudded by as he walked to the big house. Claude shivered. Deer most likely sheltered in that white pine thicket, he thought, yarded up. Come up the ridge trail from downwind and get two before they know we're there. It was a satisfying conclusion to his plan for the hunt. At the house he stripped quickly and slid into his flannel nightshirt. "Ah," he said contentedly as he slipped into bed and slid over to warm himself against the sleeping Letty.

Jones' doubts came true before he left Greenbottom five days later. Word arrived from the Gallipolis warehouse that a theft had occurred. Five kegs of Claude's dark rum were gone, along with merchandize from other owners, including Jones. Claude winced.

"That was part of Pinckney Middleton's October shipment," Claude told his friend. "It was contracted down river already. A good pile of coin gone."

Jones swore. "We better get up there fast."

Two days later, Claude and Jones faced the warehouse manager in the tiny corner office. Padgett wiped his forehead with a damp bandanna as he trembled before the grim men. His fat paunch grumbled with complaints audible to all and his bald head bobbed as he tried to reassure them. "Sheriff ain't found out nothin' yet," he said, in answer to their question. "Done fired that lazy Thad and hired those Legrange brothers. Sheriff said they won't put up with no nonsense; they's honest."

"He's right on that," Jones replied. "I been knowin' them since they was babies. Miz Julia weren't sparing of the Bible or the stick when they was boys. Taught 'em right."

"Know how to use guns," Claude added. "Both in the Seventh Infantry in sixty four and five."

Padgett sweated through his shirt before their condemning eyes. He fidgeted, his fear showing. "I ain't been here long, Mr. Jones. Got some learnin' to do about these local folks." His words spilled out. "Different in Baltimore. Don't never have no trouble like this."

Claude turned to Jones. "I'll wire down river, Cal. Those barrels got my stamp on them. If they show up at any of the taverns they can be seized and held to my account."

"We better tell Bandie," Jones said. "He'll be a'wantin' to know about this. Might turn up one of those loafers Minns uses at Point Pleasant." He drummed his fingers on the wall as Padgett waited silently. "Joshua too," he added. "Wiley don't do no stealin' himself."

Jones and Claude inspected the rest of their goods and talked to Tandy in the warehouse before leaving the groveling Padgett. But they gave him a stern warning as he ushered them out, his head still bobbing like a jumping jack. "Yes sir," he said, "ain't havin' no more breakins."

Two weeks later, time enough, Claude thought, to move the kegs by wagon, he received a telegraph from a tavern keeper friend in Cincinnati. "Your kegs here, seized and held by police. Two men escaped. One named Lennie."

* * *

"You know him, Charles?" Claude asked Searle.

"He's that roustabout that bought the timber for Minns," Searle replied. "He's shifty and a tough."

Claude puffed on his cigar for a moment. His thoughts went back to the timber deal where he had foxed Minns into a big profit for his friend Trumbull. He chuckled. Made old Trumbull mighty happy, and beholden. He knocked off the ashes and took another puff before bracing the quiet Searle.

"You reckon you can follow him for a few days? Find out what they're up to?

"Minns gettin' suspicious 'bout me, Claude. Got to take him something on you. Then I can get close to Lennie. He mostly hangs around with Josh."

The planter swung back in his swivel chair, its springs and

hinges squeaking. "See what you can do," he said. "That Josh ain't to be trusted."

It was a cool day when Tandy came in on a lathered mule, slipping off before the cabin in the twilight of early evening. He handed a note to Claude and waited.

"Get yourself some supper, Tandy," Claude said, "then come on back."

The note from Searle was terse. "Josh and Lennie and six others planning to raid your warehouse stores this Saturday night. Padgett home sick. Come quick with help."

Collecting Henry and one other trooper on the way, Claude and Tandy met Charles at the warehouse. They were in ambush when the raiders pried open a side door and entered. A fire bell pealed in the distance, accompanied by many shouts.

"You recken we git all of them barrels this time?" came out of the gloom.

Charles nudged Claude. "That's Lennie," he whispered.

"Old Padgett's laid up," Joshua's voice replied. "Them Legranges fightin' the fire you set at their mama's house. Ain't nobody around so let's git on with it."

A lantern flared at the group, revealing Josh and seven other men.

"Hands up," Claude shouted.

Joshua dived behind a box and opened fire, his weapon spurting flame. Several men raced out of the door with the remaining raiders spreading among the boxes and bales. Claude tapped Searle and crawled to the side and slipped along the side of the warehouse. One by one they boxed men between them, killing the two they found. When the firing stopped, Josh and the other men were gone. Lying on the floor in the lantern light were three bodies, two dead of bullet wounds and one by knife thrusts.

Tandy grunted. "Dat one mine," he said with a satisfied grin. He took the man's revolver and searched the body, coming up with a few coins and bills.

"Search the others," Claude said. "Keep any money you find. I'm mighty grateful."

The Negro quickly finished, collecting the guns and knives into a little pile.

"Lennie ain't here," Charles said. "Seen two of these before." He kicked two bodies. "Other one new."

Claude inspected the dead men. Plumb centered, he thought. The blood odor nauseated him, his thoughts slipping back to Rogersville and the men he had killed there in sixty three. He shook off the gloom and said, "Get the sheriff, Tandy."

Complaining about the hour and the fire, the local Sheriff finished with them quickly. After making a cursory survey of the bodies and the open door, he asked, "Joshua Minns," you say?"

"Yes," Claude replied, as the others nodded. "He had six men with him, besides Lennie, that tavern loafer in Point Pleasant. Don't know the rest."

"Know both," the Sheriff said, "an' they musta run out." He nudged the pile of weapons with his boot toe. "You aimin' to take these?"

"They're yours, Sheriff," Claude said.

The Sheriff's eyes gleamed at the booty, the revolvers alone worth a good price. He knelt and inspected the bodies closely, holding the lamp over each in turn as he turned them over and checked the wounds. Brushing straw off his knees when he stood, he passed his judgement.

"Don't 'spect no jury find no fault. Plain what they was up to. But chargin' those others across the river ain't no use. Minns lawyer's a slick weasel."

"I'm not looking for a legal fight," Claude said quietly. "We aim to take care of our own troubles."

The Sheriff nodded. "Bandie and I seen a lot of these last ten years. The war changed ever'thing to the bad." His tone turned bitter. "Seems like the law can't do it right no more, what with these slick lawyers that Minns hires, like that Hudler. You ketch 'em like tonight, no jury ever convict." Same as Bandie said, Claude thought. Got to enforce our own law.

"Get the bodies out, Tandy," Claude said. The Negro grabbed one man by the ankles, then dragged him toward the open door. Jones and Claude hauled on the other two. When the thieves lay in a row outside and the Sheriff had all the weapons in a sack, Claude said,

"Get a hammer and some nails, Tandy. We'll nail the door shut and then see Padgett and the Legranges. That poor widow has had a might of sorrow."

The resourceful Tandy hammered cut nails in solidly, persisting until the door was immovable without a wrecking bar. The Sheriff chuckled when he checked the work. "Ain't nobody goin' in this again," he said, "not 'til old Padgett loosens his purse a little." He laughed loudly. "He ain't one to spend nothin' so I 'spect it'll jest stay shut."

With the warehouse secure, the group parted, with the Sheriff promising to remove the dead men and Claude heading for the widow's house.

* * *

"What the hell did you do, Josh? Can't you do nothin' right?" Wiley's raging voice and pounding fist emphasized his anger at his nephew.

The bar was deserted at that early morning hour in Point Pleasant, as Minns met with Lennie and Joshua. Lennie wound a bandage around his lower left arm, its red spot still spreading and brightly colored.

Joshua sprawled in a chair before the fire, staring into the flames. "I tell you, Unk, they was waitin' fer us. Some damned rat told Shaw."

"It was that Searle," Lennie said. "No other. He knows 'bout all our doins, an' he works fer Shaw." He wound the cloth more tightly on his arm and used his teeth to pull one strand tight on the knot securing his bandage.

While the two Minns meditated on his remark, he said, "I don't take kindly to bein' shot agin'. Had enough o' thet in the war."

"What you plannin' ter do?" Josh asked.

"Ketch 'im and hang 'im, same's as we done to spies." Lennie calm voice continued. "You don' he'p, I do it alone."

Wiley stirred, his great bulk sagging as he rose and walked the floor. Silent for a few paces on the creaking boards, he stopped before Lennie. "You may be right, Lennie. Can't help thinkin' of that Trumbull deal. He could of been in with Shaw to snooker me out of all that coin." His resentment turned into a whine. "Old Trumbull laughed at me when I threatened to law him."

Wiley mimicked the old mountaineer. "Go ahead. Ain't no judge 'roun' here listen to you." Minns took a big swallow out of his jug. "Then he roared at me that he had the coin and weren't givin' none back."

Joshua rared up out of his chair. "He's right, Unk. You didn't make no friends hiring that no good Hudler and you ain't welcome in no courts."

They sat the rest of the night away mostly in silence, drinking until all snored loudly in deep comas, punctuated with epithets and thrashing of bodies in personal nightmares. After they fell asleep, the tipsy barmaid sneaked from her hiding place in the closet off the barroom and stole out of the door.

* * *

Planting time in 1868 in South Carolina came early, after a fine spring. Rance returned to the big house for his noon meal one damp day, responding to Aunt Susan's musical cry from the back porch. He chuckled as he recognized the difference since the war. Been a small child carrying the message before, he thought. One very respectful boy, with his "Massa" and servility. He shook off the thought as he walked to the house. He had to admit that it was much better this way. Free Negroes were different, worked harder, particularly on the small acreages he had deeded them. He clumped up the steps and onto the porch, to Aunty's protest.

"Don' you track all dat mud in here."

"You haven't changed a bit, Aunty," he replied. Shucking

his boots and sliding his feet into a pair of waiting slippers, he entered the door. Grabbing the old Negro around the waist, he squeezed her tight.

"Go 'long, Mista Rance," she said. Then with a suspicious twist to her face, she asked, "What you mean, I ain't changed?"

He faced her uncertainty with a laugh. "You're still orderin' me around, like I'm still a little boy. Don't I ever get to grow up? "

Susan swept back the wisps of gray hair peeking from her bandanna and waved a wooden spoon at him. "You ack jest like you allus do when you was small. Ain't thinkin' atall. I got ter keep Miz Ashley's house clean. Boys don't have no sense 'bout dose things."

He squeezed her again over her protests, than kissed her. "You keep on, Aunty. Miz Ashley'll lambast me if I track in."

With her mumbling protests following, Rance passed into hall. He found Ashley at her desk in the little office off the front parlor, concentrating on some lined pages. Bending over, he kissed the back of her neck and caressed the sides of her head.

His wife shook off his hands and said, "Don't bother me, Rance, 'til I get this column added up." She bent again to the task and raised up a few minutes later with a smile and a satisfied, "Ah!"

"You lookin' at the farm or your business?" he asked.

Without a word but with an impish grin, she rose from her chair and extended a hand to him. He eagerly possessed it and drew her to him for a prolonged embrace. She shivered when he ran his hands down her back but shook him off and smoothed her dress when a little bell sounded. Her skirt's brilliant green sheen and sharp pleats attested to new cloth, as well as the stiff white lace trim on the bodice. He reached for her again even as she wriggled away. "Later," she said.

Hand in hand they walked into the dining room and sat down at the white draped table, displaying sparkling crystal, fine silver and china. Rance seated Ashley at his immediate right rather than the traditional foot of the table, then took the head chair with its high, carved back. He possessed her left hand, stroking it, until Susan's kitchen help paraded in with the dishes and served them. When the Negroes were again out of the room, Ashley said the blessing, then dabbled with her fork while he attacked the roast venison.

"We're going to be rich again," she said slowly.

His fork stopped in mid air. "Why do you say that? We ain't got but a thousand in the bank and still owe that debt to Pinck."

"As you say, Rance,..it's in the cards." She placed one hand over her heart. "I feel it here."

He shook his head. "Ain't enough. Need money to get rich." He swept his hand around, circling over the table. "Got everything back in the house and can set a good meal from that big garden and smokehouse, but the work still will be hard."

"Oh ye of little faith," she said. "Here you are planting a hundred acres of cotton this spring and you think it won't yield? And you've got Jed and his cousins to help? All those strong young men? And Jed with his own woman and child?"

He shifted in his chair as his face took on a thoughtful cast. Ashley let him eat in silence as he pursued bite after bite with the fork, first venison, then sweet potatoes followed by turnips. When he broke off a piece of cornbread and nibbled on it, she spurred further.

"That sheet I was figuring on is about the weaving mill. While you been thinking only of clearing that land and setting out crops, I been working with Beulah and her granny friends. They made all the cloth we got in the back bedroom. We'll sell at a good profit."

As if he were deaf, he spread peach jam on a piece of cornbread on his plate, and forked pieces into his mouth.

She drummed a spoon on the table. When it didn't get his attention, she seized a silver bell nearby and jingled it next to his ear. "Are you listening, Rance?" she said impatiently. "Sometime I don't think you even hear me!"

Aunty Susan rushed in, slamming the kitchen door behind

her and wiping her hands on her apron. "You want me, Missus?"

"No," Ashley replied, "it's Mister Pickens I'm trying to wake up."

The old servant took a position behind Rance's chair and placed her hands on his shoulders. Kneading the muscles with strong grips, she massaged around his neck. He closed his eyes and slumped against the back of his chair. A "more" came when she stopped. Another session and he straightened up, alert and smiling.

"Thanks, Aunty," he said. "I'm ready for Ashley and her business talk. She's doing well with that mill we started."

"Dem patterns are purty," Susan said. "We all likes de color and dem reds and yallers tergether dat Beulah and Miz Ashley done got up." She flipped up her dress edge to display an abbreviated brilliant petticoat above a still smoothly rounded ankle.

"Susan!" Ashley exclaimed, as her right hand flew to her mouth. Her cheeks reddened as she said, "Cover yourself this minute!"

"Man gotta see de goods, Miz Ashley, ter appreciate what he gettin'. All dose young gals buy yer cloth sooner dan de grannies. Dose colors slay de men. No chance fur 'em atall."

Ashley gasped and her face crimsoned. She put her hands over her eyes and bent over her plate.

Rance guffawed at Susan's remarks. He reached over to Ashley and squeezed her hand. "You see, dear," he said, when she looked at him, "you can beat me. Aunty just told you where to sell all that cloth, to the young folks. They don't just want those English drabs. They want some sparkle and your cloth will give them the flower blossoms. They'll make you rich."

She smiled. "As soon as we get the money ahead I'm going to buy one of those English machines for our mill. We can add to the finer work by the grannies." She hugged herself with a triumphant smirk. "Beulah said we ought to do designs and make dresses."

"You want to get out a patterns magazine?"

"Later, maybe," she replied. She blushed. "But you ought to see some of Beulah's getups. Positively outrageous....but beautiful!"

"Dat right, Mista Rance." Susan said. "Dat Beulah got de head fer clothes. Jest come on ter our church next Sunday. Look at de young gels preen afore dem boys."

Ashley bristled. "He ain't ogling no pretty girls, Aunty Susan. He's got me to look at."

The old Negro chuckled, unrepentant and uncowed by the outburst. "You better show Mista Rance, Missus, er he ain't likely understand de difference."

She gathered up some plates and stalked back to the kitchen, pushing aside the girls ogling thorough a crack in the swinging door.

Rance imprisoned Ashley's left hand again and reached for her chin with his other fingers. She blushed as he turned her face toward him and gazed into her eyes. She is a beautiful woman, he thought, all recovered from that pinched harpy after the war. It was hard on her, ... and I didn't even realize it. Here with nothing but ache and no money. He stroked her smooth cheek with his left hand and ran his fingers down over her throat. "You're my woman, Ashley, and don't you ever think I'd look at one of those gels, as Aunty put it." He stroked her slowly as she bent toward him and her eyes took on a dreamy look. "By God, gal, you're beautiful!"

She rared back, the trance broken. "Rance!" she wailed. "Don't take the Lord's name in vain."

"I beg the Lord's pardon," he said, "but you're more beautiful than when we wed."

Her face softened. "I love that, Rance, and thank you."

She withdrew her hand and applied her fork to her plate, silent for a few bites while he ate. "Remember I told you about the merchants in Columbia?"

"Yes," he said, "but what's happening now?"

Ashley hesitated, choosing her words. "That store we dealt with before the war finally agreed to take some of our cloth. But they aren't cordial at all."

His hard voice interrupted. "You want me to talk to them? I'll not have you or Beulah mistreated."

"No. Beulah and I will open our own store. I got Miss Naughton from the school to agree to run it and we have plenty of Beulah's friends as seamstresses. Can offer cloth, sundries, hats, make dresses for ladies".... she hesitated ...."and on a second side, take care of the nigra women who want things."

He nodded. "They surely need some place decent. I swear, Ashley, I wonder why we didn't free those folks long ago. Whole different way now and I like how Jed and the others work. No slacking at all once they're working for their own money. Really good hands."

"Just like Aunty Susan and her girls here," she replied. "By the way," she added. "Got a letter from Pinck today. He was taken by those samples I sent him. Said they'd sell fine. Asked for fifty bolts for trial. Beulah and one of her cousins will take them down. They been wanting to visit Charleston."

"Wonderful!" Rance ran a piece of cornbread around the remnants of gravy on his plate and forked it into his mouth. "Heard about you in town, Ashley. Old Kramer said you were a hard bargainer...astute, he said. He admires you."

"Well, you'd never know it, looking at him. Always sitting there at that bank desk like a sphinx. I swear, but I never can figure out what that man is thinking or apt to do."

He laughed. "Good habits for a banker!'

She reached for a dish of stewed apples and spooned some into a bowl before pouring on cream. Handing it to him, she prepared her own. With her spoon poised, she said, "You aiming at a trip to Greenbottom this year?"

Rance had anticipated her oblique question. "That Shaw boy'll be about seventeen won't he? Just right for Nancy in a few more years?"

"Claudius seems like a fine young man," she said. "Can't do better that marry into a prosperous family and Letty will mold all those children into good folks. Hard workers."

"Not looking for a South Carolina boy?"

The depth of her answer surprised him. "The South needs new blood, Rance. Driving people." She paused. "Took Letty to wake me up to the pleasure of working. We been resting on the nigras too long. Our kin and the rest around here are no better, excepting old Pinck. He's a driver." She spooned up some apples and chewed thoughtfully. " The Shaw boy will be a welcome son."

"We'll go in November," he said. "Claude invited us for then, after the harvest is done. Pinck and Rose may join us."

She clapped her hands. "I'll write Rose." She grinned. "Send her some of my colored cloth too. A little present she can use on Pinck."

He finished his apples and returned to business. "If Pinck doesn't come, I'll take the two thousand gallons of rum for him. We'll go to Cincinnati on Claude's new boat. He expects it to be on the river in August."

"Sapphire," she said. "How did he choose that name?"

"Kittie Mae did," he replied. "Wife of her gambler friend, Worth Fauquier."

She shuddered. "He frightens me. So formal, but so cold."

"Fine southern gentleman," he reminded her. "His wife was killed by a shell at Petersburg along with their children."

Her head bowed and she murmured a short prayer. "He's trying to get himself killed," she said, "the way Letty talks."

He nodded and folded his knapkin. "Best I got back to the barn. Jed will be finished with the basket his wife brought him. Special for today."

"What's special?" Ashley asked.

"His son is one year old. He's playing with the boy right now." He rose and gave her a hug and kiss. "Until later."

Ashley beamed and rang for Susan. When the old Negro entered she began an animated discussion, their giggles and chuckles resounding in the large old room.

Rance labored at his desk in the late evening, penning papers. A slight rustle at his back interrupted, with a tall, rounded figure silently slipping past him in the lamp light. Glints of bright reds and yellows reflected from its skirt. Hesitating before him, a slim hand reached down and grasped the cloth. Sliding it up to mid calf, Ashley exposed a slim and smoothly rounded ankle.

* * *

"Charles?" came the whisper out of the bushes.

Searle whirled and pulled his pistol. He aimed it at the dark figure next to the growth at his front door. "Who is it?"

A feminine voice replied. "No matter," she said. "Come to warn you."

"About what?"

"Lennie and Minns had a ruckus in the tavern late the other night. Lennie figures you're working fer Shaw but Minns ain't ready fer thet."

Charles relaxed his stance and holstered his weapon. "So what's Lennie plan to do?"

The figure squatted down at the sound of footsteps passing closeby. When the man was well away, she crept closer and whispered. "He's aimin' on ambushin' you. Then hanging you as a spy,... like in the war."

He took a step toward the figure, which promptly broke and ran, vanishing around the corner of the house.

20

"You ever seen such rain?" Letty asked, when the hammering drops poured across the window in a stream. She got up and peered through the glass into the darkened yard. "It's almost like night and only three."

Claude tossed another oak billet onto the crackling fire in the parlor. The hot stones of the fireplace radiated into a warm room, with its oil lamps glowing bright. He jabbed at the burning oak with a poker, a shower of sparks carrying up the chimney. "Good draft," he said. "Enoch Kitts sure knew how to get the curve right when he laid up the brick. Thirty years old but there's no better fireplaces around than in Greenbottom."

"That's all well and good," Letty said impatiently. "But what about the rain?"

"Can't do nothing about that except wait and pray," Claude replied. "But if this keeps on another few days the river will boom."

She shivered and drew her shawl around her. "Feels cold even with the warm spell. Not like early March. Snow will melt fast with all this rain."

"We're high enough here to be dry, but I'd best see to the landings before it floods the bottoms." He made a last poke at the fire, then leaned the tool against the stones. Claude laughed. "Never thought I'd be happy about Minns but his point in the river will keep the Crown City landing safe. That spit's so high and grown up with big trees there's no chance of damage ... even if the river rises forty feet. Just like a barricade for the landing and the gravel bar at the end really diverts the current."

"I don't want this year remembered for a big flood, Claude. Too many people suffer, those in the bottoms along the river."

He shrugged. "Been happening since I was a boy. Just have to put up with it." A smile followed. "It'll give Searle a good run down river with his logs. Probably his last. Sawmilling and coal mining bringing in more money."

Four weeks later Claude and Letty trod the Crown City site, fetched in a hurry by a messenger from his brother. Minns' spit was mostly missing, vanished into the flood, along with the Shaw Landing and lower warehouse. They waded through the mud along the now receding river, Claude swearing until Letty shushed him.

"No use cursing, Claude. It's gone."

"We had a good profit last year, Letty. Now this blamed river has taken it all." He picked up a flat rock and skipped it across the surface of the water. "Six," he said, and grinned at her. Claude slapped his hands together, cleaning them of daubs of mud. Bending over, he squished some mud with a boot toe before straightening up. "Might as well get on with it. This will harden fast now that the river's going down." He took her arm as they walked to higher ground. "See Abel when we get back across the river. Can't do it without another loan."

* * *

Creadey rose from his chair as Hannibal entered his parlor. Rays of bright sunlight streamed through the windows, and soft April breezes brought sweet scents of fruit tree blossoms. A cardinal's chirp sounded in the yard, along with the chattering of a blue jay.

"Welcome, friend," Creadey said. "You hear God's creatures? They also extend greetings."

Hannibal bowed as he took Creadey's limp hand. "It is my pleasure to be here Reverend, though I grieve that you are poorly."

Recasting his shawl around his shoulders, Creadey pointed his cane to a nearby seat and took the cushioned rocker in front of the small fire. "Need heat," he said, "can't seem to get warm."

"It does help," Hannibal said, even as he wiped his face with a bandanna. "You sent for me?"

"Yes," Creadey replied, "to ask a great favor."

"Anything."

Creadey coughed and reached for a glass on a side table. Pouring out some syrupy brown liquid from a nearby bottle, he quaffed it down. After clearing his throat with a glass of water and a rasping expulsion of air, Creadey asked, "Will you preach for me while I get better?"

The request silenced Hannibal. The monumental thought staggered him ... him a black man and former slave preaching in a white church. He faced his doubts directly with Creadey.

"Some, maybe many in your congregation likely to be mighty put out, Reverend. Don't want to forget I'm a Negro and a slave. War ain't never ended in some's minds."

Creadey grimaced and bowed his head. "Do you remember the Lord's advice, Hannibal? ... come unto me all ye that are heavy laden?"

"I do, preacher, but lifting the burden can be long and hard."

"Claude and Letty freed you from your bondage and you and your Negro friends freed his soul in the escape. It's as plain as that sunlight in the window. He's a changed man, as are you." Creadey hacked and his body shook. He blew into a large cloth and cleared his throat and his nose. "The Lord freed you of your burden and called you to help others with theirs. It is your bounden duty, Hannibal. The Lord is calling you to this pulpit."

Hannibal hesitated, then reached for the Bible on the table beside the sick man's chair. He fondled it lovingly and said, "Thy will be done."

"Let us pray," Creadey intoned. With bowed heads, they

both began, "Our Father who art in Heaven ....," reciting the Lord's Prayer in measured synergy. "And now," Creadey continued, "bless Hannibal to this task, give him strength to have patience and to love the congregation, even those who are his enemies. Convert them, Lord, as you did Saul on the road to Tarsus. Make Hannibal thy instrument to lead the sinners in their rebirth. I ask all this in Jesus name, amen."

"Amen, and amen," Hannibal added. "I will do my best."

* * *

"I swear, Letty," Claude said, "but that flood last spring treated us just like the old Nile River acted in Egypt."

"Why do you say that?"

Claude seized her arm and pulled her from her chair with all her yarn balls spilling from her lap onto the floor. Her knitting needles went next, along with the uncompleted spread. Colored yarn carpeted the floor around her seat, one ball unraveling clear over to the cold fireplace.

"Now look what you've done," she wailed, as she gathered things together. "Can't you just tell me?"

He grasped her around her waist and pulled her to him. With a squeeze and a caress of her corpulent front, he kissed her and said, "You're just like our fields, a beauty and expecting a big yield."

Letty colored and dropped her head, glancing around. "Now you hush!" she said. "It ain't right you saying that where Kittie Mae or the other girls might hear. They'll find out about babies soon enough, when they're grown."

He laughed. "Can't hide that," he said. "Kittie Mae and the others already know. She's growing up, Letty. Anybody can see her blossoming."

She slapped at him playfully and a smile followed. "Well, since you're so bounden, let's get on out there."

Arm in arm, they sought the shade of the east end of the porch and sat in the wicker chairs. Claude held her hand

and they rocked for a few moments. A warm August breeze bathed them and rustled through the sheltering trees. The stand of tall, dark-green corn rippled in waves over the long, flat bottom stretching down to the river.

"Look at that corn," Claude said. "Best crop we ever had."

"It is pretty," Letty said. "The river bless't us."

He squeezed her hand and stroked her stomach and said, "Bless't in more ways than one. Going to name him Hannibal."

Letty hastily glanced around and moved his hand away. "You're terrible!" she said. "And how do you know it will be a boy?"

He laughed. "Saw it all in a dream the other night. Hannibal was baptizing Hannibal. Heard him say it, plain as day."

His remark silenced her and she squeezed his hand. "It's a fine name," she said. "A name of a conqueror and may he be worthy of it."

Upstream a series of short whistle blasts intruded on their reverie.

"Another boat passing the bend," Claude said. He listened to more ordered notes. "Must be a new one. Never heard that whistle before." Frantic blast patterns interrupted, ending in the prolonged thunder of a lower key. "That sharp bend spooked him bad."

"Can't see there, Claude. Remember that time with Cal Jones? I thought he'd run into the Celeste and closed my eyes tight. We just scraped by."

He chuckled. "You weren't the only one. Even Cal was scared." Claude whistled softly. "Mighty close that time."

Letty fingered the wicker arm of her chair and picked at a small unpainted spot. He reached over again and possessed her hand. stroking it. "You're worried about something, Letty. I can always tell."

"If the river treated us so good, it's the same for all the others. Be so much corn, you can't sell it. Won't be worth hardly nothing. Aren't you afraid of that?"

Claude shook his head. "Barge it clear down to New Orleans. Those factors there'll take all I send them. Already got Ledoux's word. He ain't never failed me before with the timber. If he says there's a market, I'll trust him."

Letty's face wrinkled and her lips tightened. "He can't control everything. I know he's your friend but his business will come first."

"Man's got to trust, Letty," he calmly replied. "And remember, we got that hundred acres of potatoes along with the timber and coal. More'n one string to our bow."

She squeezed his hand and struggled to rise. He helped her out of the inclined seat, pulling her erect against him. Stroking her head as it rested on his chest, he said, "We are bless't with the Lord's bounty. Let us enjoy it and give thanks without worry."

"What about that Wiley Minns?" she said, shivering.

Claude stroked her back and held her close. "He ain't been bothering me lately," he said. "Sheriff said he went down to Carolina in May. Ain't come back."

"He scares me, Claude. And that mean Joshua."

Claude drew back from her and laughed. "Josh found out there's women around," he said. "Sparking Trumbull's daughter, that little one that's so quiet."

"Abigail?" Letty asked.

He nodded. "That's right. And Trumbull told me that if Josh had gold like Wiley, he'd bless the marriage."

Letty's mouth fell open and her right palm quickly covered it. "I can't believe it!" she said. She jerked her left hand from his and burst out, "That's scandalous! Trumbull would sell Abigail for money?"

Claude backed off hastily. "Well, I didn't say that! They're sparking and Josh is mighty interested. He ain't asked for her yet but Trumbull expects it mighty soon. Says Abigail is willing."

His wife's back stiffened and with a contemptuous frown, she cut him up. "You men really do love that gold, don't you?" Letty marched away from him, her heels pounding down on the boards, and slammed the door as she entered the house.

"Well, Josh isn't bothering me," Claude muttered. "That's what you wanted, wasn't it?" He stared at the closed door and sighed. "If Abigail ties him down, so much the better. Nothing like a woman to make a man peaceable."

* * *

Rance and Ashley and their daughter Nancy arrived in Greenbottom on November 1, coming in a carriage driven by Charles Searle.

"Welcome, welcome!" Claude boomed out as he met Rance at the bottom of the front steps on that sunny afternoon. He leaned on his cane, favoring his right foot.

Rance bounded down from the carriage and took Claude's free hand, pumping away. "Not serious, I hope?"

"No," Claude replied, "just caught it on a root. Fool step when I wasn't watching."

The South Carolinian nodded and turned to the carriage. Ashley took his hand and stepped to the flagstone landing even as Nancy leaped from the other side into the embrace of Kittie Mae. The two girls chattered and kissed and went off arm in arm while their elders completed the greetings.

"Seems like those two got plans," Ashley said.

Letty giggled. "Kittie Mae had a letter from Nancy a week ago. Wouldn't say what was in it."

Ashley sighed and said, "I expect it's about men. Nancy does go on, now that she thinks she's almost grown. She's been telling me she wants a rich husband. No boy's going to satisfy that."

Their two mates intruded, shepherding the ladies into the house while Charles and Isaiah supervised hands moving the trunks from a second wagon. When they reassembled in the parlor an hour later, Ashley was freshly attired in a new dress of flashing color. Sunbeams reflected from the reds and the purple shades in the skirt, complementing the shining deep green of her bodice with its white lace.

Letty walked around her guest staring while Ashley pirouetted in the center of the room. Shafts of light magnified the richness of the intense reds.

"Do you like it?" Ashley asked.

"It's lovely," Letty replied. Her brow furrowed and she hesitated a moment. "But do you wear that out in public? Isn't it a little .... risqué?"

Rance waltzed to Ashley's side, seized her about the waist with one arm and bowed to the Shaws. "Meet my new bride, folks. Ashley gave up all those dull war trappings except for traveling. She's soldiering under these new colors and I'm proud to side her."

"Are those part of the cloth you wrote about?" Claude asked. "You mentioned that Ashley has a textile mill going."

Holding Ashley's hand above her head, Rance let her spin once to show off the magnificent array of colors. "We brought fifty bolts of five colors," he said, "as a trial to sell to the merchants in Cincinnati."

A clatter in the hall interrupted Claude's reply. Rushing in ahead of Nancy, a resplendent Kittie Mae squealed, "Mama, Mama! Look what Nancy gave me."

The two girls danced through the room, each in a mix of blue, green and yellow dresses. They went into the sunlight and passed through the shadows, then curtsied to the adults in a sunbeam, spreading their skirts in a display of brilliant pleats and lace.

"Gorgeous," Claude said.

At the door, Claudius stared silently. His eyes never left Nancy as she rose and greeted the Shaws. Letty hugged her and bid her welcome while Kittie Mae shyly thanked Ashley.

"It's good of you to give me this," Kittie Mae said, curtseying. "And in a Harper's pattern too. I've never had anything so beautiful."

"It was Nancy's gift," Ashley said kindly. "She wanted you both to have a pair of matching dresses for the trip on the river boat." She laughed. "You two will really shine. All the men will want to dance with you."

The two girls colored and sidled away to seats in a corner. Their heads together, they laughed and shared secrets unintelligible to the adults. Claudius edged farther around the door jamb until Claude spied him and called out,

"Well, come on in, son, and greet the Pickens. No reason to be bashful."

Ashley's face beamed as she inspected the erect, strapping youth. "Come to me first, Claudius. Let me look at you."

Rance nudged Claude and leaned over. He whispered, "She's measuring him for a son-in-law. Set on a northerner."

Claude and Letty linked arms as Ashley graded their eldest son. She grasped his hands and pulled the boy to her in a tight motherly embrace, then held him at arms length and inspected his frame. Claudius flushed but met her gaze unflinchingly.

"My," she said, "but you have grown. Six feet at least and filling out. And with a handsome mustache. Do you go to school or are you finished?"

Claudius flinched and looked at his mother in silence. He squirmed and shifted his feet, paling under the combined weight of four pairs of adult eyes.

His mother's voice pricked him sharply. "Mind your manners, Claudius. Mrs. Pickens is our guest."

The spell broken, Claudius replied, "One more year of high school, Miz Pickens, then I'll be done." Words spilled out once he was started. "I been helping Pa with the farming and have learned right much about trading along the river and keeping the records." He backed away a step and proudly added, "Made over three hundred dollars on my own account last year."

"Wonderful!" she said. "What did you trade?"

He grew more erect as he faced her and said, "Dogs. We got the best hounds in the county. Everybody knows Old Blue."

Ashley turned a puzzled face to her husband. He laughed and said, "Blue was a renowned bluetick down our way, Ashley, when Athey Minns had him. Don't you remember? West Virginia got good blood when Claude brought him north."

"We have a new litter right now, Miz Ashley," Claudius volunteered. "Two blueticks and three black and tans, but all got spots. They're four weeks old and real pretty."

"And you'll sell those when they are weaned?"

"No ma'am," Claudius replied. He warmed to the task. "I keep 'em 'til they're about a year old and started on rabbits and coons, or maybe foxes for those that's interested. Then they bring good money." Letty smiled and nodded encouragingly to him. "Even took three to Cincinnati last summer," he said. "Sold 'em right off."

The two girls had come closer, silent and intent on the conversation. Nancy placed her hand on her mother's arm and said, "Could I go see the puppies, mother?" At Ashley's, "Yes, dear," she asked Claudius, "Will you show them to me?"

Rance chuckled and muttered loud enough for only Claude to hear. "She's hot on the track!"

"We'll need to change," Kittie Mae said, taking Nancy's arm. "Those puppies are down to the barn and we don't want to get mussed." She swept the other girl out of the room while shouting back, "See you there, Claudius."

After the boy's footsteps had died out in the side hall, Ashley went to Letty and hugged her. "He is truly growing into a fine looking young man," she said. "I do hope they hit it off. We would welcome Claudius into our family."

"And Nancy into ours," Letty replied. "Our boy is a reliable hardworker," she said, "and saving, and does not smoke or drink ... unusual for these times."

They clasped their hands together in a foursome, parents hoping for the planned outcome. "Bless their union ... and ours," Rance said. "At last," he added, "the war is behind us."

* * *

"How do you like the Sapphire?" Claude asked as they cruised the Ohio River, just above Cincinnati.

"She's a beauty!" Rance answered. "Powerful, too. Look at that wake. I never have seen such a huge paddlewheel."

The party sat on the upper weather deck behind the pilot-house, their chairs arranged around a table with a pitcher and glasses. They wore only light coats on a mild day with scattered clouds. The Ohio and Kentucky banks showed more farms and hamlets as they steamed along, aided by a slow current. Smoke rose to the west, concentrated in one area.

"Cal Jones bought her for us," Claude said. "He knows more about boats than any man on the river." He stroked the mahogany railing proudly. "Brand new last summer."

As if he had heard the compliment, Jones sounded the whistle, deafening them with a long blast. The ladies clapped their hands over their ears as the steam jet was carried away by the wind. Ahead a boat steaming upriver sought the Kentucky side of the channel, passing well clear but in easy hailing distance.

When they were abreast, the pilot of the other boat shouted through his megaphone, "Any new snags, Cal?"

"One pile just below the Big Sandy is all," Jones yelled back. "But watch the bar at the Guyan. It shifted some but the channel is clear enough. You can see the eddies easy."

A wave answered and the two boats separated rapidly. Around the next bend, Cincinnati lay before them on the Ohio shore, with its columns of dirty smoke. The travelers rose and lined up along the forward railing as Jones slowed and maneuvered Sapphire into the bank alongside six more steamers. It was a clean landing, finished off with the attachment of heavy mooring lines and the dropping of the brows.

When they gathered in the lounge a week later to tally their successes, Claude and Ashley were especially jubilant.

"Look at this, Rance," Ashley said. "All the cloth sold in two days and I got orders for more bolts than we can make in six months."

"You'll need to expand your mill," her husband answered. He mournfully added, "did better than my rum. Kentucky whiskey selling better from what Claude's tavern friend tells us."

Claude looked up from his notebook. "That's right. Kelly caters to the Irish but he keeps track of the other taverns. It's whiskey the folks mostly want, along with hard cider and home brew. Easy to make those here."

"How did the Cuban cigars do?" Letty asked.

Rance brightened and sought his notes. "The best of all," he said. "Sold everything I brought at a big profit. Claude and I struck a deal with six stores and one factor. They'll take more but they'll come through Shaw and Sons."

"Shaw and Sons?" Letty asked. "What's that?"

Claude sought her hands and looked her directly in the eyes. "Rance and I talked it over, dear. Claudius needs a start and a business is the best. Then later Garrett and little Hannibal if they want. I'll get the papers straight with Judge Marvin when we're back to Greenbottom."

Tears ran down Letty's cheeks. "Claudius in business?" she wailed, "he's almost grown up." She daubed her eyes and said, "I can't bear to think of his leaving, not yet."

Ashley rushed to her side and embraced Letty, pushing Claude away. She cuddled and soothed the crying woman with murmured entreaties. With a sniff and a final wipe, Letty sat up, smiling.

"I suppose every boy must grow up," she said, daubing a few stray tears, "and every mother must cry at the first one leaving home."

"He's not gone," Claude said, "not for another year. He can help me with the coal orders as well as his dogs while he finishes school. Get started with a good stake."

"Another year?" Letty asked.

"We want him to come to South Carolina," Ashley said. "He can be Claude's agent for your business with my mill and Rance's and Pinck's shipping."

Letty's haggard face brightened. She cheerfully said, "No better way to have him and Nancy together. They'll make a fine couple."

When the Sapphire was ready to leave two days later, heading upriver, Kittie Mae and Nancy brought Worth Fauquier to the group on the upper deck. The Virginian bowed to the ladies with the two girls' arms interlocked with his. He was in a striking gray suit with frock coat, flanked by two sets of colorful dresses.

"As you can see," he said, smiling, "I am surrounded and have surrendered."

"To a Yankee and a Confederate, I see," Rance said jokingly.

They all laughed, as Worth shook off the girls' arms and sought the hands of the two men. "I am delighted to be with you," he said.

Their repartee was interrupted by the sight of a beautiful, light complexioned woman exiting the stairs up to the weather deck. She strode toward the group in a graceful, undulating step, a precocious stride that struck chords with Claude. Where have I seen her, he thought. Without hesitation, she paused before him and smiled impishly.

"Remember me, Claude?" she said. At his hesitation, she said, "I'm Iris from the Calhoun place."

He stood transfixed, silent as the others, struck by her appearance on the Sapphire, astounded at her voluptuous beauty. Dressed in the latest fashions, she was a desirable creature so different from the thin Iris of his escape. He stared at her rouged cheeks and reddened lips, a face grown from pretty into a ravishing charm. Claude flushed and pushed back his carnal thoughts. Iris? Here?

Without further talk, Iris seized Claude tightly and kissed him on the lips, while rubbing her body against his. She resisted his attempt to escape her, clinging and tantalizing and kissing him again. He stirred at her invitation but wrested free.

"What are you doing here?" he demanded angrily. Scrubbing the rouge off his lips with the back of his hand, he grabbed her arm and shook her roughly. "Why are you here?"

Iris smiled seductively and pulled her arm free of him. "Tol' you I'd be back, Claude," she said in a throaty voice.

Letty rushed in front of Claude and turned her back to Iris. "Who is this woman, Claude?" Her ominous tone and pursed lips were steady but her trembling body warned him of an explosion.

"She is an octoroon from Calhoun's," he said calmly. "Wanted Hannibal, and wanted me to help her escape. She's a meddlesome vixen Granny Esther warned me about as being nothing but trouble, so I did not help her. She threatened me and said she'd be back. I imagine she'll go for Hannibal."

Iris laughed and smoothed her dress, parading her charms. "You right on dat," she said. "Where is he? I take him from dat no-good Hester."

"Allow me," Worth said, as he stepped between Letty and Iris. He pushed the woman away roughly, then bent his head to her and said very slowly. "Now you leave these good folks alone or I will throw you in the river. Do you understand me."

Iris quailed before the steely eyes and the flinty tone of Worth's threat. Her body sagged slightly and she backed up.

"I be seeing you again, Claude," she said. As she left, she shouted loudly, "You tell dat Hester I git Hannibal good. He want me over her when I done wid him."

21

Wiley Minns rocked on his brother's porch, its view over the browning Carolina slopes one of his favorites. Next to him, Ma Minns, Athey's widow, kept her knitting needles busy, their little clicking sounds adding to the hum of insects. A bluejay screamed in the massive cedar to the right of the porch, invisible in its thick clusters of dark green needles. Two more answered down the hill, one suddenly appearing and soaring into the cedar. The second followed close on, the three jawing as they settled on their roosts.

Ma stilled her hands, tying off a knot and clipping the yarn with a pair of small scissors. "When you goin' back up to Greenbottom, Wiley? Seems like you spent all summer just idlin' here in South Carolina."

"It's time now, Ma. Been thinking and waiting for October and the crops to be about made, and for all that new gold to pile up from Jasper's sales." He moved his head sharply and swiped his hands at a buzzing fly. "Tol' Josh to range up an' down the Ohio during the summer and promise gold fer those things Shaw's tradin' for. Make better deals than him. Thet letter yestiday said him and Hank had seen about all the folks, so it's time to go."

She sighed. "Ain't you had enough o' this? You been chasin' Shaw more'n three year since the war and you ain't broke him yet."

He bristled at the implied insult and the porch floor squealed loudly at his rocker's increased speed. "Crowded him right pert last year but that damned judge took his side. This next year I'll get his things and his notes. Break him right."

She rocked a spell in silence, while her hands corralled loose strands of graying hair. Adjustment of her shawl came next, tightening it around her bony shoulders. The squeaking rockers drew protests from the unpainted floor boards, a somber crescendo of discordance.

"How come you ain't let Josh kill Shaw and be done with it, you hate him so?"

His face turned murderous and his right fist clenched. "That bastard killed Athey and the boys," he hissed. "His whole life is trade. Break him trading and I kill 'im twice, the second time when we put him under. I'm bustin' him first, then Josh can take his shot."

"Josh said he was settin' up, last time he wrote. He don' sound like no fightin' man no more."

Wiley chuckled. "That boy run onto Abigail when he was supposed to be lookin' at Trumbull's timber. Seen that girl instead an' never been the same after. Tol' everyone she was his'n."

Ma looked him straight in the eyes. "It's Athey's gold you're usin', Wiley, and you're taking more back with you. I want you to give two thousand to Josh for settin' up. You promise that?"

He nodded. "It's little enough. I'll be leaving next week after talking to Miz Pickens. Wheedle somethin' out of her about their business dealings with Shaw."

Ma brightened and exploded into a talkative stream. "She's expanding her factory, Wiley. Never seen such goings-on with a high-toned lady. Ain't no different than an overseer. Works all the time. Nigras mighty happy, got money jingling, and her cloth sells good. Purty!"

"How about the Captain?"

Her hands stilled for a moment. "He and that old Pinckney

Middleton from down to Charl'ston been gittin' trade from around the state. He's as busy as Miz Ashley. I swan, Wiley, they's goin' end up richer than a'fore the War. I never expected such folks to take to working."

Wiley stroked his sideburns and twisted the ends of his moustache. "They allus was high an' mighty. Throwed me off the plantation once before the war. Maybe I can touch them too."

Ma recoiled and her hand flew to her mouth as her chair screeched to a stop. "Don't you bother them none," she gasped. "Them folks run us Minns right outen the country."

The two fell silent, Ma resuming her knitting, deep in their thoughts until the reddish-orange sun sank to the far slope and blue and orange streaks traversed the darkening sky. Birds twittered, settling in for the night, and a hooty owl called. Ma rolled up her knitting and went into the cabin. A frying pan clattered after the poker rattled in the fire. Still rocking, Wiley muttered, "If Pickens gits in the way, he gits the same as Shaw. Ain't no Minns fergit an insult."

* * *

Leaves were a kaleidoscope of reds and yellows when Wiley arrived back in Point Pleasant on a crisp, late October day. Stretching and scratching after he stepped down from the carriage, he walked stiffly toward the Bull's Head, leaving his team hitched to the rail. "Damn," he said, "where's Josh?"

His question was answered by the sight of his nephew hurrying from the building, wiping his mouth with his right sleeve as he strode forward. Josh shepherded him into the tavern and called to a waitress for a mug of coffee.

"You bring it, Unk?" he asked.

"Shut up, boy," was Wiley's testy reply. He surveyed the large number of men in the tavern. "We ain't wantin' no folks here to know our business."

Josh nodded and moved his mug to a table in a far corner, not close to the patrons. When Wiley's coffee came, he sipped on the steaming cup and warmed his hands around the hot china. Beckoning to the girl, he said, “Hold on. You got any stew left this time of day?”

She nodded and answered, “Deer meat and pork,with plenty of taters and cabbage and onions.”

His eyes gleamed and he smacked his lips. “Ain’t no better nowhere,” he said. When his bowl came, with its biscuits and honey, he waved aside Josh’s questions until he had cleaned up the lot, polishing his bowl with a remnant of biscuit. Wiley belched and eased back from the table. “Just as I remember it,” he said. “Beats your ma’s fixin’s all hollow.”

Joshua bristled. “Don’t you go saying thet! Ma fed you all those times you come begging gold. You got fatter ever’ year thet you showed up.”

Wiley ignored the gibe and swigged from his coffee mug. Bending close to his nephew, he whispered, “You run onto any o’ Shaw’s notes we can git? Or any deals we can beat him on?”

His query was interrupted by Lennie, who burst into the tavern. Pausing while he shielded his eyes and searched the dim interior, he fixed on them and rushed over to their table. Lennie flopped down into a chair and ignored Wiley. “Thet Wilkerson boy’s sparkin’ Abigail, Josh. Saw ’em at the Tate wedding last Sunday. He was holdin’ her hand and lookin’ mighty sheepeyed.”

A pall settled over the meeting, a silence as deep as a still, dark night. When Wiley said, “You got any answers for me, boy?” Josh replied,

“Shut up, Unk, I got to think on this.”

“But we need to git to Shaw, boy.”

“The hell with Shaw! I got to run off thet damned Wilkerson. Bastard ain’t goin’ to git Abigail. Thought they all knew thet she’s mine.”

“Ma sent you two thousand gold to set up,” Wiley said. “Will that he’p change her mind?”

Joshua gaped a moment then pounded with his mug. “That’ll fetch her! Let’s git to the house, Unk. I want thet gold right now. Take it to Trumbull and show him."

When the two young men left him in the early morning, Wiley took his coffee out on the porch and settled into a rocking chair. He laughed as the men galloped away. "Damn fool don't realize he's gittin' an' anchor. Never be the same." He sipped and rocked, his plans for Shaw interrupted by desire. Mists rose from the wet countryside, obscuring his view of the lower slopes. An unseen whistle sounded from the river and a cow bawled from a nearby pasture. "Ma was right," he told the squeaking chair. "Got to settle with Shaw quick. Josh done lost to thet girl." He rocked and rocked until the sun cleared the mists but not his vision of the future. Entering the house about noon, he found the kitchen stove cold and no pot on it. "Damn!" he swore, as he surveyed the interior. "Josh ain't wantin' me around once he gits hitched. Not with Abigail a'temptin' him." He slumped into a chair at the kitchen table. "Got to settle this thing next year, fer sure."

* * *

Jubal Peavey eyed the girl as she served him his plate of fried ham and potatoes. She strolled back to the wood stove with a seductive roll of her rounded bottom, his piercing gaze following. Rattling the pots still on the stove lids, then setting them aside to the warming area, she brought her smaller plate to the table and sat facing him.

"You're a mighty fine cook," he said. "Hank did better'n I thought in pickin' a woman. An' Ruth is a pretty name."

"Took 'im long enough," she said. "Fust come over to our place sniffin' around 'bout two year ago. Waitin' to sixty eight to marry ain't right. Thought I'd be an old maid."

"Well, you're only nineteen," Jubal protested. "An' a right purty thing," he added.

The girl fluffed herself up and displayed her full bosom swelling through her tight bodice. She caressed her hair and a slight smile fleeted across her face. "You like me?" she said. She stuck out her tongue and oscillated it back and forth between her lips. He left his meat untouched and sidled around the table to her chair. Bending over her upturned face, he kissed her as his hands slid down over her bosom and rounded belly. Without a word, she rose from the chair and led him back to the bedroom.

"Where's Hank?" he asked.

She grumbled as she stripped her dress and underclothes, standing naked before him. "He's off with Josh and those other trash, drinkin' again. Had a big hangover when he took me to the preacher. Hot fer me fer months 'til he got thet Walker hound, then went roamin'." She tossed her head and preened before the dresser mirror, her reflection smooth and buxom. "Must be drunk again fer he shore can't see what he's got here."

He laughed. "Josh ain't fergot; jest tryin' his new dog."

* * *

It drizzled rain the cool March day that they buried the Right Reverend George Catlett Creadey. With most of the membership standing around the open grave in the cemetery beside the church, Hannibal read the burial service in its fullness, consigning Creadey's soul to the eternal. His ashes to ashes and dust to dust rolled out sonorously as he tossed a handful of soil onto the casket to finish the service. Creadey's wife knelt and bowed her head in silent prayer. Hannibal blessed her as he helped her up and three women took the weeping widow and her two sons away, heading for the nearby church. The crowd gradually drifted apart, with several older members pausing to toss clumps of dirt onto the box as they filed past. When the group had decreased to just Hannibal and workmen filling the grave, two men came back and interrupted Hannibal's final farewell.

"It's time to go," Henry said.

"I know, Henry," Hannibal replied, "but he was such a dear friend and his call to me so clear. I couldn't resist him and the Lord." His tearful face was framed by drops of water dripping from the brim of his hat.

"We got to talk to you right quick, Hannibal. Me an' the other deacons done decided we want you for the pulpit, now that

Reverend Creadey is gone."

"But I have my church on Little Seven Mile."

Henry and the other man seized Hannibal by the arms and turned their faces close to his. "Ain't no reason you can't do both," Henry insisted. "And they can come here ever' Sunday they choose. Easy to freight them with all our carriages?"

"You ain't worried most of them are Negroes?"

Henry growled, choking off an epithet. "We done gone through that. All as disagree left last year when you first started preachin'."

His friend nodded. "Don' you worry none, Hannibal. Folks mighty satisfied with your messages. You are one fine preacher."

"We'll do the call and installation next Sunday," Henry said, "iffen you accept." He hastily added, "Same salary as Preacher Creadey."

Hannibal wiped his damp face with a large bandanna and turned it to the sky. "Oh Lord," he said, "you have led me to this place as part of your plan for me and our dear departed. I will do my best to serve you in his dedicated spirit, always faithful."

Henry clapped him on the back and his friend wrung Hannibal's hand. "Bless you," he said, to which Henry added, "Amen!"

* * *

"Mighty fine fire," Claude said, while poking up the burning pile in the deep, stone-faced fireplace. "Can't ask for better." He tossed on several three foot long billets of split, black-barked oak, warmed his seat a few moments, then walked over to the window.

Ian McLellan stirred from his chair and joined him while Charles Searle knocked his pipe's scrapings into the fireplace. "Building this cabin sure improved your place," Searle said. "Ain't never seen so cosy a house."

Light from the fire and oil lamps revealed Claude's desk,

overflowing with papers, and a line of pale oak filing cabinets. The room had been converted from living quarters to a large office with its chairs, and benches against the walls. Deer antlers graced three walls and a long-barreled cap and ball rifle hung over deer hooves above the mantel, along with a tasseled leather possibles sack and a powder horn. Braided throw rugs of bright colored cloth brightened up the floor of polished, wide pine boards.

"You're right," Claude said as he turned from the window. "Mighty comfortin' in this kind of weather." Tree branches rustled in answer and wind shook the house, rattling windows as it gusted. A mournful howl sounded at the western end of the roof. Claude shivered and moved over to the fire.

Ian froze into a tense stillness. "Thet ain't the banshee, Claude, but it don' sound like no wind ner no human neither."

As if to answer, an even louder howl accompanied the next whistling gust. The two visitors simultaneously pulled pistols but Claude, instead, picked up a Bible from a table and opened it to a bookmark, reading, "come to me all ye who are heavy laden and I will give you rest." Closing the holy book, he held up a cross and prayed, "Oh Lord, give a peaceful rest to that man burned by the Indians long ago. Let him and us be in peace."

"Reverend Creadey and Hannibal did that when you built," Charles said. "The hant still here?"

Another gust pounded the house but the howl disappeared. The wind whipped the branches of the trees into thrashing collisions, a frenzy of activity, the sound and fury of Shakespeare without result. Claude bent his head and said, "Thy will be done." As if to answer him the gust died away into an oscillating stream of pulses against the house, a strong wind that no longer carried the eerie note.

"Time we got to work," Claude said. "Evening moving on."

The front door opened after a loud knock. A husky blonde girl came in and took a collection of supper dishes from the oval oak table in the middle of the floor, leaving it wiped clean.

Once she was gone, Claude shifted some papers from the

desk and seated himself at one end. "Sit," he said, motioning to the others.

Ian squirmed uneasily in his chair, turning to look at the door to the hall to the bedrooms. "Don' feel right, Claude. Shiv-erin'. Somethin' else in this house 'sides us."

"That's just the Irish in you thinkin' about the wind."

"No," Charles said, "it was you who prayed, not Ian. What's going' on? No nigras about an' you with Gertie, a German girl for this house."

Claude sighed. "Negroes won't come near, since the howls started. It ain't but some loose board, I think, but Enoch Kitts looked at it all. He's the finest carpenter around even if he does work on the boats. Couldn't find nothing."

His visitors shifted in their seats and Ian glanced over his shoulder, again surveying the closed hall door. It rattled at another gust and he jumped up out of his chair. Sweat started on his forehead and he moved around to an opposite position facing the door. Pulling his pistol and placing a cross beside it on the table, he relaxed and said nervously, "I'm ready, Claude."

The other men grinned at his Irish nature, always supersti-tious as long as they had known him, Claude since boyhood. The latter opened his Bible again and said, "The Lord will protect us, Ian. Ain't no wrongdoing here. Hants are for the evil."

Ian nodded and gulped. "Just can't he'p it. Our people talked about the banshees and the wee folk all the time I was growin' up. Mama an' Grandpa tol' us the tales." He laughed ruefully. "Guess we're given to being tormented, what with the demon rum an' the rest. Irish allus was driven."

"But you beat devil rum," Claude said. "I'm proud of you for that."

Charles nodded. "Mighty fine. You're a good man, sober, Ian. Even harder workin' than my Pa an' he was somethin' else!"

Reflection occupied them for a few minutes, interrupted with crackling from the fireplace as a billet broke and the fire flamed up, throwing sparks up the chimney and others to sputter out on the flagstone hearth. Claude shuffled some papers and they bent to the business at hand.

"Let's go over the coal and sawmill accounts first. Looks like last year was a mighty good one. We need to settle up your parts."

They finished with the tallies and the plans for sixty nine by midnight. At the end, Claude brought sacks of coins from an iron safe and counted out stacks of gold and silver for his partners. He hefted his remainder. "Added to that in Abel's bank, I'll have no debts starting out," he said. "Don't have to worry about old Wiley snatching something from me right off."

"He had Josh and Hank chasing your notes and land deals, as you know," Ian said. "But they ain't likely to stray far for a time. Wiley will be doin' all the dirt hisself." A laugh resonated around the table.

"Ruth and Abigail be tamin' 'em close to home fer a good while!" Charles said. "Saw both in Point Pleasant last week and they was both hanging on their wives like they couldn't see nothin' else."

The wind gusted in a rapid series of pulses but the howl was absent. Picking up his revolver and crucifix, Ian led the way out into the night, each with his sack of coins and the empty safe open behind them.

* * *

"Mighty cold," Hannibal said, as he stamped into his house on Little Seven Mile and hung his coat on a peg.

"You get the rest of the corn in?" Granny Eva asked, her hands full of steaming platters. She set them down on the dining table an instant later and wiped her hands on her apron.

"We sure did," Bub replied from his step behind Hannibal. "Pulled all those ears. Kernels plenty hard what with that big freeze." They both went over to the fireplace and backed up to its crackling flames. "Ah," Bub said. "Ain't that good!"

"It surely is, boy." Hannibal shifted his position a bit. "Fire feelin' might fine after today. Harvesting corn in November is one powerful hard job, even worse in this winter freeze."

When their two field hands came in and the family assembled around the big table with its aromas, they bowed their heads for Hannibal's blessing.

"Oh Lord, we give you thanks that we can assemble here, healthy and humble and in peace, with a fine corn crop, at least five hundred bushels. Your tithe will go for good things, Lord, and to help my ministry of those fine people of the Second Greenbottom Baptist Church that you entrusted to my care. For the families of Hank Peavey and Joshua Minns, we ask thy blessing, for they soon will have little children to love and I will seek to baptize both."

Granny Mandy grumbled and Hannibal raised his head and said, "Shush!"

He refolded his hands and bowed his head. "Bless those around this table. Bless this food to our bodies and us to thy service,.... Amen... and Amen."

"Why you do dat?" Granny asked.

Hannibal smiled. "Now you know, Granny, that the Lord loves everybody, Hank and Josh too. Since Josh bought that river farm close to us, we got to get along. Best way is to invite him into the church and be friends."

Granny shook her head, frowning, "Dat ain't no way to deal wid a snake."

"The good Lord and Abigail will reform him," Hannibal said. "His hate will melt before that little daughter he will cherish always."

"How you know it be a girl," Hester asked.

"Lord told me in a dream. Josh will reform and I will baptize them all."

Granny stubbornly persisted with her interrogation. "What about them Peaveys?"

Hannibal laughed as he reached for the cherry pie. "They's comin' into the fold too. The Lord ain't leavin' no sinners hereabouts, not when I get done with them." His face clouded as he shoveled a big wedge onto his plate. "None but that

Wiley. He still ain't nothin' but hate."

Granny nodded. "We bury him."

"Don't want it to come to that," Hannibal replied. He took a forkful of pie and chewed for a moment. Washing it down with a gulp of milk, he shrugged his shoulders. "Some hate can't be changed. If Wiley don' come to the Lord, vengeance will seek him out." With his pie eaten, Hannibal turned to the pork and vegetables, shoveling in great portions. Only murmurs and requests broke the silence during the rest of the dinner.

22

Claude picked up Letty and swung her around and around in a tight embrace, her feet kicking behind her as he put his lips close to her ear. "Did you hear the news, Letty? Iris went back south."

"Put me down," she protested. When he did not respond but stopped twirling and hugged her tighter, she squirmed to escape. Letty's face crimsoned when her maid glanced in as she slipped past the door of the bedroom. Her heels tapped out echoes on down the hall. "Heavens, Claude," Letty protested, as she freed herself and straightened her dress, "what will Rachel and the other servants think? You're acting like a bear!"

"Well, I'm happy," he responded and danced a little jig. "She's gone! No more trouble for me, nor Hannibal either."

"But why? I thought she came to stay."

"Charles told me that she about froze up this past winter. Couldn't take the cold and complained all the time to her maid." A laugh welled up, growing into a guffaw. "Stayed close inside, but she still courted outrageously. Men visitin' all the time. Gossip went all over Point Pleasant." He tickled her until she giggled. "That ain't the real reason, of course. She run onto money, big time gambler that Worth knows. Worth said he wanted her bad and she sold dear. Moved to New Orleans."

"Well thank heavens for the Lord favoring us. I can't think of a better valentine."

"True, gal," Claude said. "Sixty nine is starting out right well."

Letty moved to a wall mirror and smoothed down her hair and adjusted the lace on her bodice. "Why are they going so far? Why not Cincinnati with all the travelers passing through to the west?"

"New Orleans'll make 'em rich, according to Worth, and her friend knew it. More money around with the foreign trade. Worth says it'll be easy pickings for he's a real sharpster. Lots of partying too, for Iris to dabble in, more'n Cincinnati."

Letty's smile exploded into laughter. "I can't help but think of you when she kissed you on the boat. You looked absolutely flummoxed."

"She took me unaware, woman," he said stiffly, as he pulled her close again. Kissing her, he said, "But I am relieved. Iris's would do anything to get her way."

He led her down to the parlor and closed the sliding doors. "We got to talk about Hannibal and Josh and Hank."

"Why?"

"Because those boys both got babies comin' right quick," he answered, as he sank into his well-dented overstuffed chair. "Hannibal's fixin' to do something might not be wise and I want your advice."

"If you're fussed about his plannin' to visit them and give each a Bible...," she breathed deeply and twined her hands together in her lap while boldly staring into his eyes..., "well he's doing right. I've already told him and Hester to invite them to church service and to our Easter picnic."

He sat quietly, ruminating. How did she know all these things, he thought. Here I been worrying about this and she's already ahead of me, with big plans for the future.

"You figure it will help?"

Letty nodded. "We got to break Wiley's hold on those two boys. They both hate because of Wiley and that ain't good. He can go his own way, once we have them in the church."

"I remember Grandma Peavey bringing Hank when he was

little," Claude said. "Old Jubal wasn't much of a mind to come but he did get baptized in the creek." He mused a moment. "Hank liked the Bible stories. I read many a one to him and the other little boys in Sunday School."

"They're not bad boys," Letty said gently. "The war changed everything. It's almost four years now and time for all of us to get on with our lives. Josh and Hank just need a little push."

"Your forget Athey and Josh's brothers," Claude said. "We killed all of them."

Letty waved her hand, dismissing his notion. "It doesn't matter. That was war. Forgiveness will come."

* * *

Hannibal pulled up before Joshua's house on Saint Patrick's Day, the March weather bright and beautiful, with a warm breeze moving white clouds over Greenbottom. He and Granny Mandy descended from the buggy and fronted a stern-faced Joshua on the porch.

"What you want?" Joshua growled.

Hannibal carried Granny Mandy's bag and a huge book while she hobbled up the steps. Holding the rail, she paused and shook her cane at him. "Git outen de way, Massa Josh. I's here to see Abigail an' your new chil'." Her eyes twinkled and she grinned at him. "Right purty thing when I birthed her last Tuesday, 'spect even more terday."

Mandy pushed past him and went into the house, heading for the sounds of the woman and nursing child. "Fetch my bag," she hollered.

Hannibal followed her, trailed by Joshua, the latter sputtering as he protested. "Ain't right yer bustin' in here where you ain't wanted."

"Please, Josh," Hannibal said. "Granny's just he'pin' Abigail and your daughter. We want to make sure they both are well."

"I don't need no preachin' to 'bout my wife! Been anybody else 'roun' never would'a had Granny Mandy fer birthin'."

"Best midwife in these parts. Done delivered at least a hundred babies since she come from Carolina. Abigail better off with her than anyone."

Joshua muttered unintelligibly and stamped into the bedroom. Once there he sat solicitously at the side of the bed, gazing fondly at his wife. Granny had the baby unwrapped, checking it. Within a few minutes she rewrapped the child and placed it in a cradle which she set to swinging. A check of Abigail followed, with Hannibal in the other room.

"I'se done, Hannibal," Granny called, when the medical work was finished and the baby restored to Abigail's arms.

With all three in chairs around the bed and their hands clasped to form a circle, Hannibal began their visit with a prayer. "Oh Lord, bless this mother and child, and her daddy. May they live in good health and love and peace, always recalling that your love envelopes all. And may they prosper on Joshua's new farm, a fine land with good house, orchard and bottom. In Jesus' name, we pray. Amen."

From her sitting position backed by a pillow, Abigail looked over them all, her silent husband, Granny, and Hannibal with his book. "What's that?" she asked.

"It's a family Bible for you and Hank and little Lily Ann," Hannibal said. "Such a pretty name."

He opened it to the family record section and showed her the entries after she laid the sleeping baby aside on the bed. They stood out boldly in flowing script. The black ink on an off-white, decorated sheet cited the full names of the parents and child with birthdate and place, as well as their marriage.

"It's for you and Joshua and for all those children in the future. A full record for your grandchildren and the others in your family generations."

"It's our'n to keep?" Abigail caressed the leather cover with its imprint "Holy Bible" in gold amid floral embellishments.

"Yes, chil'," Granny said. "Fum Hannibal an' Hester an' me an' Claude an' Miz Letty. We all wish yer family well."

Abigail burst into tears. "It's the most purty and wonderful present I ever got. No," she said, "that we ever got. Look, Josh," she added, and handed the book to him.

He took it reluctantly but brightened when he leafed through and read the names aloud. "Joshua Athey Minns," he said. With a clouded face he asked, "How come you know my middle name and when I was birthed?"

"Wrote your mother," Hannibal said. "I have her letter here." He fetched out a folded paper and read,

> "Dear Reverend.
>
> It don't sound right callen a nigra Reverend but in these times, I recken I got to change jest like all the rest. You axed about Josh. He was my first, borned July 20, 1844 here at Columbia, a fine healthy boy all his life. His name is Joshua Athey Minns, atter the bible warrior and his father. Our Josh is quarter Cherokee. They was allus fighters and Josh did hisself proud in the war.
>
> I allus liked to read about Joshua in the Bible and got ter start agin on him an' Moses. Been neglecting the Good Book lately.
>
> I ain't heard much from Josh or Wiley since last summer but I'se glad he got a good gal and she's in the family way. When you see Joshua and give him and Abigail the Bible, tell him I love him and fer him to read the Good Book and to follow the Lord. Ain't no reason to hate like his uncle Wiley. The past is past and the dead buried and he ought ter fergit the war and go on. His life is to live, not ter git kilt in fighting.
>
> Rebecca Minns"

Hannibal held out the letter and Josh took it gingerly, laying the page on his knee. He fingered the paper and spent a few moments tracing out lines with a forefinger. "Ma's name is Rebecca?" he asked. "I never knowed any other than Ma."

Hannibal wiped his eyes with a handkerchief and blew his nose. "Your Ma's a good woman, Josh, with a distinguished name. Her family were Boones, so you're related to old Daniel himself. Look at the Bible."

Josh's finger slowly traced the names above his in the small family tree depicted and read slowly, "Rebecca Boone Minns, born April 21, 1824, Holston, North Carolina." His finger continued on his ancestry and his sibling's names. "You wrote all these?

"Yes," Hannibal said, "and those for Abigail and the Trumbulls. Folks should know who they come from and both you folks got good blood. Ain't no reason not to hold your heads up proud."

Josh's face relaxed and he puzzled a moment, silent as Abigail cooed to the baby in the circle of her arm and patted its bottom lightly. He peered again at the names and examined the cover of the Bible, then placed the letter inside the book and slowly closed it, placing the thick volume on a side table.

"I thank you for the Bible and fer the help with Abigail and Lily Ann." His face hardened and he harshly challenged the pastor. "We still got those killin's to settle, Hannibal ... Athey, Jeremy, Jared. Shaw ner you ain't never answered fer 'em."

"Your mother says to forget the war and go on. Those were killin' days and from what she said, you did yourself proud as a soldier. Can't you accept that Captain Shaw was a soldier too? He did what he had to do to escape. And we Negroes were part of that."

"Think on it, honey," Abigail softly implored. She put her hand in his and squeezed. "Leave the past dead and buried."

Josh pondered until his face softened and he caressed Abigail's cheek and felt the baby's warm body. "I will do that," he said, "think on it."

Hannibal seized his opportunity. "Meantime, Josh, bring Abigail and the baby to church next Sunday. We'll introduce you all to the congregation. And Abigail," he added, "in three months we'll baptize Lily Ann."

Abigail wept while holding tight to Josh's hand. "Thank you, pastor," she said. "We'll be there."

* * *

Wiley Minns paced the floor of his private room at the Bull's Head, his red face swelled and murderous in aspect. Striking with a leather quirt, he layed one cut each on the shoulders of Josh and Hank as they squirmed uneasily before him. Warm August breezes blew in through the opened window, relieving the odor of a room too long closed up. Abruptly stopping before Josh, he berated his nephew.

"You joinin' that church with the nigger preacher? He killed your Pa and brothers!" His vitriol continued washing over Josh as he railed about being a traitor to Minns' blood.

"Ain't true, Unk," Josh heatedly retorted. "Hannibal killed nobody. Claude shot Jeremy when he was about to fire at them. Pa and Jared was done in by the nigras while they protected Claude."

Wiley went rigid and exploded. "You call him Claude!" He choked, unable to speak while his body violently spasmed and he turned his face to the heavens. "Claude!" he screamed, "my God, boy, ain't you got no pride left?

Josh's temper rose. He jumped up and forcibly pushed Wiley into a seat. Thrusting his face close to his uncle's, he ordered, "You shut up fer a change. Me an' Hank got responsibilities now."

"My God, boy," Wiley whined. "you ain't even no Minns no more. You think a wife and youngun keep you from killin' that Shaw?"

"Ma said to forgive, and to fergit the war, Unk," Josh said calmly. "Good book says the same. Took me a while to study on it, but Abigail he'ped me see that it's best to go on, and join in the church. Can't hate forever an' we got a good livin' here."

Hank sided in. "Miz Letty an' Granny Mandy he'ped me an' Ruth with our youngun when she was 'bout ter die. Pulled her through fine." His voice strengthened and became combative. "I don't hev no call no more ter buck Claude, Wiley. He's a good neighbor."

Wiley stared open-mouthed. "You too, Hank? What about your grandpa?"

Hank shook his head. "Gramps ain't stirrin' up no trouble. Claude's square with him and he don' hol' no grudge. Gramps tol' me ter keep the low-lifes off the place, 'specially Lennie and them roustabouts. Sits on the porch an' rocks and croons to Marie Louise.

"Marie Louise?" Minns said. "Wherever you git names like those?"

"Ruth's got French blood kin in Gallipolis, Wiley. Both them names are in her family. Right pretty, too."

Minns paced the room, speechless, while the two young men eyed him warily. They shifted their chairs to the opposite side of the center table and Hank surreptitiously felt his belt gun and shifted its holster a bit.

His caution went for naught. Minns turned with a smile and his unctuous voice bathed them. "You're right, boys. the good book says, 'Vengeance is mine, sayeth the Lord, I will repay.' So we'll jest leave it to the Lord."

Josh smiled at his uncle's ingratiating tone. "Figuring on foxing us, Unk? I done heard you try this a thousand times a'fore. Allus got a dirty trick up yer sleeve."

Wiley's rigid stance and angry face confronted him. "Git!" he shouted, shaking a fist at Josh. He choked on his next words, unable to speak.

Josh and Hank rose cautiously and backed away. As his uncle's hand moved toward a coat pocket, Josh drew his belt gun. Pointing it at Wiley, he said, "Don' you try to pull no tricks on me, Unk, ner Hank neither. I know how sneaky you are." His jaw muscles clenched and he said coldly, "You do an' Abigail er Ruth and the babies are hurt, I'll kill you."

"Git!" Wiley thundered, his hand dropping to his side. "You ain't no Minns no more."

The two young men paused at the door to the room and Joshua took his parting shot. "I'm writin' Jasper and tellin' him you ain't welcome to no more of their gold. Ain't no reason thet he sweats while you hate. Ain't fittin'."

Wiley's face purpled and he threw a mug against the wall, shouting, "Get out, damn it! And," he added ominously, "you stay outen my way."

* * *

Letty brought coffee and cookies that cold morning in November when Claude worked on his accounts. The crackling fire made the room a cosy place, cool at the edges but warm at Claude's desk. He rose at her entrance and the door slam in the breeze, helping her set the heavy tray on the center table.

"Where's Gertie? he asked. "Why did you fetch it?"

"Wanted to talk private," Letty answered.

When he had finished one well-sugared cup, she poured a replacement and took a chair across from him.

"Well, now," he said with a laugh, "what schemes are we into this time?"

"It ain't a scheme, Claude. Hester come by yesterday. Said that Josh and Hank had told Hannibal they wanted to do some trading with you. Hannibal felt they're a little skittish because of the past. Weren't sure you'd deal with them."

"I thought we cleared that all away at the church picnic last August? We sure talked enough together. The past is past!"

Letty ate a bite of cookie and sipped at her coffee. "It takes time and prayer to cleanse a soul of hate, Claude. Josh has about lost his, now that he ain't with Wiley anymore and comes to church regular." She passed the plate of cookies to him. He picked out two and laid them on his plate. Letty poured his cup full again and said, "A deal with you will help get rid of his suspicions. Can you help?"

He reared back in his chair and stretched before picking up a cookie. Holding it out, he said, "You see this?" At her nod, he turned the cookie over and over. "It's a perfect blend of good eatin' things. Way I figure, life ain't no different. A man's got to blend the good to keep out the bad. I'll deal with Josh and Hank any time and give them a fair shake."

Letty beamed. She finished her cookie and coffee and placed her things on the tray. Bending over him, she hugged him tightly and said, "I love you, Claude Shaw."

He turned his face up and kissed her. "Tell Hester for them to let me know when they're comin' over. I'll meet both together." He paused. "Why not ask them to bring Abigail and Ruth and the babies and stay for supper. We can have a good visit.

"See her today at the church. We got a Sunday School planning meeting."

He nodded as he crunched down his last cookie and carried his cup back to his desk. When she went out with the tray, he was again unhearing, engrossed in his accounts.

When they were seated around the table a week later, Claude said, "Best to talk here, with the quiet."

Hank chuckled. "Right noisy in the house, Captain." He glanced around, focusing on the deer heads and the comfortable furnishings of the cabin. "Mighty nice place. Ruth been atter me to fix up some. I recken we do it atter we sell the crops."

"I heard you got a hant," Josh said. "Any truth to thet?"

"Not that I believe," Claude replied. "Wind shrieks like a banshee sometimes off the corner of the roof. Can't find a loose board."

"Git Enoch Kitts ter look at it," Hank advised. "He'll turn up the trouble."

"Already done that," Claude replied. "No luck." He picked up the cookie tray on the table and passed it around. When it was back in place, he said, "Let's get on to the trade. I can do it several ways, buy outright at wholesale and take my chances, take it on consignment, twenty percent commission, or you can ship your goods on my steamer and sell them yourself, paying only for freight and passage."

He waited while the young men considered the options. Hank finished his cookie and broke the ice. "We got over two thousand bushels of ear corn, Captain. Plus Josh has tobacco and dried beans and some sundries." He puffed on his pipe. "Recken I'll sell those three steers you doctored last spring. They's fattened up considerable."

Claude nodded. "You'll get a better price in Cincinnati than Gallipolis, that's for sure. Pay to take 'em there."

"We do better sellin' everythin' ourselves?" Josh asked. "We ain't never done this a'fore."

"Yes," Claude said, "except for the skins you catch in the winter. Best to go to Devereaux in Gallipolis on those." He crunched another cookie and offered the plate. It's pile rapidly diminished as the men helped themselves. "You'll make more in Cincinnati with the other freight and I'll be happy to introduce you around."

"You know, Captain," Josh said, "these cookies mighty tasty. Kin Abigail git the recipe from Miz Letty?"

"Surely," Claude said easily.

How he has changed, he thought, from a rebel filled with hate to a fine farmer asking for a recipe. He marveled at the change in both young men in such a short time. All due to Hannibal and Letty, he thought. They were right and I was wrong. But those two girls deserve even more credit, he concluded. Abigail and Ruth and their babies have calmed them down. Another few years and they'll have forgot the war. Damn Wiley anyhow, still raising fusses. Working with Lennie and those Jeter trash to burn the boat. Got a good lesson when we killed two of 'em. Shaking his shoulders he said, "Let's get on to the trip."

When the trading details were thrashed out, Josh and Hank headed for the house to join their families. Before leaving Claude in the cabin, Josh held out his hand and said, "Thanks, Captain. Ma and Abigail was right. Ain't no reason ter hate when life is so good." He looked directly at Claude and said, "Unk is wrong but I ain't able to convince him. Be careful of yerself."

"Thanks, Josh," Claude replied, with a hard grip. "I'm glad

the hatchet is buried. The war is behind us and the good life ahead. You can count on us for tradin' and friendship."

* * *

Letty sank into the easy chair before the parlor fire and kicked off her shoes. Wriggling her toes she squirmed to a more comfortable position and let out a big, "Ah!"

"Tired, gal?"

"Gettin' older, Claude. Don't know when the Christmas parties and visits have tired me so."

Claude nodded and puffed at his pipe. Tendrils of bluish smoke hung in the room, already redolent of the many bodies and habits of the earlier partygoers. The hall clock struck, it's chimes echoing into the parlor. "Be midnight in a few minutes, Letty, and another new year. Are you ready? Can you stand one more dance."

"For the great year of eighteen seventy?" She smiled. "You can bet on it. We'll see Claudius married in South Carolina in June according to Ashley. I swear, Claude, but she has turned into a bustling woman."

"She and Rance too," Claude said. They are getting rich and Claudius is marrying good, even if early."

Silence left them to their thoughts as the heat of the fireplace emveloped their tired bodies. Letty stirred first.

"Kittie Mae is next, Claude. Did you see how Joe was following her around...like a puppy dog."

"He's a good worker, Letty, solid, sober, old enough." He blew out a smoke ring. "Never saw a man so inclined to machinery. He takes to those engines and gears and pulleys like he was born for them."

"Kittie Mae said he wanted to go with the railroad. It's plannin' to build a big shop in Huntington after the city is chartered. I told Kittie Mae to wait two years until he was established."

"I'll agree to that and give my consent. Let them get betrothed in the church next month, so everybody knows."

Now how did she find out about Huntington, Claude thought? It don't matter what I know, she's always ahead. The wonder of it amused him. Man plots and woman leads him along all the time! Except for some, like Worth. What sadness in his face as he watched the girls at the parties, in bright gowns. He had refused all but polite conversations with the women, that is except for Kittie Mae. Worth had whirled her around laughing as they circled the dance floor. And the thousand gold for a dowry. It was staggering but would do wonders for Kittie Mae and Joe when they married.

At least one thing had changed in all the parties, the colors. With Ashley's explorations into fashions, the girls in the Shaw family had blossomed, following Nancy Pickens' lead. What a beauty for Claudius, and rich!

The chimes struck midnight. Without a word, Claude rose and bowed to Letty. "May I have this first dance?

Rising in her stocking feet, Letty let herself be steered around the floor until they both settled onto a couch, ready again to take their ease.

January 1, 1870 brought a white frost and freeze. Claude walked the lane to the river with his cigar, his footing impeccable on the hard ground. He was halfway there when the shot came, a light rifle from the sound, cracking in the still cold. With the practice of long campaigning, he threw himself down and sought cover. Over by the creek, he thought. Disgust filled his soul. Ain't a good shot either. Probably another of that drunken crowd from the tavern. He was hidden with his pistol ready when a heavily armed Hank ran down the hill from the house, shouting, "You all right, Claude?"

Together they planned their envelopment of the sniper. Only a pile of tobacco remnants cluttered the ambush site on the knoll, a flattened bed of dried grasses evidence of a long wait.

"Wiley ain't got no sense, Claude, " Hank said, when they had satisfied themselves fully that the sniper was long gone.

You git the chance, put him under."

With a sinking heart, Claude replied, "Don't want to kill him, Hank. Done enough of that in the war."

"Has to be, Captain. Wiley ain't never gonna change."

23

Claude settled into a chair at the head of the center table and motioned the other men to assemble around it. Captain Jones sat at his right hand with Abel House on the left. The others scraped chairs and settled in, Charles Searle, Worth Fauquier, Joe McLellan, and Hank Peavey. Claude started with a prayer.

"Oh Lord, bless these our coming year's struggles. We are met in our second annual get-together to arrange our efforts in the interests of our families and of you. We ask thy blessing on Ian McLellan, lost in the river last month and on Mary Jane and Joe here and his two brothers. May you give them solace as we pray for Ian's soul. And may you help Joe be the best mechanic in this area, a trade that he loves. We ask all this in Jesus name, amen."

Amens ran around the table as the men finished theirs.

Outside of the cabin, the March wind whistled and thrashed the trees, the big poplar still bare of leaves but whipping its low branches against the roof. Scud alternately darkened the windows but the rain had eased off, other than an occasional tattoo of big drops from the whipping tree branches. The storm had passed but the wind was still in its death throes, settling down.

"Recken the river will rise even more," Captain Jones said, "even though it has blowed off clear and cold."

"Could be," Claude replied, "but we got to move along. The Sapphire will be free to sail as soon as the river drops and the snags quit shifting. Best to be ready."

"I appreciate being asked here, Capt'n," Hank said. "Right neighborly."

"You shipped an' made money in sixty nine, Hank, and we don't forget friends. Besides," he added, "you an' Ruth are right across the road. Only fitting."

Laughter resounded around the table at yips and low barks from Old Blue, sleeping in front of the fire. His legs moved and tail thumped until he woke himself from his dream. Shifting around, he instantly went back to sleep.

"He reminds me of a hound I had," Worth said, chuckling. "Always liked the fire but never could lie still."

"Blue's pretty old now," Claude said. "We let him sleep where he likes and Letty feeds him prime."

"You never told us the whole story about Blue," Abel said.

"He fought for my life," Claude replied. "Always in his debt."

The men nodded, understanding the bond. They moved on to the first shipments on Sapphire, to move as soon as the water level dropped. A hard three hours followed as they mapped out the year's activities of the riverboat, sawmill, and farms. At the end, Claude asked,

"How does the money look, Abel?"

"You're okay, Claude. You should finish this year out of debt and with a good balance." He looked at his ledgers, open on the table. "But you should put more into the coal mine. It makes the most profit."

"I'll talk to Trumbull and Charles will get on it. Old Trumbull and Josh couldn't be here today." Claude puffed at his cigar, grinning as he said, "Sent word he had some partying to do with Abigail and Lucy Ann. I swear, it's a caution how that reb and Trumbull have got along."

"It's the grandbaby," Abel reminded him. "Made them think of the future, not of the war. Their war's over forever."

"You're right on that," Claude responded.

They had broken up the meeting and were taking convivial

drinks while the women set up the dinner, when the intense chatter of male and female was interrupted by a barrage of wind and the slamming front door. All eyes riveted on the sodden figure standing there, Wiley Minns swaying and aiming a cocked, short barreled shotgun. Old Blue tensed and crouched, his eyes fixed on the figure as he inched along the floor toward Minns. Next to him, Worth stroked his hackles and muttered, "Steady, boy."

"I come fer you, Shaw," Wiley announced in the deep stillness. "Josh done gone soft and them loafers won't take my money." He waved the double barrel around and the group slowly eased away from Claude, leaving a clear lane.

"I'm unarmed, Minns. You'll hang for murder, if the men here don't kill you first."

Outside, the wind picked up and raged, building up the thrashing of the poplar. An eerie howl started behind Minns, rising to a banshee shriek, and the cabin shook. The preacher jumped and swung his weapon sideways toward the unearthly cries. "What's that?" he shouted.

"It's Satan come for your soul," Claude screamed at him, "give it up, man!"

Unnoticed, Worth released Old Blue and prodded him with a, "Git, Blue."

Blue jumped with a roar, charging Minns. Wiley swung to the threat, emptying both barrels toward the leaping dog. Worth staggered even as Blue dropped limply to the floor. But it was Wiley all eyes riveted on. He stood erect, a surprised look on his face, then crumpled into a heap. Joe sprang to Worth's side as the gambler slowly fell, a derringer dropping from his hand. When they eased him down, red already covered his right side and he was barely conscious. He grasped Joe's arm and murmured, "Kittie Mae," before slipping into eternity.

"How is Kittie Mae," Claude asked.

"She's about over her crying," Letty replied. "But it was an awful shock, losing Worth. He was truly her second father."

"Joe will console her." Claude wiped his eyes. "Got to say,

this past week's been a terrible trial."

"You put Blue in the family graveyard, I notice."

"He'll get a fine marker too," Claude said. "That old dog did me more than one good turn, first in the war. He and Worth saved my life."

"Do as well for Worth, Claude, back to his homeplace in Petersburg."

"I will do that and more."

"It's over now, Claude. We can live in peace."

* * *

Dust swirled about the camp site in the rolling pasture that July 4. Brown eyed daisies waved their yellow petals among the grazing horses, all the motion adding hazards to the flight of grasshoppers and foraging bees. Tall, angular tents along the company street and blowing smoke from the campfires were oddly reminiscent of the men's days of soldiering in Tennessee. A small cluster of troopers sought the clutch of stools on the upwind side, habit protecting them from the acrid smoke. Their patched and faded regimentals took them back to their war days. Lively banter ensued as they retold tales of adventure. And gloom fell upon them when they reflected on the fallen. But it was news of the Negro that interested them most when the Sergeant walked up, ending his day's duty at the headquarters tent.

As usual, Henry served as spokesman for the group. He confronted the Sergeant, while the rest of the men just listened and puffed away on their pipes and cigars.

"Hear tell Capt'n Shaw got the officers to give a Negro honorary membership, Tom. That right?"

Upturned, inquiring faces stared stolidly, waiting for the information. Sergeant Tom Dickey faced the remnant of the original company as he had so many times before. Only a small number of men had gathered for the reunion, friends of many years. He shrugged his shoulders,

"You've knowed Hannibal for years, Henry. He saved the

Captain's life. More'n once, Claude said, when they was 'scapin' down in Carolina an' Georgia."

"Don't seem right givin' a Negro membership," Henry complained, "even if it be Hannibal. And as a Sergeant?"

Growls and groans seconded the spokesman's irritated protest.

"Can't change nothin', boys," Tom Dickey said. He acted swiftly to squelch the gripes, his grin infectious. "The officers decided jest like in the war. Wouldn't want 'em to take a vote would you?"

Henry's temper flashed. "Well, they might'a asked us! We ain't in the Army no more."

"You can brace Captain Shaw hisself," Dickey said, pointing. "Here he comes."

Claude met the entire company one by one, shaking hands with each and recalling old times. They laughed once again at his much told tale of the walnut dye and Colonel Will's discomfiture. It was the irrepressible Henry, finally, who brought up Hannibal.

"Hear tell, Capt'n, you asked to make your Negro, Hannibal, an honorary Sergeant."

The men gathered close around, their puffing increasing as they bent to hear their Captain's answer. Smoke drifted in blue whorls above the dense crowd but its aromatic odor hardly camouflaged the stink of old sweat on the campers.

Smells just like we were back at war, Claude thought, as they hemmed him in and he took stock of their temper. Unwashed men, camping in the smoke. They don't even look too different except maybe for the lack of long beards and straggly hair. And no graybacks, he reminded himself. Ain't too fussed, either. He looked Henry straight in the eye and spoke up forcefully so all could hear.

"Hannibal Shaw is a free man, Henry, the pastor of your church. He served with me in the battles in Tennessee." His tone turned sharp. "You know that for a fact, don't you?"

At Henry's acquiescing nod, Claude clinched Hannibal's heroism. "He carried me from the field at Rogersville when I was badly wounded. And he kept the rebs from killin' me. Saved my life."

Henry protested. "But Captain, he was your'n then. S'posed to take care of you."

The trooper shrank back at the change in Claude, his Captain's face suddenly icy stern. Claude punched him lightly in the chest with his pointed finger. "When we escaped, he fed me, protected me, saved my life again. He killed rebs."

Claude crowded Henry and stared him down. "He was just as much a trooper of this company as you and me, Henry." The Captain looked about, fixing on the uncertainty in the other men's eyes. He turned combative and challenging both in his authority and in his friendship. "Or any man here," he loudly added. "I'm proud of him as I am of you all."

Henry's plaintive voice answered for the rest. "We ain't causin' no trouble, Capt'n. It jest didn't seem fittin' to have a Negro, a reverend, as part of the regiment." The troopers' nods and grunting assents backed him up.

"Are you satisfied now, Henry?" Claude asked.

"Yep. And I 'spect the other boys too. Right, boys?"

A chorus of agreement surged out. Claude knew he had won, perhaps not their enthusiasm but their agreement. They'll get used to it, he thought, and Hannibal will win them over with his level-headed camaraderie. He smoothed over the difficulty with a tactical diversion.

"We'll make the presentation at the banquet. Gonna have some good beef." He laughed. "Different from that meat we had down by Shelbyville."

Claude poked Henry in the ribs. "Remember the cow you shot, Henry?"

Henry roared with laughter and his body convulsed. "Damn, but warn't that a tough old thing! Thought we was eatin' the hide, she was so stringy."

Howls rose from the men. Jokes and ribald remarks added to the good humor and chuckling that followed. The group broke up as knots moved off to the stools and visiting.

Claude shouted after them. "You're my friends, boys. Accept Hannibal Shaw for what he is, a fighter just like you."

"I'll give him a good cheer, Capt'n," Henry said. He fidgeted and looked shamefaced. "Didn't mean no harm."

"I know that, Henry. We been together too long."

"The other boys'll raise a holler too, Claude,when I hurrah. You and Hannibal will have plenty to cheer you at the tables."

Masons' Hall served the entire unit at one sitting, a dais holding Colonel Garrard and other dignitaries. Red, white and blue bunting hung on every wall and from the ceiling. The regimental colors and Ohio and U.S. flags clustered at the side of the platform. Claude and Letty graced a table in the front row, Hannibal and Hester their guests. Henry sat to Hannibal's right, his voluble conversation droning on while the dinner was served and enjoyed.

He winked at the planter while he chewed his meat. "Good beef, Claude," he said. "Ain't like the one at Shelbyville."

They both chuckled at their private joke and the other troopers burst out laughing, mystifying the ladies.

Letty tapped Claude's arm with her fan. "What on earth is so funny?"

Henry chuckled while he enlightened the ladies. "We had some tough, old beef down there, Miz Letty. 'bout wore out our teeth. Most like leather."

Her face remained puzzled at the incomprehensible joke, but her good humor patronized them as she reproved Henry with, "How long do you folks plan to tell all those old tales?"

"Long's we can laugh, Miz Letty." Henry turned serious and reminded her of the terrors. "Twas a hard, dangerous business, Miz Letty. Lots got killed. But Hannibal and Hester here show it was worth it. And war makes men brothers, them that's been shot at. It's good to remember."

Letty's face paled and she fanned herself rapidly. "You're right, Henry," she said tremulously. "Claude never talks of the war at home. It's only fitting he get together with you friends."

Clinking of a bell from the podium signaled an end to the dinner and commencement of the interminable order of business. Loud clapping was interspersed with private conversations as the Adjutant shouted from the podium for order and handled the long sequence of introductions, short speeches, and recognitions. Finally he motioned to Claude to come forward and introduced Captain Shaw to the assembly.

Claude drew cheers at his announcement that he would make his remarks short, and proceeded at once to his summation. "Colonel Garrard, distinguished guests, valiant members of the Seventh Ohio, I present to you a brave man, marked on his cheek by a wound from the rebs, a wound meant for me. He saved my life more than once, killed his man to preserve our cause, fed me and carried me when I was hurt and in want. He and his lovely wife, Hester, have become fine, Christian members of our Ohio River Valley community. Hester herself killed a reb who had his rifle aimed and was about to murder me. So I and our great nation are in their debt."

He paused, intent on Letty and her sudden grasp of Hester's hand. Letty sought her handkerchief, its folds receiving her tears as her shoulders shook. Never been said before, Claude told himself. Time all knew. His spirits lifting in pride and joy, he thundered out his peroration.

"It is with the utmost respect and pleasure that I present the Reverend Hannibal Shaw to you to receive an Honorary Membership in the Seventh Ohio."

Henry led the hurrahs as Hannibal and Hester stood and bowed and Hannibal ascended the dais. His solid, erect figure was imposing in its black broadcloth. A prominent dent and scar marked his cheek, his souvenir from Athey Minns in 1864. Hannibal waited at the side of the Colonel, now in command at the podium.

"Will the Adjutant read the orders," Garrard said.

The Adjutant skipped over the administrative clauses quickly and passed on to the paragraph on the award.

"........ and hereby, by unit acclaim, is appointed Honorary

Sergeant, Company L, Seventh Ohio, with all the rights, privileges, and responsibilities appertaining thereto."

Pandemonium sparked by Henry drowned out the last part of the reading, all the closing comments on orders and signatures unintelligible. The Adjutant nodded to Colonel Garrard when he was finished and took Hannibal's coat.

"Order! Order!" the Colonel shouted from the podium. He pounded hard with his gavel when the din continued, but neither his commands nor the resonating podium calmed the troopers' celebration. It took a few minutes to quell the anarchy, but eventually Garrard's commanding presence compelled a reluctant silence. Ungiven to long delays as they well knew, he presented the certificate and shook Hannibal's hand while the troopers cheered. Then he held up a uniform coat with three chevrons and showed it off to wild applause. Helping Hannibal don the garment, Garrard smoothed back the shoulders and adjusted the fit. He stepped away with a smile when the job was done and offered the podium to the new Sergeant.

Hannibal waited for the hushed silence that finally suffused the hall. He spoke slowly, with great dignity, accentuating his telling words with sign language by his hands. "I am a free man, formerly a slave. I thank Claude and you all, the present, the absent, the missing, and the honored dead for what you have done for Hester and for me and for our brethren. As I stand before you with this great honor, now free, now with learning, now with opportunity, I can attest that the Seventh and freedom are first in my heart. May the Seventh always be revered for its magnificent men and battle record. But most of all may it and the United States be blessed by God for setting us free."

THE END

EPILOG 1

With the family together, the building of wealth became Claude Shaw's object after the Civil War. He moved his family to Huntington and settled there when it had only a dozen or so houses. Family elders reported that Shaw owned real estate in downtown Huntington as it developed. Another tidbit was that the family pastured its cow on land later used to build the downtown courthouse, where the author received his Boy Scout Merit Badges in the Courts of Honor in the 1930s.

Mary Jane McLellan moved to Huntington as a widow and established a millinery shop, never remarrying. A late picture before 1920 reveals a beautiful old lady in shiny black, with a perky hat. By then she was living with her son, James Garrett McClellan, in Boston, where he was in the utility business. A family tale credited him with inventing the McClellan Boiler. His brother, Joseph Leroy McLellon, the author's grandfather, married Kitty May Shaw and became prominent, being on the Huntington City Council. He moved to St. Paul, Minnesota, in the 1890s as Superintendent of the Light Plant but caught an intestinal ailment and died in 1897. Kitty May used her three thousand dollar inheritance to move to St. Albans, W.Va., near her sister, Lillian. She built a little house, which was called the Little Green House because of its color. In the early 1900s, she married Charles H. Murrill, a true Virginian and Confederate cavalryman, from whom the author takes his middle name. Grandpa Murrill lived until the author was about twelve and made bows and arrows for him on the Kitts(Uncle Charles and Aunt Edythe McLellon Kitts) farm below Burlington, Ohio. Murrill came from the area of Union, Monroe County, Va.(now W.Va.)

The three McLellon brothers all spelled their names differently, McLellon, McLellan and McClellan. Uncle Franklin Fremont McLellan had one withered arm. He was a telegrapher and moved to Denver, Col., then to National City, Cal., the last of the three brothers to die, in the 1930s.

Claude Shaw became well off. Elders reported that he gave a dowry of a farm to each of five daughters. Kitty May stayed around the Huntington area. All of her three children reportedly were born at Greenbottom. Shaw owned an active riverboat and Kitty May learned to gamble on it as a girl, becoming a very fine games player. Thus the family contained a Riverboat Gambler. Her two brothers ended up in Charleston, W.Va.(Garrett), and in Bristol, Virginia. The latter, Uncle Claude, had a veneer factory. The most famous uncle was Uncle Pike Trowbridge. He married Lillian Shaw, Kitty May's sister, and was prominent in the sheriff and tax collector's offices in Kanawha County, W.Va. Two aunts, Emma Shaw(Aunt Em) and Edna Shaw(Aunt Ted), and Kitty lived in the Huntington, W.Va. area until they all died within about two months of each other in 1944, the last of the seven Shaw children.

As the decades wore on, his war wound bothered Claude Shaw. He died early because of it, according to elder's accounts. He was 67 when he passed away in February, 1894. Captain Shaw was buried at Crown City, Ohio.

All contact with the African Americans associated with the family was lost after 1905. When Clyde McLellon, the author's father and Kitty May's son, visited in 1905, he was met at the Huntington train station by an elderly black man, who came to greet him and to help with his baggage. A photo of Lutetia at the time includes her Negro maid. No other contact has continued.

This book is fiction, with a family flavor of the times added, based on known facts and family tales.

EPILOG 2

Fine snowflakes drifted in the opened front door of Greenbottom, its initial small crack forced wider by the strong February wind. Hannibal stamped his feet and shook himself before he entered the hall. But the invalid was his concern, not the snow or his dripping garments.

"How is he, Miss Letty?"

"Poorly, Hannibal," she replied. "The doctor gives him a few more days, at best."

Letty shivered in the cool front hall. She drew her shawl around her shoulders while Hannibal removed his hat, gloves and scarf. His overcoat followed. A tall Negro footman received the whitened garments, their melting snowflakes leaving puddles on the polished floor. Once free of the wrappings, Hannibal took Letty's hands in his great palms. Her brimming eyes and drawn face attested to her grief as she was drawn to him. His still erect but now bulky body and graying hair attested to the decades since he and Claude had made their epic escape. Patting Letty's hands, he soothed the sobbing woman with the melodious voice that he had cultivated as his learning improved, one that thundered from the pulpit on the glory days of Easter and was hardly less silent on other Sundays.

"The Lord is with him, Miss Letty, and with you. We all must pass the river and Claude goes as a good man. He will be welcomed."

"He needs you, Hannibal. He was asking that you come,

over and over. 'Where's Hannibal?' he'll cry out. 'I need Hannibal to save my life again.'"

"Where is he?"

"In the front parlor. We moved him downstairs where he could look out the big windows. He so loves the stretch to the river."

Hannibal strode swiftly toward the closed, double-sliding doors while Letty instructed the waiting footman.

"Put those things to dry before the big fire in the kitchen, 'sephus. And have Silas take Hannibal's team to the barn. No reason those poor horses should stand out there in that freezing wind."

"Yessum, Miss Letty."

Letty turned from the retreating Josephus and followed Hannibal into the sick room. An odor of medicines, sweat and mustiness filled the air, and the smell of decay and impending death penetrated to any visitor. The bed was shadowed from a turned-down lamp and drawn blinds kept the room in semidarkness. Logs crackled in the fireplace. Orange light from the flames reflected from the high ceiling and the room's decorative wainscot and picture molding.

"We keep it shut up close," Letty said, "because of the awful cold and so he can sleep. Claude has trouble keeping warm in this terrible weather."

"It has been mighty raw, Miss Letty. Bitter this winter. Eighteen ninety four starting our real bad. Hard on everyone."

The sleeper stirred and his eyes inched open. A wide smile and flushed cheeks greeted Hannibal when Claude recognized him and tried to sit up, mouthing all but inaudible greetings. Letty rushed to help the invalid but Claude waved away her protests as he struggled. Between Letty and Hannibal they wrestled him upright, a cluster of pillows bracing his back and neck. Sweat beaded Claude's forehead when they finished and he sank into the softness of the pillows with a sigh.

"I'm grateful you came," he said. Claude's weak whisper barely carried, its timbre no longer the rich baritone of the strong planter.

"Anytime you call, Claude," Hannibal said. "But it hurts me to find you so poorly."

"I'm dying, Hannibal." Claude's voice grew stronger, its vibrant tone welling from some last reserve of strength. "Doc's been whisperin' to Letty," he said. "Thinks I don't know." He placed his hand over his heart. "I know it here. It's my time and place."

Hannibal nodded and his face twisted sorrowfully. He picked up one of the invalid's gaunt, transparent hands, its blue veins showing, and gently clasped the cold fingers in his warm, bulky grasp. Claude returned the pressure as their eyes locked and Hannibal accepted the coming visit of the angel of death.

"The Lord moves in mysterious ways," he intoned. "He tells us we will go to the Kingdom of Heaven if we believe. You do believe, don't you, Claude?"

"I was saved long ago, Hannibal."

Claude's mind wandered as the others kept their vigil in silence, a reverential quiet broken only by the crackling of the fire and a few stirrings of bodies. Letty sat in a chair nearby with her hands folded on her lap and her face peaceful, while Hannibal bowed his head. A sudden intake and Claude came alive, his eyes bright and his strong voice calling out to Hannibal.

"Would you pray for me?"

Hannibal knelt by the side of the bed, his forehead on Claude's hand clasped in his. "Our Father. Here is thy servant Claude, one who believes in and who has honored you. I ask thy blessing on him as he passes to your side. May you make his travel easy and without pain. May you receive his soul into your loving embrace and comfort Letty in her great loss. And help the rest of us, all those he has befriended, to accept this loss of a good man, gone to everlasting life. Amen."

Claude eased back with a happy smile and a whispered thanks, his hand pressing Hannibal's on the brightly patterned quilt. A burning light came into his eyes as the Negro stroked his hand, and once again his voice boomed out of the wasted body.

"Hester? And your chil'ren? How are they?"

Hannibal's eyes lighted up and he chuckled. "They're fine, Claude. Hester sends her love and prayers. She's over to Gallipolis. Got another grandchild this week."

Claude smiled. "And her school?"

"Got forty six chil'ren this year. Gets bigger every time. She has one may go to college in the fall. He's smart!"

An approving nod was cut off by a sad grimace and a wince from the invalid. Letty hurried to his side and pulled his body up as he arched and groaned. Greasy droplets of water ran down his cheeks, their rankness adding to the fetid odor of the stuffy room.

"He's about tired out, Hannibal," she said, "and he's got those spasms. He can't talk much more."

Claude struggled up and pushed her away.

"Remember Granny Mandy?" he asked. He didn't wait for Hannibal's grin and nod, going on in haste. "She said, 'We'uns jist like you,' an' she was right. No reason for all that misery of the slavery. Just a terrible burden."

"Freedom, Claude. It's needed by every man."

"You've proved yourself better'n most white men, Hannibal. I'm proud to be your friend."

Letty rushed in when the invalid's mouth began dribbling. She wiped off the spittle and sponged off his sweaty face with a wet cloth, cooing and soothing him and alerting his friend to his fatigue. "It's time he slept, Hannibal."

Claude whispered one last request. "Will you preach at the funeral?"

The pastor's strong voice reverberated through the room. "I promise, Claude."

Hannibal waited at the door for Letty, while she fluffed up the pillows and adjusted them around the dying man. A flare from the fire sharpened the hollows of the death mask. The shades were gathering another soul for entry into eternity. Hannibal saw not the mask but the young Claude, a strong man who had beaten his first master, rescued him and treated him kindly, a man on the run from the prison camp, dyed black to match his color, a scarecrow covered with cockleburrs in front of Colonel Wills at Dalton, a staunch friend who had helped him win freedom. Freedom! How wonderful it was!

Only a dying coal in the fireplace lit the room. Nearby, Letty dozed in the easy chair while Claude sank deeper into sleep. He stirred and sighed when a shadow approached the bed and a faint breeze fanned his brow.

"Claude?" a voice called softly in his ear. "Wake up, Claude."

The musical whisper cut through his unconsciousness, adding to the pull of the soft hand on his. He struggled to wake, to escape the darkness. His ravaged body called him deeper into sleep but an inner voice told him to rise and go out into the sun of the new day.

A quiet voice from the side encouraged him. "It's time, boy."

Granny Rose's smiling brown face bent over him when he opened his eyes. Her hands straightened his night clothes and pulled at him to follow. He yawned and rubbed his eyes and felt of her fingers. The gentle pressure of her hand reassured him, calming his fears about his day of journey just as she had in all the times past when he was a boy. Hopping out of the bed, he followed her. The floor surprised him. February but it wasn't even cold! Somewhere in the blackness of the parlor, soft piano music played and the sweet chords of 'Nearer My God to Thee' wafted over his halting steps.

He was amazed that his strength had returned when he tramped through the large front hall. An erect, lustrous young Claude gazed back at him from the long wall mirror, dark haired, unwrinkled, strong and confident. Granny backed him closely, her luminous light bathing him in an inner peace. It struck him like a bolt, his ethereal presence, his steps silent on the hard floorboards. Never a tramp of boots, just a whisper as he passed. Grieving for Letty and her suffering from his illness, he prayed for her soul and peace until she joined him again. Somehow he was not surprised that a warm, dark tunnel faced the front door when Granny pushed it open, a tunnel radiating light at the far end, where glowing figures beckoned.

Greetings wafted down to him as he strode along it toward the radiance. Gabe's halloo boomed above the rest, the voices from the past tugging at his heart. Gentle voices of welcome and hurrying figures transformed into the luminous shapes of Granny Mandy, Beulah, Granny Owdoms, Granny Esther, and Aunty Mittie. The sweet-voiced ladies rushed into a loving circle around him to lead him toward the light. A bark sounded faintly and a hound with a wagging, long tail bounced among them. Old Blue's grinning jowls snuffled at his legs in greeting. Claude's hand went right through when he bent to pet the old bluetick, the hound's spots now a royal blue, brilliant and beautiful. All Claude's grannies and aunties hugged him while Gabe beamed nearby, his friends celebrating his release from pain, and his entry, and his freedom, as he joined them in the free land.

THE FINAL END

ABOUT THE AUTHOR

Waldron M. McLellon, PhD, P.E. enlisted in the Navy in 1936 as an Apprentice Seaman. Twenty seven years later he retired as a Captain, Civil Engineer Corps. Intervening years saw him busy as a seagoing officer on WW II combatant ships, in naval Public Works and engineering, and in nuclear weapons testing. He was the naval representative on the National Fallout Shelter Survey at the time of the Cuban Missile Crisis in 1962 and did much work on nuclear weapons effects and radiation safety.

Following retirement, he attained the PhD in environmental engineering and served fifteen years as a faculty member, first at Clemson University, then at the University of Central Florida. He is a Professor Emeritus from the latter. After leaving university life, over five years were spent in an engineering consulting firm.

He has numerous publications in professional journals and other locales, has been author of four other books, and contributor to four more. His historical novel, LEATHER AND SOUL, treated of the escape of his Greatgrandfather, Lt. James Claudius Shaw, 7th Ohio Cavalry, from the Confederates in 1864. It received very complimentary reviews and the 1994 FALLOT LITERARY AWARD, National Association of Independent Publishers. His sequel, ONE STEP — TWO STEP, picks up the relation of his GGPa Claude Shaw and Hannibal Shaw from LEATHER AND SOUL, in their changed association of white and black, formerly master and slave, through the succeeding years to 1870.

McLellon lives in Fern Park, Florida with Naomi, his wife of 57 years.

Other Books by Waldron Murrill McLellon:

Megabyting my Mind,
59 plug-ins to add power

LEATHER AND SOUL;
A Civil War Odyssey

Correspondence Course Manual
For Water Treatment Plant Operators, Class C,
2nd Edition.(Co-author)

The ONO Book (Co-author)

Contributor to:

Biological Nutrient Removal
Editors: M.P. Wanielista and W.W. Eckenfelder

Health Physics Operational Monitoring
Editors: C.A. Willis and J.S. Handloser

Environmental Engineering Unit Operations and Processes
Laboratory Manual
Editor: J.T. O'Connor

Studies in Atomic Defense Engineering
NavDocks P-290, U.S. Navy

PROCUREMENT DATA

ONE STEP — TWO STEP
A Civil War Sequel

ISBN 1-884489-02-8
6X9 TRADE PAPER, PERFECT BOUND

by

Waldron Murrill McLellon

To order "ONE STEP — TWO STEP" direct from the publisher for U.S. destinations, send your check or money order for $14.95, plus $3.75 shipping, to Butternut Press, Publishers, 1913 Winnebago Trail, Fern Park, Florida 32730-3015. Florida destinations include the Florida sales tax in addition. When ordering more than one copy, add $1.50 shipping for each additional copy.

MAKE CHECKS OR MONEY ORDERS PAYABLE TO BUTTERNUT PRESS, PUBLISHERS.

For quantity purchases, telephone Butternut Press, Publishers, (407) 339-9244, or write to Butternut Press, Publishers, 1913 Winnebago Trail, Fern Park, Florida, 32730-3015. FAX number is (407) 339-9244.
e-mail: wally79497@msn.com

For PURCHASE of the precursor book, "LEATHER AND SOUL, A Civil War Odyssey," see following.

PROCUREMENT DATA

LEATHER AND SOUL
A Civil War Odyssey

ISBN 1-884489-00-1
TRADE PAPERBACK, PERFECT BOUND, 1994

by

Waldron Murrill McLellon

To order "LEATHER AND SOUL"(limited numbers are available) direct from the publisher for U.S. destinations, send your check or money order for $16.95, plus $3.75 shipping, to Butternut Press, Publishers, 1913 Winnebago Trail, Fern Park, Florida 32730-3015. Florida destinations include the Florida sales tax in addition. If ordering more than one copy, add $1.50 shipping for each additional copy.

MAKE CHECKS OR MONEY ORDERS PAYABLE TO BUTTTERNUT PRESS, PUB.

For quantity purchases(limited numbers are available), telephone Butternut Press, Publishers, (407) 339-9244, or write to Butternut Press, Publishers, 1913 Winnebago Trail, Fern Park, Florida, 32730-3015. FAX number is (407) 339-9244. e-mail: wally79497@msn.com

DISCOUNT: 20% OFF RETAIL BOOK PRICE IF BOTH BOOKS ARE ORDERED AS A SET.